THE
INNOCENTS
WITHIN

THE
INNOCENTS
WITHIN

A

NOVEL

ROBERT DALEY

VILLARD

NEW YORK

Copyright © 1999 by Riviera Productions, Ltd.

All rights reserved under International and Pan-American Copyright Conventions.
Published in the United States by Villard Books, a division of
Random House, Inc., New York, and simultaneously in Canada
by Random House of Canada Limited, Toronto.

VILLARD BOOKS and colophon are registered trademarks of Random House, Inc.

Library of Congress Cataloging-in-Publication Data
Daley, Robert.
The innocents within: a novel/Robert Daley.
p.   cm.
ISBN 0-375-50178-9
1. World War, 1939–1945—Underground movements—France—Fiction.
I. Title.
PS3554.A43I5   1999   813'.54—dc21   99-14155

Random House website address: www.atrandom.com

Printed in the United States of America on acid-free paper

9 8 7 6 5 4 3 2

First Edition

Book design by JoAnne Metsch

"He's armed without that's innocent within."

—ALEXANDER POPE

"You must have chaos in you to give birth to a dancing star."

—NIETZSCHE

THE

INNOCENTS

WITHIN

I

ALREADY he could hear the bombers overhead.

The hut was unheated, a row of sinks, a row of toilets. The pilot, whose name was David Gannon, shaved in cold water because there was never any hot this early. He was twenty years old and there was not yet much to shave. Brand new to the squadron, he had blue eyes, crew-cut sandy hair, a fair complexion, and nice teeth. He stood five feet ten, the limit for a fighter pilot in that war, and weighed 150 pounds, which was under the limit. He tended to move quickly, decisively, like the athlete he still thought himself to be. At college he had played varsity basketball—he was more than tall enough for the game as it was played in those years, the tallest man on his team being only six-three. Stripped to the waist as he was now, his ribs showed. Later, if he lived, he would fill out. He had a long neck, prominent Adam's apple, and long fingers with well-bitten nails. He had a man's job but the body of a boy.

Major Toft came in and took the sink next to him. Toft was the oldest man in the squadron, twenty-five.

"Morning, Davey."

"Morning, Major."

Toft wore long johns open at the throat, and he set his towel and shaving kit on the shelf. The squadron's top ace, as well as its commander, Toft had already shot down sixteen enemy planes. To Davey he was not only an ace but an older man besides, and he was in awe of him.

At all of the mirrors men were shaving. They took their time about it, shaved carefully, for missions lasted six hours or more, and oxygen masks made the least stubble chafe.

At the sink Davey stared back at himself. The mirror did not show what was most important about him: that he was still unblooded by life. He had not yet killed anyone, which the entire squadron knew. He had not yet known a woman either, which no one knew, and which he would have died rather than reveal. He did have a girlfriend, Nancy, who was a sophomore at a college in upstate New York. He wrote to her nearly every day, described for her every new plane he flew. She wrote to him less often.

Dressed now in flight jacket and flight suit, he stepped outside and found his bike on the rack. The night was still dark and cold, and as he pedaled off it began to rain. There were other bikes ahead of him and behind. The bombers were still passing overhead, but the overcast was too low and thick to see them. The North Sea—cold, clammy—was about a mile away, so close Davey could smell it. The bombers passed over him in boxes, thirty or more planes to the box. The noise was so heavy that the ground seemed to tremble. After each box came a gap that was almost silence, and then the noise increased as the next box came over.

The headlight was dim. He pushed his face into the thin English rain. It should have been dawn by now but wasn't; the darkness hung on. The cold had congealed the mud of the path. The wet air bathed Davey's face, made his cheeks red. He breathed it in. Because of the ruts, steering was difficult. Even keeping upright was a problem. The bike was old, no rubber grips. It had belonged to several other pilots before him. Though the collar of his flight jacket was turned up, his ears were cold, his hands too. Cold steel against his fingers, cold rain on his knuckles.

At the operations hut, he leaned the bike against the wall, then entered the briefing room. The pilots were all chattering. They stopped when the colonel jumped up onto the dais and the curtain parted, exposing the wall map. Every day there was a different tape fixed to the map. Today's extended all the way to Stuttgart.

The silence seemed to deepen.

The bombers would take out the industrial complexes around the city, the colonel said. Two of the group's three squadrons, supported by two squadrons of P-47s from the 56th, would fly escort.

Sixty-four fighters to cover the many boxes of bombers already on their way.

Davey kept glancing over at Major Toft. Toft was nodding calmly, he saw. On the day Davey joined the squadron, Toft had taken him up to check him out. Three times Toft gave him a five-hundred-foot height advantage, and they had mock dogfights. The first two times Toft had escaped; Davey was not able to bring his guns to bear. He had had mock dogfights in flight school and had usually won them. Looking across into the other cockpit he could see that Toft was laughing at him. It made Davey furious. He climbed the five hundred feet again, the third dogfight started, and this time the squadron leader could not shake him off no matter what he tried, and Davey nailed him. Still laughing, Toft had pointed for them both to go down.

Enemy resistance was expected to be heavy, said the colonel on the dais. He was using his pointer. Expect concentrations of enemy fighters here, here, and here. Expect heavy flak over the target. Expect more fighters on the way back.

The colonel stepped down off the dais. Replacing him, the assistant operations officer gave out the compass heading, rendezvous point, coded distress call, escape procedures. The pilots had plastic boards fixed to the thighs of their flight suits. Using a red crayon that could be wiped off in the event of capture, they jotted down coordinates. Major Toft never used the crayon. He wrote in ink on the back of his hand, so Davey did too. Though he had never dared brag to other pilots, the mock dogfight had left Davey proud, sure of himself as a pilot. As soon as he got the hang of it, he had beaten the great Toft.

The weather officer spoke of heavy overcast over England, breaking up a bit over Holland. Eastern Belgium mostly clear. Target area probably clear. Expect high cumulus. A little stratus low down. For their return much of the overcast would have burned off, and the rain should have stopped. Ceiling over the base should be at least five hundred feet by the time they got back.

The briefing lasted forty-five minutes. When it ended the pilots went to the board at the rear of the hut where red and blue disks hung, each with a pilot's name on it. The disks were laid out to show each man his formation, and his place in it.

Davey saw he was in red flight and that he was tail-end Charlie again. It would be his job to protect the flight's rear. Clear the air-space behind the flight—and keep clearing it. After an hour his neck would be chafed and sore. If enemy fighters came down on them unseen out of the sun, he was the one who would get picked off first. Flying tail-end Charlie was not a popular role, but as the new man he had expected it.

The pilots issued from the hut. The clouds hung dark and low. There was a clatter of bikes as they mounted and started for the mess hall. The rain had turned to mist. They pedaled into its cold wet kiss.

There was still time left, though not much.

The mess hall was another Nissen hut. Breakfast was powdered eggs, fried spam, canned orange juice, and coffee. The hut was heated by a cast-iron stove. The pilots had pushed the tables as close to the stove as they could. They talked about the latest pilots who had been killed, all from other bases. They named and ex-plained them. Who? Why? Two guys from the 56th had collided over Hamburg; another, diving after an Me 109, had augered in; a Brit in a damaged Spitfire had flown into a bridge trying to get home. They laid slices of bread on top of the stove to make toast, and while waiting for it they enumerated the mistakes of others, explained away every death. Like Davey, most of them had crew cuts, and they were all young. In an hour they would be at thirty thousand feet dueling with other youths trying to kill them. Talk-ing like this was part of the ritual. Mention death enough and it lost its reality, could not happen. Whether realizing it or not, they talked to make death commonplace, and to make themselves brave. They buttered their toast. Bravery was words that could be grabbed out of the air and added to their psyches in layers, like clothing.

Davey too laid out bread to be toasted. Guys had been killed in flight school, but it was always their own fault. Combat was differ-ent. He realized he could be shot down, and sometimes considered getting killed, but at his age could not visualize it, could not imagine himself dead. He liked talking about death though. It made him feel superior to boys his age back home, who had never seen it, or faced it. It gave a special importance to being a pilot.

As he buttered his toast the heat came off the stove and through the shoulders of his flight jacket. English bread was heavier than American bread. Because it was different he didn't approve of it, but as always on mornings he was to fly, he was ferociously hungry. He made himself a peanut butter and jam sandwich for later, wrapped it in paper napkins and put it in his pocket.

He went into the latrine: six open commodes side by side, all taken, pilots squatting, flight suits at their knees, all of them at this point feeling their nerves coming on strong. Fighter pilots were never bothered by constipation. Davey waited his turn. A commode was vacated and he took it. His first six months in the army he couldn't bear doing this in public. He used to wait until the middle of the night. Now, he voided his bowels, his bladder. The mission would be aloft five or six hours. There was a relief tube in the cockpit, but at high altitude it froze.

He pedaled in the direction of operations. The rain had stopped. Under his wheels, the frozen ruts had become chocolate mud.

He drew his parachute from supply. Major Toft, behind him in line, said: "How you feeling, Davey?"

"Fine," Davey said, "fine." His Adam's apple moved when he nodded.

A weapons carrier drove the pilots out to their planes. The day was still dark, the overcast still low. It hung over them, heavy and substantial, it loomed like a mountain.

Davey appraised the P-51 Mustang that had been assigned to him. Its gunports were taped over to keep out moisture and possible foreign objects. Just looking at the plane gave him pleasure. It was new, as virginal as he was. It had a white spinner and green wings. It was as sleek as a girl, and as beautiful. He loved the way it looked. As a boy he had read books about World War I aces. These had fascinated him, given him dreams of being a fighter pilot. World War II had made him one.

He glanced over at Toft's plane, which gleamed more than the others. Toft paid his crewmen to hand-wax its wings, its fuselage.

Said it added an extra ten miles an hour. Could be the difference someday between life and death. Davey was determined, as soon as he made first lieutenant, to use the extra money to do the same. Right now he sent all his money home. His mother put it in the bank for him. When the war ended, if he wanted to get married and start a family, he would need to have sufficient money. Getting married, he figured, required at least two or three thousand dollars in the bank.

That he might get killed first was not, to him, a consideration.

His crew chief on the wing told him everything was fine, and he nodded and climbed in. While in college he had worked summers as a garage mechanic, learning and doing. He couldn't think of it as a career—socially it wasn't acceptable—but he had loved that job. Machinery fascinated him. In a sense an airplane was only a car with wings. As soon as he knew he was to fly P-51 Mustangs, he had studied the plane, how it worked, what it would do. He had come to understand it far better, for instance, than he understood older men, or girls.

He was wearing fleece-lined flying boots over two pairs of socks, and his flight suit and leather jacket, and over all of it the yellow Mae West. He sat on top of his parachute, clipped the dinghy in its package to the parachute harness, and began the cockpit check. He wore the standard thin leather helmet, his goggles still resting on his forehead. In a shoulder holster, out of the way of all the harnesses, rode a .45 automatic. He checked his instruments, his oxygen, the numbers on the back of his hand. The crew chief gave him the thumbs up, and jumped down to the ground.

Just as he used to do before taking the court at the start of a game, Davey made a quick sign of the cross, then reached for and pushed the energizer button. Sixteen feet of propellor began to turn, the four blades moving more and more quickly until, with a puff of dense blue smoke, the engine caught.

Along the line all the engines caught. Toft taxied his flight to the end of the runway. With one hand on the throttle, one on the stick, Davey watched for Taft's take-off signal.

The planes took off two by two, the pairs starting forward every five seconds, one pair from the right side of the runway, one from the left to minimize propwash. The runway was linked steel matting that rattled and undulated underneath, and it was short. Loaded to the top with fuel and ammo, the planes used up every inch. However graceful they looked in the air, each one weighed over five tons, and coaxing them up was tricky.

One by one the planes disappeared into the scud.

Davey, part of the last pair off, retracted his wheels and entered the overcast. Unable to see anything, he turned ten degrees left as instructed so as to avoid a possible collision with his wingmate, and kept climbing. It was dense and dark in there. The scud was thousands of feet thick. He began to think it would never end.

Climbing at identical revs, identical speeds, the planes popped out into brilliant sunshine almost together and quickly formed up, still climbing, heading east in flights of four, sixteen planes in all, four shallow Vees, Davey flying rear left of the rear flight.

Toft rocked his wings, which meant tighten up, and everyone moved in closer.

The North Sea was below them, a hundred miles wide where they crossed it. They couldn't see it. Under them, the undercast stretched rumpled, dirty gray, to the horizon. Presently a steady drone filled their earphones—the enemy trying to jam their VHF radios—and from this they knew they were over the continent.

Davey switched on in his oxygen mask. The cockpit was not pressurized, and although the sun warmed his face and shoulders, his legs and feet were getting cold, but would get colder. At eighteen thousand feet the supercharger kicked in hard. Toft on the radio ordered them to activate gun sights and guns. The orange sight ring appeared on the optical glass in front of Davey.

At 28,000 feet they stopped climbing. By then Davey's head was on a swivel, up and back, up and back, his eyes raking the sky for enemy fighters that weren't yet there, but soon would be, if the briefing was correct. It was his responsibility to spot them first and warn everybody. His neck began to ache. The fleece of his collar was soft, but chafed anyway. He had long ago understood why fighter pilots wrapped their necks in silk scarfs. It wasn't because it made a romantic image.

Specks in the distance. The bombers. Davey pushed the transmit button: "Big friends at twelve o'clock low." In flight school he had acquired a reputation for the keenest eyes in the class. He was proud of this, of course he was, but in the fighter pilot's world, the young man's world, modesty was the thing. Davey had been careful then and was careful now to let no pride show. If he had called out about the bombers, moments before everybody would have spotted them, it was because he was new here. He wanted to be trusted. He wanted the men around him to know he was paying attention.

The bombers got bigger. Contrails floated back from their engine exhausts, wispy man-made clouds, elongated, thin imitations of the real thing.

They came up on the rearmost box of bombers. "Glad to see you, little friends," said a voice in Davey's ear, in all their ears.

They overtook one box after another, then hovered, throttling back, flying lazy esses to hold position above and to the side. There were more bombers ahead, wings creaming the air, a squadron of P-47s drifting back and forth above them. On and on they droned, penetrating ever more deeply into enemy sky.

More specks far off, to the left, climbing. "Bogies nine o'clock low," called Davey.

"Drop tanks," ordered Toft.

Thirty-two auxiliary tanks tumbled lazily away, gaining speed as they fell. Most still contained some fuel, and would explode like bombs when they struck, gigantic Molotov cocktails, incinerating anyone who happened to be standing there.

Sixteen pairs of eyes stared at the specks coming up from the side.

"They're P-47s," a voice said.

"They are not," said Davey, "they're Focke-Wulfs."

"Let's go down and see, shall we?" said Toft softly.

They dove. Davey's cockpit was blasted with heat from the engine. The pressure forced him down in his seat. G-suits had not yet reached combat squadrons, and he tried to clamp his stomach muscles to keep blood in his head. Repeatedly he cleared his ears. Below him the specks increased in speed and girth until the white bordered crosses appeared on the wings, the swastikas on the tails.

"There must be sixty of them," a voice said.

"Sixteen against sixty," said another voice.

They dove into them, guns firing, and went through and zoomed up the other side, and the dogfight started, the wild confusion of aerial combat. The squadron broke down into elements of two—leader and wingman. Otherwise there was nothing orderly about it. Planes filled the air like a roomful of flies, all zooming in different directions. The radio filled up with shouted warnings, cries of triumph, curses. Davey's leader was a first lieutenant named Buxton. Blasting enemy planes from the sky was Buxton's job. Davey's was to fly wingman, sticking to Buxton whatever he did, guarding his rear, and he did this, though what he wanted to do was shoot down planes himself. He saw a 190 explode. The wing came off another and lashed back and nearly hit him. Buxton wrenched his plane all over the sky, Davey likewise, erratic maneuvers impossible to track, two partners locked in a dance, closer than any dance, virtually an embrace.

Wingmen not only did not shoot down anything, they were frequently shot down themselves. Trying to protect Buxton's tail and his own as well, Davey was aware of this every moment.

The P-51 Mustangs darted this way and that, trying to find and single out the weakling, the cripple, or simply the unlucky enemy who flashed in front of their sights—someone who could be murdered. Lieutenant Buxton found a 190 that may have been already damaged. They were in a turn together, Buxton clinging to his tail, pulling Gs, gaining, Davey right behind pulling the same Gs, and a second 190 came out of nowhere and was on top of Buxton. "Break left," shouted Davey. He saw Buxton's plane stand on its wing and dive, the 190 after him, Davey right behind, Buxton's prey forgotten.

Davey was too far back for effective shooting but fired anyway, hoping to distract the enemy, make him let go of Buxton. He saw his tracers curling around the enemy plane, and then it veered sharp right, and Buxton was in the clear.

Concentrating on Buxton, Davey never saw the 190 that came in behind him.

The sky by this time was full of parachutes, and also of pieces of airplane, lethal junk either drifting or falling depending on what it was, some of it below him, some raining down from on top, and when his plane gave a kind of stagger, Davey's first thought was that he had flown into debris. Then he realized he was taking hits.

His head jerked around. The 190 was almost on top of him, so close he could see the gun flashes, thought he could see the bullets coming at him. A hole was ripped out of his right wing.

College basketball had honed his reflexes, his hand-eye coordination. In flight school he had worked hard, and in addition he had something which could not be taught, something inborn—or so it was said of certain pilots at that time and since. That is, he understood through his fingers, through the way the straps cut into his body, through the noises the engine made, exactly what he could make a plane do, and what it would refuse to do, how hard it could be pushed. He knew where it would stall, or spin. He knew when the rivets would pop if he dove it any steeper. He knew the exact moment when it would become contemptuous of its pilot.

About to be shot down, he did not have time to think, and did not need to. Instinctively he pulled back on throttle and stick, pulled back so hard he felt the plane quiver, on the edge of a stall. This tactic, plus probably the hole in the wing, caused such a sudden deceleration that Davey was thrown hard against his straps, and the enemy pilot had to sail under him to avoid a collision.

Immediately adding power, Davey dove, and now he was the one with the advantage, being behind and slightly above the enemy pilot who, turning tightly, could not shake him. The turn got tighter and tighter, with Davey on the inside of it, gaining, for Mustangs could turn tighter than any plane in the sky, until finally the 190 filled the circle on the optical glass twelve inches in front of his nose, filled it from wingtip to wingtip. Davey had only to exert pressure with his right forefinger. His six .50-caliber machine guns, three in each wing, would do the rest.

Instead he hesitated. He wanted his first kill well enough, but there was a young man like himself in that plane, for he could see into his canopy. A boy who, like himself, hoped to go back to school one day, see his girl again, get married—and who was desperate to escape, trying one evasive movement after another while Davey hung on, the two black crosses still framed in his gunsight. If his object had been to confront the other pilot with the inevitable, to torture him with the waiting, he could not have done it better.

Suddenly Davey saw his face, for his head was twisted all the way around trying to see where Davey was. He looked shocked, scared, frantic.

Not much time had passed. At such speeds, only an instant. As time is measured, nothing at all. An eternity, during which Davey made a speech to himself. You have to do it. You've been trained to do it. This is war. Him or you.

He pressed the trigger. His guns poured forth hundreds of rounds. Though blinking rapidly, he saw them take root.

The enemy plane disintegrated. He saw this much because he had to avoid the chunks and pieces that came sailing back.

"Good shooting, Davey." Toft's voice in his ears. Toft had had the luxury to glance around him and now to speak because the dogfight was petering out. Dogfights are like spasms. They consume themselves. By their nature they cannot last.

Davey did not know the dogfight was over, did not turn his head to find Toft or anyone. Sweating from exertion, panting from fear, his concentration was elsewhere. There had been no chute. He was following the wreckage down. Earlier there had been chutes in many directions. They had blossomed like hope. But this time there was none. He followed the wreckage almost to the trees, all the time praying for the other young man to jump. But no chute ever showed.

When he flew back upstairs he was alone in the sky. No dogfight anywhere. Not a plane in sight. He closed his eyes, saw the dead pilot's face, and opened them again. He had no idea where he was, and he began to select compass headings at random, trying to find his comrades. There was an armada out there somewhere, and he was trying to find it but couldn't. He saw that he was getting low on fuel.

His arms and shoulders ached, his neck. Manhandling a P-51 at four hundred miles an hour in a dogfight required strength. The controls were not hydraulically assisted; they got heavy. Moving them required enormous effort. Physically, emotionally, mentally, he was close to exhaustion. He was also seven or eight hundred miles from home, and he was alone.

He started back to England.

He flew northwest, and as he picked up landmarks below, he was able to set a course. He left Germany, began to cross Holland.

Alone he was intensely vulnerable. Any pair of fighters could pick him off, even a single fighter he did not see in time. He watched the sky for someone who might kill him—tried to watch all of it—watched the fuel gauge too, for that could kill him just as fast. In the last hour the needle had collapsed almost completely.

Below him the overcast thickened, closing in, but he caught a glimpse of the Zuider Zee. He was safe now from enemy fighters, or believed he was, and so let down below the overcast where he could take his oxygen mask off, rub the stiffness from his cheeks, move his numb legs, shift around on his cramped buttocks, crack the canopy to let in some fresh air to breathe. The cockpit stank of oil, gas, and stale sweat. He was ferociously hungry and he got out his peanut butter and jam sandwich and ate it, while watching the fuel gauge. He was thirsty too, but had nothing with him to drink. Sweating out the fuel made him thirstier still. He pushed the air-sea rescue button on his radio and asked for a compass check, and got it, and there was nothing more for him to do except watch the North Sea below. It was well-lathered, and he knew it was cold. If he went down in the water his life expectancy was twenty minutes. Not enough time for a launch to find him.

When he could see land ahead—the field—he lowered his wheels, heard them thump and lock, another relief. He spotted the tower, aimed himself down the runway, saw one other thing as well, that the fuel gauge was empty. He flew straight in, landing hot, rolling fast, feeling rather than hearing the click and rattle of the steel mats underneath. Having taxied over to the hardstand, he shut the Mustang down. From one instant to the next all of the violence went out of it. All the violence, such as there had been, went out of him too, and he felt the momentary exhilaration of someone who has risked death and survived. He breathed the air, felt its coolness on his face.

In the officer's club later he had to buy beers for everyone. He pretended to be ebullient, though he was not. Every pilot who bellied up to the bar made him describe his kill and so he told the story ten or more times. He did not mention the enemy pilot's face, though he kept seeing it.

Between rounds he stared at the floor and wished he was still in school, still playing basketball. Once Toft came over and clapped him on the shoulder, saying: "Nice job, kid."

Already one of the top aces of the war, Toft had got two more kills today, but no one was making him celebrate it.

That night in his bunk, still seeing the dead pilot's face, Davey felt tears come to his eyes, and then, trying to do it as silently as he could, he was crying.

II

ANDRE Favert was a Protestant pastor in Le Lignon, a village in the center of France. The pilots, gunners, bombadiers who made war from the sky were not a factor in his life. He never saw warplanes overhead, and Le Lignon was too unimportant in an industrial way ever to attract them.

His role in the war did exist, but it was diametrically different from theirs, just as his problems on this particular day were different.

For some years the roads of France had swarmed with refugees, mostly foreigners, mostly Jews, people without papers, without money, and now almost without hope, all trying to elude the Gestapo and the Gestapo's servants, who were the French police. Some refugees had children. Some were children themselves: either adolescents traveling alone or tots whose parents had disappeared in roundups and who had attached themselves to whatever adults they could find.

Certain of these people came to Le Lignon. It started early in the war and continued, a few dozen people at first, followed by hundreds, then thousands. For as long as one could buy black market gasoline they sometimes came by car or truck. After that they came in on the one o'clock train and asked directions to the presbytery, where they found that the whisper that had spread through the refugee community was correct. Pastor Favert took them in. He fed and sheltered them and then found them lodgings where they would be safe. Forged papers were prepared for them, and although some had been there now for years, hundreds of others had been smuggled to safety in Switzerland.

By the beginning of 1944 there was not a house for kilometers around that did not harbor a family of refugee Jews, and there were schools, pensions, and hotels in the village itself that housed thirty or more at a time. Favert had a wife and four children and was under no illusion about what would happen to him, and perhaps to his family, if what he was doing were discovered.

Le Lignon sits on a vast flat plateau a thousand meters high in the Massif Central. The mountains around it go up twice that high, but are a good distance off. The village consisted at that time of five or six streets of gray stone houses, in some of which animals were quartered on the ground floor, the people living above; most days the streets out front were clotted with dung. There was a village fountain with its adjacent *lavoir* in which many of the women still did their laundry, in winter having to break the glass off the water first, then rubbing sheets and shirts against the smooth stone. There was a market square with most of the village's dozen or so shops clustered around it, and a few small hotels that in normal times were empty most of the year, though there was a little tourism in summer.

Le Lignon was a poor place, and always would be. There was an almost constant wind. The river wending through was not much of a river. The wind blew down the river and through the narrow streets. In winter it could blow icy cold. The outlying farms were small and unprofitable, for the soil was poor and the growing season short.

The population of the village itself, not counting refugees, was about nine hundred, and in the outlying commune lived nine hundred more. All but about ten percent of these people were Protestants, for Le Lignon was an anomaly, a Protestant village in a Catholic country, one of several in or near the Massif Central, all of them left over from the time when the Huguenot minority had had to find isolated places in which they could huddle together for protection, and worship in secret. Their temple at the edge of the village was an austere building that dated from about 1820. True freedom of religion had not existed all that long. Of course, the village had its Catholic church as well. The church and its handsome steeple were over four hundred years old. Its priest, who had very few parishioners and who had refused to take part in the conspiracy to save Jews, lived in the house next door.

The wars of religion, the massacres and executions of Protestants by Catholics, and in off years the discrimination, had lasted, with intervals, for centuries. All the old stories were still alive, part of the psyche of Le Lignon. The people of the village understood in an almost personal way what persecution was; they were sympathetic to those who suffered it, and they listened to their pastor—Favert had been pastor since 1932. Mostly they did what he asked. Although there was an elected mayor who might be an electrician one year, a bar owner the next, the pastor remained the pastor, the principal authority figure of both the village and the region. Communal decisions, and these days there was great risk attached to most of them, were made not in the mayor's office but in the Protestant temple under the aegis of the pastor. In this time of betrayals, reprisals, assassinations, tortures, deportations, and death camps, not to mention the mass slaughter perpetrated by the armies fighting on the various fronts, what he preached from the pulpit, what he had urged on his parishioners at the beginning of the war and still did, was nonviolence, passive resistance, love of neighbor. "No government can oblige one to kill," he preached. "One must find some other way to fight Nazism, must look for it every day in obedience to the Bible. As the hardest metal yields to sufficient heat, the hardest heart must melt before the sufficiency of the heat of nonviolence."

His sermons were sometimes described as violent—the violence of a Christian trying to convince. "Man," he preached, "is a soldier against all forms of evil that reside in the human spirit and that war brings out." He asked his parishioners to be caring, Christian people. Above all, he asked them to open their doors to people in need.

As his own was open.

The world had fallen into darkness, but Le Lignon had not.

Pastor Favert, then forty-two, was a big lumbering man, balding, with a thin mustache under thick glasses that he was forever taking off to clean. He could be clumsy and loud. He was also open and gregarious, talkative, warm, a man who, although he lived in a cataclysmic time, tended to hug people a lot.

His name had become known to every religious community in France, and to all of the charitable organizations that still functioned there, some of which funded him, sending the money in from Switzerland by couriers who, when they got through—they didn't always—came to his door and handed over paper parcels full of cash.

So far no one had given him up to the Gestapo.

There was an underground buzz about him everywhere, and he knew this. He had the energy of two men, and the goodness, it was said, of twenty. He had achieved a kind of fame, and although he had started as a mild, meek kind of man, lately he had become somewhat domineering, even at times arrogant—people had begun to remark on this. He would no longer brook criticism or dissent. He was the one who decided which refugees were sent where, how much of the precious but always inadequate money to distribute each day, and to whom.

On this particular morning Le Lignon was to be visited by a cabinet minister from the collaborationist government in Vichy, and by certain other dignitaries as well. Pastor Favert saw this as a special problem, and it had kept him awake much of the night.

The cabinet minister's schedule had already been determined—instructions had come from Vichy: luncheon, followed by a march to the sports field where he would make a speech to the youth of Le Lignon, who were to be assembled for this purpose. The cabinet minister's name was Deshaies, and Favert knew about the speeches he liked to make to young people. He would lecture them about patriotism and obedience, about their duties to the state, and especially to the person of Marshal Pétain, the head of state—his object was to instill in French youth the cult of a father figure. He would urge the youngsters to join the Companions of France and to attend the government-sponsored youth camps with their bugles, uniforms, parades, and fascist salutes. They were sure to find these camps, which were modeled on the Hitler Youth, exciting and fun.

Deshaies could be very seductive, and this speech was one of the two principal reasons for his visit, Favert believed. The other was a confrontation with himself, for Deshaies must know—everybody knew—how often and how strongly he had preached against these same youth programs. Thanks to his preaching, the boys and girls of Le Lignon had shown no enthusiasm for any of them so far.

Deshaies's speech was to be followed by a reception in the Protestant temple, and finally by a religious service.

Tossing and turning beside his wife, Favert had puzzled over what to do. What his posture was to be. Only when he had decided on a program of his own, and the people he would use to implement it, did the pastor finally fall asleep.

When morning came he got his program started.

Previously, almost like a military commander, he had divided his village into segments, each with its leader. Some of these people he reached now by phone. Because the village phones were on a party line—anyone could listen in—his instructions had to be cryptic. After that, moving hurriedly through the streets, he met others in person, and to one of them he handed something he had written.

The final part of his plan involved a refugee girl who lived in his house. Her name was Rachel Weiss, though she now carried false papers identifying her as Sylvie Bonaire. She would be one of two people serving at the luncheon, the other being a waiter from one of the hotels. Rachel was three weeks short of her eighteenth birthday, and he told her what he wanted her to do. When finished he asked if she thought she could do it—if she was willing to do it.

"Yes," she said.

"All right," said the pastor.

Born in Berlin, Rachel Weiss was the daughter of a Jewish textile merchant. At the age of eight she had been sent to a British boarding school to learn English, not a word of which she spoke. Her father took her to the school, which was sixty miles south of London, and the tears, when he got ready to leave, rolled down the child's face. He dried them with his handkerchief, told her to be a good girl, and then he was gone.

After that, traveling back and forth to Berlin by train and ferry and then train again, Rachel saw her parents only during Christmas and summer vacations. For a young girl these were very long trips. She was too young to know about the rise of the Nazis, whose laws against Jews got stricter. Finally her father sold his business for half of what it was worth, got much of his money, not all, out of Germany, applied for visas to America, and moved to Paris to wait until they were accorded. So during her last several vacations Rachel saw her parents in their rented flat near the Eiffel Tower. Stamped into her German passport was a British visa good for the duration of the school year, and a French visa good for thirty days. The passport was new; she had been obliged to turn the old one in—she and everyone else—and the new one gave her a different middle name. For female German Jews it was Sara, for male Jews Israel. By then she spoke English with an upper-class English accent. She was an intelligent girl certainly, though starved for affection.

In September 1939, then thirteen years old, Rachel was spending a week with the family of a girlfriend from school in a resort in the French Alps. It was a time of hormonal change, and she had developed a fierce crush, her first, on her girlfriend's brother, who was twenty. Then war broke out, the brother went into the army, and Rachel rushed back to Paris where her parents had abandoned their flat and were already on the run. Male aliens who had registered with the police had been ordered to report to sports stadiums in and around Paris—Stade Rolland Garros, the Stade de Colombes—and in these places without roofs or heat or beds or hot water they were being held. The law-abiding Herr Weiss had registered, for he had wanted no trouble from the police, but now, seeing that trouble was upon him anyway, he knew better than to report. He was not going to be imprisoned in a sports stadium, and after that most probably in a French concentration camp. Instead, he and his wife were going to keep moving, and hope the American visas came through before they were caught. There were, however, two problems. One was money—he still had some but could no longer get at it. The other was Rachel. He needed to put her in a place where she could go to school and where she would be safe, however long the waiting took. It had to be a place that would not cost much.

Already in the refugee community there were rumors about Le Lignon.

They went down there on the train. No one checked their papers en route. They enrolled Rachel in the village school and got her a room in a pension. Again Rachel wept when they left her.

For a while there were letters from her parents, and once a phone call. Then the letters stopped. The money stopped as well. She never heard from them again. Pastor Favert and his wife took her in, a scared, skinny child with jet black hair and nearly black eyes, who might be beautiful in a few years, when she filled out. They treated her like their daughter. They gave her a new name, together with forged identity and ration cards. She began to learn French, and soon spoke all three of her languages without accent, something that is possible only with children.

She had lived with the Faverts now for four years. They had given her the first real affection she had had since she first went to England. After a time she had asked if, like their other children, she could call them maman and papa.

It was just before noon when the official cars rolled into the village, coming to a stop in front of the *mairie,* where a small group waited: the recently elected mayor, who was a plumber by trade, and the adjunct mayor, who was the owner of one of the village's small hotels, plus Pastor Favert and his assistant pastor, whose name was Henriot. The mayor ran down the steps and opened the car door for Cabinet Minister Deshaies who, as he stepped out, was seen to be a tall man of about forty, tanned, with a big smile, and although he was a civilian in a civilian government, he wore a uniform that looked new and fit him perfectly. It somewhat resembled the uniforms favored by Hitler and his entourage, except that it was blue.

Monsieur Deshaies began to glance around somewhat self-consciously, perhaps because he had expected the old stone buildings to be decorated with flags and bunting in his honor. But there were no decorations. Perhaps he had expected the streets to be lined with cheering throngs, but there were none; the streets were empty. Perhaps he had even expected a band, but the village was silent.

His aide had joined him on the sidewalk, as had the occupants of the other two cars: the prefect and subprefect of the department, plus several local politicians, all noticing the lack of the expected welcome, all looking uncomfortable.

There was a communal hall attached to the *mairie,* and this was where the luncheon took place, catered by the hotel owner and served by the hotel's one waiter and by Rachel Weiss. At today's luncheon the fare was to be spartan. The mayor had wanted to treat the visiting dignitaries to a feast. By pooling their ration coupons and buying on the black market they could just do it. But Pastor Favert had suggested that this might embarrass their guests, who might prefer to be treated as family. "They might prefer to eat as we do," he said.

At this stage of the war, even in villages like Le Lignon, people were hungry much of the time.

So the first course was to be a rather thin soup. Rachel brought in the tureen, which was not only a big one but so heavy that she carried it in her two arms. She went to serve the principal guest, Deshaies, first, but as she bent over him she apparently lost control of the tureen, did not quite catch it in time, and so spilled part of its contents onto the back of his uniform.

Deshaies gave a squeak and jumped to his feet.

Favert jumped up also, and with his napkin attempted to wipe the soup off Deshaies.

For a moment Rachel stood as if stricken. She put the tureen down, both fists went to her mouth. Then she turned and bolted from the room.

"I'll have her punished, if you like," said the pastor.

"No," said Deshaies, "of course not."

"Poor girl," said Favert. "She's mortified."

Rachel did not return, and the rest of the luncheon was served by the hotel's waiter.

Presently they all pushed back from the table. Everyone was careful not to step in the puddle of soup.

Next stop would be the sports field. "How far away is it?" said Deshaies.

"Not far," answered Pastor Favert.

"Do I need my overcoat?"

"I'm not taking one."

It was December, the sports field was eight or nine hundred meters distant, and they had stepped out into a biting wind, which was perhaps doubly biting to a man whose back was soaked through to his shirt. Although Pastor Favert seemed not to mind the cold, and walked slowly, Deshaies was shivering well before the field came in sight.

As had been requested by Vichy, the youth of the region had been assembled there, and they waited in ranks. Some were small children, and some were adolescents, including a contingent of Boy Scouts in their neckerchiefs and brown uniforms.

A section of flooring had been set up at one end of the field; on it stood two smallish loudspeakers and a microphone. Deshaies stepped onto it, shivering slightly but all smiles, and unrolled his speech, which he had been clutching. He gripped the mike with his other hand, and prepared to start, but he was interrupted as the Scouts came forward. Each of them wanted to shake his hand, it seemed, and to make a small welcoming speech of his own, and for a time Deshaies grinned and accepted this homage as his due. But as it continued his grin faded. Behind the Scouts the other kids had pressed forward for their turn, not as if they had been coached, but as if they thought that emulating the Scouts was expected of them, each one wanting to shake Deshaies's hand too, and make a speech to him. The crush around the cabinet minister was so great that several times he was jostled, and once almost knocked off his feet. Behind him the other dignitaries turned their backs to the wind, turned their coat collars up, and stamped their feet to keep warm, all except Pastor Favert, who studied the sky.

Deshaies's hand got sore, for some of the kids, particularly the Scouts, were wringing it like a dish towel; and by now he was visibly trembling from the cold.

The hand-shaking ended finally, but by then less than half the kids remained on the sports field, and when the mike was turned on it was found not to work. The half-frozen cabinet minister stepped to the front of the platform and began his speech. He urged the youth of Le Lignon and its surrounding area to obey the new racial laws, to do their duty by the nation. He had to shout to make himself heard and most of what he said was carried away on the wind. After less than sixty seconds he rammed the rest of the speech into his pocket and hurried from the field, the other dignitaries trooping after him.

The next scheduled event was the religious service in the temple. At the invitation of Pastor Favert a prominent Swiss theologian had come across from Geneva—it was he who climbed to the pulpit to give the sermon. He spoke of Christian love: Christian love does not permit one to do wrong to a neighbor, he said. He spoke of obedience to the state and to the law, which was mandatory for all Christians, provided the laws were just, provided the state did not try to force the people to violate the laws of God, for the laws of God were preeminent, and the first and most important of these laws was love of neighbor.

When the sermon ended, hymns were sung. Pastor Favert, who was standing beside Minister Deshaies, handed him a hymnal and urged him to join in.

And finally there was a reception in the church hall. The entire village had been invited, and glasses and bottles of wine had been set out for the expected throngs, but few people came.

Suddenly the door opened, and a group of schoolboys, the oldest about twelve, came forward and handed Deshaies a petition. The cabinet minister tried to thrust it unread into the pocket of his uniform, but the boy asked him respectfully to please read it.

"Now?" he said.

There were five boys standing before him. "Now," said one of them, and the others nodded.

"Later," said Deshaies.

The boys stood their ground. "Please, Monsieur," said the group's spokesman.

So Deshaies read it. About halfway through his face got dark, and his lips began to move, and when he had finished he handed the paper to the prefect of the department who, reading, began at once to mutter, and who, when he had finished, or perhaps before, crumpled the paper into a ball and threw it to the floor. The Swiss theologian picked it up, read it, and passed it on to Favert.

This paper was later posted on the bulletin board at the *mairie* so that everyone might read it, and this is what it said:

We have recently learned of frightening scenes where French police, on orders of the occupying power, broke into homes and seized Jews who had committed no crime, who had hurt no one, tearing fathers from their families, mothers from their children, all these people to be deported to camps in Germany or other Eastern European points against their will.

We feel obliged to tell you, Monsieur Deshaies, that there are among us a certain number of Jews. But we make no distinction between Jews and non-Jews. It is contrary to Jesus' teaching, and God's law.

Should our comrades, whose only fault is to be born in another religion, receive an order to let themselves be deported, or even detained, they would disobey this order, and we would try to hide them as best we could.

"Sir," said the boy who seemed to be spokesman for the group, "may we have a response from you?"

For Deshaies it had been a trying day, and his reply was perhaps harsher than he intended, for it came out almost as a snarl: "I have nothing to do with Jews, who in any case are enemies of the French state. These questions are not my affair. Speak to the prefect of your department."

He turned, shook hands with no one, and strode from the hall. In a moment they heard his car start up outside. The engine roared and he was gone.

The prefect, whose name was Brin and who was the civil governor of the Haute-Loire department in which Le Lignon lay, turned on Pastor Favert. Ignoring the boys, he demanded furiously: "Who wrote that paper?"

"Should we ask one of the boys?" said Favert.

"No twelve-year-old boy could have written it. Don't make me laugh." But the prefect wasn't laughing.

"The children in this village write excellent French," said Favert, smoothing his mustache. "Our schools concentrate on it."

"This was supposed to be a day of national harmony," said Brin with increasing heat.

The pastor frowned. "There can be no question of harmony

when our brothers and sisters are threatened with deportation, with imprisonment in camps—extermination camps, if the rumors are correct."

"Foreign Jews who live in this village are not your brothers," shouted Brin. "They do not belong to your church or your country."

"They are innocent people."

"It is not a question of deportation anyway," said the prefect, who appeared to be trying to calm himself down.

"Not a question of deportation," said Favert. "I see."

"I have it from Marshal Pétain himself, and the marshal does not lie. Nor does the Führer, who is an intelligent man."

Brin was a fervent Catholic, a fervent anti-Communist as well. It was the Communists, the Freemasons, and the Jews, he said, who had caused the downfall of France, as was well known, and all had to be extirpated if the nation was to become healthy again. He said: "Just as the English have created a Zionist center in Palestine, the Führer has ordered all European Jews regrouped in Poland. There they will have land and houses, and a life that is suitable to them, and they will cease to corrupt the west."

Prior to the occupation Brin had served as a mid-level *fonctionnaire;* now he and his family lived in the prefect's official residence, which was a palace. He had been furnished with a big office, a car and driver around the clock, and other perks. He said: "In a few days I will send people to detain all Jews living in Le Lignon."

"We do not know what a Jew is," said Favert carefully. He took off and polished his glasses. "We know only men."

Brin was shouting again: "I have received my orders and I will carry them out."

"Orders from the occupying power," commented Favert. "And you a Frenchman."

"Monsieur Favert," said Brin, his voice icy, "you would do well to take care."

The pastor turned away.

"If you are not prudent," shouted the prefect to his back, "it is you whom I shall be obliged to have deported."

And he too, followed by his entourage, made for the door.

III

THE pilots stood in the adjutant's office, Davey and Major Toft among them. The adjutant was handing out forty-eight-hour passes, and the men were waiting their turn.

"Been to London yet, Davey?"

"Not yet, Major."

"Joe," said Toft.

Davey nodded.

"You're welcome to come along with us, if you like."

On the train they took over a first-class compartment. The countryside began to pass. Davey sat at the window looking out. It was raining. Everything looked soaked.

One of the pilots had a bottle in a paper bag, and it began to pass from hand to hand, though skipping Davey, who politely said he didn't want any.

"Where'd you go to school, Davey?" said Toft beside him.

"Fordham, Major. Only two years so far."

"Joe," said Toft.

Davey smoothed the seat fabric with his hand. Toft was a field-grade officer. He was his mentor and idol both.

"Fordham's Catholic, isn't it?" said Toft.

"Yes, Jesuit."

"Coed?"

"No. No girls. I've never been to school with girls in my life."

After a moment Davey said: "How about you?" He couldn't call him Joe, and from then on didn't call him anything.

"Ohio State," said Toft.

"Good school," said Davey, "but we whomped you in the Garden two Christmases ago." A nice memory, though from another world. Davey himself, only a sophomore, had scored eighteen points that night, mostly from outside, and now, remembering, he felt a glow that made him smirk. It was the first time he had made the starting lineup, the first time he had heard fifteen thousand people cheering him, many of the voices shouting his name. His two-handed set shot was really working. He was putting it through the cords from almost anywhere. This experience and similar ones had given him, though he did not realize it, an inner strength that was unusual in boys his age.

"Got my master's from Ohio State too," said Toft. The squadron commander's résumé ended there, though he did not say so. He had been in the army ever since.

All of their résumés were thin, and some would never grow thicker.

Toft's master's degree surprised Davey. "What subject?" he asked. Once you had seen Toft in a P-51 over Germany, it was difficult to imagine him in a classroom.

"American lit."

"That's what I was studying too. You going to teach it, or what?"

"Maybe," said Toft, "if I get out of this thing." And then after a moment: "We're all in college still. The college of life and death."

The bottle, making the rounds, again reached Davey. "Really, no," he said.

The pilot proffering the bottle seemed puzzled. He said: "It's scotch."

"No, thanks."

"Pilots are men who like to drink."

"I never knew a pilot didn't drink, did you, Dave?" said one of the others.

" 'Specially fighter pilots."

"Maybe he's got the clap. Guy has the clap, he's not allowed to drink."

"You got the clap, Dave."

"That must be it. Got the clap."

The jeering, friendly at first, had become not so friendly.

"This here's good scotch. Just try it."

"I don't like scotch," said Davey, adding quickly: "I like to drink though. Just not scotch."

"Cocktails," said the pilot. "Manhattans, I bet. Old-fashioneds."

"Sweet stuff."

"Women's drinks."

"This here's a man's drink."

"If he doesn't want to drink," said Toft, who was swigging his share, "he doesn't have to drink. He's a better pilot than any of you. Leave him alone."

Outside the window it was still raining. Davey watched the procession of damp fields. The overcast was very low and dark.

A little later, a slight slur to his words, Toft said: "First thing to do is get hotel rooms."

"Take us a hot bath, have dinner in a swanky restaurant," said the pilot opposite him.

The pilot with the bottle had taken it out of the bag and was peering at it. " 'S empty," he said. He reached for the window. When he pulled it down, cold wet air rushed in.

"Close the goddamn window," said Toft.

The other pilot heaved the bottle out into a field, then pulled the window up.

"After that we pick up some girls," said Toft.

They checked into a hotel in Picadilly, three double rooms. In college they had slept two to a room, in the Air Corps the same. They were at an age when a double room constituted as much privacy as anyone could wish for. Besides, the hotel was expensive.

"You and me, Davey," Toft said, "that okay?"

His idol had again singled him out, and Davey was pleased.

While Toft took a bath, Davey lay on one of the beds. He thought about Nancy, who was far away and had not written this week. Something was wrong; he did not know what. There was nothing he could do about it. To meet a nice English girl tonight would be nice. Talk to her, maybe dance with her. He missed being with a girl. But there were millions of troops quartered in England. All the nice girls would be taken, leaving only the other kind. The kind that had hung around every base at which he had trained. As a good Catholic boy, he had a romantic view of girls and of sex. He had never been near a prostitute, and the idea of them perhaps scared him.

Another thing: Following Toft and the others through London could cost plenty. How much, he wondered. He had to save his money. Marriage was expensive. He would need thousands of dollars.

They dined at Hachetts, one of the most popular restaurants in wartime London. An orchestra was playing as they came in. The dance floor was crowded with couples dancing.

They were shown to a table well back. The nightly bombing of London was long over; rationing, on the other hand, was stronger than ever. They could have fish, the waiter told them, including lobster. Or chicken. And of course as much of any wine or liquor as they wished. They ordered above the din of the music, starting with scotch for the other men, and a manhattan for Davey.

Most of the men at the other tables, most of the ones dancing as well, were officers in uniform, Davey saw. Americans, British, French—even Polish. Many were colonels and generals sitting with, or dancing with, well-dressed older women.

But there were girls too, some in dresses, others in uniform: British WRNS, American WAACs, nurses of various nationalities. They looked to him older and more sophisticated than he would be comfortable with. They were all taken anyway. Often their dates were pilots with silver wings on their chests, and the girls leaned into their arms, or into the glow of the candlelight above the tables, and listened raptly as the pilots talked.

At his own table the pilots kept ordering drinks. Davey downed a number of manhattans, the others much scotch. For a time two nurses were seated with them. Then the nurses were gone, and two of the pilots as well. Davey was very hungry. His head had got fuzzy. Couples kept moving past the table to or from the dance floor. People seemed to dance all the time. They danced while waiting to order, and between courses, even while waiting for the check.

Davey said to Toft: "When you shoot somebody down, does it affect you?"

They were alone at the table—their two remaining comrades had moved to the dance floor where, flushed and giggling, they pushed into the crowd to cut in on one couple after another.

"I try not to let it affect me."

"I keep seeing that guy's face."

"You always see their faces," said Toft. "Even if you didn't see them."

"It bothers me, Major."

"Joe."

"Bothers me a lot." Davey felt tears building up behind his eyes. "What am I gonna do, Joe?"

"Don't think about it," Toft said. "Goes away after a while. Have to wait."

A new round of drinks was delivered.

"How would you like to be my wingman?" said Toft.

The question made Davey more or less sober. It seemed to him that his entire future was at stake, and that he had best pay attention. He said carefully: "I'm flattered, of course."

"Together we'd wipe out the whole Luftwaffe."

"Yes, well—"

"You don't want to."

"It isn't that."

"You're the best pilot in the squadron."

"Thank you."

"After me, of course."

"What about Buxton?"

"You're better."

"He's an ace."

"You'll be an ace too."

"You think so?"

"I do, I do."

"Can't get to be an ace flying on somebody's wing." There. Davey had wanted to say this for a week, and now it was said.

Toft signaled to the waiter, who approached the table.

"Sir?"

The glass in front of Toft was still half full. "Another round here," he said.

"I've got eight missions in," said Davey doggedly. "I've been meaning to ask you—"

Perhaps it was the fumes in his head that had given him the nerve to speak out. "I want to lead. Maybe it's time somebody became my wingman."

"You think so?"

"Yes."

"Eight missions?"

"Yes."

"I didn't know it was that many."

"So how about it?"

"Have to think it over. Need some time to think it over."

The new round of drinks was set down on the table. There were now two full glasses in front of Davey, one and a half in front of Toft.

"I thought it over," said Toft. "You ride my wing for a while, we see how it goes."

Davey said nothing.

"My way's better."

Again Davey said nothing.

"Good experience for you," said Toft.

"I think we should eat something," said Davey.

The waiter came and they ordered the chicken.

"My way's best," said Toft, when the waiter had left them. "You'll see."

The other two pilots were still on the dance floor. Davey and Toft found themselves, suddenly, with not much to say to each other.

The waiter came back with their dinners. Mashed potatoes. Chicken legs poking upwards. Davey ate hungrily, cutting and chewing. Toft only picked with his fork.

"See that girl over there?" he said.

He was pointing, which embarrassed Davey: "Don't point, she's looking at you."

Like Toft she was in her middle twenties. A blond girl in a tight black dress. Toft said: "Go over and ask if she wants to have a drink with me."

"She's with somebody."

"Doesn't matter," said Toft.

"Probably it would be better if you approached her personally."

"You think so?"

"Girls like to be approached personally, usually."

"Never mind," said Toft. "Not important."

Their plates were taken away. Their two comrades, showing off for each other, were still on the dance floor cutting in on unknown women. Toft and Davey drank and watched.

"Cutting in on babes you don't know takes balls," said Toft.

"You wanna dance," suggested Davey, "go dance."

"Don't have the balls."

Davey found this comment incomprehensible. His idol was afraid to ask an unknown woman to dance. So was Davey, but then Davey had no desire to dance with anybody, or if he did, not much. Whereas Toft wanted to, but didn't have the nerve. "You shot down eighteen planes," Davey said. "You got the biggest balls in the world."

"That's planes, not girls," said Toft. He was staring at the blond girl in the tight black dress. "You dance with her, Davey. Go ask her."

"Not me," said Davey, "you should ask her."

"Can't."

"Why not?

Toft said: "Don't know how to dance."

"Don't know how to dance?"

"Never learned."

"That's a problem."

"Should have learned."

"I learned. When I was sixteen, my mother sent my brother and me to Arthur Murray."

Toft emptied his glass. "I don't really want to dance. I want to pick up a girl and screw her. This is not the place, Davey. To pick up girls. Come on."

They went back to the hotel, where Toft waved a twenty-dollar bill at the night concierge. He said: "We want some girls. Want you to get us some."

"Girls?" said the concierge stiffly.

"You know what a girl is, don't you? Do you want me to describe one for you?"

"It might be difficult, sir. At this hour." But the bill had vanished.

"Want some girls," said Toft. "Send 'em up."

They went up to their room, where Toft turned the lights down low. "Girls like soft lighting," he murmured.

Having removed their shoes they reclined on the beds. Toft lay with his eyes closed.

"I'm not sure this is such a good idea," said Davey.

"'S wonderful idea."

"Well, I'm not so sure." Both had drunk a great deal, but under the pressure of the moment, Davey was suddenly cold sober.

They waited.

"Wish there was a radio in the room," Toft said. "Help keep us awake."

Davey said: "We could possibly catch something."

"Use a rubber."

"I don't think I have one."

Toft raised his head. "Didn't bring rubbers?"

"I guess I forgot."

"There was a box of them beside the door where you sign out."

"I didn't see them."

"Jesus, they were right there."

Davey had seen them clearly enough. "I must have been preoccupied," he said.

Toft again lay back with his eyes closed. "I got some extras. I'll lend you what you need. How many you think you'll need?"

"We should have got two rooms," said Davey.

"You want some privacy, I'll take mine in the bathroom."

Davey said nothing, and they continued to wait.

"Joe?" Davey had never felt more alert in his life.

"Don't let me fall asleep," said Toft. "Almost fell asleep."

"Joe, suppose the girls are a couple of dogs."

"They're not going to be film stars."

"I wouldn't want to do it if she's a dog."

"They're not going to be Betty Grable and Linda Darnell."

After a moment Toft mumbled: "So turn the lights out. In the dark, you won't be able to tell."

On the next bed his breathing became regular, and then Davey realized he was asleep.

At the sound of a scratching at the door, Davey sat bolt upright.

The scratching became discrete taps, and then louder ones. After throwing a glance at the man on the other bed, Davey dropped down on the pillow, where he lay with eyes screwed shut pretending, in case Toft woke up, to be asleep.

Presently came the noise of high heels receding down the corridor. For a while longer Davey remained tense, eyes still shut tight— perhaps they'd come back.

He was awakened by sunlight streaming into the room, and by Toft shaking him. He sat up, rubbing his eyes.

"What happened?" demanded the squadron commander.

In their rumpled uniforms the two pilots stood facing each other.

"We must have fallen asleep," said Davey.

"Did the women come?"

"I guess not."

"Don't you know?"

"Yeah, I'm sure of it. They didn't come."

Fuming, Toft began to curse the concierge. "Sonuva bitch owes me twenty bucks. I'm going down and break his fuckin' neck. Fuckin' thief."

They washed, shaved, and went downstairs, where Toft stormed toward the concierge's desk, but the night man had gone off duty; a different man was there.

They went into the dining room and ordered breakfast. "Fine couple of fighter pilots we are," Toft said pouring out tea. "Come to London with money to burn and can't even get laid. That's amazing, wouldn't you say?"

Davey gave a weak smile. "Amazing," he said.

IV

Ｉ N the presbytery the telephone rang ten times, perhaps more, before Favert found his glasses in the dark, got his bathrobe on, and got out of the bedroom to answer it. By then, except for the smallest child, the entire household was awake.

"They're coming," said the voice in Favert's ear. It was someone who worked in the *mairie,* Favert believed—he did not know who—or perhaps someone in the police. The same voice had called in the night in the past, each time warning of a raid.

The pastor started to ask questions but was too late. The other man had already hung up.

"What is it?" The phone was in Favert's office. His wife in her long woolen nightdress, barefoot, stood in the doorway.

His wife's name was Norma. Behind her crowded all the children, including Rachel in a similar nightdress, and for the first time, perhaps because of the stress of the moment, Favert saw that the girl had somehow grown into a young woman. When did that happen, he asked himself? What had become of the child he had taken in, who was so scared, so desperately anxious to please, so in need of love? Somehow she had become as much a part of his family—he was sure Norma felt the same—as their real children.

The pastor didn't know how many Jews were hidden in and

around Le Lignon. Over a thousand, certainly. A plan existed for emergencies such as tonight's, and Favert picked up the phone again to put it into operation.

But the line, he found, had gone dead.

This meant that the raid must be imminent, and was the worst news of all. The Jews, who were scattered as far as the most outlying farms, would have to be warned almost individually. The police would come from Le Puy, which was to the west. Jews who lived in that direction would have to be warned first, and he would have to do it himself because whoever rode out that way risked running into the police and being arrested. Would it be the French police again or, this time, the Gestapo? How much time did he have? He would be traveling by bicycle, for he had no car.

"I have to go out," said Favert to his wife, and he looked at Rachel. She could not stay here, he decided. Unlike most of the refugees, she spoke French and might get by, but he was unwilling to take the chance with her life. "Get dressed, Rachel," he said. "Dress warmly. I want you to do something for me."

In his own room he threw on his clothes. "Put the kids back to bed," he said to his wife. "If anyone asks about me, I'm visiting parishioners who are in need."

Rachel was waiting in the big room. He took her out into the night and gave her instructions. She was to pedal east, alerting his section heads who lived in that direction, and then stopping at farms as far as the border of the commune. She was young and strong and would be all right, he believed. She should ride as far as St. Agave and wake up l'Abbé Monnier, the priest there. Ask him to open the church. Tell him that other refugees would be riding in behind her. Monnier was not part of the conspiracy to hide Jews, but he had agreed to help on a temporary basis in emergencies such as this.

Favert got bikes out of the shed, and he put Rachel on Norma's, which was in better shape than her own. The night was dark and cold, and he hoped she would be warm enough. She wore several layers of sweaters, for she owned no coat or jacket, and one of Norma's old skirts cut down to fit, and woolen stockings. She had a kerchief on her head, and a long scarf wound several times around her neck and tied in a loose knot, the ends hanging almost to her waist. There was hardly enough light to see her face, but she was rosy-cheeked as always, young and blooming, smiling up at him, and he saw that she was unafraid, saw no risk, and was anxious to be off. To her, this was an adventure. He also saw that she had no gloves, so he made her take his own, and then gave her a push start down the road.

He himself pedaled first to the schoolmaster's house, and together they woke up several of the students who boarded there, and sent them out on other bikes to knock on the doors of section heads, after that stopping at the various pensions, hotels, and private houses inside the village where Jews lived, telling them to be dressed and out on the street as fast as possible. The schoolmaster had a truck and would pick up as many as he could and drive them to the church in St. Agave. They were to take food and a blanket and nothing else. If the schoolmaster did not come for them in time—he would be collecting children first—they were to run into the woods and hide. The truck could carry thirty or forty refugees at a time standing up, and the schoolmaster had enough carefully hoarded black market gasoline to make four trips, possibly five, if there should be time before the roadblocks went up that would isolate the village.

Next, Pastor Favert started out on the road to Le Puy, knees churning. The road was bordered on both sides by poor farms, each one housing, in addition to the farmer and his family, a refugee couple, sometimes with children, sometimes without. And he began knocking on doors. The farmhouses were widely separated, and behind them on both sides rose dense forest.

The night was dark and very cold, the wind blew, and his hands on the bare handlebars felt frozen. He was pedaling hard between farmhouses, and his legs and back began to tighten up, and he worried about being able to make it as far as the outermost farms. It was by then close to four o'clock in the morning, the darkest and coldest part of the night. There was no other traffic on the road, and from time to time, forced to stop to catch his breath, he listened for the cars and police buses he knew were coming. He pedaled with his mouth open, panting. The wind never stopped. It blew icy cold across the plateau, most of the time he was pedaling directly into it, and it blew into his mouth and made his teeth ache.

He wrapped his scarf around his lower face, but this did not seem to help.

None of the farmers had gasoline, but some had tractors and trucks that had been converted to run on charcoal. He urged them to load up as many refugees as they could carry, taking the very young, the very old, and the infirm first, and then if there was time and room, some of the others. Refugees who had bicycles could follow. Some of the refugees immediately became frantic, and he was able to speak German to them, for he had studied in Germany, and he tried to calm them down.

If they kept to the farm lanes and back roads they should be safe, he told them. They should make for the village of Hingeaux. The mayor there was sympathetic and would open the basement of the town hall.

Those refugees for whom there was no transport should take blankets and food, ground cloths if they had them, and disappear into the woods behind the farms, and stay there until the crisis was over.

The sun began to rise. The exhausted Favert had reached the last of the farms. He watched a refugee family clamber into a cart drawn by a tractor and go down a lane into the woods. The farmer's wife offered him a glass of wine, which he refused, for he never drank alcoholic beverages, and then a glass of cold water, which he accepted gratefully.

When he came out into the yard again he saw the police cars go by, and then the khaki-colored buses full of gendarmes.

He thanked the farm woman, they shook hands, and he straddled his bike and began to pedal slowly back toward the village. His thighs were chafed and his back hurt, but the sun was up above the trees, it was a little warmer now, and the wind had dropped.

The roadblock when he came to it was about two kilometers out from Le Lignon, a gendarme on a motorcycle, only one man but more than enough when dealing with frightened refugees. Favert was held up there for a time. He had to show his papers, explain who he was. The gendarme, if he had read his rank correctly, was a noncommissioned officer, a *maréchal des logis chef,* and his orders were to stop traffic coming out from the village; apparently he didn't know what to do with someone coming in. But presently he decided to let Favert through.

When the pastor pedaled into the market square he saw the four khaki buses drawn up there, plus two cars, and standing beside one of the cars were the mayor, and Prefect Brin, and a third man who wore a leather overcoat down to his shins and a trilby hat. Gestapo, thought Favert. To put some backbone into this raid, to make sure the French did it right.

Two of the buses were filled with gendarmes, who sat with kepis off and tunics unbuttoned, but looked uncomfortable anyway. The other two buses were empty.

Empty buses to take away whatever Jews they catch, thought Favert.

When he got down off his bike his thighs started to quiver, and he almost fell down. He waited for this to pass, then wheeled the bike toward the three men, where he shook hands with the mayor and with Brin.

"Where were you?" demanded Brin.

Favert studied the German officer, who was clean-shaven, narrow-faced, about thirty-five.

"I want to know where you've been," said Brin.

Pastor Favert nodded to the German.

"This is Monsieur Gruber," said Brin.

Bracing to attention in the German manner, Favert said in German: "Herr Gruber, *Guten Tag.* Gestapo, is it?"

The man's eyes narrowed.

"It is good that you are here," the pastor said in German. "You and men like you stiffen the fabric of French life."

"You speak German quite well," said Gruber.

Brin and the mayor, not understanding, kept glancing from one to the other.

"Classic German, yes," said the pastor. "What I have trouble with is modern German. New words. 'Reinforced interrogations,' for instance. Is that a euphemism for something? What does it mean?"

The German looked at him, but said nothing.

So the pastor turned to Brin and the mayor and switched to

French. "I was just asking him about reinforced interrogations. According to SS regulations dated June 12, 1942, reinforced interrogations can only be applied if a previous interrogation shows that the prisoner has important information that he refuses to divulge."

Pastor Favert had a source of information denied to most of his compatriots: Swiss pastors who moved freely across both borders.

"Of course," he said to Brin and the mayor, "the law is very strict—reinforced interrogations can only be applied against Jews, Communists, Marxists, Jehovah's Witnesses, Bible students, saboteurs, terrorists, resistance agents, or Polish or Russian vagabonds. So I suppose we shouldn't worry about it too much."

"I know who you are," said Gruber in German.

The pastor did not know who Gruber was. If he had, would he have held his tongue? "Another new phrase that puzzles me," the pastor said in German, "is 'final solution.' What could that mean?"

"I want an answer," said Brin in French. "Where were you?"

"I am the pastor," Favert answered. "When any member of my flock has need of me I must go there, even in the middle of the night."

Brin nodded coldly. After a moment he began what was almost a prepared speech. "Pastor," he said, "we know in detail the suspect activities to which you are devoted."

Speaking German, Favert said to Gruber: "You did not answer my question."

Gruber's eyes may have narrowed further. Otherwise no emotion showed. His rank was *Obersturmbannführer,* the equivalent of lieutenant colonel. He commanded all Reich Security forces for Lyon and the center of France—this included the Gestapo and the SS both.

Brin's speech, meanwhile, had continued. "Pastor, you are hiding in this commune a certain number of Jews. I have an order to lead these people to the prefecture for a control. You are therefore going to give me a list of these persons, and of their addresses, and you will advise them to present themselves and not try to flee."

"Sorry," said Favert, "I've never known the names."

This was true. All had been furnished with forged identity

cards—not by him, because a forged identity card to him was a lie, and although he recognized the necessity, he would only acquiesce in the forging, not take part in it personally.

Except for Rachel's, he had been careful not to learn the false names.

"The modern police have motorcycles, cars, radios," said Brin. "Against them resistance is useless." Once again his anger showed. "We know where your protégés are hiding."

"Well, then, you should have no trouble finding them."

"We've already made a house-to-house search of the village," Brin said. "We did not find Jews. You have hidden them. I want to know where."

"There used to be Jews here," said Favert. "But they left some time ago."

"How long ago?"

Favert was a man of such strong conscience, or of such pride—there may have been an admixture of arrogance as well—that he refused ever to lie. Or perhaps he felt that to lie was to demean himself. Whatever the need or provocation, he would not speak an untruth. To lie now was out of the question.

"Answer me. How long ago?"

"Different ones left at different times, I suppose."

"You're lying."

"I don't lie."

"We'll find them."

"Good luck," said Favert. He nodded at them and moved off.

"Come back here," shouted Brin.

"It's Sunday morning," said Pastor Favert. He took off and polished his glasses. "If you will excuse me, I must prepare for the church service." He gave another nod, and left them.

When he came into the presbytery he found his wife waiting just inside the door. Wordlessly she embraced him. She was not a woman to burst into tears, but he realized from the way she clung to him how worried she had become. It was an extremely close marriage, but the things he did had begun to terrify her.

The embrace ended. She said: "I'll fix your breakfast."

He sat at the kitchen table and watched her do it.

She said: "The Gestapo's here."

"Yes. I just met one of them."

"The mayor has had to sign a paper. They sat him down between men with guns. He had no choice."

"A paper?"

"All Jews are to present themselves at the *mairie* by five P.M. today, so that an accurate census may be taken. A routine control."

"A routine control," said Favert, and he gave a brief laugh. "Is anyone supposed to believe that? With armed gendarmes standing by, and two empty buses to take them away?"

"They have a truck with a loudspeaker. First they sent it through the village. Now they're sending it down all the roads."

For the service the temple was crowded to overflowing. People stood in the vestibule, in all the aisles, all of the women wearing hats, the men with their hats in their laps or their hands, the village men wearing shapeless black suits, many of the peasant farmers in the rough clothes of their station.

The pulpit was attached to the center of the wall high up and was reached by a flight of stairs. When Favert, wearing his cassock and split white bib, had climbed up there to begin his sermon he saw that Brin and the Gestapo man had pushed their way in from the vestibule. Because they had removed their hats he saw that Gruber had light brown hair that was parted in the middle and almost shaved at the sides.

They were there to hear him preach, he realized, and possibly, if they did not like what they heard, to arrest him afterward.

He took as his text the thirteenth chapter of St. Paul's epistle to the Romans: "Let every person be subject to the governing authorities . . ." And he began to explain the meaning of Paul's words. Christians must do their civic duties, pay their taxes, honor officials to whom honor is due, obey just laws. But Paul went on to say, and Pastor Favert quoted him in part: "Owe no one anything except to love one another, for he who loves his neighbor has fulfilled the law. The commandments, 'Thou shall not kill, thou shall not steal, thou shall not covet,' and any other commandments, are summed up in this sentence, 'Thou shall love thy neighbor as thyself. Love does not do wrong to a neighbor.' "

No one coughed, nor even stirred. The church was absolutely

still. "When there is conflict between the laws of God and the laws that any government may seek to impose," Favert preached, "then the good Christian must obey God, not man. To be against evil is to be against whatever is destructive of human life, including also the passions that motivate that destruction. There can be no defense for the shedding of innocent blood."

The service ended, and he stood outside greeting his parishioners, some of whom had tears in their eyes. Many, as they shook his hand, seemed unable to speak. He looked for Brin and the Gestapo man, but did not see them.

He had lunch, then got down on the floor and played with the smallest of his children. Without Rachel the presbytery seemed emptier than he was used to. After a brief nap, he put on a dark suit shiny with age, and his thin overcoat, and went out of the house, for he expected to be arrested, and he did not want his children to see this happen.

It was nearly dark. On the square there was no one moving about, no villagers visible at all. Except for the lights in the houses the village might have been empty. The parked buses were still there, and the empty ones were still empty.

Brin and the Gestapo man came out of the cafe on the square and crossed to where Pastor Favert was standing.

"It's five P.M.," said Brin ominously.

"So it is," said the pastor. "Are you leaving now?" There was a chance, he saw, that he was not to be arrested after all.

"Monsieur Gruber and I have urgent business in Le Puy, and must get back."

"Did you find any Jews?"

"No.

"I'm not surprised," said Favert. "There are none here."

"Because you're hiding them," said Brin. "I hold you responsible for this unacceptable resistance to the laws of your country. If you continue to oppose authority, it is you who will be arrested and deported." He gave an ugly little laugh. "You will give me those Jews, Pastor. I will have those Jews."

"But how can I give them to you when you have seen for yourself there are none here."

"The roadblocks will remain in place until we have them."

Muttering to himself, Brin moved toward his car. The Gestapo man, who had said nothing, followed.

"Auf Wiedersehen, Herr Gruber," said Favert to his back, and as he again braced in the German manner he believed he had seen the last of him.

It would be three days before the roadblocks were removed, and the Jews came trooping back.

V

FROM Le Lignon, Obersturmbannführer Gerhard Gruber had gone on to Le Puy where he had other business. By the time he started home it was very late, he could feel a migraine coming on, and he was in as foul a mood as he could remember. He was sick of the high-ranking Frenchmen with whom he was obliged to deal—they never got anything right and they practically drooled with obsequiousness—and he had been chewing on his earlier humiliation for hours. A Protestant pastor who was of no significance whatever had made a fool of him.

Home to Gruber was a fine big apartment, formerly the property of a Jew, in Lyon. It was on the Quai Gailleton overlooking the Rhône. He was not responsible for the Jew or the Jew's family, who had been arrested and deported before he ever came to France. The apartment was not only spacious, but had big windows with balconies, and it had come with servants' rooms upstairs under the mansard, which was where Gruber's own servants lived. He had two assigned to him, a valet and a cook. Like all members of the support staff in Lyon they were Germans, for the work that Reich Security performed was too sensitive to permit French nationals to get close.

His car stopped in front of his building and his guards accompanied him upstairs in case terrorists should be lurking somewhere inside. There were terrorists everywhere these days. As the bird-cage elevator progressed upward the guards stood to either side of him, their guns in their hands, feeling no doubt as trapped as he did, easy targets in that cage.

They got out on his floor, he inserted his key in the door, and as it opened he dismissed them, for he could hear the familiar foot-steps coming forward. He recognized her footsteps even before the opening was big enough to disclose the girl herself, a superb twenty-four-year-old blond named Claire Cusset, formerly a nude dancer at the Folies-Bergère.

He stepped inside, closed the door on the guards, and as he em-braced her he immediately felt a little better.

Gruber was thirty-seven years old, tall and thin, though a bit hippy. He was a university graduate who had nursed ambitions of becoming an opera singer. Instead his father had made him study law. He got his degree, and then for two years went around audi-tioning for the impresarios of provincial opera houses, most of whom he believed to have been Jews. They told him he had a nice baritone voice, a good voice, not a great one, and then hired some-one else, usually one of their co-religionists.

His father would give him no money.

He gave up opera and took a commission in the navy. He would sing in officer's clubs and at official ceremonies, and was popular with other young officers, and with girls, but he got a general's daughter pregnant and was fired for having besmirched the honor of the navy. He would have married the daughter, almost did, but the general (the girl too of course) had some Jewish blood, which, under National Socialism, would have put a crimp in his future. It was a tough decision, but he made it. Out of work, penniless, he joined the SS. Because he could see war coming, and because he be-lieved Hitler had the correct outlook on the world and the Jews, it seemed a good place to be. Recruits first learned, then employed certain SS maxims. "An order is an order" was one of them. "We must have the will to kill coldly and tranquilly" was another.

Gruber got into trouble again during the Norway expedition in 1940—some funds were missing. This landed him on the Russian front in one of the four *Einsatzgruppen.* The mission of these groups was to terrorize the Russian population through mass murder. Gruber had overseen the executions of as many as seven hundred people at a time: Jews, Gypsies, Communists, partisans, hostages. He had watched them dig the mass graves, and sometimes had watched the eventual machine-gunning too. You got used to it, he would have said. He thought himself no more ruthless than he had to be. In a manner of speaking he had closed his eyes and done what he was told, for he could afford no more blots on his record. He became known as an efficient officer, and he progressed upward in rank: *Untersturmführer, Obersturmführer, Hauptsturmführer*. These were SS ranks. All had army equivalents, the last of them captain.

Transferred to Paris, he hired teachers and worked hard perfecting his schoolroom French, four or more hours a day, and as soon as he had become fairly fluent he began to cultivate politicians, entertainers, and the very rich—important people only. Off-duty he seldom wore the SS uniform, and claimed if asked to be a Wehrmacht officer. When foul deeds had to be done, he was now of sufficient rank that his hand never showed. He was friendly, deplored "excesses," and at any party where there was a piano and people who wanted to hear him, he would sing. French officials with whom he was obliged to deal considered him cultured, suave, and not at all like the other Germans, those brutes all around him. He wrote frequent letters to his wife and children in Berlin, but did not lack female companionship. At first, knowing no one, he had been obliged to frequent brothels, but eventually he had acquired Claire Cusset. After watching her dance at the Folies he had sent in his card, and after that he gave her presents, principally food. To keep her body round in the right places, essential in her line of work, Claire needed food—scarce in Paris—which he supplied. His own needs were something else, which she supplied.

In November 1942 the German army had swarmed across the demarcation line, occupying all of France for the first time. Promoted to his present rank, Gruber was sent to Lyon to take over Reich Security—technically it was called the *Kommando der Sipo und SD*—for the city and most of central and southeastern France. The KDS was divided into six sections: administration, judicial, economic, and so forth. Section 4, repression of political crime, was the Gestapo. When the Resistance assassinated someone or blew up a bridge, that was a political crime. Being a Jew was a political crime also. Section 4 had by far the most manpower, and the heaviest workload, and on the success or failure of its operatives rode Gruber's career.

His principal charge in Lyon was the same as it had been in Paris, no change: seeing to it that trains loaded with Jews left on schedule for the east.

Gruber had had enough of killing, and wished now to live the good life. No one was close enough to know what he was doing— not his wife, not his masters in Berlin, not even his masters in Paris. Ensconced in his splendid apartment, ministered to by servants, going to bed with Claire Cusset every night, Gruber would have been content to let the war go on without him. The good life should have been possible, but was not, and the principal reason was that the collecting and deportation of Jews had recently become Berlin's top priority; it seemed to take precedence even over the winning of battles. There were constant telegrams from Eichmann's Jewish Section in Berlin. The empty trains kept pulling in, each of about twenty boxcars, and the pressure on Gruber was relentless. Needed was a minimum of a thousand Jews for each train, but there had come to be a shortage of what he and his colleagues referred to as "inventory." That is, Jews in large quantities had become increasingly difficult to find, making it harder and harder to keep filling those trains.

Gruber saw himself losing Lyon, losing Claire, losing all he had gained.

At this point a rumor reached him. That Jews in great numbers were being hidden in a village called Le Lignon.

So he had gone there with buses, gendarmes, and the prefect of the department, no violence of any kind, no threats, which was the way to do it if you could, but had been thwarted and then humiliated by a Protestant pastor, and had come away without a single Jew.

That night after sex, sitting up in bed in the dark, hip to hip with Claire, their bodies bare and warm, both of them smoking, the shutters and drapes closed because of the blackout, the two coals flickering like miniature stars, Gruber said: "Did you ever hear of a Protestant pastor named Andre Favert?"

"No," answered Claire.

Because she could not see his face Gruber allowed himself to frown. But he was not surprised by her answer. Except for singers and film stars, he told himself, she never heard of anybody. Ask her what's the name of the Führer, and probably she wouldn't know.

He gave a sigh and said: "Let's get some sleep."

Having felt for the ashtray on the bedside table, he rubbed out his cigarette. Claire did the same, and when they had slid down into the bed, she reached over and found his hand, which was nice.

He lay in the dark brooding. The events of today were supposed to have been part of something bigger, but he saw now he would have to go back and start again—this Pastor Favert had turned out to be a solid impediment. Hundreds of Jews were hidden in and around Le Lignon, Gruber believed—today he had become convinced of it—but Favert would have to be eliminated before he could get at them. An experienced leader himself, Gruber knew how to recognize a fellow leader when he saw one. Eliminate the leader—Favert—and he could go back and pluck Jews off the trees like apples. He might be able to fill an entire train, maybe two trains.

Eliminate Favert and expunge today's humiliation as well. Revenge would be extremely sweet.

Gruber's staff car was waiting downstairs in the morning. His office was in the Hôtel Terminus next to the railroad station, close enough to walk to, though walking the streets of Lyon these days was out of the question, for there had been assassinations, and although the French paid dearly for each one, always at least ten hostages shot for one German, and sometimes more, still they continued. His car was impressive, a big Mercedes. He had the use of a motorcycle with sidecar as well—if he had to get through narrow streets in a hurry, the sidecar was more practical, though in it you were more exposed.

Upstairs in his office he brooded a bit longer, then began making phone calls. The wise way to go about this was to work through the French, which meant, in turn, that nothing was going to be accomplished overnight. He could arrest Favert himself immediately, but it would cause a stir. The French did not seem to mind too much when Jews got arrested, but a Protestant pastor was another thing. Better to let them do it themselves. Better to lodge his "suggestion" in high places, and then wait while it was turned into an order and made its way down the chain of command to officers in the field. Doing it this way would take time, how much time he could not say, but there were no trains scheduled at the moment, so he could wait. It shouldn't take too long.

As he hung up the phone he was smiling. Revenge was even sweeter if you couldn't have it right away. Like sex. Better to be tantalized first. Anticipation was part of the eventual pleasure which, because of it, would be all the greater when it came.

VI

After the group briefing, Toft called half his squadron to one side. Seven young men in flight jackets and the crushed uniform caps that pilots affected clustered around him, one of them Davey.

Today, as the bombers plastered Düsseldorf, he was to lead eight Mustangs to a different target. They would climb up into the bomber stream, following along as if part of it, but then veer to the south to find and strafe what Intelligence described as a major Luftwaffe repair base. The base was supposed to be about twenty miles south of Munich. It was supposed to be heavily defended, ten or a dozen antiaircraft batteries, maybe more. There were supposed to be upward of two hundred planes on the ground there.

This much Toft's pilots had heard in the group briefing.

"We go for the batteries first," Toft told them now. "Knock them out, the danger's over, and we can strafe the aircraft on the ground till we run out of ammo."

He was silent while all of them contemplated what they were being asked to do. The Mustang was the supreme fighter plane of the war. It had the longest range, the fastest speed, the fastest climb, and it could outmaneuver anything in the sky, but its engine was liquid cooled, which made it vulnerable to ground fire. This was its weakness; take a hit in the coolant, and you were going down. Most of the Mustangs lost so far had been brought down by ground fire.

"Keep kicking your rudder so as to spray bullets," said Toft. "You kill a lot of enemy gunners that way, and you discourage the rest. No place to hide. Clear?" Of the seven young men, six were smoking nervously, every face somber. "We come in from up-sun. That way anyone who gets hit has a clear run to try to get home.

Again he paused.

"My element will make the initial pass. The rest of you stand off and see what sort of fire we draw and where it's coming from. Then we go in two by two and blast the guns."

He glanced all around but no one said anything.

"At the end of each pass everybody does a climbing turn to the left. To the left, got that? I don't want us colliding with each other."

Some of the men nodded. The seven faces looked back at him.

"If we knock out the guns we should be able to make seven or eight passes on the parked aircraft."

Again he waited for comment that did not come.

"If the field turns out to be too heavily defended, too many guns to knock out, we abort. I'm not going to trade planes and pilots for planes." He looked around once more. "If I'm shot down, Captain Conner decides whether the fire is too heavy, whether to continue the attack, or break off and go home."

Still no one spoke. "Man your ships," he said.

Because they had to lag behind the bombers, it took three hours to reach their target, and they could not at first find it. They peered down from 29,000 feet. The countryside was painted with snow. Otherwise nothing. Toft brought them halfway down and the autobahn became a black string. They could see miniature farm buildings under white blankets, miniature trees with snow in their hair.

Davey thought he saw something. "Check the autobahn," he said into his throat mike. Even for Davey those were mere specks down there. "That thing moving is, I believe, a tractor, and the vehicle it's pulling could be a plane."

At this stage of the war no traffic moved on autobahns by day.

"Drop tanks," said Toft.

The sixteen silver tanks floated away.

"Check gun switches, sights," said Toft. "Down we go."

When they leveled off, the lead vehicle was seen to be a tractor, and it was towing a plane without wings. "They may be using the autobahn as a runway," called Davey. "That field over there may be the base."

The field was surrounded by snow-covered fir trees. They circled, losing more altitude, while the two vehicles left the autobahn via a gap in the trees.

Now they could discern two snow-covered runways, and snowy shapes near or under the trees that could only be more planes.

"My element goes in first," called Toft. "The rest of you watch to see where the batteries are. You ready, Davey?"

They set up to the south, and then Toft and Davey turned and angled steeply down. They were making over four hundred miles an hour as they reached the field. Davey aimed at one of the parked planes. He saw powdered snow pop off it. Then it exploded, the smoke rising above the trees almost before he and Toft were clear.

Only two batteries had opened fire, one to the left, the other to the right, which news was relayed to them as he and Toft came around to form up. This was minimal opposition, and the pilots were all pleased.

"Anybody see anything else?" inquired Toft.

No one had. Eight pairs of eyes had raked the ground, and continued to do so. The bulk of the parked aircraft were dead ahead, some of them relatively far back in the trees. But there were no hidden batteries anyone could perceive, and if they existed, why hadn't they fired already?

Toft detached two planes, one to hit the right-hand battery, the other the left. There was no reason to wait until this was done. The remaining Mustangs would give them a few seconds head start, then sweep over the field six abreast, guns hammering.

"Pick a target," Toft called. "Let's go."

This time they came up over low hills at treetop level at top speed. At this height they could see parked planes everywhere, even far back in the trees, and then a flare rose up over the middle of the field which no one at first understood, though all soon would.

Davey at this time was on the extreme left of the formation, pointed toward an FW 190 that was parked broadside to him, and that expanded with incredible rapidity in his sight ring, the easiest target he had ever seen, the sight ring nearly filling up with it, but even as he prepared to press the trigger he knew that something had gone wrong. The flare had barely distracted him. Nor did all the snow that seemed to fly off the trees ahead, but an instant after that the air was filled with blobs of orange and red fire. At first they had no shape, and then they became orange and red golf balls traveling toward him with fantastic heat at fantastic speed. Davey had never seen fiery golf balls before, twenty-millimeter shells, he supposed, and the onrushing Mustangs flew right into them.

Still he maintained focus on the 190, his bullets kicking up snow and dirt, then climbing onto its wings. All the while his Mustang shuddered and bucked from the recoil of its guns, and from the incredible barrage of flak through which he was flying. The 190 burst into flames, chunks and pieces flying in all directions, and as he lifted over the trees, he glimpsed something else too—only a glimpse—where the antiaircraft fire was coming from.

Then he was past, they were all past, though some of the Mustangs had taken hits. Toft requested a roll call to be sure everyone was unhurt, every plane still functioning. "All of you test your controls," he ordered.

They were very low and well away from the field, coming around, forming up for another pass, if that was what Toft would decide on.

Someone said: "Jesus, that was heavy."

"There must be twenty batteries down there," said someone else.

"Anybody see where they are?" called Toft.

"In the trees," said Davey. "When they fired it shook all the snow off the trees. They're on platforms about twenty feet up."

"Spray those trees," said Toft. "Get those guns."

They came around and down. The golf ball hailstorm repeated itself, and they flew into it.

The gunners in the trees had bigger weapons, cannons over machine guns, but they were immobile, and no longer in ambush, for the fall of all that powdery snow had given away their positions.

There were green trees and white trees down there, and the planes came at the green ones at tremendous speed, and forty-eight guns threshed the branches, threshed the men, turned the trees to stalks.

On that pass the Mustangs cleared about half the platforms, denuded them of guns and men, and on the next pass the rest. After that they methodically destroyed every plane on the ground that they could see.

By the sixth pass some resistance had been reestablished. Fiery golf balls reappeared in the air. The Mustangs flew through them with insouciance, believing nothing could hurt them now, and formed up for another pass and came through intact still again.

"Last one," Toft said. He was nearly out of ammunition. They all were.

Down they went. Davey had already destroyed at least three planes on the ground, seen them go up in orange geysers of flame, had hit others as well; this time he had a parked 109 in his sight ring, but before he could pull off a burst there came a kind of sudden sodden crump, then some thuds. Part of the canopy came in on him, and his side and hip felt stung by a dozen powerful bees.

He was hit and knew it, but there wasn't time to worry about that, for the Mustang had seemed to stop in midair, and when he glanced over, he saw that part of his right wing was gone. And the plane began to drop.

He was so low he did not have much air to lose. He gave full left rudder trying to compensate, and pushed the throttle to the stops, simultaneously lifting the nose to the point where he was sure the plane would stall, though it did not, and then higher still, trying to keep the Mustang in the air as long as possible, at least give himself time to figure out what had happened, what to do.

At the same time he was being lifted up higher and higher in his seat, and when he looked down he saw that the dinghy he was sitting on had begun to inflate. The wind was whistling into the cockpit. The dinghy was whistling too, or rather the cylinder attached to it, which must have been set off by a bullet or shrapnel.

"I'm hit," he gasped into the radio. "I don't know how bad."

His head was being forced forward against the canopy as he rose higher and higher in his seat, by now it was as if he sat on a throne. He grabbed the sheath knife out of his boot and began trying to stab the dinghy to death, obscene hissing monster that it was. Down plunged the knife, but the dinghy kept expanding. Again and again he stabbed it. He couldn't watch what he was doing because he was trying to fly the plane, and so managed to stab himself in the leg. He was insane with rage and fear by that time and hardly felt it, except that his pants leg rapidly got wet. His waist was already wet, his side. But at last the dinghy subsided. One final outgoing hiss and it was done, flat.

He thought of trying to land on the autobahn below, assuming the Mustang would do it for him. At least he would be alive, unless the survivors of the slaughter back there found him, and cut his throat. If he did survive the landing, the best he could hope for was a prison camp, perhaps for years, for the war might have years to go, there was no break in sight as yet.

The autobahn ran west so he followed it, deciding he had best put as much distance as possible between himself and the smoke and carnage he had helped cause, before bailing out or going down.

In his radio he heard Toft send the others back to England, and then the squadron leader was flying alongside him.

"I'm with you, Davey. I'll get you home."

Davey flew holding his rudder full left. His left leg was losing strength on the pedal, beginning to go numb. The stick was pushed that way too as he tried to hold the broken wing high. He was proceeding crabwise through the air, trying for altitude but not getting much, and Toft alongside was throttled way back but had to fly esses to keep from leaving him behind.

They began to pass over Lake Constance. To the south were the snowcapped Alps. Davey knew exactly where he was—still over Germany. Being a fighter pilot had improved his geography, he realized. He realized also that he was bleeding badly. How bad, he didn't know, didn't want to know.

To the south was Switzerland. They had the whole width of it to go, a hundred miles or more, then part of France, all of Belgium, and finally the North Sea. He would have to cross the North Sea in winter in a crippled plane and no dinghy. There was an emergency base at Manston just beyond the cliffs of Dover, if he could get that far. Did he have enough fuel to get there crabwise? His mind was getting fuzzy. He had both feet on left rudder now, for his left leg had lost all feeling, and his right had cramped up solid. His arms and shoulders ached, and he was soaked in sweat and blood.

"Suppose enemy fighters find us," said Davey. He was talking to keep himself conscious.

"They won't."

"If they do?"

"I'll protect you," said Toft

Avoiding cities and the antiaircraft guns around them, they moved slowly west.

Davey's head drooped forward. "You have any ammo left?" he said, rousing himself still again.

"No."

"How are you going to protect me?"

"I'll get on their tails and scare them to death."

This comment was perhaps amusing, but neither laughed.

"I'm running hot," said Davey a little later.

"Crack your cowl flaps."

Each emergency roused him for a time. "I already did."

"Open the mixture to full rich."

Raw gas acted as a coolant, Davey knew. The temperature went down slightly. But the gas needle began to go down fast.

"I think we're out of German airspace," the squadron commander said. "We're over France."

Davey was too weak to answer.

"How's your fuel?" said Toft.

There was a long silence while Davey tried to study the needles. "It's fine," he said, though he thought it wasn't. He bit down on his lip.

"We need to go more north," said Toft.

Below all was smoothly white. Above was a thick gray overcast which at least protected them from high-flying fighters. The wind was blowing them steadily south.

"Try to fly more north," said Toft.

"I can't," said Davey. He was no longer enunciating clearly.

"Try, Davey, try."

"It won't go that way."

Davey's engine began to run rough. He tried to focus on his gas gauge but couldn't. During lucid moments he worried about Toft, whose fuel must be dangerously low. "I'm all right now," he said. "Go on home, Joe. Go home."

But Toft stuck with him.

Davey's Mustang began to shudder. He had to blink his eyes to see at all, but glanced out at his ruined wing and saw another shred of surface aluminum tear off and sail away.

After that nothing he could do would hold the plane in the air, and he had to drop the nose to keep from stalling.

"I'm going down, Joe."

"Bail out, Davey. Bail out."

His head had gone stupid, but he made what seemed to him a wise decision. He said: "I think I'd rather ride it in."

"Get out, Davey, jump before it's too late."

"It looks smooth down there."

Toft was shouting at him: "You don't know what's under that snow. For God's sake bail out."

Davey's Mustang was sinking fast, the ground coming up to meet him. "I've never bailed out of a plane," he said. "It's too late anyway."

THESE were the last words Toft heard him speak. The Mustang pancaked into a snowy field, bounced twice, and slid toward a forest, which it entered, chopping down bushes and trees as it went. A large tree fell down, and Toft thought he saw that both wings had been torn off. Though he flew back and forth over the spot for some minutes, he saw no movement in or near the plane.

VII

Tʜᴇ forger, who carried papers identifying himself as Henri Prudhomme, but whose real name was Pierre Glickstein, heard the planes overhead, one of them dropping lower and lower, obviously in trouble, and he got to the window in time to see it pancake in. The sound this made was a hollow thump like a bass drum, though louder and heavier, much heavier, and from the impact the floor seemed to jump under his feet.

On an afternoon this cold his window was nearly frosted over, and the snow, which had fallen for two days, was falling again, but as the plane rebounded he could see the white star on its side. It bounced four meters in the air, five tons bouncing, sailed a short ways, came down, and bounced again. The second bounce was lower than the first. There was no third bounce, it only skidded on, digging up the field, then entered the forest scything. Bushes vanished. Trees toppled. It scythed down everything it touched. The forest smothered it. By the time it stopped it could barely be seen.

Pierre Glickstein witnessed all this from the room in which he lived and worked, which was attached to a barn on a farm three kilometers out of Le Lignon. The farmhouse, the barn, and all the other buildings were made of stone, with walls nearly a meter thick, and they crouched under heavy slate roofs and, today, heavy snow. All had been built at least two hundred years ago, perhaps much more, the date now lost, though some had been added to along the way, the forger's room for instance, and the farm had stayed in the same family all that time. It added up to eight generations of people, thirty of beasts whose lives are shorter.

A long enough period, one that had encompassed many wars, though not yet all of this one.

In the farmhouse lived the farmer and his wife, both getting on in years. Their several children had moved away long ago. The outbuildings were clustered around the house: barn, toolhouse, shed for manure, creamery, lean-to for firewood, a privy of course, and a long shed that was a kind of garage. It held plow, carts, bicycles, a small rusted truck altered to run on charcoal, and a 1928 Renault, bought secondhand, the only car the farmer had ever owned, already old when he bought it, older still when the war started. After France fell, men came by and requisitioned its tires, which were needed by the German war machine. He was given a paper for them. It didn't matter, there was already no gas. The car sat now on blocks, its wheels bare, waiting for a time when fuel to run it, and tires to run it on, would again be available.

The farmer owned about thirty acres, plus three cows, a horse, and two pigs. For Le Lignon this counted as a big farm, and a rich one. That is, the scores of others hereabouts were smaller and poorer. The land was planted mostly in cabbages and potatoes, which were the staple crops these days. The farmhouse was without electricity or telephone, for the government's rural electrification program had been abandoned because of the war. There was no central heating of course, nor running water. Water came from a well, and a hand pump over the kitchen sink brought it into the house.

Pierre Glickstein's room was about the size of a jail cell. It had been built onto the barn at the end of the last century. It had a dirt floor and a sloping roof, and contained an iron cot, the table on which he performed his meticulous work, two chairs, and a coat-tree on which hung his few clothes. Pushed into one corner were some old farm implements, for the room had previously been used for storage. Heat was provided by a small stove which, no matter how much wood he shoved into it, was insufficient on a day like this. His single window had long ago been cut into one of the outside walls, but the room was entered from the barn, and it was the forger's habit, searching for every bit of warmth, to keep this door open so that the heat of the animals might drift in on him. Of course their various aromas drifted in too. The peasants hereabouts believed that to breathe such air was healthy. They all lived beside or above their animals, and some lived a good long time, so perhaps they were right. The forger was a city boy from Nice. He was studious, not very tall, slight of build, wore glasses. He had no previous knowledge of farms or farmers, and so had no firm opinion on the subject of barnyard air. He had had no previous knowledge of forgery either.

In November 1942, as soon as the Germans had crossed the demarcation line, they had begun to round up Jews in the south, who had previously considered themselves safe, and one of these people was Glickstein's mother, who was held in a camp to await deportation to Poland, or Russia, or wherever Jews were being sent, and from which none was ever known to have returned. Glickstein had been a student hoping to become an architect, and the roundup missed him. He had found out which camp his mother was in, and which papers were necessary to get her out, and he had forged them, and this had been the start of his present career. He had turned her into a Hungarian. Hungary was Germany's ally, and Hungarian Jews were, for the time being, not being molested. He had brought her to Le Lignon, where Jews were said to find sanctuary, and after asking around had set her up as housekeeper for the Protestant pastor two villages away.

Glickstein himself had taken up residence in the unheated room with the dirt floor, and had become the principal forger for Le Lignon and the villages all around, provider of new identities for the refugees who lived on the plateau, or who passed through as they tried to get to Switzerland or Spain. For most of them he was the difference between life or death.

On his table now lay the tools of his trade: compass and ruler for tracing, two typewriters whose type size differed, and whose ribbons were in different ink; a mimeograph machine for printing out false military orders; bottles of inks in various colors; and a selection of tax stamps, rubber stamps, blank identity cards, ration cards, and official letterheads, most of them provided by sympathetic mayors or functionaries, or stolen from the offices of unsympathetic ones, others of them run off on clandestine printing presses. These were, so to speak, the forger's raw materials, all brought to this room by a woman he knew only as Madame Jeanne.

Glickstein worked all day every day, and usually into the night, forging by daylight for as long as it lasted, and then by the light of innumerable candles. He tried to complete ten sets of papers a day. There were by this time so many counterfeit documents floating around occupied France that in the event of a control by the Gestapo or the *Feldgendarmerie* it was no longer sufficient to show identity and ration cards only. Backup documents were needed to reinforce them: birth, baptismal, and marriage certificates; driver's licenses; declarations of change of domicile; and so forth. The wary Frenchman, not to mention the wary refugee, carried everything he could get.

For each refugee Glickstein provided all these papers, the complete set, and when he had a batch ready, he delivered them to an innkeeper in Rence—never to Le Lignon itself—who would distribute them further. The innkeeper and Madame Jeanne were his only contacts. Everyone knew there was a forger operating on the plateau, but not that it was he. He was seldom seen in the streets of the village, and had never spoken to Pastor Favert. He pretended to be the farmer's hired hand, and was accepted as such. The work done in and around Le Lignon was compartmentalized. No one asked what anyone else was up to, which was part of the reason why so many Jews had remained hidden so long. Certain details of the conspiracy were unknown even to Favert, and he was the moral force behind it.

Delivery of Glickstein's forged documents was always by night. With a thickness of documents under his shirt, he would set out by bicycle, running without lights on tires that were stuffed with straw because they had become too thin to hold air, and this was the most dangerous part of his job. If he ran into a patrol at such an hour, he would be stopped, and because there could be no satisfactory explanation for why he was out on the road so late, he was almost sure to be searched.

Once in fact he did get stopped.

A police car with two men in it. Both got out: a French gendarme in uniform, and a *mec* in a leather coat who spoke with an accent. Gestapo, probably.

The forger's chest was puffed out almost like a woman's, and he held himself round-shouldered to try to compensate. The flashlights moved from his papers to his face and back again, and from time to time he glanced with pretended innocence up at the stars. His own papers were good ones, the best he could make. They identified him as born in French Algeria, which was now in Allied hands, meaning that the birth of Henri Prudhomme there could not be checked. He had given himself a Protestant father but an Arab mother, for Muslims circumcised their boy babies too. If this Gestapo *mec* in the leather overcoat ordered him to undo his fly and show what he had, this would be his explanation, and it might possibly save him. Then again, it might not. If they found the wad of papers inside his shirt, being a Jew would be the least of his problems.

In response to the gendarme's question, he said he was on his way to visit—he had no intention of jeopardizing either his mother or the innkeeper—his girlfriend.

"At this time of night?"

"She's sick."

The gendarme gave him a traffic ticket for running without lights, and then, without a body search, without even patting him down, they let him go, and he pedaled on into the town, and delivered his papers to the innkeeper. He then returned to his room, and went back to work. He was the provider of documents on whom everyone depended. He was *the* forger.

He was nineteen years old.

And now through his window he had seen the P-51 bounce off the ground, then skid into the forest, and he ran through the barn and outside into the snow. It was late in the day, the light was beginning to fail, and the snow was falling harder. He could see no movement in or around the plane. What he did see was the other plane coming back, very low this time, and he crouched against the barn wall afraid of being strafed. It made several passes. After the first of them he felt safe enough against the barn wall, and his principal thoughts became personal. The second plane's repeated passes served no purpose he could see except to localize the site for anyone who hadn't heard the crash itself, and if somebody notified the *Boches* they would come swarming around within hours, you could count on it. He would have to move himself and his equipment somewhere else, though where? Even then, assuming the *Boches* arrived quickly and found the wrecked plane quickly, the risk to him personally would become enormous. They would zero in on the farmer or his wife or both, and force them to divulge secrets they didn't even know they had. The *Boches* were experts at this, as every Frenchman knew. They would learn of the existence of Pierre Glickstein, alias Henri Prudhomme, and they would track him down. He would not be able to get away far enough fast enough.

Finally the other plane flew off. He heard its engine diminish into the distance, and with that he ran across the field toward the forest. Because his room was so cold he was already dressed warmly. He wore two sweaters, both raveled, and over them a sheepskin vest whose wool was turned to the inside—he had made the vest himself by sewing together the hides of two recently slaughtered sheep, and then cutting out armholes. He wore thick corduroy pants over long underwear, two pairs of socks, and the traditional wooden shoes of the region, the soles an inch thick, the uppers of leather. He was even wearing gloves, though with the fingers cut off so he could work.

He was bareheaded. The snow came down on his hair as he ran. Underfoot the snow was about half a meter deep except where the plane had skinned it off, so he was obliged to run slowly, high-stepping.

When he reached the plane he saw that both wings had been sheared away, leaving stubs. The canopy had been smashed too, for he noted shards of it stuck in the snow. He could not see the pilot. This was a spruce forest here, and there were so many branches crowded on top of the cockpit that he could not tell if he was in there or not, much less whether alive or dead.

The propellor blades were bent back over where the engine must be. The engine was still hot, for he could hear it ticking. There was an odor of raw gasoline, but no fire, at least not yet.

[6 6]

Glickstein jumped up onto one of the stubs and tried to free the cockpit, but he was fighting branches that were dense with needles, extremely elastic, and folded together in several layers. He could discern no sound or movement underneath them, and as fast as he pulled one branch away it sprang back. Above him the wind was blowing hard. It kept blowing puffs of snow off the trees and down his neck.

He needed an ax, and was about to go back to get one, when he saw the farmer himself coming forward, eyes studying his ruined field. He was carrying a pitchfork, not an ax, having grabbed it up as a weapon most likely, the only one close to hand.

"Is he alive?" the farmer said when he was close.

"I don't know. Help me get these branches off him."

The farmer's name was Daudet. He too wore a sheepskin coat, though his had sleeves. There was a beret on his head, a muffler wrapped around his neck, and an unlit cigarette butt in his mouth. There was little or no tobacco in the cigarettes these days. Dried grass was more like it, and not much of that. Cigarettes had become mostly paper, and had to be continually relit.

The farmer stepped onto the same stub as Glickstein, his wooden shoes making a ringing noise, and together they pulled away enough branches to reveal the top of the pilot's thin helmet.

"Bastard took out most of my cabbages," the old man muttered.

To him this was a serious loss. One of the few foodstuffs not rationed, cabbages went into most of the soups that kept people alive. The farmer had just been robbed of much of his principal cash crop, and Glickstein understood this.

They bent the branches back, and with two men working were able to break most of them, until finally the pilot's head, slumped well forward, came into view.

"Is he alive?" Glickstein said.

"There's blood all over the place," Daudet said. "Probably bled out." The farmer was not wearing his false teeth, the forger saw. He had only one tooth of his own, for the favored method of dentistry in rural France at that time was extraction. The one tooth was clamped down on the butt. His false teeth didn't fit very well, apparently; the farmer used them only to eat.

Just then the pilot moaned.

"He's alive," Glickstein said. "Let's get him out."

The forger was no expert on the release mechanisms of P-51 seat harnesses. It took a moment to puzzle them out, after which he got his hands under the pilot's arms and pulled, but it was dead weight, and he was unable to lift him.

"Maybe we shouldn't move him," suggested the farmer.

"He'll freeze to death out here. Get up on the other wing."

Together they got the pilot out of the seat, pushed him to the edge of the cockpit, and lowered him into the snow. The parachute pack and the ruptured dinghy to which he was attached came with him.

"You smell that?" The farmer was sniffing the air. "There's still fuel in those tanks."

"Help me with him," said Glickstein.

"That fuel is worth money. I'm not leaving it for the *Boches*."

"Come back and get it later. Help me get him into the barn."

They laid him on the dinghy and half carried, half dragged him through the snow to the barn, where they set him down on some straw. He was covered with blood but still breathing. They looked down at their hands, which were bloody now too.

"What do we do with him?" said Daudet.

Before closing the barn door, Glickstein peered out. The snow was still coming down. Already the track of the plane had been obscured, the field again entirely white.

"We can't keep him here," the farmer said. "The *Boches* will come looking."

"I don't think they will," Glickstein said. To the forger the danger no longer seemed so immediate. Who was going to notify the Germans? A local farmer? Every farm out this way harbored one or more families of Jews. A passing motorist? There weren't many at the best of times, and none at all in the two days the storm had lasted.

"I think we're safe if it keeps snowing," Glickstein said.

"You think so?"

"Longer. Until the snow melts."

"Look at him," the farmer said. Kneeling, he had peeled off the pilot's helmet. "He's just a kid."

It was the ruined cabbage field that had made the old man surly earlier, Glickstein judged, but he had got used to that now, and the surliness had passed. He was a solid churchgoing Protestant who considered the harboring of refugees normal, the thing any good Christian would do. He took no credit for it. He knew exactly who Glickstein was and what he was doing and did not talk about it, even to Glickstein himself. The forger gave him money whenever a refugee was rich enough to pay a small sum for the new papers. Otherwise the farmer charged no rent, and Glickstein ate at his table every day.

"That's some lump on his forehead," the farmer said. "He needs a doctor."

There was only one doctor in the village. "One of us could go in and bring him out," Glickstein said.

"Take too long, the roads the way they are. I'll take him in to the pastor. He'll know what to do."

"No," said Glickstein, "I'll take him." He had a proprietary interest in this pilot. He had discovered him, and he wanted to know what would be done with him.

The farmer nodded. "Take him, then. I'll hitch up the sled."

This was the first Glickstein realized he would have to manage a horse.

"Get a wet towel, clean him up a bit," the farmer said. "I'll get the horse out."

The barn contained five stanchions for cows, only three of them occupied, and a stall for the plowhorse. There was a cage for the rabbits, and straw on the floor in which a dozen or more chickens rooted. The hayloft was overhead. The farmer went into the stall, and Glickstein heard the stirring of the horse. After a moment the farmer came out pulling it along by a bridle.

Glickstein got a rag from his room, filled a pail with water from the pump inside the barn door, then knelt and sponged some of the blood off the pilot's face and hands—off his own hands too. If the pilot died they could inform the Germans, give up the body, the plane too, and be in the clear. But to Glickstein he didn't look like he was dying. He was breathing steadily, and even seemed to grimace with pain from time to time.

The farmer was hitching the horse to the sled, which was not what Glickstein commonly thought of as a sled; it was used to drag loads of firewood in from the forest.

"Do me a favor," the farmer said, "stow your gear before you go."

When not in use, the forger's gear was supposed to be stowed in one of the beehives out back. This was the only request the farmer had ever made of him. In the event of a police raid, they would never look there, the farmer believed. It would not occur to them. If it did, they would be afraid of the bees.

"No one will come today," Glickstein said.

"Probably not. I'd feel better though."

"Okay, I'll do it."

By the time he returned from the hives the horse had been harnessed, and the sled dragged close to the door. On it lay the dinghy, on top of which a bed of straw had already been prepared by the farmer. They lifted the pilot onto the straw, packed him in blankets off Glickstein's bed, then folded the dinghy over him and tied it. It would serve as a windbreaker, and also as a kind of tent over his face.

Glickstein had found the pilot's survival kit, which he decided to bring into the village and give to the doctor. He held up the parachute in its pack. "You want this?"

The farmer shook his head. "Eventually they'll find the plane. I don't want them to find that too."

"I read someplace these things are silk." All cloth had become rare, and silk almost priceless.

"Give it to the pastor," Daudet said.

"What about his gun?"

"You take it."

Glickstein had it in his hand. He was afraid of guns, and this particular gun would connect him to the pilot. "I don't want it," he said.

"I'll take care of it," Daudet said.

"Don't get caught with it. Pitch it into the forest."

The farmer was opening the barn door. "You better get started."

But Glickstein, the city boy, was studying the horse. "I don't know too much about horses."

"You snap the reins if you want him to go, pull back if you want him to stop."

Outside, the snow was blowing.

Glickstein walked from one side of the horse to the other. "What's his name?"

"Who?"

"The horse."

"You're not trying to make friends with him."

The farmer handed him the reins, and Glickstein stepped onto the sled. "Does he have a name?"

"The horse?"

"Yeah, the horse."

The farmer grinned, his one tooth showing. "I always called him 'horse.'"

"'Horse?'"

"Just 'horse.'" The farmer swatted the animal on the rump and it moved forward, staggering Glickstein. It dragged the sled out of the barn onto the snow.

The cold was intense. When Glickstein pulled on the left rein, he found to his surprise that the horse obeyed him. He got the sled pointed in the right direction, and steered it around the barn and out past the house. For a moment he even coaxed the animal into a high-stepping trot, an accomplishment that was absurdly pleasing.

The road when he got to it was as smooth as whipped cream, no marks on it at all, but the cream was half a meter thick. He looked back at the wide smooth track he was making—nothing could move on this road tonight except sleds like this one. Or a tank, maybe. For the time being, it seemed to Glickstein, they had nothing to fear from the Germans.

The snow was cold and dry, and it blew off the surface into his face. He watched the wind form dunes that then dissolved as if by magic. The plump, narrow road climbed through a forest, past white spears of trees, and then came out, and the country opened up into a series of small farms to both sides, sweeps of white up to the clusters of stone buildings and beyond, nobody visible outside of course, the dim light of candles or oil lamps showing in some of the windows, smoke issuing from the chimneys and then blowing away.

The day was turning toward night. The snow smothered all sound. It was very cold. The horse's head was surrounded with smoke, and he kept shaking it, breaking stride as he did so, shaking the sled, and soon he was only plodding along. Nothing the forger could do would coax him back into a trot.

At the speed of a horse walking they moved through another forest and out the other side, and the forger watched the scenery pass. It passed exceedingly slowly, and the cold came through his clothes and he began shivering and stamping his feet, and he wondered how the wounded pilot was holding out. Once he heard him moan. "Just a little farther, my friend," he said in French, doubting the boy could understand even if he was awake. The wind blew more and more briskly, skinning crystals off the crust of snow, slamming them stingingly into his face.

It became full dark, which was fine with Glickstein. He did not want to enter the village in daylight.

They were nearly there now, and he said as much to the horse, and then to the injured youth behind him, getting no answer. The road turned, came out of the trees, and ahead he could perceive the village. The moon hung like a cantaloupe. There was a faint glow to the smoke that rose above the houses, a kind of halo in the blowing snow. The road dropped downhill toward the river, the sled sliding, the horse trotting again; they crossed the bridge and began to climb up the other side. The Protestant temple on its small square passed by, and then the street narrowed, and the forger steered the horse into an even narrower street, the rue de la Grande Fontaine, and pulled him to a stop in front of the presbytery. The snow in the street had been packed down by feet, which surprised him slightly—what could be the explanation for that?—and he jumped off the sled and banged on the door.

It was opened by a girl about his own age—Rachel—whom he did not know.

"Where's the pastor?"

"He's not here."

Inside were lights, warmth. "I have an injured man. Help me with him."

They carried the pilot into the presbytery. A fire burned in the hearth. The pilot was heavy but they lifted him high enough to lay him down on the dining room table.

The girl wore two sweaters, Glickstein noted. Compared to outside, the room was warm, though not very. "Phone the doctor," he said. "Get him over here."

He undid the ropes around the dinghy, and pulled back the blankets enough to be sure the pilot was still alive.

"He's bleeding," the girl said.

"Not so much now," said Glickstein.

He stood with his back to the fireplace. He had never been in the presbytery before. From the hall he could hear the girl on the phone with the doctor. Compared to his own room this place was a palace, but the furniture was heavy and of poor quality: an armoire, a buffet, chairs, frayed upholstery. The table under the pilot was quite thick. And the fireplace seemed to be the only heat.

The girl came back into the room. "He's on his way."

She stood looking down at the pilot's face. "American?" she asked.

"Yes."

"A flier?"

"Yes."

"He's very good-looking, isn't he?"

This caused a silence between them.

"What's your name?" Glickstein said.

"Sylvie," said Rachel.

"Sylvie what?"

She looked a him a moment.

"Sylvie Bonaire."

"I thought at first you were one of the pastor's daughters."

"No."

"Where do you live?"

"Here. I look after the children."

It was a long time since the forger had talked to a girl, and he wanted to talk more. Out at the farm he lived like a monk; he had almost forgotten that girls like this existed, that in an earlier life there had been dances and movies and school and sports and other teenagers to talk to.

But this girl seemed focused on the pilot, whose crew-cut head she suddenly stroked, a gesture, it seemed to Glickstein, of great tenderness.

When she glanced up and found him gazing at her she snatched her hand away. "I was trying to see if he has a fever," she said, embarrassed.

"Where are you from originally?"

Again she hesitated. "Nice."

"I'm from Nice too. Whereabouts did you live?" Glickstein was not so much probing for information as searching for a topic of conversation.

"I don't remember."

"You don't remember?"

She wore wooden shoes, thick wool stockings, and a wool skirt to her knees. She was a girl in a place he had not expected to find one, and he was trying to make contact.

"We left there when I was very young."

"Where are your parents?"

"They died a long time ago."

Glickstein decided she was lying to him, and he studied her.

"A traffic accident," Rachel said.

She sounded French, but he doubted she was. It was her choice of words, perhaps, or the darkness of her eyes and hair. She did not lie very well, and Glickstein became certain she was a refugee, and if so probably Jewish. They had that in common, if they could mention it, which they couldn't. Perhaps it was he who had provided her papers—they were perhaps connected in this way too. But he had turned out so many hundreds of sets of papers that he had no specific memory of working on hers.

He wanted to know more about her, but the only questions left him were the ones that in this village were never asked, so he said:

"Where is everybody?"

"Out." She gave a smile that seemed to him uncertain.

"When will the pastor be back?"

"I don't know," she said, and to his astonishment burst into tears.

Glickstein took a step toward her. "What's the matter?"

He wanted to touch her but it had been years since he had touched a girl and he did not know how to do it. "You better tell me."

Finally he took her shoulders and shook them, which was not the way he wanted to touch her at all, but it made her stop blubbering. She said: "He's been . . . arrested and taken away."

"When?" said Glickstein sharply.

After wiping her eyes on her sleeve, she told him that some men had come that afternoon.

"Gestapo?"

"Frenchmen." But apparently she noted the alarm that had come over his face for she added with a certain bitterness: "Don't worry, they're gone."

"Frenchmen, you say?"

"When there's dirty work to be done, the Germans make the French do it, don't they. They took the assistant pastor and the schoolmaster as well."

All three of these men were vital to the conspiracy to harbor Jews, and Glickstein knew it. The assistant pastor was in charge of the escape networks to Switzerland. The headmaster produced the ID photos that went onto Glickstein's forged documents. And the pastor was the pastor. "They decapitated the village," he said. "They lopped off all three heads."

And then: "Where did they take them? What charge?"

"Nobody knows."

"And Madame Favert?"

"She was allowed to accompany them."

"What about their children?"

"The wife of the assistant pastor has them."

"But you're to stay here?"

"To keep the fires up so the pipes don't freeze," said the girl.

And to deal with any couriers or refugees who turn up at the door, thought Glickstein.

He tried to calculate what the arrests meant, both to the overall picture and to him personally. Obviously the Germans ordered this. Were they acting on specific information? If so, was he next? Did they know he was the forger? How much time did he have?

Were they planning massive raids on the now leaderless village? Or were they only trying to rid themselves of what they considered minor annoyances?

There came a banging on the door. The pastor's door was never locked, as everyone knew, and they heard it open and close, and the doctor entered the room, a little man carrying a big bag. Nodding to both of them, he went straight to the pilot on the table, threw back the blankets, and studied the gashes in the clothes, the places where blood had run freely. He took the pilot's pulse, fingered the lump on his forehead, pulled back his eyelids to study his eyes.

The doctor was fifty-eight years old, a Czech from the Sudetenland. His name was Blum, but he carried papers according to which his name was Ligier, a naturalized Frenchman licensed to practice. This made him one of the few refugees in the village able to support himself. He spoke poor French, but the village had never had a doctor before and was glad to have him.

"You," he said to Glickstein, "table to fire we carry." To Rachel, whom he also knew as Sylvie Bonnaire, he said: "You help."

The table was heavy—with the pilot on it heavier still—but there were no rugs on the floor. The three of them half carried, half dragged the table in front of the hearth.

To Rachel the doctor said: "You make fire big big big." And to Glickstein: "His clothes we take off."

They got the pilot half sitting up and peeled off his flight jacket. Rachel was throwing logs into the fireplace while trying to watch what they were doing. As they pulled and tugged at the top of the flight suit, and then on the woolen undershirt sodden with blood, the fire blazed up, and in its glow the boy's face took on a grimace, as if he was experiencing torture in a dream. "You're hurting him," cried Rachel.

They kept pulling off clothing, and each time the pilot groaned, they saw that the girl winced. The naked torso appeared, exposing gashes and blood down its side, the chest hairless and bloody as well. The wounds made Rachel wince still again.

"Nothing, he feels," muttered the doctor. "Concussion."

"How bad a concussion?" said Glickstein.

"Bad, but better than broken skull. Skull not broken I think."

Certain of the pilot's wounds had begun bleeding again. They laid him back down, and the doctor took his blood pressure. "Low, not too low," he said, repacking the gear in its box. "Not tonight die. Now boots we remove."

The left boot came off with no difficulty, and the two pairs of socks under it. Bare toes pointed at the ceiling.

But the right boot would not come off. "Is very swollen in there," the doctor muttered, manipulating the boot. "Is bone broke I think." Beads of sweat formed on his forehead as he worked. "I not like cut off boot." In France in 1944 boots were as precious as food. More so, for they could not be replaced, and this pilot was going to have to try to make it to Switzerland or Spain on foot. "Big sin if ruin boot," the doctor said. "Ask pastor about sin." This was an attempt at humor, and was accompanied by a half smile. But the next comment was serious. "When he heal up, boot he need."

Finally it came off, and after it, carefully, the socks. From mid-calf to instep the flesh was badly swollen, badly discolored too.

"X-ray machine don't have," the doctor muttered, "also no whole blood here." His fingers palpated ankle, shin, and foot. Le Lignon's farmers got injured often enough, schoolchildren too, and were taken for X-rays or blood transfusions to the hospital in Le Puy, forty kilometers away, an option not open to downed American pilots.

"Now remainder of clothing," the doctor said to Glickstein, and together they pulled off the flight suit, the long johns.

There was still another wound in the fleshy part of the hip, making five in all, all on the right side, plus a deep stab wound in the left thigh that seemed to puzzle the doctor. With his fingers he puckered it several times, as if to squeeze out more blood.

Rachel stood watching. A corner of the blanket covered the pilot, but suddenly it slipped off. Conscious of the presence of the girl, Dr. Blum lunged for it, and pulled it back.

The doctor was irritated with himself, almost appalled that the blanket had slipped. "You go in kitchen, boil water," he ordered Rachel.

The girl hesitated, eyes downcast, then nodded and left the room, while behind her the doctor shook his head several times.

Glickstein held out the Air Corps survival kit. "There's this too, Doc."

The doctor studied the kit's contents for some minutes, fingering everything: sterile bandages, adhesive tape that stuck, sulfa powder to prevent infection—material he did not have and that was impossible to get.

Now he followed Rachel into the kitchen, where he washed his hands, and thrust his instruments into the water she had boiled. Presently he carried the instruments in their pot, together with soap, a basin of water, and a sponge back to his makeshift operating table in front of the fire.

Rachel followed behind him. The fire was throwing off much heat. The pilot, decorously covered, lay as before, and as the doctor moved back and forth in front of her, the light flickered on the bloody body, the smooth young face, the crew-cut hair.

Staring at Rachel, the doctor pointed with his chin toward the kitchen. For a short time the girl held her ground, but he stared at her wordlessly, not moving, so that at last her eyes dropped and she retreated.

Though not all the way. As soon as Dr. Blum had washed the areas around the wounds, and begun stitching, she silently returned, advancing as far as she dared. Totally engrossed in his work, Blum never noticed, whereas Glickstein kept looking across at her, and did not know what to do or say, except to be especially observant about the corner of blanket, quick to rearrange it each time it slipped.

The hip and side wounds contained metal—whether shrapnel or parts of the pilot's plane no one present was competent to say. Blum probed for and extracted eight fragments, holding them out on the end of his forceps before dropping them pinging into a bowl Glickstein had found; and after that sewing up each of the wounds. He had small delicate hands and, sewing, he was very quick. He sprinkled on American sulfa powder, applied American bandages held in place by American tape, and when finished he wrapped the pilot in blankets so that only his head and part of the broken leg were visible. It was at this point that he again noticed Rachel. He glared at her a moment, but said nothing.

Rachel, Glickstein saw, did not drop her eyes, and she looked back at him with what he took to be defiance.

"Now the leg," said Blum, fingering it. "Is broke here in foot I think yes. Maybe here too. Through floor of plane he try to push foot when crash."

"I think the floor of the plane is armor-plated," said Glickstein.

"He try. Not succeed."

Blum moved toward the kitchen, passing Rachel coming and going, each time shaking his head at her with irritation. At the sink he mixed up plaster from a sack out of his bag.

Back in front of the fire he twisted the swollen joints into the shape he wanted, then caked on the plaster, molding it with his now-clotted fingers.

When the plaster had set he and Glickstein carried the pilot, blankets and all, into the bedroom nearest the fireplace, Rachel's suggestion. The door could be left open, she said, providing some warmth.

In fact this was Rachel's room, though she did not say so, and when Dr. Blum had inspected it there was no way he could tell, for she owned no perfume, no jewelry, no cosmetics, no magazines or photos of film stars, and her few clothes as she outgrew old ones had been made for her by Madame Favert out of bedspreads, drapes, upholstery—whatever could be spared or found. The family had textile coupons, as did Rachel with her forged papers, but there was little in the shops, sometimes nothing, and besides, the pastor had very little money. Rachel owned one set of underwear, and was wearing it; she washed it out every night.

Nothing suggested this was the room of a teenage girl.

She was made to leave the room while the pilot was installed in the bed and tucked in. Glickstein was given back his blankets.

When the door opened again she was still standing outside, and she gazed in at the boy in her bed, his head on her pillow, but the view was cut off by Dr. Blum who again took his pulse, and again peeled back his eyelids.

"He soon wake up I think," Blum said, and he gave Rachel her instructions. The patient had lost much blood. When he woke up she was to make him drink a certain herb tea, the same tea as was given to women after childbirth to replace lost blood—Dr. Blum removed a package of it from his bag. As much of it as he would swallow. She must keep him covered. If he ran a fever or became agitated, Rachel was to telephone at once. When he woke he would have a terrible headache. He could be given aspirin—Dr. Blum handed over aspirin out of the survival kit, for there was none in the presbytery. Tomorrow he was to be given no hard food, only soup, much soup.

"I can stay with her, Doc," said Glickstein, "if it will help out." A young man alone in a house all night with an unmarried girl? In 1944 this was a preposterous suggestion, as all knew, and Glickstein's voice trailed off at the end. It was out of the question, and Blum did not deign to reply.

He said: "I send Madame Lambron." This was the village midwife. In fact, she had gone to assist earlier that day at a birth on one of the outlying farms. Babies came when they chose, the new mother might require help afterward, and because of the storm the midwife might be unable to get back anyway, so Blum added: "If her I can find." To Glickstein he added: "With me you come home. My wife a nice soup fix."

With that he bade Rachel good night, and made for the door, dragging with him the glum Glickstein and his blankets. Rachel shook hands with them, closed the door and they were gone.

She went into the kitchen and brewed a pot of tea. When the boy woke up she could heat it quickly and it would be ready. She felt suddenly much better. She was not alone in the house anymore. She had something to do, someone to care for who would take her mind off the pastor. That she was risking her life by nursing an enemy pilot never occurred to her. She was already risking her life by being Jewish.

While the tea steeped, she made soup, for there was none left. In this house soup was kept permanently on the stove but the visitors this afternoon, before taking the pastor away, had eaten it all. Now she cleaned and diced potatoes, carrots, turnips, onions, cabbage. There was a piece of bacon left—it was more lard than bacon, about the size of a deck of cards. She cut it into squares and browned it in the bottom of the pot. When it had given up most of its fat, she tossed in the vegetables and stirred them around in the sizzle, then added herbs, salt, and finally water, and set it to boil.

BY then Glickstein sat at dinner with Dr. Blum and his wife. Because Madame Blum spoke much better French than her husband, he had waited until now to ask the question that had been tormenting him for an hour. He said: "What can you tell me about the pastor?"

But neither could tell him much more than he knew already, and after a time they sat in silence, speculating, imagining the worst.

VIII

THEY had come for the pastor not from Le Puy but from Lyon, which is much farther away, a major city down on the plain beside the river, capital then as now of a different department. Most of all, Lyon was outside Le Lignon's orbit. They had calculated well. The pastor received no advance warning.

They came for him in two cars and a truck, a convoy.

They had started out in the dark, intending to reach Le Lignon before dawn. This was standard police practice in France as elsewhere. Empty streets. People still asleep, or in bathrobes, and therefore unlikely to resist. In and out quickly. Resistance, if there was to be resistance, would not have time to form.

But these policemen had not reckoned on so much snow.

All three vehicles were equipped with chains, but the snow had been falling for the last two days, and up on the plateau the world had gone silent in more ways than one.

The streets of Lyon, as the convoy started out, were not too bad, even slushy in spots. The tires crunched and jangled. The snow danced and blew in the headlights.

But the road as it began to climb became narrower, steeper. There were many switchbacks, and the snow got deep and then deeper. There were no tracks of previous vehicles. Possibly none had been this way in days. The truck was in the lead. Sometimes the driver could discern only with difficulty where the road went.

It began to be dawn. A little after that the snow stopped falling, and all three drivers doused their headlights. None of the vehicles was heated, and the windshields kept frosting over. It was very cold. They had to keep scraping the glass clear.

Once on top of the plateau the snow was blowing in all directions. It was almost a meter deep. The truck was pushing snow like a plow, but was not a plow, and its flat nose inflated the snow into a series of gigantic white balloons. Sometimes these balloons burst. Sometimes they merely got so heavy they immobilized the truck, together with the cars behind it of course, and the three chauffeurs had to get out with shovels. They shoveled and batted at the snow until the truck could move again. But ahead of them the dunes continued to rise, enormous piles, cream cheese couldn't have been heavier, until the chauffeurs were forced to get down with their shovels still again.

In this way the convoy proceeded, reaching Le Lignon just before lunch, five or six hours late. At the entrance to the village the vehicles split into three directions, for there were three arrests to be made in all.

The officer in charge was a *commissaire de police* named Robert Chapotel. He had reserved the pastor for himself, and he got out of the truck, waded toward the presbytery, and pounded on the door.

Chapotel was French, as were all his men. He was forty-four years old, a graduate of the Sorbonne, who, in the course of twenty years in the Sûreté Nationale, had risen to his present high rank. He had enforced the law before the occupation, and still did. For him, nothing much had changed. He believed in the law, and in the power of the state to make and enforce laws. Public order, especially in times like this, was more important than any individual. The state must function smoothly, and this meant controlling those who broke the law. He realized that certain of the new laws perhaps should not have been enacted—the arrest of Pastor Favert was in a murky area, perhaps. But in Chapotel's mind it was not a policeman's job to dwell on such questions. The law was the law.

When he had made arrests of this kind in the past two or three years, he had each time asked himself only if the orders of his superiors were within the law. If so, it was his job to do what he was told.

As he waited for the pastor's door to open he was not happy and he was not relaxed, for he expected, as soon as he announced himself and his purpose, to be scorned, cursed. Probably he would be accused of working for his German masters—he had long ago convinced himself that he wasn't. This was the least of the abuse he could expect. Usually the man he had come for was cowed, but the wives sometimes spat in his face. When this happened, Chapotel wiped the spittle off, and without a word clapped handcuffs on the prisoner and dragged him out.

It was Madame Favert who opened the presbytery door. He saw that she was a big stern-looking woman wearing a cardigan sweater over a housedress that reached almost to the floor. Her hair was black with a bit of gray in it. It was pulled back severely and rolled into a bun in the back. She looked to be about forty years old.

He had come for the pastor, Chapotel told her. He did not show an arrest warrant for he had none. He did not read out charges for he did not know what they were. Before the war warrants and charges would have been required. Without them no arrest could be made. Under the occupation this was no longer true. The legal code had been streamlined. Since September 3, 1940, the law allowed the arrest of anyone "dangerous to the national defense."

He understood vaguely that the pastor had preached passive resistance to the legally constituted government in Vichy. He supposed this was one of the charges against him. In addition, according to rumor, he was said to harbor Jews. Under the law this was a crime as well.

Chapotel saw the consternation on Madame Favert's face, but it only lasted a moment. The pastor was out but would be back soon, she told Chapotel, and invited him inside.

He declined.

"He may be a while," she said.

Chapotel heard his men stamping their feet in the snow. Behind them was the unheated truck they had come in.

"He's at the bedside of a parishioner who's dying," the woman said apologetically.

The snow, Chapotel saw, had begun falling again. He wore a fedora, a muffler around his neck, and an overcoat that was worn thin in places. He had two men with him who were as cold as he was. His ears felt on fire, and the fingers in his gloves were like ice.

"You'll freeze to death out there," said the pastor's wife. "Come in."

Chapotel gave a slight inclination of his head, kicked the snow off his boots, and stepped into the house, his men following. Inside, all removed their fedoras.

There was a fire in the hearth, and Chapotel allowed it to warm his back. He saw that the table was set, and that the family had been about to sit down to the noon meal, which, in a country village like this, would be dinner. He counted five children staring at him, including a rather beautiful teenage girl. Some of the children were too young to know why he was there, and their expressions showed curiosity. The older faces showed fear. The girl's especially showed fear. Chapotel had a son about her age, or a little older, who had been deported to Germany as part of a forced labor battalion. The boy's letters sometimes got through. The work was hard, he wrote, and there was not enough to eat.

"You'll have dinner with us of course," the woman said. "You and your men."

He answered stiffly: "That won't be necessary."

"Nonsense." And to Rachel: "Set three more places."

He watched the girl as she selected cutlery from a sideboard. Her back was thin. She was not yet a woman, but soon would be. Except for her bosom and her bottom she was as slim as a boy. Her figure did not look like a French girl's to Chapotel. Nor did she resemble the other children, so she was not the pastor's daughter. She could be Jewish, he thought, and this gave him pause. She was perhaps not even French.

"Why don't you sit here," said Madame Favert. "And your men here."

Chapotel's men were hungry. He could see it in their faces, and so could she.

"It will take the rest of the day to get back to wherever you've come from," she said.

They had been six hours on the road in the snow. He said: "I cannot presume on your hospitality."

"And in a storm like this nothing will be open along the way."

On the table stood a tureen of soup, a basket of rough bread, some cheese, and a bowl of what looked like applesauce.

"Even if you have the coupons for it," she said.

In general, merchants did not ask policemen to produce ration coupons. It was one of the perks of the job. Subject to shortages, policemen could usually get food.

"So please sit down."

His men watched him. With a slight nod of his head, he acquiesced. Everyone sat down, and the teenage girl filled his dish with soup.

"There isn't much, I'm afraid," said Madame Favert. "Times are not the best."

"No," Chapotel said, "they're not."

She passed the basket, and he took a piece of bread. "It's rye," she apologized. "Rye is the only grain that will grow up here. The season's too short."

"This is very generous of you," he said. Realizing that these people did not have much, he ate sparingly, while trying to signal his men to do the same.

"There's no wine, I'm afraid. The pastor won't allow it. He says wine is the first step toward alcoholism. I don't entirely agree. But, well . . ."

Her conversation, he realized, was an attempt to put her guests at ease.

"We give our wine ration to the butcher. In exchange he gives us a bit of meat, when he happens to have any."

The front door opened. They heard the stomp of boots, and then the pastor entered the room. "I came as soon as I heard," he said, glancing around. There was snow on his shoulders like dandruff, but in a moment it had vanished.

"This is the *commissaire*, Chapotel," his wife said.

"I've been ordered to bring you in." Chapotel had stood up. So had both his men.

"Yes, I've heard. Do I have time for dinner first?" The pastor had offered his hand. There was nothing for Chapotel to do but take it.

"Yes, of course," he said.

"I understand you've been ordered to arrest the assistant pastor and the schoolmaster as well. Your men were having trouble finding them, but I've sent word that they are to come in."

"I'll have your papers, if I may."

The pastor looked surprised, but handed them over, and Chapotel shoved them into his pocket.

Rachel ladled out soup, and the pastor sat down at the head of the table. As he began to eat he spoke to one of his children about school, and to his wife about the parishioner whose bedside he had just left. His voice sounded as unconcerned as if today was just a normal day, as if getting arrested was unimportant.

Now came a series of knocks on the door, followed by parishioners who trooped in bearing gifts for their pastor—news of the arrests, Chapotel realized, was all over the village.

Before long there were fifteen or twenty men and women dripping snow onto the floor, and more coming, the pastor jumping up each time to shake hands or hug people, smiling, thanking everybody, the gifts piling up on the table, so many that Rachel had to clear away dishes to make room. Gifts of food mostly, and this surprised Chapotel. In a country where people frequently went hungry, no one gave food away. But there it was: jars of vegetables and jams put up last summer and sealed with wax; bags of carrots and potatoes out of root cellars; a bottle of local honey; a bag of chestnuts; a small tin of sugar and another of tea hoarded, probably, since before the war. There were sweaters, socks, and scarfs too, all hand-knitted; and three of the scarcest and most precious commodities of all, candles, a bar of real soap, and a roll of toilet paper.

Having deposited their gifts, the parishioners stood around with long faces while the pastor finished his lunch. From time to time he laughed and assured them he'd be back soon. Judging from their faces, none of them believed him. Some had tears in their eyes.

To the embarrassment of Chapotel, the gifts kept coming, and from the people who brought them he was obliged to endure stares of contempt. Finally another of his men entered, leaning over the table to inform him in a whisper that the other two prisoners had been arrested and were in the truck.

It was what Chapotel had been waiting for. Enough. The show was over. "Pack a small valise," he ordered the pastor. "Change of underwear, warm clothes, a blanket."

The pastor started toward his bedroom. With a jerk of his chin Chapotel sent one of his men to watch him. He did not expect the pastor to grab a weapon or attempt to escape, but detectives learned early on never to trust prisoners.

Waiting, Chapotel stood with his back to the fire as if trying to store up warmth.

With his valise in hand, the pastor came back into the main room where he embraced each of his children. He still seemed cheerful. He embraced the older girl too, holding her rather longer than the others, it seemed to Chapotel, perhaps because she was weeping so hard. But her weeping had set off the other children. The caterwauling got on Chapotel's nerves. The pastor embraced his wife, who by this time had arranged a parcel of the gifts. No tears from the wife. She was made of stern stuff, thought Chapotel.

"Outside and into the truck," he ordered curtly. To Madame Favert he said: "Thank you for lunch."

The wailing of the children followed them out the door.

BEHIND him Madame Favert was busy, and she was in a hurry. She telephoned Giselle Henriot, the assistant pastor's wife, then drew Rachel toward the front door: "Take the children up to the Henriots'. Fix a bag for them, clothes, toys, whatever. They're to stay there until I come back." As she spoke she was putting on coat, hat, and gloves. "They'll be less traumatized with the other children around."

She wrapped a scarf around her neck.

"You'll be here alone. Can you manage?"

Rachel nodded.

"I'm going with my husband." She had decided not to tell her children she was going. It would be easier for them that way. She would just go. "Dry your tears, girl. I'll be back in a couple of days, the pastor too, you'll see."

She had the door half open. "Keep the house warm. Any refugees come, send them to the pastor at Buzet. If a courier comes, take whatever he gives you up to Madame Henriot."

The door opened fully, then closed, and she was gone. Rachel went back into the room where the fire blazed and the remnants of dinner waited on the table. Though the children clustered around her, the big house that had always rung with movement and noise had gone silent. In it Rachel Weiss was now alone, her parents ripped away from her still again.

ABOUT a hundred people had tramped down the snow outside. They had waited against the walls of the buildings, and as soon as Pastor Favert appeared they had begun singing hymns. Chapotel's vehicles were there, and as he approached them with his prisoner he could not help glancing nervously around.

The afternoon had got very dark. It was intensely cold, and the air as he breathed it felt heavy. This meant, it seemed to him, more snow coming.

At first only a few people sang, it was almost like humming, but other voices quickly joined in, the noise swelled, and soon everyone was singing, a mighty choir in the snowy street as if it were Christmas and they were singing carols. Chapotel was a Catholic, though he rarely went to church anymore; he did not know Protestant hymns. Nonetheless he discerned most of the words:

> *Lord help us find true freedom*
> *Hatred and fear*
> *Are like high walls around us*
> *They have dried out our hearts*
> *We are their prisoners*
> *Lord help us find true freedom*

When the pastor stopped to listen, Chapotel pushed him roughly toward the truck, so that he stumbled slightly. It made the singing perhaps falter for a moment. Otherwise there was no reaction Chapotel could see.

The truck was an army-type personnel carrier. It had a canvas roof tied down over hoops. Chapotel lifted the rear flap and peered in at the other two prisoners, who sat on the benches that ran along each side. They looked back at him, but neither spoke.

"Here are their papers, *Patron*," one of his men said, handing them over.

Chapotel glanced down at them, then into the truck. "Which one is Henriot?"

"That one, *Patron*." Henriot, the assistant pastor, was a big heavy man who looked to be about forty.

Chapotel was trying to ignore the singing, which seemed to him louder than ever. "And the other's Vernier, the headmaster?"

"*Oui*, Monsieur."

The headmaster was smaller, with thick glasses.

None of the prisoners had been handcuffed as yet, though according to regulations they should have been. But that could wait. He did not want to risk provoking the crowd. A crowd this big could take the prisoners away from him if it wished.

He motioned Pastor Favert to get into the truck. The pastor handed up his valise and parcel, but it was a steep climb, and until hands from inside reached down to help, he could not make it.

The crowd had started a second hymn. It sounded louder and more irritating than the first.

"Where are you taking him?" a woman's voice said.

Chapotel glanced around and saw that it was Madame Favert. "Lyon," he said.

"And after that?"

"Someone else will decide."

She was dressed warmly, a thick wool hat, gloves, a heavy cloth coat that was shiny with wear.

"You don't care what happens to him, do you?"

"No."

"What you're doing is outrageous." He saw that her reserve had finally cracked. "And you are outrageous. And don't tell me you're just obeying orders."

"I'm sorry."

"You're not sorry."

"As it happens, I am."

"Prove it."

He gave a rough laugh.

"Let me go with you."

"You can't go where he's going."

"As far as Lyon."

"Why?"

She said: "I want to be with my husband as long as I can," adding stubbornly: "And I want to find out where your orders came from so I can get them countermanded."

A silence fell between them while he considered what response to give.

"There's room in the truck," she said stubbornly, "and it's covered. No one need know I came along."

"You can ride in the cab with me," he said after a moment.

"That wasn't what I asked for. I asked to ride in the back of the truck."

"It will be cold back there. Very cold."

"Cold for your prisoners too, did you ever think of that? They shouldn't be back there either. I'll ride with them."

"Suit yourself."

He had had enough of her. He had had enough of all of them, and he marched toward the cab where his men waited. The truck bed was too high for her to get into by herself. That was not his problem, and he was not going to help her.

"You and you," he said, pointing to two of his men. "Get in the back and guard the prisoners."

"Jesus, *Patron*."

"We'll freeze back there, *Patron*."

"I don't like being here any more than you do."

"You don't have to shout at us."

They were shivering and stamping their feet, exaggerating it to get him to change his mind.

"Just do what you're told."

The shivering and stamping stopped. The two men stared at him, and then down at the snow.

"I'll see that you're relieved in an hour," he said. "We'll do it in shifts, one hour on, one off."

The engines started, and the three vehicles moved off in the direction from which they had come, the truck again in the lead. Behind them the parishioners were still singing, the voices audible even at the edge of the village, which was where Chapotel stopped the convoy and ordered the three prisoners handcuffed to the hoops inside the truck.

Ignoring Madame Favert, who was sputtering with rage, he stood by the rear flap watching it done.

"Prisoners in custody are to be kept handcuffed at all times," he told her. "That's regulations."

"I don't care if it's regulations, it's inhuman."

The hymn singing had finally stopped, or at least he could no longer hear it. He said: "If you don't like what you see, get out and go back."

They stared at each other.

The village streets, sheltered from the wind by houses and partially tramped down by feet, had been passable. Out here the snow crystals blew around. They stung his face like sand. He got back into the cab, and the convoy moved on, the truck plowing its path, the two cars following as closely as they could as if trying to cling to it.

Chapotel had nothing against Protestants, though he had never known any, nor against Jews either—he did know Jews, some of whom he liked—but the law must be obeyed. He was not working for Germany. He didn't care about Germany, only about France. He didn't entirely believe the rationale behind the present French racial laws as decreed by the head of state. He did believe, given the present emergency, that Marshal Pétain considered them necessary. A man needed something to believe in, and Chapotel had chosen to believe in the Marshal. The Marshal had saved France during the last war. Chapotel had been only a boy at the time but he had heard the stories. They had impressed him then, and still did. Ultimately it was from the Marshal, who was now eighty-eight years old, that his orders came, and he would continue to obey him and them.

In front of the truck the snow continued to swell into dunes that brought them regularly to a halt. The three vehicles had come this way only a few hours ago but the snow they pushed against was as smooth and deep as before, and Chapotel, though he looked for the tracks they had made earlier, saw no sign of them.

Just then he heard the noise of planes flying low. Sticking his head out into the swirling wind, he saw that there were two of them, one clearly in trouble, and he identified the American star on its fuselage, even as it dropped below the trees on the other side of the village. Higher up, the second plane circled around several times alone, so the other had surely gone down. Chapotel had heard no sound of the crash, whether because of the muffling effect of the snow, or because the convoy was too far away, was impossible to tell.

The pilot of the downed plane, if still alive, should be found and arrested. This much to Chapotel seemed certain, and he determined to report the crash and its approximate location when he reached Lyon. For the good of France, not Germany. France did not need an armed and desperate man on the loose, perhaps hidden by the Resistance, which, to protect this biggest of all trophies, would not hesitate to ambush any German troops that came looking for him, which in turn would lead to reprisals—the Germans were good at reprisals, a minimum of ten Frenchmen murdered for every German.

Snow had begun falling again.

If Chapotel could get over there, take command at the scene, he could stop all that in advance, he believed. But under present conditions on such roads as this it was impossible, and he ordered his driver, who also had seen the plane go down, to push on ahead.

A little later one of the cars slid off the road down into some trees. Since the truck could get little traction itself, it took them more than an hour to drag it back up. The prisoners in their handcuffs, having been allowed down from the truck, stood stamping their feet and watching.

A hundred meters farther on the second car slid off, though not so far. They dragged it out. The snow was still coming down.

It became late afternoon, the light failed fast, and then, from one minute to the next it seemed, it was night. In the headlights the road could barely be discerned at all, and they were still not off the plateau, hadn't even reached Rence, the next town north, another Protestant stronghold and only ten kilometers from Le Lignon.

It was madness to try to continue, Chapotel decided when they had at last come into the town. Rence had a detachment of gendarmes, he remembered, the only law enforcement presence on the plateau. Having found the gendarmerie, leaving his prisoners still handcuffed in the back of the truck, he banged on the door, and when it was opened showed his police card and asked for a cell for his prisoners, and shelter for the night for himself and his men.

Gendarmes, strictly speaking, were not cops. The gendarmerie was a branch of the army. Gendarmes operated only in rural areas, and if anything big happened, they called in the Sûreté Nationale, meaning men like Chapotel. They well understood that real cops considered them clods.

The gendarme in charge of the Rence unit, the one who opened to Chapotel, asked who the prisoners were, and even pulled his boots on and went out to shine his flashlight in on their faces. Then he refused both of Chapotel's requests.

In Rence as elsewhere, gendarmes lodged with their families in the towns they served. They became part of the community. The town's interests became their interests. They had no wish to earn the emnity of their neighbors.

Unable to believe his ears, Chapotel made his request for shelter a second time.

The gendarme again refused him. A Protestant himself, he knew Pastor Favert by reputation, and had even gone to Le Lignon several times to hear him preach. He wanted nothing to do with Chapotel or his prisoners. He wanted nothing that could connect him with the arrest of Pastor Favert.

"Where do you suggest I go?" asked Chapotel tightly.

"There's a Protestant temple farther down this street," said the gendarme. "Maybe the pastor there will help you."

"You'll hear about this," snarled Chapotel, and he went out into the snow-blue night and got back into the truck.

The pastor of Rence, whose name was Marles, did not have room for everybody, especially since Chapotel refused to be separated from his prisoners.

"We'll sleep in the church," said Chapotel. "Open the church."

"The temple," said Marles. "Yes, certainly. Of course it's not heated."

Chapotel shrugged.

The church—temple to the Protestants—was cold, but at least there was no wind. When Pastor Marles had put the lights on and led them inside, Chapotel saw that the temple did not resemble a Catholic church at all. Pews, a pulpit, but no candles burning, no saints in niches, no decorations of any kind. A stark, austere hall, that's all it was.

"I can send over some food," offered Marles. "What, I don't know."

"That won't be necessary," said Chapotel stiffly.

When Marles had left them he sent one of his men into the street to buy something to eat. The man came back with two baguettes of coarse rye bread. The *boulangerie* had been the only store still open, the man said; this was all that was left on the shelves.

Just then one of Marles's children came in with a pot of soup and some bowls. Chapotel tore the baguettes into equal pieces and distributed them. The bread was stale, and there wasn't much of it, but they dunked it in the soup.

When dinner, if that's what it was, was finished, Chapotel ordered Madame Favert to spend the night in the presbytery, telling her she needed her privacy. In any case he did not want her here. He locked the door behind her.

He and his men and the prisoners slept on the pews in the unheated church, and in the morning the convoy pushed on toward Lyon.

IX

F ROM an early age Rachel's world had kept changing in what were for her violent ways. She had had to learn two new countries, two new languages, two new parents. The only way to fit in was to learn to please—a difficult job, at which she was not always successful. The pastor, though affectionate in his way, was stern and often remote. His wife had her own children, who got most of her time and affection. Rachel was never mistreated, but there was no place she felt she belonged. As a child, and then as a teenage girl, the image of Prince Charming had sometimes comforted her. One day he would ride into her life on a white horse, and she would live happily ever after.

For some time she had considered herself too old for such fantasies, but as she stood in the doorway and gazed at the unconscious pilot, it occurred to her that something equivalent might actually have happened. The boy lying there swathed in blankets was perhaps not a prince, but to a refugee girl in an isolated village in the center of France, he seemed as glamorous as one, a warrior against evil who had done heroic acts in places she could never go. An American too. Her image of Americans was in no way unusual for that time and place. Americans had engaged themselves in a crusade to save the world. They lived big lives, were rich in all the ways that counted. And this particular American, unlike Prince Charming, had come into her life not on a white horse but, even better, out of the sky.

The experience, however, was not as ethereal as she might have supposed—the prince in question was of flesh and blood. She had seen his blood, his flesh too. His eyes were closed now, but his eyelashes were as long as a girl's, and his hands, as she remembered them, were nice, with long thin fingers—sensitive hands, she thought. Though only in glimpses, she had seen all of him, and he was already in her bed, a new twist on an old story, and part of what made it seem to her so real.

The tea was made, the soup made, she wanted to know more about him, so she went back to the living room, and in front of the fire ransacked his leather jacket, and then his lacerated flight suit, until she had laid bare everything in them, including his billfold, which she rummaged through. She was consumed with guilt as she did this, believing herself no better than a snoop. In addition she was afraid the midwife would come through the door and catch her at it. Her heart had begun to pound, and already she was preparing a defense for Madame Lambron: I just wanted to know his name so I could take care of him better.

The pilot's name, she saw, was Second Lieutenant David R. Gannon, U.S. Army Air Corps, and he was two years older than she. Having learned this much she lost her nerve, thrust the ID card back into the wallet, and the wallet into the bloody pocket, then glanced furtively around, pulse still racing.

But Madame Lambron did not appear.

When she had calmed down a bit she examined the survival kit—what was left of it, for Dr. Blum had taken away all the medical stuff—telling herself this examination was neutral, the survival kit was neutral, she could not be blamed. But included, as in all such kits, was a bar of chocolate, and as soon as she realized what it was, her mouth began to water.

Sugar was rationed, and often could not be found even if one had the coupons for it. Chocolate on the plateau was nonexistent. Fruit jellies existed, but weren't very sweet. For cookies there were macaroons that tasted of sand and bran. When she was still in school two cookies had been served every day during recess; they were supposed to be filled with vitamins, but the kids said they were made of fish meal, for they smelled of fish. Most kids, Rachel included, had refused to eat them.

And now she stared at a bar of chocolate. Since she held it in her hands, she must have picked it up, though she couldn't remember doing so. Surely the young pilot wouldn't begrudge her a piece of his chocolate.

And so she struggled with herself, at last winning what seemed to her a great victory. She put the bar back where it came from.

Feeling now exceedingly virtuous, she decided to wash out David R. Gannon's flight suit and underwear, and she gathered it up, but in so doing became aware again of the wallet in the pocket.

Madame Lambron wasn't coming. This seemed clear to her. There was nothing to fear from that direction.

She withdrew the wallet and, having put down the clothes, again spread its folds. Her heart raced once more, but not as much as the first time.

There were some photos. In one, wearing his uniform, David R. Gannon stood with what she took to be his family: an older couple, another boy who resembled him, a younger girl. The next photo showed him grinning down from the cockpit of an airplane, perhaps the one in which he had just crashed. She tried to imagine him encased in this machine or another, thousands of meters up in the sky, but she had never been in an airplane or even seen one close up, so the image that formed was vague.

The third photo was of him with a girl about her own age—his girlfriend, Rachel decided. Who was not as pretty as all that.

In the wallet also were twelve British pounds, and a letter. Rachel had not seen a pound note since she left England in the summer before the war, almost five years, but she knew what she would buy if she were in London now with twelve pounds to spend: new underwear, a lipstick, and an afternoon in a tearoom eating sweets. She began to think of other things she wanted: a hat with a veil, white gloves, high-heeled shoes—in these things she would feel like a lady, she believed. She wasn't sure, but she thought they might cost much more than twelve pounds.

There was a deeper meaning to those few pound notes of which she was perhaps only half aware. They represented boarding school and girlfriends to her, and a time when she had had parents of her own to go home to, just like other kids.

As she spread the wallet to replace the money, the letter fell out. It looked crumpled and therefore well read. It was perhaps a love letter, such as one read about in romantic books, and she picked it up.

Placing the wallet and its letter on the mantelpiece, she went to look in on David R. Gannon. He was still not awake, would surely not wake up for another few minutes.

Next she opened the front door and peered out. The wind blew. Snow still fell. The streetlight—there was only one—hung from a building farther down the street. Every village in France was supposed to be dark at night, but this one defied that law, as it did certain others. A cone of snow swirled under the light. She looked up and down for Madame Lambron, but did not see her.

Back in front of the fire, Rachel stared at the flames. To read someone else's mail was an awful sin, maybe a crime.

Unable to help herself, she plucked the letter from its envelope.

Dated three weeks previously, it was addressed "Dear Davey" and was signed "Love and Kisses" by a girl named Nancy, but it did not seem a very warm or intimate letter to Rachel. A hero such as the young man in her room deserved a girl who would love him more than that, she believed, as she herself would in Nancy's place.

She read the letter only once. Her guilt was so strong that she read it fast and put it back where it came from fast.

If David R. Gannon ever found out he would despise her, she believed. She had done a terrible act. She was not virtuous at all, and might as well stop pretending, a notion that was strangely liberating. Since she was bad, she might as well be bad all the way, and she went back to the survival kit, pulled out the bar of chocolate, broke off a piece, and rammed it into her mouth.

She let it melt on her tongue. It was as luscious as she remembered chocolate to be, more. Never, she thought, had she tasted anything so delicious.

She would only eat one square, she promised herself, perhaps two, but when next she looked down, half the bar was gone. This came as a shock, was accompanied by an amazing amount of guilt, and at once she stopped, and folded the wrapper over. What to do with what was left? She couldn't put it back half eaten. Where to hide it? The woodpile beside the fireplace, she thought, and as she pushed it under some logs she was already thinking up lies to tell David R. Gannon when he woke up, if he asked for it.

With guilt had come remorse. It was so strong that she returned to the idea of washing out the bloody clothes and she carried them into the kitchen where she sponged the blood off the leather jacket, and washed out the socks, underwear, and flightsuit, scrubbing hard, obliged to work in cold water because of the blood.

The woodstove in the kitchen served both for cooking and heating—it and the living room fireplace produced the only heat in the house. By the time Rachel had hung the clothing in front of the stove she was humming to herself, and she took the jacket into the bedroom and sat beside David R. Gannon, and by the low light that came in from the hall began to mend the leather with needle and thread, not the proper equipment for leather perhaps, but all she had or would be able to find in Le Lignon. She wondered how long it would take him to heal, and how long he would stay. He could get another jacket when he got back to England, if he got back. She was coming down to earth as far as fantasies were concerned. He wasn't really Prince Charming and he wouldn't stay long. This brought her thoughts to England itself which, these last few years, seemed more home to her than Berlin had ever been, and she was invaded by a desperate longing both for the place, particularly her school, and for the years of her young life that it represented. The emotion was only a kind of homesickness, but tonight it hit her hard, so that tears came to her eyes.

Having glanced in on the pilot—there was no change she could see—she continued into the kitchen where she ladled out a bowl of soup, sliced up what bread was left, and sat down and ate her dinner.

When finished, she heated up a bowl of the herb tea and carried it back to the bedside, for the doctor had promised that David R. Gannon would wake up soon. There seemed to be more color to his face than before, and he was breathing regularly. He was more Sleeping Beauty than Prince Charming—even fairy tales can get confused—and maybe she should bend over and kiss him awake.

A crazy notion, it made Rachel smile.

She was impatient for him to wake up so she could do things for him.

She sat with a book in her lap that her young eyes were able to read even in the dim light from the hall, but she began to worry about the pastor and could not concentrate on it. The pastor had committed no crime and wasn't Jewish either, she told herself, so they would have to let him go, wouldn't they? In her eyes the pastor was a gigantic figure. As soon as he got where they were going he would put a stop to it, whatever it was, she believed. It was the French he would be dealing with, not the Gestapo. And Madame Favert, her foster mother, would be back tomorrow, probably. Madame Favert, who was so strong and so kind. Unless they arrested her too. But the pastor would stop that as well.

Rachel kept stealing glances at the boy beside her. Though blanketed to the chin, he was naked underneath. She was aware of this, and it made her uncomfortable.

Then she must have dozed, for she was awakened by the thrashing of David R. Gannon, who was fighting an aerial battle in his head, or so she imagined. He kept shouting warnings: "Look out . . . I've got him . . . break right." She understood the words if not their significance, and for as long as the thrashing continued she cradled his head against her bosom. "Hush," she cooed in his ear, "you're safe now, no one's going to hurt you, hush." She held him close until the thrashing stopped, then lifted the bowl of tea to his mouth, saying: "Drink this."

His eyes opened, and he looked at her in a fuzzy way, then began to drink. The tea was only tepid, but she got him to drink all of it.

"I'm cold," he murmured, and went back to sleep.

She laid his head on the pillow and then, turning, realized for the first time that he had kicked the blankets almost completely off. Although this gave her a shock she told herself that, since one of his bandages might have come loose, it was okay to look. She could have touched him if she wished, he wouldn't have known, a notion that caused an erotic reaction for which she was not prepared, and as she covered up that part of him her knees went so weak that she had to sit down a moment before she could continue. But finally she tucked in all the blankets, and went to get more tea for the next time. He woke again about an hour later, and she forced more tea down his throat, and after laying him back down she gently wiped what had spilled from his chin and neck.

Back in the living room she put more logs on the fire, and as she watched it blaze up she chided herself for her behavior—she had stolen his chocolate, read his letter, and satisfied her curiosity about men by staring at his body. The fire did nothing to ease her confusion, only confronted her with emotions she could not sort out. Presently she got a blanket off one of the children's beds, then settled down in the chair beside him, but he slept through until morning. And so, after a time, however much she tried to stay alert, did she.

IN the morning in the street outside the temple Commissaire Chapotel renewed his offer to Madame Favert. It was a bright day, sunny, cold. She could ride up front with him if she wished. She again refused and climbed into the back of the truck. A blanket over their shoulders, she sat beside her husband the rest of the day, sometimes holding his free hand though both wore thick gloves, sometimes staring at the floor, or the canvas wall while he talked and talked.

Some of the talk was instructions: about the next batch of money which would be coming in from Switzerland—who to pass it on to; and about additional refugees who could be expected to arrive as soon as the snow melted enough for the little train to start running again; he told her which pastors of which neighboring villages they should be sent on to, and what code word they should be furnished with—otherwise the pastor in question might get frightened and turn them away. For false documents, the person to approach was Jeanne Escudet—this was the woman Glickstein knew as Madame Jeanne. And some refugees would need to be guided to Switzerland; three men of the village did this work, and he named them—a barman, a schoolteacher, and a seventeen-year-old Boy Scout in short pants. There were three routes, he told his wife. None of the guides knew about the other guides, and each knew only one route. Refugees approaching them would need a code word, however, and he told her what it was. Previously, he added, the man in charge of the escape routes had been the assistant pastor, and both of them looked across at Henriot, who would not be doing any guiding for a while, and he gave them back a weak grin.

To Norma Favert it was as if her husband were a bishop laying on hands, anointing her as his successor, a job for which she was not suited, did not want. Her job was to raise her children. It was his job too, but he had never seen life or the world that way. He believed himself the moral conscience of Le Lignon, and by extension the world. He wore this conscience like armor plate, believing that since he was such a good man nothing could hurt him.

Or those who depended on him either.

In the back of the truck the prisoners and Madame Favert were alone—their guards of yesterday rode today in the cars. There was a fierceness in her husband's eyes, she saw. The sun's glow through the canvas could not compare with it. He loves all this, she thought. Passwords and code words and secrets. To be arrested, handcuffed. To be on his way to a concentration camp, from which he would be deported to a worse one in Eastern Europe from which he might not come back. Leaving her a widow, her children without a father.

She was thoroughly exasperated with him.

But she didn't say so. He was proud and stubborn and would not have understood. These might be the last moments they would have together. She didn't want to fight with him. If she lost him, she would not want to live.

They could not see out of the truck. They could feel the tires sliding sideways in the deep snow, hear the treads spinning and whining.

Her husband began to speak of the children. If he did not return she was to raise them just so, and he gave explicit instructions. He named the schools they were to attend, the subjects they were to study, the boys and girls they were to date, and later marry. Especially she was to safeguard their faith. It would be nice if his son, who was ten years old, decided on the church, became eventually a pastor.

"It's possible I won't come back," he said. "I don't expect that's what will happen, but you should be prepared."

She stared at him and for a moment was unable to speak.

"Don't misunderstand me," he said.

"No."

"No one wants to be a martyr."

"No."

"I'd like to be buried in the churchyard of Le Lignon, if that's what happens. Assuming that my body is returned."

Did he even consider what her feelings might be? she asked herself. What, listening to such instructions, was she expected to feel? She did not believe in his God, and he knew this. She was not sure she believed in God at all, and he knew this too. He was a man of enormous tolerance. His own faith was unshakable, but he had no difficulty whatever accepting the faith or lack of faith of Catholics or Jews or anyone else, including his wife. He asked only that they be good persons.

He began to talk about God who took care of his servants, in the present case himself, so there was nothing to worry about, not now, not ever. This irritated Norma Favert anew, for she simply did not believe it. She did not see how any grown person could believe it.

"God's will," he said, "will be done. One has only to submit to it." And he began to quote from memory from the Bible.

Then he said to Assistant Pastor Henriot on the opposite bench: "As soon as we get to the camp we'll organize services."

Henriot was a good man too, Norma knew—and totally in awe of her husband. Henriot had five children but did not seem too worried, perhaps relying on her husband to rescue him. The third prisoner, Headmaster Vernier, did look worried. He had a wife and three children and was no mystic.

Norma Favert had been brought up a Catholic but had given it up to marry this man whose gloved hand she was holding, this earnest, good man, this brilliant preacher who could and did enthrall an entire church every Sunday. Before asking her to marry him he had said to her: "I want to live a life of poverty." She had accepted this at the time and still did. She had loved him and borne his children. She had believed in his work, especially the harboring of refugees, and had helped him in it, but she gave now an exasperated shake of her head, which her husband never noticed, because she saw the events of the last two days as proof that principle was more important to him than she was, than their children were.

"Is there someone you know, some contact who might be able to arrange your release?" she asked him.

"I really don't think that will be necessary."

He isn't even going to try to get himself out of this, she told herself, and realized she would have to do it, and she began thinking of the steps she would take once they reached Lyon.

On dry roads they could have got there in two hours, but the snow on the plateau was as deep as ever, the road without guardrails, narrow, all descents perilous. The cold penetrated more and more, and the slipping and sliding were sometimes scary, for there were occasions when the truck slid off the road and hung there at a tilt, and the tires spun as they tried to get it back on. They never stopped in any of the villages they went through, never even stopped for lunch. They did stop once so she could slog off the road into the deep snow behind a spruce tree, and pee. She was so angry at everyone by then, her husband included, that she wasn't even embarrassed.

The most dangerous part of the ride was coming down off the plateau. After that the snow was less deep, and then at last night was falling, and they were moving through the slush of Lyon.

At the Hôtel de Police, where the three prisoners were to be locked up in holding cells, Norma Favert kissed her husband good night.

She found shelter in the presbytery on the rue de la Lanterne. She knew the pastor's name there, Ducoté, although she had never met him. When she had told him her story, he promised to go with her tomorrow as she tried to find out who was responsible for the arrests, and how she could get them countermanded. After that Madame Ducoté gave her a bowl of soup and some bread and then led her to a room that was cold, and she got between sheets that felt colder still, and worried about tomorrow.

. . .

THE doctor came, hanging his coat on one of the pegs beside the door, kicking the snow off his overshoes which, like the ones worn by many people on the plateau, had been made by the village cobbler out of pieces of old automobile tubes.

"I examine him," the doctor said, banishing Rachel. "You outside wait."

About ten minutes passed. Rachel stood in the hall. When the door opened again finally, she looked past the doctor at the pilot.

"He wake up yet?" the doctor said.

"Yes, briefly."

"How much times?"

"Counting last night, four. Each time I got him to drink tea."

"How many he drink?"

"The bowls were pretty big. Almost a liter, maybe."

"Is good."

"How is he?"

"No fever has. Means infection has not got. Blood pressure up. *Gut. Gut.*"

The doctor went out to the hall. His shoes had once been black but were now gray, they were misshapen as well, and as he tugged his overshoes back over them, he said: "Madame Lambron not come home to village yet."

"You don't need to send her," said Rachel. "I can manage."

"Better I send."

"I really wish you wouldn't." She wanted to take care of the pilot herself, and as she walked Blum to the door an argument came to her, and she spoke it. "The fewer people know he's here, the better."

The doctor, his hand on the doorknob, looked at her. Finally he said: "About this pilot, who you tell?"

"No one," said Rachel.

"Good. Continue no one. With tea continue also. After that, soup. I come tomorrow."

Opening the door he said: "About this, if someone ask, I never came here, know nothing. Who sewed up wounds, not me."

Rachel returned to the bedroom where she stared pensively at

David R. Gannon. Alone with him she had imagined the presbytery as a cocoon that sealed them off from the rest of the world, and would keep them safe. But in Europe in 1944 there were no cocoons. She had not been worried about the Germans, but the doctor was, which meant she should be too. If they found out she was nursing an American pilot, what would they do to her?

There came more banging on the door. Hearing it she felt instant terror. A single word came to her head: Gestapo.

The banging was repeated. As she heard the door being opened, her heart was slapping. But then a voice called out in French, not German: "Anybody here? May I come in?"

Not the Gestapo then. She took a deep breath and went to the door; it was the young man who had brought the pilot in yesterday.

Pierre Glickstein had a sack over his shoulder, and he stepped inside stamping the snow off his feet.

She was not glad to see him. Partly this was because of the fright he had just caused her, partly because his presence reminded her that he was in on the secret too, and if he was, how many others, any one of whom might talk?

"I brought you some food," Glickstein said, and handed over the sack.

Rachel placed the sack on the chair behind her.

"How's the patient?"

"Fine."

"Good."

"How many people know about this pilot?" She had to know the answer to this question.

"He crashed on the farm where I live. The farmer helped me bring him as far as the barn. So he knows. Probably his wife knows as well. If he told her."

Rachel stared at the sack on the chair, not seeing it, making her calculations.

"I brought you some eggs, butter, cheese, some milk, a couple of cabbages, and a rabbit."

A rabbit was meat, and should have brought a smile to her face but did not.

"The reason is, you're going to have to feed him, and I figured you wouldn't have any coupons for him."

"Thank you," said Rachel. Aware finally of her rudeness she was ashamed: "Won't you come in?"

They walked into the living room and stood before the fire.

"By the way," Pierre Glickstein said, "my name's Henri Prud-homme."

"Mine's Sylvie—"

"Yes, you told me."

This was followed by a long silence.

"Because of the snow I had to walk in from the farm," Glick-stein said. "The sack got pretty heavy."

It was not until that moment that she became aware of his interest in her. The admiration of young men was nothing new to Rachel. She was surprised she hadn't noticed it previously. He didn't bring that food for the pilot, she told herself, he brought it as an excuse to see me.

It was flattering of course, but her life seemed to her complicated enough already. However nice this little guy might be, she didn't need him making soft eyes at her as well.

They stood in front of the fire.

"He's still unconscious?" Glickstein asked.

"Sleeping, yes."

"Could I see him?"

Rachel led the way into the bedroom, and they gazed down on the pilot.

"The doctor was here earlier," Rachel said. "He said he's doing fine."

"Well, good."

They trooped back to the fire.

"If he's going to stay," Glickstein said, "he should have identity papers and ration books."

"Maybe he'll leave pretty soon."

"With that broken leg I don't see how you can move him for a while."

Rachel was silent.

"I know a *mec*," Glickstein said. "He may be able to get papers for him. Good ones."

Not knowing how to respond, Rachel said nothing.

"The pilot didn't have a photo of himself in his things, did he?"

"I don't know," lied Rachel.

Together they went through the pilot's wallet.

"Here's something," said Glickstein. He held up the photo of the pilot with his girlfriend.

"That's not exactly a passport photo," said Rachel.

"Trim her out of it, might be enough left for an identity card."

"You think so?"

Glickstein said cautiously: "This *mec* who forges them, I'd have to talk to him."

After a moment, Rachel said: "What do you think of his girl-friend?"

"She's okay, I guess." After studying the photo, Glickstein put it in his pocket. He gave Rachel a smile. "Not my type, though."

She offered to fix dinner for him. For both of them it would have been a chance to talk to someone their own age. But he refused, saying the food was for the pilot.

"If this *mec* I know can do anything," Glickstein said, "I'll come back tomorrow or the next day with papers for the pilot."

Rachel walked him to the door.

"At least then you'll be able to buy food for him."

"Thank you for what you brought," said Rachel. "Especially the rabbit."

She closed the door on him.

X

OBERSTURMBANNFÜHRER Gruber's alarm woke him
early. Beside him Claire Cusset grunted, turned over, and went
back to sleep. She usually slept naked and was naked now, so before getting out of bed he lifted the covers off her, the better to admire the roundness of her bottom. He even stroked it hopefully a
time or two, but she did not wake up, so he sighed and went
through into the bathroom where he bathed and shaved. His dressing room was attached. He put on a gray double-breasted suit and
black shoes shined to a gloss. Today was for him an important day,
he looked forward to it, and he wanted to look his best. After today
the way would be clear, he believed, to roll up a great many Jews.

He went out into the dining room where his valet served him a
breakfast of eggs, sausage, bread with real butter, and English tea.
All of this and more was available on the black market, if you had
money to pay; the French didn't mind gouging each other, but they
did not dare gouge the Gestapo, which exacted a percentage of the
produce in exchange for letting the black marketeers operate.

It was still winter outside, far too cold for Gruber to eat breakfast on his balcony, but he did stand in the window as he finished
his tea, looking out over the river and the city, contemplating the
day to come.

. . .

THE prisoner's personal belongings had been taken from them and also, lest they try to hang themselves, their belts, shoelaces, and ties. Now they were made to shuffle into a room, where they stood with their pockets empty, their collars open, their shoes loose. After being fingerprinted and photographed they were made to sit beside men at desks who read them lines on forms and typed out the answers they gave.

Chapotel had chosen to interrogate Pastor Favert himself.

"Name, date and place of birth," he began.

Favert told him.

The policeman showed no emotion of any kind.

"Parents' names, dates and places of birth."

Just then a short fat man of about fifty came into the room. He wore a well-cut suit which was not only relatively new but seemed to be made out of real wool, not rayon like most men wore. It was clear he was important because the interrogations stopped at once, and the detectives rose to their feet, Chapotel included.

This was Commissaire Divisionnaire Mollarde, chief of the Sûreté in Lyon. He was smiling. It was a smile, the pastor would learn, that rarely left his face.

He said, smiling: "What have we here?"

"Two pastors and a teacher," said one of the detectives.

"Oh yes," said Mollarde. He knew about them. He had been told to order their arrests, and he had done it.

Nodding his head, still smiling, he looked them over. "And what are you men guilty of? A little black marketeering here and there? A little swindle on the side?"

Pastor Favert said: "We don't know what we're guilty of. We have not been charged."

Mollarde looked perplexed. "Surely, my good man, you must have some idea."

"Perhaps," Favert decided to say, "it is because we have been trying to shelter refugees, to keep them from being deported." And he watched for Mollarde's reaction.

"Refugees," the *divisionnaire* exploded. "You've been sheltering Jews, that's what you're telling me. Jews."

Favert nodded.

"You don't think I see through you, I see right through you." Mollarde was sputtering. "*Refugees* is another word for Jews, and everyone knows it. It's Jews and Jew lovers—the Jewish conspiracy—who have brought France to his point. The law says—"

"There are higher laws," said Favert. He could feel everyone watching him, the detectives with curiosity, the other two prisoners probably wishing he would shut up. But he could not remain silent. "The laws of God and—"

"France is in the abyss, and it's the Jews who have done it—"

"—and the laws of humanity."

"Are you Jews yourselves?" Mollarde shouted. "Admit it, you're Jews yourselves."

"We're Protestants," said Favert.

"Protestants," snorted Mollarde, "you think they're any better? Upheaval everywhere they go. It's been going on centuries."

The *divisionnaire* continued to rant. France, unlike other countries, had been good to minorities, even Protestants, and especially Jews, he said. "We let them live among us, never persecuted them, treated them like any other citizens." He had had Jewish friends himself, he said. And what was the result? The Jews had betrayed France, that was the result. Because of them and their well-known money grubbing, France had collapsed.

It was almost a sermon, and to the pastor it sounded devout—obviously the *divisionnaire* believed such rot, and this had implications that left him shocked and appalled.

"You'll pay for what you've done to France and to the Marshal. This time you'll pay. Oh, how you'll pay."

The *divisionnaire* was not smiling now. Turning to Chapotel he said: "Ship them to Le Vernet. Bring me the order and I'll sign it."

Le Vernet: the most dreaded of the French concentration camps. The name made even Favert blink.

"See how you like Le Vernet," snarled the *divisionnaire*. "Lots of Jews there. See how many you can shelter there." Turning again to Chapotel he ordered: "Measure their noses, check their penises first."

Under the French racial laws promulgated by Marshal Pétain,

the measuring of noses and the checking of foreskins had become standard police practice with suspected Jews.

The *divisionnaire* waited for Chapotel to acknowledge the order.

"*Oui, Patron,*" Chapotel said.

"If you find what I think you're going to find, stamp their papers 'Jew.' I want them out of here in thirty minutes."

He turned and strode from the room.

When the door had slammed behind him, Favert said to Chapotel: "Shall we unbutton our flies here, or do you do that kind of examination in the toilet?"

Chapotel went to the door to make certain Mollarde was gone. Returning, he sat down behind his desk: "Names of parents," he said, "dates and places of birth."

The questioning continued about twenty minutes more, whereupon the policeman stood up from his typewriter and said to two of his men: "You and you, move them out."

They were given back their small suitcases, their belts, ties, and shoelaces. Again handcuffed, they were herded toward the stairs. But Pastor Favert resisted being pushed. Turning, he said: "You have some packages of ours."

"The food, the toilet paper," said Chapotel, "yes."

There was a pause. The two men gazed at each other. Favert was not going to beg, and this was clear to both men. Chapotel said to a detective: "Give them their packages."

"Thank you," the pastor said.

While this was done, Chapotel stepped to the window where he peered down at the street. "I'm sorry about Le Vernet," he said over his shoulder.

The last Favert saw of him was his back.

In the staircase there was a man coming up who stood aside to let them pass.

Favert saw that it was Obersturmbannführer Gruber. "Herr Gruber," he said, "*Guten Tag.*"

The Gestapo officer said nothing.

Favert said in German: "I haven't seen you since you visited Le Lignon but didn't find any Jews."

After a brief inclination of the head, Gruber continued up the stairs.

Favert, turning to watch him go, supposed that Gruber was the reason he and his companions had been arrested.

"Move," said one of the detectives, giving him a push.

In the courtyard waited the same truck as last night. As soon as the prisoners were loaded into it, the engine started and it drove out into the slush.

Favert sat on the bench between the headmaster and Assistant Pastor Henriot. Their cuffed hands were in their laps, and all three were continually jolted by the movement of the truck. Opposite sat two uniformed policemen who watched intently, hands on their guns, not knowing if they were dangerous or not.

At first the prisoners were silent. Henriot and Vernier were too shaken to speak, their fear showing in their faces. Favert was unnerved as well, but in a different way.

"My thoughts are fixed on Commissaire Divisionnaire Mollarde," he said. "He seemed to me a patriotic, sincere kind of man. Did he to you?"

Neither of the other men answered.

Favert said: "Do you think he really believes those hate-ridden clichés he spouts?"

Still no answer.

"I think he does," said Favert. "He's high ranking, he's educated as well, yet he's swallowed them without thought, without evidence to back them up. He regurgitates them the same way."

Again there was no response from the other two.

"I always thought there were only two forces in the world," Favert murmured, and he blinked behind his glasses. "Good and evil, God and the devil. But there's a third force as strong as the other two: stupidity. The devil, God, and the halfwits are all struggling for control of the world."

Now he too lapsed into silence. Le Lignon had been immune to such stupidity, a place without compromises, without murders. Stupid people, if any, had been afraid to take harmful action or, indeed, to open their mouths. One simply did not see such stupidity in Le Lignon. Isolated from France and the war, immune to the slaughter elsewhere, the village had tried to cloak itself in goodness.

Favert resumed brooding aloud. "How does one fight against stupidity? Evil can be fought, but stupidity is simply there, one can do nothing about it."

There were some similar ideas that he tried to communicate to his companions as they bounced along, but the other two men were too self-absorbed to listen, too closed in on their fear of what lay ahead: Le Vernet, deportation, death.

Seeing this, finally, Favert stopped.

"I'm sorry I got you into this," he said. "It's my fault."

"It's not your fault," said Henriot. "We knew what we were doing."

"I wish there was some way I alone could be facing whatever we're facing."

The pastor meant this. For some time he had been hoping for a test. Proof that he was the man he was trying to be. Something difficult. So far everything he had accomplished had been too easy. I want to know what I really believe, he had told himself. Who and what I really am. Now that such a test was upon him he felt very little fear, was almost happy. But it distressed him to have led the other two men toward the same test, toward a future that could be terrible. They had not wished it, had merely been walking behind him. He believed himself stronger than they were. He would support and protect them as much as he could.

But supposing he wasn't strong enough either?

As was usual with him, he sought strength in faith. "God looks after his servants," he told them. "All we need do is believe."

DAVEY woke up. Outside the bedroom window it was just beginning to be light, for he could discern daylight through the slats of the shutters. Not knowing where he was, he tried to lift his head to see more, but the movement caused nausea, and such faintness that he fell back.

He had a ringing headache, a throbbing leg, and thought there must be stitches in his side for each time he breathed he could feel them pull. He was naked in a bed someplace, but didn't know where, and he explored his flesh, finding the bandages, prodding them one by one, wondering what was under them. He felt the lump on his head. He measured the cast on his leg with the toes of his other foot. He was terrifically thirsty.

With his crew-cut head creasing the pillow, he tried to scroll backward through memory, but there wasn't much there. He could remember straffing the gunners in the trees, and then shooting up the parked planes. He remembered being hit, and trying to hold his ship in the air, and even the beginning of the flight to get home. He seemed to remember crossing into France, but nothing after that. He doubted he was in England.

In the chair beside him the sleeping Rachel did not stir. She had thick black hair and was very pretty. She was not dressed like a nurse, so he was not in a hospital, and if he were a prisoner he did not think she would be there at all.

Which meant what? He lay with his pain and thirst and tried to figure it out, but his head wasn't working properly. He watched the light between the slats get brighter, and wondered how badly he had been hurt, and finally he reached out to the girl beside him, and to wake her tried to rub or squeeze her knee. But his too weak hand kept sliding off.

In fact Rachel was locked in a dream in which she was a small girl in bed with her parents, warm and cozy, much loved by them both. And then mingling with this dream in the beginning of conscious time she became her present age, in bed and maybe not alone, for a disembodied hand was stroking her knee. Prince Charming's hand perhaps, in any case someone's—suddenly the dream had become intensely erotic, for the hand seemed to be moving up her thigh.

She sat up with a start, which made David R. Gannon's hand fall away.

"Do you speak English?" His voice was so weak it could hardly be heard.

The preposterous brightness outside was bouncing up through the slats. "Yes," she said, giving a kind of frantic smile, for she had not washed her face or combed her hair, perhaps even smelled of sleep, and her first thoughts were: I didn't want him to see me like this. What will he think of me?

Then she realized how pale he was, how thin his voice sounded, and she grabbed up the bowl of now cold tea. "Drink this," she said, and although not daring to hold him against her bosom as previously, she helped him sit up enough to do it.

"Ugh," he said, turning away.

"It's good for you. Drink it."

He made a face.

"It's meant to replace the blood you've lost. Drink it."

He drank it down.

"That's better." She lowered him to the pillow. But for a short time she had held him in her arms, face-to-face, close enough to kiss, and now he was staring at her.

I must look a sight, she told herself, and brushed her hair back from her face.

He said: "You're English."

"No." What was she anymore, she asked herself. Germany didn't want her. She wasn't French, despite her forged identity papers. She had no nationality. She certainly wasn't English, though she often wished she were. She said: "I did go to school in England."

"I like England a lot."

Here for the moment the conversation rested.

Out of nervousness she stood up. "Are you hungry? Would you like some soup?"

"Where am I?"

She told him, naming the village, and then, to orient him better, the nearest great city: "We're not too far from Lyon."

Later he would tell her how much, even in his dazed state, this shocked him, for it put him hundreds of miles off-course. To have missed England by that much made him ashamed.

"I have to get back to my squadron."

"Soon," said Rachel soothingly, "soon."

"There's a cast on my leg."

"You're lucky to be alive."

"Are the Germans here?"

"No."

"Police?"

"No. The village is too small. The nearest gendarmerie is ten kilometers away."

"If someone saw my plane go down—"

"It was snowing quite hard."

"—and notified them."

"I don't think so. You're safe for a while."

His eyes closed. He breathed deeply, then opened them again. "Whose house is this?"

She told him it was the presbytery.

"Where is the priest? Can I see him?"

"He's not a priest. He's Protestant pastor. He's got a wife and children. This is a Protestant village."

She saw him trying to digest this.

Rachel decided to say: "The pastor's away at the moment."

"Who else lives here?"

"They're all away temporarily."

"I have to get back to England."

"As soon as you're better. Now rest."

He said: "My clothes—"

"They must be dry by now."

In a moment she was back with an armful, which she dropped on his chest. He lifted part of his flight suit, stuck his finger through one of the shrapnel holes. All of his movements were in slow motion.

"I got most of the blood out last night. I'll sew them up for you now if you like."

"Let me get dressed."

"You're pretty weak."

His hand lay on top of the clothes.

"Would you like me to help you?"

"I don't have anything on."

"I don't mind."

This reply seemed to discomfort him. "Who put me to bed?"

"It wasn't me," the girl said. For reasons unknown to her, the question had made her blush. Which made him blush too.

"The doctor put you to bed."

They blushed at each other.

"Now how about that soup?"

When she came back with it he was asleep again, his clothes still piled on his chest. She woke him, helped raise his head. With their faces close together she spooned soup into him, and wiped his chin afterward.

"Are you a nurse?"

"No."

"Do you live here?"

"Yes."

"The pastor's daughter?"

"No."

The soup was finished. She had a hand towel with which she wiped his mouth and chin.

"You're awfully nice to me," he said.

His eyes closed, and in a moment he had fallen asleep again.

She sat beside the bed a while longer. Their conversation had been insufficient to keep him awake, it seemed.

Presently she became bored. Annoyed with herself, she went out into the hall and found gloves and a stocking cap. She put on a leather jacket belonging to the pastor and rolled up the sleeves, and stepped into an old pair of boots of Madame Favert's. Pulling the cap down over her ears, she went out of the house into the snow.

The stores were open. She noted a few women with string bags doing their marketing. The village was soundless, and soon she was above the houses. The sun was blinding, the glare as hard as noise. It seemed to reverberate off the snow.

Keeping to furrows other people had made, trudging farther up-hill, she met some girls she knew and they walked up as far as the theology college that the pastor had founded some years before, and a number of future theologians came out and began pelting them with snowballs. The girls fired back, and it was war. When Rachel returned to the presbytery an hour later her gloves were soaked, there was melting snow down her back and in her boots, but her cheeks were red, her eyes sparkling.

David R. Gannon was awake. He had tried to sit up, he said, but had nearly fainted. "I was afraid you weren't coming back."

She saw how alone he felt, and how vulnerable. It made her feel more kindly toward him than ever.

"What's your name?" he asked.

She started to say: Sylvie Bonaire. Instead, realizing how much she wanted to tell him the truth, she hesitated. She wanted to be Rachel Weiss again to someone—and he was probably safe. But she was too afraid.

"Why do you want to know?"

"Please tell me."

"Rachel," she said finally.

"Rachel what?"

She had decided to compromise. "Rachel Bonaire."

"That's a pretty name."

To start with a lie was a bad thing. If she were superstitious, she could take it as an omen, a curse on whatever came next. The smile left her face and she said: "You need some more soup and some more tea."

"Do you have anything to eat?"

"Nothing but liquid today. Doctor's orders."

In the kitchen she started to worry about food: what would she give him in the days to come. There was little food in the house, apart from what the forger—she had no reason to doubt that his name was Henri Prudhomme—had brought. The root cellar this far into the winter was largely depleted, she knew. Left were some turnips, a basket of potatoes, some desiccated apples, and limp carrots. The preserves put up last summer were nearly gone too. There were jars of stewed tomatoes and stewed prunes down there, and several jars of blackberry jam that were unsweetened because there had been no sugar to put in them.

She saw she would have to buy food in the shops, but there were not enough coupons in her own ration book for two people, and he of course had no coupons at all. The children's ration books had gone with them to Madame Henriot's. Also Rachel had little money. This was a poor region, the pastor's collection baskets did not collect much, and every sou that came into the house was kept in a jar in the kitchen, a jar that never overflowed. But Madame Favert had taken most of it with her. What she had left behind for Rachel wouldn't go very far.

The girl had no idea how long her foster mother would be gone, and she began to worry about her, and about the pastor.

. . .

THE door to the big office was open, Mollarde seated at his desk, and when Obersturmbannführer Gruber knocked on the jamb the *divisionnaire* got up and came forward. The two men wished each other good morning, and shook hands.

Speaking correct French but with a heavy accent Gruber said: "I understand the arrests have been carried out."

"Arrests?"

"I passed your prisoners on the stairs."

Mollarde was not comfortable in the presence of this German. "There'll be no more trouble from those men," he said unctuously.

Though nothing showed, Gruber felt an emotion akin to glee. An insult had been avenged, a score settled. Better still, the way had been opened to collect hidden Jews, perhaps a trainload, all from a single village. He said: "Where will I be able to find the prisoners?"

"Find them?" Mollarde would never have admitted to feeling now a slight admixture of fear, but it was there.

"The two pastors, the schoolmaster," said Gruber. His voice was flat, his face expressionless, while inside he nursed his great pleasure. When he sang to people, of course, he smiled into the applause. That was part of show business. Most other times, he permitted no emotion to show. In his business a man made enemies, many of them, and to display one's human side was a weakness an enemy might exploit. He said: "Where are you sending them?"

"I thought Le Vernet would be just right."

Gruber frowned. "That's quite far away."

"Well, I thought it would be just right."

"I wanted them close, so they would be, shall we say, available."

"Well, they're gone now," said the *divisionnaire* stiffly.

"Call them back. Change the destination."

"If you wanted to control the case, you should have arrested them yourself."

"St. Paul d'Eyjeaux, for instance."

This camp was near Limoges. The Gestapo culled its inmate population regularly, Mollarde knew. The trains left for places like Auschwitz. What happened there he did not want to know, but he had heard rumors.

Mollarde did not consider Gestapo officers, including this one, to be policemen. Cops—*flics* in French—obeyed the rule of law. They worked within constraints and restraints, and if they didn't they were answerable to the courts, the public prosecutor, the prefect, the minister of the interior, and ultimately to the public—unlike these Gestapo *mecs* who made their own law, who were answerable to no one. They were men without culture, had had no formation, and for the most part were nothing but thugs. Mollarde had no respect for them, and his fear now was passing.

He said: "I did what I thought you wanted." There was nothing Obersturmbannführer Gruber could do to him, he believed, and he was suddenly in no mood to be pushed around by the current masters of France.

"You want them," he told Gruber, "you know where they are. All you have to do is go and get them."

"As you say," said Gruber, and he bowed and left.

DOWNSTAIRS, opposite the reception desk, Norma Favert still waited to see Chapotel.

Earlier she had walked alongside Pastor Ducoté toward the *commissariat*. Most of the sidewalks had been shoveled, but the streets had not been plowed, and hordes of bicycles rolled through the slush. The streetcars passed with bells clanging, and people got down from them. The lines outside the food shops were quite long. Other women were hurrying to work—men too, of course, but it was the women who interested her, and she looked them over carefully, noted their hairdos, the clothes they wore. Fashion played no part in Norma Favert's life. In Le Lignon there was no such thing, but Lyon was a big city, the third largest in France. The women here would be dressed in the latest fashion, whatever it was, and she was curious about it and about them. Their hair was mostly piled high, she noted, their necks bare, small hats on top of their hair, and veils down as far as their noses. Their shoulders were square and built up. Their shoes had thick soles of either wood or cork. At first she thought they were all wearing stockings, though stockings were supposedly unobtainable now, silk was unobtainable. Then she realized that they had only painted their legs the stocking color; some had even painted seams down the backs of their legs. You could hardly tell. With the high hair and hats, and the thick soles, most of them looked very tall to her, and their wooden soles hammered the pavement as they passed.

She felt a little embarrassed about her country clothes, about the way she wore her hair—the severe bun at the back of her head.

Upon reaching the *commissariat* she had been told to take a seat in the vestibule. About then, unknown to her, the truck bearing the three prisoners was driving out of the courtyard.

In the vestibule Pastor Ducoté sat beside her. The hours began to pass.

They waited so long that she began screaming at the policeman behind the desk, and at others who passed in the hall. Few cops are able to withstand an irate woman, few men, so this produced results of a sort—she and Ducoté were at last led to Commissaire Chapotel's office.

He was sitting at an upright typewriter at a desk whose edges were scarred with cigarette burns. There was a butt in the side of his mouth, and he was working on his report. He glanced up at her sourly. When she introduced Pastor Ducoté, he rose from the desk and the two men shook hands.

Chapotel was not the one Madame Favert wanted to see. "Who's your superior?"

One eye half closed, Chapotel gazed at her through smoke. Finally he said: "That would be Commissaire Divisionnaire Mollarde."

"Where's his office?"

"End of the corridor." Chapotel decided to add: "But I don't think he'll see you."

"Oh no? Just watch."

The *divisionnaire*'s door was closed. Throwing the door back, Madame Favert burst in on him, then stood there breathing hard.

By the nameplate on the desk, she knew she was in the right office. Not quite daring to enter, Pastor Ducoté remained in the hall just outside.

Mollarde, who looked up at her startled, was in shirtsleeves. The shirt was monogrammed but the sleeves were too long for his pudgy arms and so were held up at the biceps by garters.

"I'm Madame Favert, the pastor's wife. I want some information."

"But of course, Madame. Please sit down." He waved Ducoté into the office as well. "Mollarde," he said, his pudgy hand outstretched. "And you, Monsieur?"

"Pastor Ducoté."

"Ah yes, I've heard of you."

Had he? It gave Norma a rush of hope.

Mollarde seemed to listen cordially while she spoke; there was even a half smile that never left his face, but when she had finished he shook his head. His own orders had come from the prefecture, but probably the prefect's orders came from elsewhere. He sounded to Norma Favert sincere, almost pious. All he could suggest, he said, was that she go over to the prefecture. She was welcome to use his name. Perhaps the prefect could tell her where to go next, what choices she had.

As she continued to question him, his smile remained in place, his cordiality, his fine manners. Beside her Pastor Ducoté said not one word.

She had run into a wall of politeness that was harder to break through than any of the other kinds of walls—animosity, for instance. Anger, hatred, whatever. Politeness, being resiliant, was a wall you kept bouncing off, damaging yourself and doing no damage whatever to the wall.

She never suspected Mollarde of lying to her. This was an honest man, she believed.

Finally she said: "May I see my husband?"

"I was afraid you would ask that," said the *divisionnaire* sadly, cordially. "If it was up to me, of course you could. But unfortunately the prisoners are gone. I tried to stop it, but I could do nothing."

"Gone? Gone where?"

To internment somewhere, the *divisionnaire* said, but he had no idea where. The first stop was likely to be Clermont-Ferrand, he believed, though he wasn't sure.

He had named the first city that came into his head.

Clermont was the shipping point for the deportation camps near Paris, as everyone knew. "Clermont?" said Norma Favert.

"Don't be alarmed, Madame."

She was more than alarmed, her head spun. If her husband got into the hands of the Gestapo or the SS they would torture him to make him talk. But he didn't know anything worth telling them. He was against violence, had refused to have anything to do with the Resistance. When suspects couldn't or wouldn't talk they were tortured to death. She stood up, and as she walked from the office, her knees were trembling.

"*Au revoir,* Madame," said the *divisionnaire* behind her.

As Mollarde closed his door, he thought he had handled her well. The last thing he needed was some harridan screaming through the halls of power. She needn't fear Clermont-Ferrand especially. For all practical purposes the Gestapo and the SS had been combined. These days they were everywhere. Didn't she know that? He thought: and we all take our orders from them.

"What do we do?" said Pastor Ducoté when they had reached the street.

They sat down in a café and ordered coffee that, when it came, tasted awful. Not real coffee—what the cynics called the *café national.* It was brewed that year mostly from ground up barley.

Norma Favert considered her choices. She could go directly to Clermont, but the trains were both infrequent and slow. By the time she got there, her husband could well have been moved elsewhere. She might not even be able to find him.

Or she could try to see the prefect here, try to follow the arrest procedure back to its source. Once she knew who that source was, only then would she be able to come up with a plan. But she would have to hurry.

RACHEL slept in one of the beds in the boys' room, and was troubled by nightmares. In the last of them, the only one she remembered later, she had been captured by the Gestapo and tied to a chair; as punishment for nursing the pilot her face was to be branded with irons being heated red hot in a brazier.

The nightmare was interrupted by noises out in the hall. A strange series of thumps. Doors that opened and closed. Her eyes popped open and she saw that it was morning.

She sprang out of bed, rushed to the door, and found herself face-to-face with David R. Gannon. She was wearing her thick flannel nightdress which reached almost to the floor. He was wrapped in a blanket to his chin. His arms were inside the blanket, the better to hold it closed around himself, she supposed, and he was standing on one leg.

"Let me help you."

"I'm fine."

Nothing showed except his head and the white cast sticking out behind him. He wasn't teetering, but she knew he was weak, and probably subject to dizzy spells as well.

"You'll fall, and then where will you be?" If he lost his balance with his arms inside the blanket he wouldn't be able to catch himself as he went down.

He said: "I was just glancing, you know, around." He looked and sounded embarrassed.

He had been searching, she suspected, for the bathroom, but was too embarrassed to say so in front of a girl.

"I think what you're looking for is there," she said, pointing.

"What room is that?"

"The bathroom."

"Oh."

They looked at each other, and neither spoke.

"Well," he said, "I guess I wouldn't mind washing my face, you know. Maybe have a drink of water."

He started hopping toward the door.

"I wish you'd let me help you."

He went into the bathroom.

"I'll bring you some hot water and a towel."

It was hard to remain standing. He sat down on the edge of a kind of tub—a sitz bath—such as he had never seen before.

She returned with a towel and an enormous steaming kettle. After half filling the sink, she put the kettle down, and went out and closed the door.

Some of Davey's strength had returned. He used the toilet, which was a great relief, wiping himself with old newspaper cut into squares. These people are really poor, he thought. He found and stropped the pastor's spare razor. He had never used a straight razor before, and worried about it cutting his throat. He found some soap that was more like a block of clay. He could not get it to make a lather. He washed his face as best he could, shaved as carefully as he could.

His body was covered with dried blood. In places the hair on his arms and legs was caked with it. He emptied the sink, poured in more hot water, and bathed himself, sort of. He had never bathed standing up before, but did the best he could.

By the time he came out he felt not only better, but also stronger. Rachel was waiting for him in the hall, fully dressed, her hair combed. She's really beautiful, he thought.

He had the blanket wrapped around him as snugly as before. Again refusing help, he hopped back to his room and sat down on the bed.

"I have to get back to England."

"When you're better."

"Do you know how to make contact with the Resistance?"

"No. The pastor won't let them operate in the village."

"There must be someone who knows."

"When you're ready, maybe I can find out."

"They can get me back to England."

"Maybe."

"Are you sure there are no Germans here?"

"Yes."

"No police either?"

"No."

"All right," said Davey, and he seemed to relax.

They looked at each other, and then both smiled. "Get into bed," Rachel said, "and I'll tuck you in."

"Well . . ."

"Well what?"

"I can't while you're here."

"Why not?" she asked, but now she was teasing.

"Well, you took my clothes away again. I don't have anything on under this blanket."

"What would you say if I told you I've already seen you?"

"When?"

"Suppose I was the one who undressed you while the doctor was getting ready to sew you up?"

"You didn't," he said. "Did you?"

"Would that bother you?"

"I don't know. Yes, I guess so."

"Get into bed," she said.

"But you said you didn't."

This brought a smile to her face. "Haven't you ever got undressed in front of a woman before?"

"Sure." His eyes had dropped. "Plenty of times. How old do you think I am?"

It was the kind of teasing that constituted also a sexual invitation, which Rachel realized only vaguely, or perhaps not at all. Nor did he at first. Finally she left the room, and he got into bed and dragged the covers over himself.

After a brief time Davey heard her voice again, still teasing: "Is it okay to come in? Nothing showing that might shock me?"

He lay in bed loosely covered by one sheet and two blankets, his broken leg comfortably arranged, and she tucked him in, and at the end, since her face was very close to his, she kissed him very lightly on the forehead. Why she did this she would never know—perhaps because she had read such a scene in a World War I novel about a nurse tending a wounded soldier. Her lips just brushed his forehead, not a real kiss at all. But before she could get away she felt his hand behind her head, and he pulled her down and kissed her on the lips. It was a brief, chaste kiss, but it was the first one between them, and it caused Rachel to back somewhat flustered to the door.

XI

T HE search plane went over late in the afternoon. It was a Fieseler Storch, with black crosses on the wings. Back and forth it flew. The forger, Pierre Glickstein, heard it, and put down the documents he was working on and went out through the barn into the snow and watched it. He didn't know it was a Storch—he knew nothing about German military aircraft—but he knew it was a search plane by its altitude, which was very low, and from the patterns it flew. He knew what it must be looking for as well, and he glanced out across the snowy field at the forest into which the Mustang had plunged.

A single glint of metal might be enough to bring a truckload of troops out here.

He could not be sure what showed from the air. Even if the wreckage was fully hidden by snow and fallen trees, what about the field leading up to it? The sun was low and slanting and might show gouges or furrows in the snow. It might show the track he and the farmer had made dragging the wounded American to the barn.

On its next pass the plane flew over his head only about two hundred meters up, and he waved to it, as if to convince the pilot that this particular farm was innocent. No sense wasting time here.

The plane made two more passes, then flew off to the northwest toward its base—Lyon, Glickstein supposed. Lyon had an air base, the only one he knew of hereabouts.

The farmer came over to where Glickstein stood.

"Do you think they saw anything?"

"I don't know."

The day was cold. They were blowing vapor at each other as they spoke.

The farmer peered out toward the forest. There was a dead butt in his mouth, his one tooth was clamped over it, and a beret low over his eyes. "I'd like to go out there, make sure everything's covered over."

"No, don't. You'd leave tracks."

From where they stood they could see nothing of the wrecked plane. It was perhaps invisible from the air as well.

"Did you go out there after we brought him in?"

"For the fuel? Yes."

Glickstein winced.

"Got about forty liters," the farmer said.

"Was it before the snow stopped?"

"It was still snowing a little, yes."

They stood in the cold in the sun's harsh light.

"I don't think I should keep my gear in the beehive," the forger said. "I've left tracks. If they come, they'll see them."

"Maybe."

"I should keep it someplace else."

The farmer stamped his feet in the cold. "Where then?"

"I was thinking, well, how about the privy."

The farmer nodded.

"I'll finish what I was working on, and we'll rig something up."

They put the gear in a sack which they carried into the privy. It was a bench privy with three holes. The farmer reached into the left-hand hole and drove a nail up into the underside of the bench, and bent it over to form a hook, and Glickstein hung his sack on it.

"Guy would have to put his head in the hole to see it," the farmer said. "I don't picture them doing that."

"What will we tell them if they come?" Glickstein said.

"Plane crashed in a blizzard. We didn't see or hear anything."

"Will they believe that?"

The farmer shrugged. "We'll see what happens."

They left the privy and closed the door. "For the time being I'm out of the forgery business," Glickstein said.

THE naked Davey lay in bed. Elsewhere in the house he could hear Rachel doing her chores. He listened to her, and was pleased to think that in a few minutes she would come into the room. Then he got up, hobbled over and locked the door. In the room stood a small armoire in which he hoped to find his underwear and flight suit. Its one door was a full-length mirror, and before opening it he glanced at himself—at the many bandages stuck to him.

The few clothes that the armoire contained were those of a girl. This was the first Davey realized—guessed—that the bed he was sleeping in was Rachel's, and he touched some of them.

His long johns and flight suit, neatly folded, lay on a shelf in the armoire. Sitting on the bed he put them on. To pull the cloth over the cast was a struggle; it made him dizzy. Several times he had to stop. Also he had tugged against his stitches, some of which, it seemed to him, started to bleed.

He ignored this. Once dressed he opened the door again, the better to hear Rachel.

When she came into the room he was sitting on the bed. "You're dressed," she said, smiling at him. "Well well well."

She was carrying a tray. "Lunch," she said.

On the tray were tea and toast for them both, and soup for him, and he drained both bowls and ate the toast.

"You're feeling better, aren't you?" said Rachel.

"Much."

When lunch was over Davey suggested they play cards. "Do you play gin rummy?"

"There are no cards in the presbytery. The pastor won't permit it."

"Why not?"

"He says they lead to gambling and to sin. The devil's pasteboards, he calls them."

This seemed a quaint idea to Davey, who smiled.

"Anyway, I have to go out."

"Could you bring me something to read while you're gone?"

"In English? There's nothing in the house, I'm afraid."

"Nothing?"

"A Bible perhaps."

"That would be the Protestant version. Catholics are not allowed to read the Protestant version." This sounded harsher than he had intended, as if the Protestant version was immoral, so that he added: "I mean . . ."

"You're Catholic?" said Rachel.

"I didn't mean to offend you."

"You didn't offend me. I'm not Protestant."

"I thought you were, living in the pastor's house."

"Well, I'm not."

"You're a Catholic, too?" he said.

She hesitated. He wasn't a Nazi, but plenty of Americans were anti-Semites, she supposed. She liked this boy, liked taking care of him, and would tell him in time, but it was better to wait until they got to know each other better.

For now she would equivocate. "Everyone in France is Catholic," she said, "except here on the plateau, where everyone is Protestant."

"Everyone?"

"No, not everyone."

After a moment, testing him, she said: "France has a few Jews too, of course. Though less and less lately."

"What does that mean?"

"That the Germans are rounding them up and deporting them to concentration camps in Eastern Europe."

"That's just a rumor," he suggested.

"Is it? The deportations are real. People have seen Jews loaded into boxcars like cattle. There's another rumor that when they get where they're going they're put in gas chambers and exterminated."

"That's impossible," said Davey. "I don't believe it for a minute." And then: "Who told you about gas chambers?"

"The pastor heard if from some Swiss pastors."

"I don't believe it."

His naïveté annoyed her. "Well, no Jew has ever come back to say for sure." For the moment she had had enough of Second Lieutenant David R. Gannon. In the doorway she said: "I'll see you later."

She dressed warmly and went out. In the butcher shop she was able to buy two small slabs of bacon, for which the butcher scissored coupons out of her book. The bacon was mostly fat, but with it she could make two pots of soup. In the bakery she bought the last loaf of bread on the shelf, and gave up another coupon. She bought onions and some beets. At this stage of the war even tomatoes were rationed, even radishes; of course both were out of season right now.

She had one other chore, and it was one she was obliged to perform twice each day: to pick up the five smaller children at school, take them to the assistant pastor's house, and stay to help with lunch or dinner.

Having slogged up the hill to the school, she rounded up the little ones—the other four were old enough to get home by themselves. It was a very cold day, and she led them still farther up the hill to the Henriot house.

Madame Henriot still knew nothing about the pilot. After lunch, sitting in front of the fire sipping tea, Rachel wondered again if she should tell her.

In Le Lignon in those years much went on that was secret. Keeping such secrets made one liable to arrest and deportation. But imparting them to the wrong person could result in people getting tortured and shot. Secrets, therefore, were a burden. Young as she was, Rachel realized this. Madame Henriot, who had enough burdens of her own, did not need to know about the pilot, and perhaps would not want to know.

This had been the girl's first decision, but she was eighteen years old, and the weight of David R. Gannon had become like carrying a continent on her back. Now she put her cup on its saucer and the saucer on the table, and said to Madame Henriot: "There's something I haven't told you."

Just then the telephone rang.

It was Madame Favert calling long distance. The phone was in the hall. Rachel heard only one side of the conversation. Apparently her foster mother asked after each of her children, and after Rachel too, for she heard Madame Henriot say: "She's right here beside me."

Because long-distance calls were so expensive, this one was short.

"She's in Lyon," Madame Henriot said when she came back into the room. "She's staying in the presbytery there. She's trying to find out where our husbands and the headmaster have been taken, and who ordered their arrests. She is very hopeful."

Madame Henriot sat down and stared pensively into the fire. "That's what I am too," she said, "hopeful."

So Rachel never told her about the pilot.

When she got back to the presbytery she put away her purchases. Still ignoring Davey, she washed and dried the few dishes they had used, and as she did so she worried again about the pastor. But he was an important man, and he wasn't Jewish. He would get this straightened out and be back. She scrubbed the stove and sink, and mopped the floor, and with that her chores, except for keeping the fires up, were over for a while.

In the bathroom she washed her face and hands and torso standing up in front of the mirror. She washed under her arms, which moved her breasts around. She washed out her blouse and underwear. Since she had no other underthings, she would have to do without for a few hours. She put a fresh blouse on over her skin, and tucked it into the same longish skirt as before, and put on her usual two sweaters, and looked at herself. No one was going to know she wore nothing underneath.

She went out and hung her blouse and undies in front of the stove. Her annoyance had worn off. She wanted to be with Davey again. But when she went into his room she saw that he was asleep.

THE Centre d'Hebergement Surveillé was near the village of Le Vernet on a flat, barren piece of land just before the abrupt rise of the Pyrenees. The words translated to "Supervised Lodging Center." A concentration camp is what it was. From behind the barbed wire the snow line could be seen moving up and down the wall of mountains, but on the day that the pastor and his companions arrived there was no snow in the camp itself. The winter had been bitterly cold and there was a constant icy wind off the mountains. Whatever snow had fallen had been blown away. What was blowing now was mostly dust off the rock-hard ground, and the pastor had to squint his eyes against it.

He had just spent most of five days in a sealed boxcar, one of six pulled by a coal-burning locomotive. He and his two companions, wrapped in their blankets against the cold, had sat close together on the floor, their backs against the thin wooden walls, sometimes praying or singing hymns, an island of three among thirty other men. The others were mostly Communists. Communism had been outlawed, and the police had been busy rolling up Communist cells. The Communists jeered or scoffed at the praying but seemed to enjoy the hymns.

Some days the train did not move. It would sit in sidings while a number of trains went by. Other days it advanced, but not much. Twice it moved considerable distances in reverse, presumably forced to come at Le Vernet from a different direction because the track ahead had been destroyed. From time to time, having been stalled for hours, the prisoners were let out in small groups for short periods. They stood beside the train. The gendarmes guarding them were armed with submachine guns. The prisoners stood blinking in the light. Sometimes they were allowed to walk back and forth beside the track. They never saw any of the occupants of the other boxcars.

Inside the boxcar the prisoners shared a bucket of fresh water, and another bucket for their toilet needs. Irregularly, they were fed: buckets of thin soup were passed inside. The men from Le Lignon had their farewell gifts from their parishioners, and the pastor suggested they share this food with their fellow prisoners. After a slight hesitation his companions agreed.

Their food did not last long after that.

Finally the train reached Le Vernet, and stopped on a siding outside the camp. It was the morning of the sixth day.

The camp perimeter, Favert saw, was delineated by a deep moat, and then by three rows of barbed-wire fencing. There were watch towers every hundred or so meters. On them stood men with machine guns.

As other armed guards herded the occupants out of the boxcars, the pastor noted a number of individuals in ragged clothes who watched in silence from inside the barbed-wire. They were dirty, unkempt, emaciated, with unhealthy pallors.

They looked to him like walking cadavers, and the sight of them removed most of the optimism and confidence that had sustained him thus far. We're not going to get out of this place, he thought. If he felt his heart drop a long way, it was not so much for himself as for his two companions. He had led them down this road—had led his whole village—and now he asked himself by what right had he done so. Who was he to decide what was right and wrong for others? Who was he to defy the French government and the German occupiers? What kind of shepherd was he to risk the lives and freedom of the flock entrusted to his care?

Then he asked himself a philosophical question. Which type of faith was the stronger: to believe without any doubts, or to believe despite doubts? It was a question that in no way calmed him. Doubt frightened him. Doubt was pain. If he lost his faith he would have nothing with which to go on living.

And so he prayed: Lord, let me not doubt.

When one prayed one became a believer, prayer itself carried one toward faith. And if a man had enough faith, he needed no sign that his prayer had been heard.

And yet a sign was precisely what Favert had begun to hope for.

Five days in a boxcar were not pleasant, but Favert was luckier than he knew. During these same five days Obersturmbannführer Gruber had been trying to find the train. He wanted it intercepted. He wanted Favert off it, and the other two as well. He didn't care as much about the other two, though they too were Jew lovers, and leaders of a Jew-loving village. Mostly he wanted the pastor.

But the train could not be found.

Gruber then sent officers to pluck Favert out of the Le Vernet camp, but the train hadn't reached there yet, and they came away empty-handed.

THE doctor returned, this time bearing crutches. It was ten o'clock at night, and once more he banished Rachel to the outer room.

When she was gone, he pulled the blankets off Davey, helped him get undressed, then changed all the bandages, sniffing each of the old ones before discarding it. There was still no infection, the lump on the patient's head was almost gone, and the leg swelling seemed much reduced too.

Rachel showed the doctor out. By the time she came back Davey was dressed again and sitting up in bed. "He says you're doing fine," she reported. "Saturday he'll take the stitches out, and maybe cut the cast down a little."

"What else did he say?"

She laughed. "That's all I understood. He speaks such terrible French."

"When can I go back to the war?"

"Do you want to go back to the war?"

"I have to. As soon as I'm able to walk."

"That will be a while."

"Yes." It would be weeks, he supposed, and more weeks after that before he would be fit enough to fly a plane, if he could get to England. He supposed he had been listed as missing in action. Maybe killed in action. His mom was no doubt distraught, and he wished he could telephone her, or at least write her a letter. But he could do nothing except wait to heal, worry about being discovered by the Germans, and enjoy talking to, and looking at, Rachel.

They were living an almost domestic life, took their meals together, listened to songs on the radio together, or else the war news—all of which was fictional, according to Rachel, unless it came over the BBC from London. But the London broadcasts were hard to bring in, for the radio was old, the tubes worn out.

Rachel had found and borrowed books in English for Davey: the Brontës, Thomas Sterne—nineteenth-century classics not to his taste, though when she was out he read them. Mostly he stared at the ceiling, chafed at the forced inactivity, the monumental boredom, and longed for her to come back.

Often they played chess in front of the fire. Rachel always kept the door locked now, so they would not be surprised. Because they found each other more interesting than the game, there were long periods between moves when the conversation went off in some especially fascinating direction. The future, for instance—what they would do if the war ever ended. The pastor had promised Rachel she could go to the university, she said, either Paris or Lyon. Davey would go back to finish college, but after that he didn't know. His father wanted him to go into advertising—plenty of money in advertising—but that sort of life no longer felt attractive to him, and he had begun to think he wanted to stay in aviation, perhaps become an airline pilot for a while, and then an executive. Flying was going to boom after the war, he said. It would be fun to be part of it.

Both of them thought they would marry quite young. Both of them, when discussing this topic, avoided eye contact. Neither, it seemed, was thinking about the other, and yet they were. Davey thought he wanted four children. Rachel said two would be enough, and she hoped they would be girls so they wouldn't have to fight in the next war.

"I shouldn't laugh at the doctor," Rachel said now. "He's just a poor displaced person, like me."

Davey knew something of her past. They had talked about it. That her parents were dead, that she was an only child with no surviving relatives, that she had come to Le Lignon from Paris nearly five years before.

Earlier he had been unwilling to probe memories that he supposed were painful for her.

Now he said: "How did your parents get killed?"

"Nobody knows."

"Maybe they're not dead. Maybe they're only missing in action, just like some of the rest of us."

"If they were alive," said Rachel, "I think they'd have got word to me somehow."

He put his hand out, a way of showing sympathy, an excuse to touch her as well, and as she took it she gave a smile of gratitude.

Lately there had been many touches between them. Any excuse to touch each other seemed to be enough.

"I was a child," she said. "They wouldn't just abandon me, would they?"

To understand what happened to them, she thought, to understand anything about me, he needs to know I'm Jewish. I should tell him, she told herself. But what she wanted even more was for him to think she was just like other girls.

It was nice that he wanted to hold her hand, and she let it lie there a while. "There are thousands and thousands of kids who have lost their parents," she said. "I was luckier than most, because the pastor and his wife took me in."

After a moment she added: "I hardly think of my parents anymore." This was true. What she remembered most was belonging to them, and the promise of a life that was bigger—and of course safer—than this one.

She stopped there, took her hand away, and asked brightly: "What's an American college like?"

She knew about his parents—that his father was president of a bank. Now he told of taking the trolley car across the Bronx to college each day, and of majoring in modern American literature, but she was not familiar with any of the books or authors he mentioned. He talked of basketball games in the campus gymnasium, and the bigger games in Madison Square Garden, most of which his team had won, of the boards thumping under his sneakers, and the noise of the crowd and the even better noise of the ball going through, how much he had loved all that, even though it was all really kid stuff compared to, well, this. And he gestured all around him as if to include the war, Le Lignon, and Rachel herself.

She sat in the chair beside the bed.

When the war came he had enlisted rather than wait to be drafted, because that way he could choose the Air Corps. He told of learning to fly in T-6 training planes at first, and then P-39s, though he saw that these designations meant nothing to her. He told of how much he loved flying, loved gunnery too, shooting at targets towed through the air.

He just didn't like killing people, he said.

She put her hand on top of his.

Her outer sweater today was red, the one under it blue. Some days she reversed them. They were bulky and hid her figure. She wore no makeup or perfume, and wooden shoes that clomped when she walked, and thick socks instead of stockings. Nonetheless to Davey she was sexier and more beautiful by far than any of the pampered scented girls he had ever danced with or taken to football games.

For a minute or more they gazed at each other in silence, long enough for an abrupt change of mood to occur in the room.

"You look cold."

Rachel gave a mock shiver. "It's cold in this house."

He lifted his blankets. "Get in here, it will warm you up."

She gave him a smile. "Why would I want to do that?"

"Just to get warm." He had slid over to make room for her. Invitingly, he held up the covers. "Don't you want to get warm?"

"I don't think so."

"You're fully dressed. What could possibly happen?"

"You. You're what could happen."

"I've got a broken leg. What can I do?"

"Huh," she said.

Because it was very late, because the doctor had come and gone, because no trains were running yet, because at this hour no one was likely to knock on the front door—which in any case was locked—she allowed herself to be pulled onto the bed. "But all we're going to do is talk," she said.

She kicked the wooden shoes off and sat down on the bed, but high up, her back against the wall, only her legs under the blankets.

"That's no good. You'll be just as cold like that."

She moved down a little lower.

"Come lower still."

She laughed. "No."

Davey hoisted himself up until he sat beside her. They pulled the blankets up to their chests.

"All right," he said. He turned off the bedside lamp. Now the only light was what came in from the hall. "What shall we talk about?"

"This is going to wrinkle my skirt," Rachel said.

"Take it off, then. I won't mind."

"I prefer not to, thank you."

And then after a long, long silence, he said: "Where'd you learn to kiss like that?"

"You like my kissing, do you?"

"Oh yes," he said. This answer came out with more feeling than he had intended, and made them both laugh.

"I've been kissing boys since I was, I think, twelve years old."

"You're kidding me.

"At boarding school in England the boys used to hang around the fence. We'd hand them money through the fence and they'd buy us sweets. What you Americans call candy. Finally I made a date with one of them. An older man actually—he was fourteen. We used to go to the beach and climb up into the lifeguard's chair and kiss."

"I thought you were never allowed out except in the company of a matron."

"They did allow us out to attend religious services. If you weren't Church of England, which I wasn't, you didn't have to attend services at school. I used to go out with this other Jewish girl—" A Freudian slip, which she covered—tried to cover—with an immediate lie: "I told them I had to go to confession." Regretting the lie the moment she spoke it, she hurried on with the rest of the story: "I don't know what the other girl did, but I would meet this boy and go up into the lifeguard's chair. We couldn't be seen—it was out of season and there was no one on the beach."

The details of her life—those she had told him—were so different from his that he found them fascinating. He was fascinated by everything about her.

"Did he ever, you know, fondle you?"

She laughed. "What was he going to fondle? I was twelve years old. There was nothing there."

And then after another silence, a longer one this time, punctuated only by sighing, breathing, the rustle of bedclothes: "Is this the way you used to kiss?"

"No. We were very much more chaste. Mouths closed."

"I love kissing you." He thought he had never felt closer to a girl than he did to her tonight, alone with her in this house in this village in the dark, and he wanted to tell her so. To him it was a poetic moment, but to speak poetry was beyond him. Subtlety of any kind was beyond him. "I love love love kissing you."

But his goal—their goals—kept shifting. Very soon kissing wasn't enough. "Aren't you hot in all those sweaters?"

"A little."

"Take them off."

"Well, I'll take one of them off," she said, and sat up. Her arms made a gigantic X. "Because it really is rather hot in this bed," she explained, as she lay back down again.

But she didn't mind the remaining sweater being moved a little, or even a lot. He found her ribs, which were as hard as his own and uninteresting for this reason, and then above them an incredible softness that had no counterpart on his own body, incredible smoothness too, and to his surprise, she began groaning softly, pressing herself into him, almost writhing, though not from pain.

"Your skirt is getting more and more wrinkled."

"I'll iron it tomorrow."

"You could take it off."

"No."

"Take the other sweater off."

"No."

"Why not?"

His face was wet from her kisses, and hers from his, and she did not answer. It was an ordinary twin bed, rather narrow, and although they were down in it now, more than big enough for them both.

Davey reached the point where something he would not be able to stop was about to happen. He tried to start a conversation that might calm him down, though Rachel did not seem interested in talk. He tried to exert muscular control over the tension that was in him, but Rachel only went on with the kissing. There was no way she could know the state he was in, he believed. Unless he told her. But he could never have told her, he would have been too embarrassed. She in no way helped him now, wouldn't let them stop, let what they were doing stop.

Lying half on top of him, her tongue caressing his lips, her body pressed on his, she was in no mood to stop herself.

Finally the spasms started. Davey could not hold off any longer, could do nothing but give into them, while keeping the rest of his body still, trying to show nothing, saying nothing lest she be disgusted by him or offended. As far as he could tell she never guessed at what had occurred.

They lay in each other's arms, tightly embraced. They breathed the same air, murmured endearments, kissed each other for each one, and he thought he might just rest his eyes for a moment. As they began to close he had another thought, this one about life. Contrary to what older men had been trying to drum into him in the year and more just past, flying airplanes and killing Germans was not the limit of what you had to do to be a man. There was so much more to life. Being loved by a woman, for instance. This was an important thought, though an incomplete one, and he couldn't quite figure out the rest of it right now, it was too complicated, he would do it another time, there wasn't room in his head for all that and for Rachel too, and right now he preferred Rachel. And he fell asleep.

Rachel lay in his arms and was content. She soon realized he was sleeping, and thought herself lucky, for she had never known desire like that before, and did not know how much longer she could have restrained him, restrained herself. She did not now feel unfulfilled. She did not know for sure that there was anything more fulfilling out there. Imagining that she had never been happier, she kissed his nose, his eyes, and thought about getting up and going into the next room, and getting this wrinkled skirt off and hung up, and getting her nightdress on and going to bed. But first she thought she would stay where she was just a little longer, just look at him there a little longer, and then she too fell asleep.

In the morning both of them came awake.

Finding herself still in bed with him, Rachel was embarrassed. She said. "I didn't plan to, I mean, spend the night with you, sleep with you. I'm sorry."

Before Davey could stop her she was on her feet, had bent for her other sweater and had pulled it on.

She stood looking down at him, looking grave, but then smiles came onto both their faces. "I guess you've slept with plenty of girls."

"Well, not all night."

This pleased her. "With me was the first?"

"Yes."

"But you've done . . . other things with girls?"

"Sure."

"Different girls?"

"Sure."

"How many?"

"Hundreds."

"Tell me."

"No."

"How many girls have you made love to?"

"I'll tell you after I make love to you."

She laughed. "I guess I'll never know, then."

She washed her face at the kitchen sink and dried it on a dish towel. As she prepared breakfast she was singing, though in a soft voice that could not be heard even as far as the hall.

THE Le Vernet camp had been there a long time already, and the pastor knew this. The long rows of wooden barracks had been built to house the residue of the Spanish Civil War, for refugees from the losing side had fled across the border, whole armies of them, and the French had chosen to lock them up in camps like this one, not knowing what else to do with them, and the months had become years.

Then World War II started. Immediately the government ordered the police to hunt down every refugee on French soil, most of whom were refugees from Hitler, because they had now become enemy aliens. They were arrested by the tens of thousands and shipped to about twenty camps, most of which were down here close to the Pyrenees. Le Vernet had collected its share and when the new inmates had overfilled the camp, a quantity of Spaniards were released to make room for them.

Although Le Vernet no longer received newly caught Jews, many remained from the early days of the war, and these were culled whenever the Germans could put a train together, but lately there were fewer and fewer trains because Wehrmacht commanders were vying for them each day, and because fighter planes from England, Davey's squadron and others, kept blowing them up. To put together a train took time. These days most newly caught Jews were held in transit camps in the north, and from there were deported to Auschwitz and such places every time a train became available. A load of Jews was due to go north on the train on which Favert had just arrived.

Outside the camp stood an administration building. Upon arrival, holding on to their suitcases, Favert and the others had waited on line in the cold, going inside in turn to be processed, and to be read the rules of the camp. There were many of these, and they were strict. Even minor infractions, the newcomers learned, were punishable by eight days of "prison," the first day without food or water, the next three days on bread and water only. There would be four roll calls a day on the parade ground, each lasting half an hour: inmates were obliged to stand at attention during roll calls. Lateness for roll call was punishable by prison. Moving or talking during roll call was punishable by prison.

Within its perimeter the camp proved to be further divided into three sections, each separated from the others by more moats, more fencing, more barbed wire. Section A was for aliens with criminal records, Section B for political prisoners, principally Communists, and Section C was for all others. Most of the criminals in Section A were refugees with no papers who had committed the crime of working, and usually they were Jews. Ordinary criminals—stickup men and the like—went to ordinary jails in the cities in which they had been convicted, and resistance fighters who got caught, whether or not they had assassinated German troops or blown up bridges, got executed on the spot, shot or hung on meat hooks usually; they did not make it this far.

The pastor, the assistant pastor, and the headmaster, being political prisoners, were assigned to Section B.

The barracks in which prisoners were housed were long and narrow, measuring about thirty meters by five, and there seemed to be two or three hundred or more. They stood in neat rows and extended almost out of sight.

Followed by his two companions, Favert stepped into the one to which he had been assigned.

Inside, in place of beds or bunks there were upper and lower sleeping platforms that ran the length of the barracks on both sides, leaving a narrow aisle down the middle.

An emaciated, one-legged man sat on one of the bunks.

"How many men in here?" Favert asked him.

"Two hundred," the man said, "a hundred on each side of the aisle, half on the lower platforms, half on the upper."

"I see," said the pastor.

"Feet toward the center, forty centimeters of space per man."

Favert nodded. Forty centimeters was about the width of a kitchen chair.

"You got any extra clothes, you tie string around them, hang 'em from the rafters or the rats will get them."

Favert noted other bundles hanging down.

"I don't think we have any string."

"Better get some."

"Maybe we can get some," said Favert. "Where do we bunk?"

"Empties down there, on the top."

There were windows at either end, but they were without glass, and the pastor could feel the wind even now. Winter this close to the Pyrenees would be not only cold but long, and if today was any indication, windy as well. Two or three lightbulbs hung down, but according to the clerk who had processed them, the electricity was on only two hours each night—from six to eight.

Favert went down to the corner, carried his suitcase up the ladder, and claimed his narrow space. Straw the thickness of a man's hand had been spread on the boards. Probably early in the war, for it was mostly packed down now. There was no other bedding. No blankets had been issued. There was a stove at the other end of the barracks, so the bunks closest to it were probably the prized ones.

"I've been asking some questions," said Assistant Pastor Henriot beside him. "The toilet is a latrine trench dug into the ground. There's plenty of water but no soap. The men complain that they're never able to get clean."

"Well," said Favert, feigning cheerfulness, "a little dirt never hurt anyone."

"As for the food . . ."

Favert laughed. "Don't tell me."

"Breakfast is black coffee."

"I wonder what they make it out of here."

"Acorns, I'm told. Ground-up acorns."

The headmaster watched them and said nothing. He looked sick.

"Lunch is probably filet mignon," said Favert.

"Lunch and dinner is soup made mostly of rutabagas."

"I don't like rutabagas," said the headmaster in a low voice.

"Which may be why all the men we've seen so far have that yellowish complexion," said the assistant pastor. "Sometimes the soup has chickpeas floating in it, plus a small amount of boiled meat that's mostly gristle."

"Looks like we're going on a diet," said Favert.

"The gristle is difficult to eat. The men like it though. They say it's good to have something to chew. Keeps the teeth from falling out."

"We can all afford to lose a little weight," said Favert. "Don't worry, we'll be out of here before you know it." And he gave them both what he meant to be a cheerful grin.

Off across the camp somebody was banging on a bell: roll call, the first they would attend in this place.

RACHEL walked up through the snow through the village. The day was cold and very bright. She had nothing on her ears, which began to burn from the cold.

Hearing the noise of a train she continued up to the railroad tracks, passing people she knew along the way and greeting them, and being greeted in return.

A locomotive equipped with a plow was just forcing its way up the hill toward the station, which it reached as she watched. The driver from his cab talked to the stationmaster for a time, both of them bundled up to the eyes. The stationmaster then retreated into the station, which was heated by a woodstove, and the locomotive continued on, its high chimney spitting steam, moving very slowly, still in view for the longest time, but finally turning the corner at the outskirts of the village, and although she could still hear it laboring, it was no longer visible.

The steel of the tracks now showed, with big banks of snow to either side. Obviously the line was now open from St. Étienne as far as Le Lignon, and even beyond, and she expected that tomorrow the trains would run normally—as normally as they had ever run since the war. Madame Favert might be back on the first of them, and if not, then on one of the following ones—soon, in any case. That would put a stop to what was going on in the presbytery. By objective standards not much was going on, but it was a lot to Rachel.

She loved the pastor and she loved her foster mother, but she wished they would stay away for a few more days at least, for David R. Gannon was really nice; she was really getting to know him. Not to be alone with him after so little time would be regrettable. Without admitting to herself that she enjoyed the kissing, enjoyed being fondled, enjoyed the excitement of the direction in which they were perhaps heading, she told herself instead that her enjoyment came only from "getting to know him."

Turning away from the tracks, she started back to the presbytery. The cold was intense, her fingers were freezing, her ears too, and she wished she had worn a hat. As she walked downhill she pressed her hair to her ears, sometimes varying this by beating her gloves together to warm her hands.

As she turned into the rue Centrale she saw that two buses and a personnel truck had pulled up in front of the Hôtel des Voyagers. The truck bore German army markings. The buses were white with red crosses on their sides, and chained wheels, which were clotted with snow. Rachel approached closer. Men, some of them in bathrobes, were being helped or lifted out of the buses by German soldiers, before being carried inside.

A number of villagers were watching.

"What's happening?" she asked a woman.

"They've requisitioned the hotel."

Rachel tried to overhear what the Germans were saying to each other but was too far away, and so took several steps forward, and an officer came out of the hotel and made straight for her.

She went stiff with fear.

"*Bonjour*, Mademoiselle," he said, saluting her. He brace-bowed, and seemed to click his heels as much as a man can wearing snow boots.

"Don't be afraid," he said in quite good French. "I mean you no harm."

She looked at him and was too frightened to speak.

He said: "We're putting convalescing soldiers in the hotel, together with a small staff. Some have been badly wounded, but they're recovering."

Rachel still said nothing.

"My name is Lieutenant Ziegler."

Rachel could see him only in quick glimpses. The rest of the time she studied the snow on which she stood. But she had now detected his interest in her, which was in no way official, was in fact no different from the interest of French boys she had known. He was blond, blue-eyed, smooth-skinned. About twenty-five years old, probably.

"We have a doctor. He will treat the people of the village if they come to him. No charge."

Behind Ziegler some of the other soldiers had stopped to watch. Voices called out ribald comments in German. Rachel tried to pretend that she did not understand them, but felt her cheeks redden, and feared she had given herself away.

Ziegler, meanwhile, had turned on them, cursing them out, reducing them to silence.

"May I know your name, Mademoiselle?"

In the last year or two, strange men had often enough tried to talk to Rachel; some had asked her name. She did now what she had done then, spun on her heel and walked away. She did this without the assurance of the past. Her knees were so weak she was afraid she might fall down. Ziegler was the enemy. He could arrest and deport her just for being Jewish. If he came to the presbytery he would find her guilty of a worse crime still: harboring an enemy pilot. He would have her shot, Davey too, probably.

Behind her the other soldiers were hooting Ziegler, which meant that temporarily she was in the clear. A few steps more and she was in another street.

She ran home and told Davey: the occupying forces had established a permanent presence in Le Lignon.

The news sobered him.

"I've got to leave," he said. "I'm a terrible risk for you. For the whole village."

"You can't even walk."

"Another couple of days and I'll go."

She looked down at the floor. "I don't want you to go," she said.

XII

Sunday neared. Though assemblies of any kind were forbidden at Le Vernet, the pastor was determined to conduct a church service. Assistant Pastor Henriot would read from the liturgy, he said, the headmaster would lead the hymns, and he himself would preach the sermon.

Once this decision was made he began to work on what he would say.

There were more than a thousand men in Section B. Not one was a Protestant. Nearly all were hard-core Communists arrested as enemies of France. Favert had talked to a number of them, and most, he had found, were as fanatical as any religious zealot. In fact, he concluded, it was zealotry that kept them alive in here; they wanted to be on hand when the Red Army smashed through to Paris, and France became a Communist state.

The pastor did not, therefore, expect his service to draw a crowd. He did expect to be arrested afterward, and to do time in "prison," but the idea did not frighten him. He would stand up for his God, whatever the consequences might be.

Assistant Pastor Henriot was opposed to the idea of a service, and the frightened headmaster was militantly opposed. Favert would not go to "prison" alone, Henriot told him. They would all three go, since all three had taken part in the service, and that would mean several days of near starvation. Their job here was to survive. They had wives and children. Already their caloric intake was too small. They could not afford to give up what little food was available. Why not hold a private service for the three of them, in which case the authorities would never know?

The pastor would not be swayed by this argument, or any other. Henriot, he decided, was speaking mostly for the headmaster, whose fear was plain to them both. But the service itself would instill courage in the man, the pastor told him, and he began to make a kind of sermon to his two companions. "The men in this barracks are atheists," Favert said. His fingers smoothed his mustache. "It's our job to be witnesses for our faith, to show them the strength that faith confers."

He added: "You two men are not obliged to take part in the service, and I will understand if you do not wish to."

He was willing to conduct the service alone, he told them, and afterward pay the price alone. Whatever his companions might decide, he was determined to conduct a service in public for however many men would attend.

Henriot was so alarmed that he began to scurry about the camp trying to get one of the guards to carry a message to the commandant. The message was a request for an audience.

There followed a number of surprises.

First, all three men were summoned to the commandant's office, which was in a brick-and-stucco building outside the barbed wire. There, after dismissing the guards, the commandant asked the prisoners to explain who they were.

He sat behind his desk as Favert responded, and the expression on his face did not change.

He said: "And you wished to see me for what reason?"

His name was Motier. They knew this from the plate on his door. He had gray hair and looked to be about fifty. Favert, who had no experience decoding epaulettes or uniforms, did not know what branch of the police he represented, nor what his rank might be. He was commandant of this camp. Otherwise they knew nothing about him, and his face gave nothing away.

The pastor explained that they wished to hold a Sunday service.

"One service only?"

"Every Sunday that we're here, Monsieur le Commandant."

"And how long will that be, in your opinion?"

"I don't know," said Favert. "Perhaps until the end of the war."

"I don't think so."

The men from Le Lignon looked at each other.

"Some Gestapo *mecs* were here the other day asking about you. They said they'd be back."

This time the three prisoners stared at the floor.

"So don't count on a long stay."

Favert said stiffly: "We want to hold services."

They waited in silence for whatever the commandant's reply would be.

He said: "I'll think about it."

"We plan," persisted Favert, "to hold the first service tomorrow."

The commandant stood up and they saw that he was tall, but had a potbelly. When he went to the door to speak to the guards outside, they saw that he walked with a limp.

He ordered the guards to return the prisoners to the camp.

For about ten minutes after that he sat brooding. Finally he sent for his second in command, a captain whose name was Pertinax.

As the commandant explained Favert's request, Pertinax sat nodding his head, saying nothing.

Commandant Motier was forced to say: "What do you think?"

"Interesting."

Motier said: "France is a free country. Was. Religious freedom guaranteed, and all that."

"Yes."

He's not going to commit himself until I do, thought Motier. This idea put him in a rage, which he was careful to conceal.

"What would you do in my place?"

"That's a tough one."

The commandant had been wounded in action during the retreat of 1940. The limp he had acquired was not going to leave him. He did not like what had happened to France, was still happening, not only the occupation and deportations, but the way Frenchmen now behaved toward each other. There was not much honor left, and no trust, informants everywhere. On the subject of a Protestant service in the camp he did not know what Pertinax's feelings might be, and his subordinate was not going to take the risk of telling him.

"I've never blamed the disaster of 1940 on the Jews or any other minority group," the commandant said. "It was the fault of the politicians and the generals, if it was anybody's fault."

"I know a lot of people who think that way."

Repressed for so long, Motier's rage was swimming up toward the light. He said: "And I hate being commandant of this camp, without the means even to improve conditions. Some days I can barely resist the desire to open the gates and let everybody run."

He stopped there. Because he had a wife and children and a career, he had never dared do it. He would be cashiered, would go to jail, his family would likely starve.

He did not dare even to act on Favert's request alone, and he was looking for support from his second in command, and not getting it.

Pertinax was nodding, and Motier watched him. Nods were easy, but what did they mean?

"It really galls me to be forced to obey the orders of our German masters," Motier said.

"It galls us all."

"Bunch of gangsters."

"Yes."

"These people here are innocent of wrongdoing."

"Most of them."

As an admission of solidarity, this was as much, Motier judged, as he was going to get.

To allow men to congregate for religious purposes was dangerous, Motier knew, freedom of any kind in a camp like this was dangerous. Under the guise of religious services the men might begin to foment plots. One of his predecessors had put down a riot by firing into the camp, killing 150 inmates. It stopped the riot, but also ended the man's career.

Because his brother was married to a Jewish woman, Motier

knew about Le Lignon, and to him Pastor Favert and the other two men were heroes such as he wished he had the courage to be himself.

"All right," he said, hesitated, and then ordered Pertinax to permit the pastor to conduct any religious service he wished, anytime he wished, and that went for any other religious denomination in the camp as well.

After a moment, because of nervousness, or perhaps fear, a thought came to him, a way to tie his subordinate into the decision—or conspiracy, if that was how someone should later choose to regard it—in such a way that he would be unable to extricate himself. "Attend the service yourself," he ordered Pertinax. "Take notes. Make sure no subversive ideas are preached." There, it was done, they were together on this church service business, whether Pertinax liked it or not. The commandant saw no way his subordinate could denounce him now, and any higher authorities that might try to punish them would be facing two men, not one.

As Pertinax stood up there was no change of expression on his face either. "*Oui, Monsieur le Commandant,*" he said, and saluted and went out.

WITH a welcoming committee behind him, Obersturmbannführer Gruber stood on the quai watching the private train pull into the Lyon railroad station.

"*Achtung, achtung,*" he called out as the train slid to a stop, and he felt the men behind him snap to attention, as he did himself.

In a moment Helmut Rahn, the SS general commanding in France, stepped onto the quai. He was a small man wearing an impeccable uniform and carrying a baton. He seemed almost to be sniffing as he glanced suspiciously around, and Gruber stepped forward, braced, and saluted.

Lyon was to be Rahn's first stop on an inspection tour of the south.

To impress him, Obersturmbannführer Gruber had arranged a banquet in his honor. The site was to be the Mere Brazier on the rue Royale, said to be the best restaurant in Lyon, which Gruber had ordered closed for the occasion. Earlier that afternoon he had caused to be delivered to the restaurant various meats and delicacies that had become virtually unobtainable in France, as well as champagnes from the north, and he had stationed SS cooks in the kitchen both to guard it and to supervise preparations lest something untoward be slipped into the dishes. The restaurant had been ordered to provide the best of the neighboring Rhône wines.

General Rahn was taken to his hotel, at which guards had been posted, and was given time to rest and freshen up.

The banquet started at eight P.M. About thirty officers had been invited. Some were local, including the Wehrmacht general commanding Army Group G, and some were part of the substantial entourage/bodyguard that had accompanied Rahn. The local officers brought their own women, none of them wives, for when transferred to France they had been obliged to leave families behind. Gruber himself entered the restaurant with the superb Claire Cusset on his arm.

For the visiting officers he had provided girls out of Chez Blanchette, one of the two brothels that catered to and were regulated by the occupying forces.

As the party progressed, great quantities of champagne were consumed, plus some fine reds from the Côte-Rôtie and Châteauneuf-du-Pape. The war, which had begun to go badly, was not spoken of at all. Before long things got a bit boisterous. Some of the prostitutes were sitting on laps. Some had their blouses undone. There even were cries for Claire Cusset to perform her act on top of a table, but Gruber, who was at heart a prude, found this idea unseemly and would not permit it. However, in response to demands from his junior officers, he did agree to sing. An upright piano was wheeled in. Having stationed himself beside it, nodding to the pianist to get him started, he began to sing Schubert *lieder* in his rich baritone voice.

> *Now chase away the flowers of our dreams*
> *Rise up into God's bright morning*
> *The lark throws its trills into the air*
> *And from deep in one's heart love makes play*
> *Of torments and sorrow.*

The applause was tumultuous, so he went on to sing many more songs.

All of you flowers that she gave me
Let them lie you down with me in the grave.

Men had tears in their eyes. They were on their feet weeping and clapping. The women too seemed admiring and impressed. He was giving voice to the noblest expressions of the German soul, and his audience would not let him stop. The Germans were a sensitive and artistic people, he believed, and for the moment he was the expression of that artistry and sensitivity, and he was very proud.

Now he switched to songs by Hugo Wolf set to verses by Goethe.

You must rise or fall
You must reign and win,
Or else lose and serve.
Between hammer and anvil
You must suffer or triumph.

The songs were all so beautiful, and so German, that he felt terrifically proud to be who he was, where he was, and as he looked into the shining faces and moist eyes, as he listened to the applause, he was riding a terrific high.

Finally he could sing no more. He was out of practice and his voice gave out. When he stopped finally the men began to stomp on the floor. He could only grin stupidly back at them. They stomped so long and so hard he thought the building might come down.

General Rahn came forward. "Gorgeous," he said. Gruber saw that Rahn's eyes were unfocused. "Gorgeous."

"Thank you, General."

"After the war I foresee a career for you in opera."

Gruber was coming down off his high. Unlike his superior, he was cold sober, had needed to be sober to sing as he had just sung. In addition, during the last three hours and more he had been watching every detail of the party. Nothing must spoil its success.

"Just one thing." Rahn was slurring his words. "There's a train. Very soon a train."

"A train. I understand, General." Gruber decided to take the liberty of shaking hands with Rahn, as if they were not only intimates but equals. "I'm removing obstacles one by one. The train will be full."

Rahn nodded, and moved drunkenly off.

The party ended very late.

PASTOR Favert's first service at Le Vernet drew twelve curious Communists, plus Pertinax, who sat in the front row but whose notebook, if any, was not in sight.

It was Pertinax who had offered the use of an empty toolshed as a church. When asked, he had also provided a blackboard on which Assistant Pastor Henriot had written out the words to the hymns.

It was a bitterly cold Sunday at the end of February. The sun was very bright. A cold wind came in through the door which could not be closed because there was no other light with which to read the hymns and the liturgy. Except for Pertinax, who wore his uniform and greatcoat, the "congregation" sat huddled in blankets.

Assistant Pastor Henriot read the Sermon on the Mount and the parable of the good Samaritan, and then Headmaster Vernier led the hymns. At first only a few voices joined in, but Vernier had made the decision to sing each hymn twice, and by the second time around the repressed, half-starved prisoners had grasped the tune and were singing at the top of their lungs.

Finally Pastor Favert rose.

He began in a low voice that was barely audible, making the men lean forward to hear, his phrases gradually increasing in volume and power. He was an accomplished orator, and this was a technique he often used—he knew every technique there was. Shafts of light glinted off his glasses, and sometimes the vapor of his breath curled about his head like a halo. He was a big man who seemed bigger, and emanating from him was a force greater than that of any man present, and he dominated the room.

His sermon was in no way tailored to this particular audience, and yet it was. He was looking as always for converts—not to his religion but to his ideology—and so he spoke of nonviolence and passive resistance in a way that these men, militant Communists all, might understand. "Nonviolence does not mean total submission," he preached, "it does not mean being a rug that other people walk on. There are other kinds of resistance, just as there are other kinds of bravery." And he began to describe Le Lignon, of standing with pastors from neighboring villages as each train came in, and meeting Jews of all ages and nationalities, most of them terrified, many of them without a word of French, and apportioning them out among themselves, and then finding families that would take them in.

"We did this because our consciences were revolted with regard to what had been done, is still being done, to the Jews. It's a humiliation for Europe, and for us as Frenchmen. The Christian church should get down on its knees and demand pardon of God for our incapacity. I myself could not be silent. I say that not in a spirit of pride or anger but in sadness and humiliation for the human race and for our country. Our duty is and has always been to help those in need, in this case Jews, to hide them, save them by any means possible. The Bible tells us what is right and what is wrong. We must resist submitting to anything contrary to the orders that are written there. I challenged my village to do it with regard to the Jews, and they rose to that challenge, and I challenge you to do the same with every breath and thought that is in you, with every opportunity given to you.

"People ask me, the lessons you preach, do they apply to this world, or only to the next? If it's this world, well and good, we're interested. If it's only the next world, we're not interested, for the next world perhaps doesn't exist. To this I answer: faith has the power to change our everyday lives, and in measuring the power of faith, eternity counts for less than efficacy. Sure it's difficult to believe in things like the resurrection. There's no shame in that. There are other kinds of faith. I'm speaking of faith that works on earth. Faith that can make our lives and the lives of others more precious. It can work in our towns and villages, in our homes. I know no more about heaven than you do. The faith I'm talking about is for use here and now."

He spoke altogether about twenty minutes, and he concluded: "In our time it is almost shameful for a man never to have been in jail, as you are, as we are. One of the great lessons of the Bible is this one, that imprisonment never silenced the prophets, nor the apostles, nor any of the saints, death itself never stopped their work, and each time a man of God fell and was silent, another stood up and began to speak. What is the Bible if not history? The word of God, the work of God cannot be stopped."

The service ended with more hymns. The voices rose into a paean that could be heard all over that part of the camp.

Afterward Pertinax stepped into the commandant's office.

"Well?"

"Nothing," Pertinax said. He flipped through his notebook to show that all the pages were blank. "A religious service is all it was."

The commandant wanted to smile, but forebore doing so. Instead he only nodded in a noncommittal way. "Good," he said.

The following Sunday the service drew about fifty men, too many for the toolshed to hold. More than half had to stand outside, where they listened to Favert and took turns peering in at him through the door, and were mostly too embarrassed, because of other men walking by, to join in the hymns.

The Sunday after that the congregation had swelled to more than two hundred, and they held the service in one of the barracks, the men sitting in neat rows on the edges of the sleeping platforms top and bottom, the feet of those on top dangling close to the ears of the men below.

RACHEL had brought most of her things—there wasn't very much—into the room next door, and had made space for them in a drawer normally shared by two little girls.

Now she got ready for bed. Her door was open, and she could hear Davey in the next room. Having got completely undressed, she folded her clothes carefully, neatly, and then began shuffling through the drawer she had appropriated, looking for a clean nightdress. The room was cold, her feet were bare on the icy floor. Her nipples were standing out, she had gooseflesh all over, and at any moment he could walk in and catch her like this. She found the nightdress she wanted, taking much longer than the task required. Like her other nightdress it was a rather thick flannel. However, she did not immediately put it on, but instead held it clenched in one hand while eyeing the doorway, prolonging the dangerous moment, the delicious risk. If he came in she hadn't invited him, she thought, excusing herself in advance, it wouldn't be her fault.

But if he did come in and found her standing like this, what would happen next?

The excitement made her shiver, or else it was the cold. There was no movement in the other room, so finally she sighed and pulled the nightdress over her head. After that she put panties on under it, proof that she planned nothing untoward. Nothing was going to happen.

In a moment she was as modestly clothed as any girl should be when going to bed.

She had already bid Davey good night, had tucked him in and turned out the light. There had been a few kisses, not too many. He had tried to make her get in bed with him, but she had refused, telling him they were not going to indulge in any more foolishness of that kind, they were both going to get a good night's sleep. She did not know if he would accept this decree, nor did she know if she herself meant it. Perhaps she was only testing her hold over him. How strong was his desire for her? Were a few words from her, which she perhaps didn't mean, enough to keep him away? The answers to some of these questions certainly existed, but they were buried too deep in her psyche for her to know for sure what they were.

So far there was no significant movement on the other side of the wall, and she was a little disappointed. A little, not entirely. The passion they had so far revealed to each other, that she had revealed to herself, had somewhat frightened her. She had no intention of "going all the way," as the euphemism of the time had it. Next time—tonight for instance—her resolve might not be as strong. She knew boys never wanted to stop, that the girl had to do it. Still, she was confident that she had been, and would remain, in control of him, and in control of herself as well. And perhaps part of what she now hoped for was the chance to prove again how in control she was.

She had turned out the light but left her door open in case he called out in the night from pain or a nightmare—this was the explanation she gave herself. She got into bed, but her hands were tingling. Her whole body was tingling.

"Rachel," he called from the other room.

She did not answer, but as she waited to see what he would do she could hardly breathe.

She heard every move he made. Now he had got out of bed. Now he stood in her doorway, saying: "Can I come in?"

She had turned to face the wall. "I'm sound asleep. Go away."

But he hopped over, sat on the edge of the bed, and stroked her hair.

"Can I get in with you?"

When she did not answer he lifted the bedclothes and slid in beside her, his flight suit pressed against her nightdress, his erection pressed against her spine so that she butted him with her rump, saying: "Can't you see I'm sleeping?"

The butting continued, him grappling with her, trying to stay in place, both of them laughing, and then he got her turned over and the laughter stopped and the kissing started again.

He kept trying to pull her nightdress up. She kept trying to pull it down. He seemed to her to have more hands than she did. Before long the nightdress was up to her neck, and she was conscious of the roughness of almost the whole length of the flight suit against her skin, against her. His face was buried in her breasts, and his hand had begun a slow glide down her body. She knew where it was headed and got it stopped, holding it against his efforts, but a great weakness seemed to have come over her. He was too strong for her, she did not have the strength to control that hand any longer, interfere with wherever it might choose to go, whatever it might do when it got there. It moved downward.

She told herself she did not mind being touched in the places he had reached so far but had been resolved from the beginning not, under any circumstance, not to open her legs. However, they seemed to want to part of their own accord. She tried to make them stop but could not. A little might be all right, she told herself, as the hand kept moving. She could not be blamed if they parted only a little. Now the hand was below her ribs, now it had reached her navel, where it encountered the band of her panties. It climbed back up a bit, slipped under, and continued down. Now it was crossing the plain of her abdomen, now it was moving down the cleft of her, but slowly, slowly. She thought it would never reach its destination.

She was unaware of how loudly she gasped, of how her body began to move, but Davey wasn't, and added to all his other emotions so far was astonishment. He had indulged in sexual fantasies in the past, but what he was seeing and hearing now had not been part of any of them. Davey's view of love was conditioned by his Catholic background. Sex was considered to be for men, girls were for pedestals, and he had taken this, as he had taken much else, on faith, part of his college education. During all his previous romantic contacts, such as they were, nothing had caused him to change his mind.

The light in the room came from the hall. It was dim, but more than enough for him to see Rachel's face, which was contorted, and in addition to the writhing she moaned, sometimes almost screamed. He did not mistake these noises for cries of pain, and so he was astonished. She was covering his face with kisses. Maybe it's because she is European, not American, he thought. This was about as deeply as he was able to think at that moment, and he went on with what he was doing, and found that he was astonished also at what pleasure it gave him to give her pleasure, to put her into this state of passion, or rapture, or whatever it was, and to keep her there.

But enough was never enough, and he conceived the notion that he could do even better for her, and for himself, that the great pulsing ache inside him could be satisfied too, the physical and intellectual ache both, the need to know the rest of the mystery, to bring it to its logical conclusion, to know all that he had never known before.

"I want to make love to you."

Her teeth were clenched, but she gasped out the word: "No."

He got one leg over her, the rough flight suit between smooth thighs. What he wanted to do was what people did who were in love, and in a moment he would be there, they would both be there.

He knelt up and worked to get out of his flight suit. It had a long zipper, now halfway down. She tried to stop him. "No, please don't."

"I'm in love with you."

"No. Please no." There was a realization on both sides that something irrevocable was about to happen, that afterward everything would be changed. But the immediacy of this was more apparent to her than to him.

"There's nothing to be scared of."

"Suppose I get pregnant." Though worried about far more than this, she had brought forth her strongest argument first, or at least the one it would be easiest for him to understand.

"I won't get you pregnant."

"The pastor will throw me out, and I have no place to go."

"You won't get pregnant."

"Don't make me. Please don't make me."

"What's the difference between making love and what we've been doing?"

What he wanted to do, what they might be about to do together, was a big step for her, and he realized this. It was a big step for him too, though less, and in a different way, a hurdle to be got over, and if a young man afterward was a changed person too, this was considered both expected and necessary.

"I promise I won't get you pregnant."

"If the pastor even finds out I've done it, he'll throw me out."

"He won't throw you out."

"He will. You don't know him."

"I'll be here for you."

"You'll be back in England or America or somewhere."

That she was young, afraid, and flinching from the revelation that was to come was only what he had expected, and he felt a great outpouring of sympathy both for her, and for the position in which she found herself. Nonetheless he went on with what had now become a failed seduction—not that he saw this as yet—employing the same kisses, touches, and endearments as before as he attempted to make her change her mind, his own passion increasing even as hers diminished.

He tried—went on trying—in every way he could think of to convince her but soon knew he had failed. His disappointment was intense, but he was no less in love with her. Short of forcing her, a possibility that never occurred to him, the place to which he had so much wanted to take them both was for now out of reach.

"I want to see you," he told her. "I want to see all of you." And kneeling, he reached for the bedside lamp. If she was shrinking from the ultimate intimacy, then he wanted whatever other intimacy he could get.

The glare of light was enough to make her sit up abruptly, so that, as her nightdress fell back into place, he was afforded only the briefest possible glimpse.

He wanted her to see all of him also, wanted to show her how great was his need for her, as if this alone proved his love, and he slipped his arms out of the flight suit so that it fell to his knees.

She never looked directly at what he had revealed. Her eyes never left his face, but her slim fingers wrapped it up and she leaned forward until her lips touched his. "Maybe tomorrow," she murmured, and kissed him.

Given his condition, this was enough to send him over the edge. Quickly he got her hand away, and himself inside the flight suit, the zipper zipped up just in time. If she knew what was happening to him, what continued for the next few seconds to happen to him, she gave no sign, nor did he, except that perhaps his eyes blinked one or two times.

"Tomorrow," he said.

And so nothing further transpired that night, and they fell asleep in each other's arms.

IN London, Major Toft had been able to talk his way into Norgeby House on Baker Street. From the outside it had not looked to him anything like what it supposedly was. It might have been someone's town house, maybe even a small museum. Inside he was struck by the starkness of the place. He was led past a staircase down a short corridor and into a room and the door was closed on him. So far he had seen no decoration of any kind. Nothing hung on the walls, no flowers or plants stood on sideboards— and the English were big on flowers, he knew.

In the room in which he stood there was a table that might have sat six people for dinner; nothing lay on it. The walls were bare too. Against them were ranged four straight chairs that looked functional, meaning uncomfortable.

It was not a room in which one wanted to sit down, so Toft didn't.

After about ten minutes a woman entered. She carried a yellow pad with a fountain pen clipped to it, and made no effort to put him at his ease.

"You wished to see me?" she said.

Toft felt as uncomfortable as if he had walked into a ladies' room by mistake. He said: "I don't quite know who I want to see."

She looked to be about thirty-five, maybe a bit less. In any case, far older than he was. To him an older woman. "Or even if I've come to the right place." He tried a smile to which she did not respond.

"State your business, please, Major."

She was very good-looking in a stern way. Dark red lipstick. Firm chin. She wore her hair upswept in front and curled under in back. Toft was no expert on English accents, of which he now knew there were a great many, but hers seemed to him upper class.

"You're Vera Tompkins?"

"Vera Tompkins, yes."

"May I call you Vera?"

"Miss Tompkins would be better."

So that was the first setback.

Toft tended not to notice what women were wearing, but he noticed her clothes because he felt so off-balance and needed something other than her face to look at. He was in a place that dealt with many secrets, and it was British, not American. He was not supposed to be there, and he was trying to compose himself.

He said: "And this is headquarters of the Special Operations Executive?"

"Major, I'm really very busy."

"You don't exactly have a signboard outside."

She wore a dark wool dress with the high shoulder pads then in fashion. The dress had a shirt collar, buttons down the front, and was belted at the waist. It fit her tightly enough to show that she had a nice figure, but it was unpressed, even wrinkled. It looked almost as if she might have slept in it.

He would have felt better if she wore a uniform so that he could read her rank off her sleeve. "I was told you control communications and activities with the Resistance in occupied France."

"What is your need to know, Major?"

"Parachute drops of supplies, moving agents in and out, landings, that sort of thing."

"Who told you that?"

"Friends in the American Intelligence community. They're supposed to have called you about me."

"Perhaps the people you want to see are the Free French."

"The Free French," said Toft. He had no way of knowing who or what he was dealing with. A bare room. A woman who reeked of authority but wore no rank.

"They're on Duke Street, behind Selfridges."

"Yes."

"Selfridges is the department store."

"I've been to Selfridges."

"Or even your own OSS."

He had arrived in England thinking of it as the forty-ninth state. He had learned that it was a separate country entirely, that things were done differently here, and that even the language was used in a way that was not always clear to him.

He said doggedly: "I was told I should see you."

"Why us, Major?"

"You personally." He had been told she was second or third in command of the French section of an intelligence agency of fourteen hundred people, with training schools all over England and Scotland, that the general and colonel above her were useful mostly for the political struggles against the multitude of other intelligence agencies running around London, but were otherwise window dressing. He had been told she had more agents in France than any other agency, more radios and radio operators too, and therefore the best intelligence.

"I know you had to show identification to get in here, Major, but if you don't mind I'd like to see it again."

Toft produced it.

She looked it over, and then him over, and finally asked him to sit down. They pulled up chairs—he attempted to help her carry hers but she froze him with a look, and he let go of it.

They sat at opposite sides of the table.

He said: "I like the way you talk."

She frowned.

"I don't mean to get fresh. I like your accent. You speak like the queen."

The smile this time lasted a tiny bit longer.

"You make our accent sound, well, common."

"What do you fly, Major? Bombers, fighters?"

"Fighters. P-51 Mustangs."

"Based up in Norfolk, is it?"

"Yes."

"Very wet up there."

"It's wet everywhere in England, I've found." Toft tried another small smile, and this time got a smile back. He definitely thought it had been a smile.

"If I have seemed rude to you, Major, I apologize. I haven't been to bed yet."

"It's ten o'clock in the morning."

"Yes, well, we had some trouble last night."

"Trouble, Miss Tompkins?"

"Something."

He let it go. "I'm surprised to find a woman in charge of an operation like this." Wrong remark, he saw at once.

"That's quite insulting, Major."

"I mean a woman as young as yourself."

"It's still insulting."

"Sorry. I didn't mean it to be."

"What is it you want from us, Major?

Toft wondered if he should tell her how many planes he had shot down, but decided she wouldn't be impressed, and so didn't.

"One of my men went down in France recently. I wondered if you had heard anything about him."

"Where was this?"

"Near Le Puy in the Massif Central."

She nodded, but said nothing.

There came a knock on the door, and a dispatch rider came in, handing her a package for which she signed. The rider was a middle-aged man in a leather jacket and leggings, and she nodded at him, and he went out.

"And now I've got to go read these, I'm afraid."

"The pilot in question is one of my men. Is he alive or dead, that's what I want to know."

Another frown. "You must understand, Major, I can't talk to you about what we do here, or what we don't do here."

"Do you know the answer?" he said bluntly.

"No."

"But you're in a position to find out?"

"What makes you think that?"

"You have radio operators all over France."

"That's a comment on which I can't . . . comment."

"Is it the type of intelligence that comes in here?"

"Does intelligence of that type reach London? Sometimes. Quite often, in fact."

"If you, or someone, receives such intelligence, do you notify the airmen's base?"

"It's done through channels, I think."

"Suppose, for sake of argument," Toft said, "that a pilot goes down in France, do you, does someone, send a plane in to pick him up?"

"Did you come all the way to London to ask me these questions, Major?"

"No. I came down because I had a few days leave." He felt like adding, just to see the expression on her face: "And I got laid last night, Miss Tompkins, what do you think of that? Picked up a girl and laid her."

"Were you with him at the time?" asked Miss Tompkins.

"Yes."

"He crashed?"

"Yes."

"What do you think? Did it look to you that he might have survived it?"

"I couldn't tell. But he was a pretty tough kid."

"Are you sure of your location?"

"I had to fix my position in order to find my way home."

"What's his name?"

She made a note of the name on her pad.

"All right, a pilot goes down in France," Toft repeated, "does a plane get sent for him, or what?"

She shook her head. "Far too many pilots go down in France to send planes for all of them."

"How do they get out?"

"They walk out through Spain, I expect. Those that can. Or they walk to the coast and get on a fishing boat."

"Those that can."

She shrugged.

"But planes go in all the time, I'm told. They bring in dispatches, radio equipment, people, and they bring people out."

"It's not regularly scheduled, like a railroad. And the people brought out are important people."

"You mean not just ordinary pilots."

"I didn't mean to offend you, Major."

"Suppose you had someone, and a plane, willing to go in there and bring someone out?"

"What are you suggesting, Major?"

"Nothing. First see if you can find out if he's alive. Let me leave you my telephone number."

"Do you have a telephone beside your bed, Major?"

"You know what I mean." Reaching for her pad, he slid it across to his side of the table and on it scrawled the address of his air base, together with some phone numbers: operations, the officers' club, and several others.

He stood up. "You're a very good-looking woman," he said. Exasperation had made him bold. "Suppose I asked you out to dinner."

She gave a kind of girlish giggle, and he was surprised.

But she recovered quickly. "Let me apologize to you, Major. I do know your name. I am aware of how many planes you have shot down. I have often wondered how a man like you stays alive. When you came in here I was curious to meet you. Having met you, may I say you're a very impressive man."

She got up from her chair, pushed it to the wall, and started to the door.

It was almost the first applause he had heard except from other pilots—if applause was what it was. "How about dinner?" he said to her back.

"The next time you come to London, perhaps," she murmured, without turning around, and was gone.

He went out of the building and down the stoop. It was raining. He had a plastic cover over his cap, and he turned up the collar of his raincoat. It had been raining for five days, which was why he had decided to come to London on leave at this time.

He saw that Baker Street was crowded with people moving along under umbrellas, and he moved along with them, and for a time it was possible to believe there was no war going on only a short distance away.

XIII

RACHEL was awakened by a loud banging on the front door. She stood stupefied beside the bed, then found her shoes, and started for the living room. Halfway across she remembered the two bedroom doors hanging open, the two unmade beds, in one of which lay a wounded American pilot, and she ran back and closed them both. "Don't make a sound," she hissed at Davey before shutting him for the time being out of her life.

Her caller was Giselle Henriot, the assistant pastor's wife, who seemed surprised to catch her still in bed at this hour—the clock on the mantelpiece read quarter to nine.

She had had trouble getting to sleep last night, Rachel explained, and when Madame Henriot looked at her in a quizzical way she added: "I lay there for hours worrying about the pastor." Immediately she chided herself for lying still again, for she had not had a thought in days not connected to herself and Davey. I don't seem able to tell the truth at all anymore, she told herself.

"It's freezing in here," said Madame Henriot, and she glanced around the room.

Quickly and nervously, Rachel did likewise, but there was nothing pertaining to Davey that she could see.

"I'll get the fire going," she said. Kneeling, she shoved brush in among the still-glowing coals—on the plateau people started their fires with *genet*, a kind of gorse or broom which reached a blazing yellow color in summer but smelled bitter in winter when it burned. She laid out logs on top. In a moment the fire flared up, and the two women stood with their backs to it, Madame Henriot dressed for outside, Rachel in her flannel nightgown trying not to shiver.

"I've been trying to call you," said Madame Henriot, "but your phone is out."

"I hadn't noticed," said Rachel.

"The snow I guess. I've signaled the PTT to come fix it. I don't know when they'll get here."

"Would you like some tea?"

"I've come directly from taking the kids to school," said Madame Henriot as Rachel led the way down the hall.

The kitchen was even colder than the other room had been. Kneeling before the woodstove whose fire she had banked before going to bed, Rachel stuffed in brush and small logs, blowing hard to restart the fire.

Madame Henriot said: "Go put some clothes on, girl, before you freeze to death. I'll make the tea."

Rachel entered the bedroom with her finger pressed to her lips to warn Davey, but when she started to leave, he demanded a kiss first. She gave him a smile instead, and went out, and into the bathroom where she washed and dressed.

When the kettle finally boiled the girl and the woman carried their tea back into the main room where they sipped it in front of the fire.

Madame Henriot said: "I came to tell you that the church is sending in a substitute pastor to conduct the service tomorrow."

He was coming from Clermont-Ferrand and was expected on the noon train, Madame Henriot said, or one of the other trains, if the trains were running. Service had been so unreliable lately.

Also, she had had another call from Madame Favert. She sent her love; she was now in Vichy, still trying to find out which ministry had ordered the arrest of the two pastors and the headmaster, and where they were. As soon as she had her answers she would have only one other stop to make, and then she would be home. She was making progress, she said, and would call again soon.

Madame Henriot no longer sounded particularly worried about her husband. Rachel thought of her as one of those women who believed that if you were a good girl and went to church regularly, everything would work out for the best—that bad things never happened to good people. Young as she was, Rachel had learned differently long ago.

Besides which, Madame Favert was taking care of it. What a difference between this woman and Mother Favert, Rachel thought.

Madame Henriot was something of a nonstop talker. Rachel, with most of her mind in the other room, had to do little more than nod from time to time. The substitute pastor was named Pelletier and it was not known how long he would stay. Probably he would go back Sunday afternoon, for he had a family after all, and Clermont was a less spartan place than here. He would of course expect to stay in the presbytery overnight, and for however long he would remain in Le Lignon, and if it made Rachel uncomfortable to be alone in the house all night with an unknown man, this was understandable and she was welcome to stay with Madame Henriot and all the children. "I'm sure we can find room for you," she said.

"No," said Rachel, coming alert with a start, "I don't see a problem." But what would this mean for Davey, she asked herself. "Pastor Pelletier will need somebody to take care of him," she said, "and I want to keep the house warm for when Mother Favert comes back."

Madame Henriot nodded, and then she was talking again.

At long last the woman finished her tea and departed. Rachel rushed right into the other room where Davey awaited her eagerly. He was to wash and shave and then get himself and his things up into the attic, she told him. There wasn't time for anything. Another pastor was coming in today, perhaps any minute.

"The attic?"

Though it was going to be cold up there, she couldn't think of anyplace else to put him. "He mustn't know you're here. We have to get a mattress up there, blankets. You can have the electric heater out of the pastor's room."

"Why mustn't he know I'm here?"

"Because he might turn you in, that's why. We don't know who he is, or what his sympathies might be."

"He's a Protestant."

"Plenty of Protestants in the Nazi party, friend."

"That's Germany. This guy's French."

"Plenty of Frenchmen work for the Germans." To Rachel, at that moment, Davey fitted the image many people seemed to have of Americans. Young and strong, sure, but ignorant and naïve as well. "Frenchmen who believe the Germans will win," she said. "Some of whom even think the Germans are just what's needed to straighten the country out. Believe me, you can't take the chance. It's too dangerous." Davey might be an officer in the American army, but she felt suddenly years older. "If he turns you in, he turns me in too."

He remained silent.

"There may be somebody coming to fix the telephone too," she said. "Plus who knows who else might drop by." He looked so crushed that she wanted to soften her rebuke, so she added: "As soon as the pastor leaves you can come down."

Davey, who had been hoping for something else today, embraced her.

She stroked his cheek.

There came another knocking at the door.

"Jesus," said Davey.

She closed the bedroom door on him. There wasn't time to get him up into the attic, which was served via a trapdoor, out of which a ladder folded down.

But at the door was only the forger, Pierre Glickstein, alias Henri Prudhomme. He had come bearing an identity card and ration books for the pilot, he said. Rachel led him into the bedroom where he presented them.

"This *mec* I know made them for you."

Davey said to Rachel: "What did he say?"

Rachel translated.

Davey put the papers down on the dresser. "I don't know," he said to Rachel. "If I use those things I become a spy, I think. If they catch me I can be shot."

"What did he say?" said Glickstein.

"He thanks you," said Rachel with a smile. "He doesn't know what the future holds, but he's certainly glad to have them."

Glickstein beamed. "He's got a new name—take a look. According to those papers he was wounded and demobilized from the French army. Take a look at those demob papers."

Typed across the sheet were the words NOT VALID FOR TRANSPORT. "What does that mean?" asked Rachel, seeing how proud he was.

"It's just to make them look real. It's even in a different colored ink than the other signature on the same page. This *mec* I know is pretty shrewd."

Some of the other papers carried typed endorsements as well, additional signatures. Glickstein pointed some of them out. "Makes it look more authentic," he said.

For the first time in his career Glickstein was taking bows for his work. The American looked unimpressed, but the girl was nodding and smiling and looking at him with what might have been new respect.

However, almost at once the forger seemed to become conscious of the way they looked at each other. It seemed to him that secret messages passed between them without a word being said—that he had no chance here.

"Tell him," Glickstein said, "that there's been a German scout plane flying around over the farm where he went down. It comes back every few days."

Even before she translated, Rachel looked alarmed.

"I don't know if they've seen anything yet," Glickstein said, "but if they keep looking they're going to spot his plane, because the snow isn't going to last forever."

Now Rachel and Davey were both alarmed, and they asked questions, most of which Glickstein was unable to answer. He didn't know if any of the wrecked P-51 showed from the air, he said. He didn't know if the scout plane would come back still again.

He watched them talking to each other in English, his eyes going from one face to the other, and the intimacy between them was clear. It had not been there the other day. He said: "Tell him he better start thinking about getting out of here, one way or another."

There came another knocking at the front door. The three young people looked at each other. Glickstein's face showed immediate terror. If caught here with an American pilot all the forged documents in the world were not going to help him.

Rachel saw his fear and became frightened herself, and the combination was enough to frighten Davey.

"It's probably the substitute pastor," Rachel said, trying to calm the other two, trying to calm herself. "His train's arrived." But she knew it hadn't. To reach the station the little train had to cross streets. Its warning hoots could be heard all over the village, even inside houses. But she had heard nothing. No hoots meant no train, which in turn meant that the person at the door—and the knocking now sounded a second time—was not the substitute pastor.

"I'll go see," she said, and closed them into the bedroom.

Left alone, the two young men stared at each other. Since they had no common language, neither spoke.

A moment later they heard footsteps returning, and the door opened—a relieved Rachel, smiling, followed by the doctor.

He said: "The stitches maybe I remove."

Having banished Rachel and Glickstein to the other room, he did remove them, snipping with tiny, needle-nosed scissors, drawing them out with tweezers.

Entirely concentrated on his work, the doctor kept saying, "Gut, gut," for the wounds showed no sign of infection, were healing nicely, and he covered them over with fresh bandages, in some cases with Band-Aids out of Davey's survival kit. After that he took the patient's blood pressure, which was normal, and his temperature, also normal, and he felt for the bump on the head, but it was gone.

"How quickly the young heal," he muttered in his own language, and felt a spasm of jealousy. His own wounds were to the spirit, and did not heal at all.

He moved the patient's toes around, which caused some pain, not much.

"*Gut,*" he said again.

During this time Rachel and Glickstein sat facing each other in front of the fire. It was the first time Glickstein had been alone with her with time to talk, but he found himself tongue-tied—he could think of nothing to say. Rachel was no help to him. The silence did not seem to bother her. She did not even seem aware of it, and he suspected her attention was in the next room with the doctor and his patient.

Presently the doctor, followed by Davey on crutches, issued from the bedroom.

"Can you ask him how long I'm going to be cooped up here?" said Davey to Rachel, and he listened while this was translated.

"He says three more weeks minimum. He doesn't have an X-ray here. He can't really tell. Next week he may cut the cast down a bit."

She's interested in the pilot, not me, thought Glickstein, watching this exchange.

Rachel did not offer her two guests tea or anything else. She was anxious only that they should be gone and Davey safely hidden before the substitute pastor arrived. As a result the doctor departed almost at once, and Glickstein, despondently, soon after.

MADAME Favert was on a train between Vichy and Lyon.

Outside it was night, and cold. The train was unventilated and, except by bodies, unheated. Only the oldest, most dilapidated trains rolled in France, the Germans having requisitioned the others. The seats were wooden benches, the entire coach rattled and creaked. Small blue bulbs glowed in the near dark, painting every face with an unhealthy pallor. The rails clicked. From time to time someone would slide a window down to get some air, and soot and cinders would fly in, together with the cold. The train smelled principally of soot. One breathed it in, it got into one's clothes.

The compartments were all full—over full. Compartments for eight had become compartments for twelve. The overhead racks were full. Having forced their way inside, people sat on their suitcases or on the floor, their backs against the sliding door, or the outside wall of the car.

In the corridors, there being no racks, the baggage was piled on the floor. People straddled it, sat on it. The corridors were full from end to end; the platforms between the cars were full as well.

Madame Favert had been on the train eight hours. At first she had had a seat in a compartment. She had lost it when she had to go to the toilet. The toilet didn't work. When she came back one of the standees from the corridor was in her seat, his hat pulled down over his eyes. She told him off, but he pretended to be asleep. She had no choice but to back into the corridor where, seated on her suitcase, she tried to sleep but could not because her legs began to cramp. It was not possible to move them because they were pinned in by other bags with people sitting on them, by other people's knees and feet.

Her suitcase, with all the air squeezed out of it, had partially collapsed.

At Roanne, half a compartment emptied out. A dozen people forced their way in from the corridor—more than a dozen—but she was quick and got a seat.

Opposite her, she noted, as the train began moving again, was the man who had stolen her seat earlier. She glared at him, but he again pulled his hat down and pretended to sleep. Beside him sat a woman with a baby on her lap.

The train stopped at Feurs, Montrand, St. Étienne—there were no expresses anymore. It did not even approach Lyon on a straight line but wandered about the countryside hours late, stopping everywhere. At Rive-de-Gier the train stopped again, and this time the police came through checking papers. In the corridor everyone had to stand up. The police pushed their way through, at times high-stepping over luggage. Looking out the window, Madame Favert saw they were in a station. She didn't know which one. There were no signs on stations anymore. The police poked their heads into every compartment, waking everybody up.

The man who had stolen her seat said to the woman next to him: "Why don't I hold the baby for a few minutes, Madame. Give you a chance to stretch."

By the time a policeman pushed into their compartment the baby was on his lap.

"Papers," the *flic* said. He was in plainclothes. French from the sound of him. There were men behind him still working the corridor. They had leather overcoats and German accents.

The flic shone his flashlight on documents. Norma Favert had hers ready: identity card, baptismal certificate, marriage certificate, ration book. The *flic* scanned them, handed them back.

"And you, Monsieur," he said to the man with the baby.

"In my back pocket," the man whispered. "Look, we just got him to sleep. If I wake him up suddenly he's going to start wailing, keep everybody awake the rest of the night. Give me a chance to do it gently. Check a few more compartments and come back and I'll have my papers ready for you."

"You've got two minutes," the *flic* said curtly.

They heard him move down the car. In the compartment no one spoke. They heard the voices moving away from them.

"Police," the voices said, "papers." The voices got dimmer.

Having handed the baby back to its mother, the man fished his billfold out of his pocket, leaned out into the corridor and waved it at the *flic,* who was by then at the end of the carriage.

The *flic* started to come back, but rather than clamber over people and baggage a second time, he changed his mind, gave a brief nod, and crossed into the next car.

When the train started up again the man let out a long breath. "Thanks for the loan of your baby," he said to the mother. "He's done me a real service."

No one asked who he was or why he had no papers. No one said anything at all.

At the Lyon station Madame Favert saw him disappear in the direction of the toilets. A Jew? An escaped prisoner? A member of the Resistance? She would never know, did not want to know.

It was then five A.M. The waiting room was as crowded as the train she had just got off. Lyon was the great crossroads of France. People waited for the arrival or departure of trains that followed no schedule, that might come, might not come, that ran when they ran. All the benches were taken. People slept against the walls or on the floor. Men in plainclothes and others in German uniforms moved among them examining papers.

Madame Favert had nowhere to go this early. She had been to St. Étienne, Clermont, Le Puy, and finally Vichy. She had ridden a dozen trains like tonight's, had waited days in anterooms hoping to see someone who might help her find her husband and get him out of custody. Most of the men she had got in to see had been kind, but none could help. Or had refused to help. Or had given her false leads, whether by accident or on purpose was usually difficult to tell. There were nights like this one that she had spent on trains. Otherwise she had taken shelter in presbyteries, eating the food of people who didn't have much.

Her money was almost gone.

Now she was back in Lyon again, her last hope. But it was too early to wake anybody up, and the station restaurant did not open for an hour or more. She went into the ladies' toilet and washed the soot off her face and hands. There was no soap, but then she hadn't expected any. Soap was rationed. And of course no towel either. She washed with soap out of her suitcase, and dried herself on her own towel. She dragged a comb through her hair, then pinned it up in the same bun as before.

Out in the waiting room she settled down against the wall, and attempted to doze, her back against her suitcase lest somebody steal it.

"Papers."

A Gestapo *mec* in a leather overcoat.

She had perhaps been sound asleep—did not at first know where she was. She stood up blinking and got her papers out.

The German handed them back and went on.

She looked at the big clock and saw she had dozed an hour or more. The station café was now open, so she went over there and sat down, and the waiter came.

She had enough coupons for a café au lait, a slice of bread, and a little butter, so that was what she ordered, and he cut the coupons out. As she paid him she was appalled to see how few bills remained in her purse. She ate and drank slowly, making it last.

There was a line of pedicabs waiting outside the station, but they were surely expensive. Asking one of the drivers to pedal her over to the Hôtel de Police was out of the question. Several of the little red streetcars passed her as she walked, and she considered jumping onboard. But no, it was better to save the fare. Her valise, as she dragged it through the streets, got heavier and heavier.

She went into the building, asked to see Commissaire Chapotel, and was made to wait. This time she did no screaming in the halls. She was too beaten down for that. There was very little courage left in her.

Finally she was led to Chapotel's office.

He looked up at her, a butt hanging from his mouth. "How can I help you, Madame?"

There was a toughness in her. She did not enumerate the cities she had been to, nor the officials she had waited to see, nor the nights trying to sleep in strange presbyteries, nor the overcrowded trains. She did not admit that she had tried and failed to go over his head. She did not plead with him. There were no tears. This man had eaten at her table. He owed her something.

"I have been unable to find my husband. I thought you might know where he is—or can find out."

Chapotel squinted at her through smoke. "I do know where he is—where he was, anyway."

"Are you going to tell me?"

"He was sent to the camp at Le Vernet."

It made her take a deep breath.

"If you'll step outside, Madame, I can perhaps find out if he is still there."

THE visiting pastor, Pelletier, did not arrive until early afternoon. He came into the presbytery bringing his own food and complaining to Rachel about the trains—between Clermont and Le Lignon, a distance of 180 kilometers, he had had to change four times, and the trains had stopped twice while German police went through the cars checking papers, a damned nuisance.

He showed Rachel the food he had brought with him. Two oranges. A whole roast chicken. Her mouth began to water. He always brought his own food when visiting other parishes, Pelletier explained. In these times it wasn't right to eat other people's food that they had had such a hard time procuring. Of course he would share what he had with her.

"Thank you," said Rachel automatically.

But where did he get a chicken? Where did he get oranges? Chickens were rare, and she had not seen an orange since Papa Favert had presented her with one on the day of her sixteenth birthday.

Who was this man, and how far could he be trusted? She glanced in the direction of the attic over her head and prayed silently that Davey would be absolutely silent up there. If he gave them away . . .

To worry about another, even to worry about herself, was new to her. Previously her worrying was done for her by Papa Favert. When she had had choices to make, he made them. Suddenly he was gone and she was left—the idea reached her only vaguely—face-to-face with womanhood in all its forms. Worries, choices, responsibilities were suddenly hers alone, and whatever decisions she made carried with them risks to her person and to this house, not to mention to the young man upstairs who, being both wounded and a fugitive, could not exist without her help.

She could not think of Davey dispassionately because he stirred in her emotions and needs that she had never felt before and that she could not sort out. All she knew was that, ready or not, she was on her own. Another vague thought came to her as well: that this was only the start of it, that the more people and things she would come to love, the more directions she would be pulled in, and the more anxiety and pain she could expect.

She installed the visiting pastor in one of the children's rooms.

Later she ate supper with him, refusing the chicken he offered, saying she rarely ate meat, but accepting one of his oranges because she had not had one in so long and was too weak-willed to say no.

During supper he talked of Jesus for some time, perhaps preparing tomorrow's sermon in his head. He was perhaps the holiest of men, but he also asked her about herself, her name, where she came from. She told the usual lies, and when he asked about Jews being hidden in Le Lignon she claimed ignorance—no one had ever talked about Jews in her presence, she said.

Pastor Pelletier then recounted to her a good many stories about

Jews saved by Pastor Favert, and some of them she already knew, though sometimes there were accompanying details she had not heard before. If Pelletier was who he said he was, obviously he would know these things, for within the church they were spoken of far and wide, Rachel assumed. But there was no reason he should regale her with them, unless he was trying to draw her out on the subject, and so she smiled and nodded in the appropriate places, and otherwise kept silent.

Mostly her thoughts were upstairs with Davey.

While she was clearing the table she suggested that Pastor Pelletier might like to go over to the temple to see how the organ was placed, the pulpit, the pews. In his absence she could have talked to Davey, offered him encouragement. But the holy man gave a short laugh and declined. It was too cold out, there was too much snow, he said.

After supper he sat in front of the fire working on his sermon, from time to time trying out a phrase aloud. Rachel sat nearby pretending to read a book, but she kept listening for sounds from above. If Davey moved a muscle up there, she and Pelletier would both hear him, she believed. He was being very silent, but she did not imagine he was in any way comfortable, and she wondered how much longer he could keep it up.

Finally Pelletier bade her good night and went to bed.

Having banked both fires, having pulled tight all the heavy drapes to hold as much heat as possible within the house, Rachel followed. There was still no way she could voice her concerns to Davey. She got in between the icy cold sheets and worried about him.

BY then the temperature in the attic, Davey judged, was about thirty degrees and dropping.

Earlier he and Rachel had forced a mattress up through the trap, Rachel on the ladder pushing, Davey seated on the edge pulling. When the mattress was in place, blankets, a pillow, and bottled water had followed. Also bread, some dried fruits and nuts, a lamp, an electric heater, a bucket, and the crutches.

Rachel had carried up his unused parachute. "I don't like having it around. I wish I had made that other young man take it away." She dropped it on the mattress. "You can use it as a pillow."

"The identity card that guy gave me—do you think he forged it himself?"

"Maybe."

"I can't use it."

She shrugged. It was the parachute that was still on her mind. "Anybody finds it . . ."

"Lot of good silk in that pack."

"Mother Favert is a great dressmaker and she has seven people to clothe."

"Maybe she'll make you a silk blouse."

While waiting for Pastor Pelletier to arrive, the trap open to hear him when he came, they had sat on the mattress, blankets over their shoulders, and had talked of other things too, of his brother and sister, of his parents, of songs and radio programs he liked that she had never heard, or movies she had never seen. On her side she talked of England, especially of her school—how she had started there without a word of English, and had later won the English composition prize. She had also become the best girl in the school at tennis and field hockey.

They talked of how long the war might last, and about the pastor, whom Davey had never met, and whom Rachel idolized.

Several times he had tried to pull her down on the mattress, but she had resisted. Pelletier could come at any moment, she said. She did permit a few kisses. It didn't take many to inflame him, she realized. She kept saying to him in French *Du calme,* though she wasn't very calm herself.

Finally she put a hand over his mouth and said: "Stop, stop." And then: "I have a confession to make. Several of them, in fact."

He saw that she had become troubled. "So what do you have to confess?"

The time had come, Rachel decided, to recant all her lies. There was not going to be a better moment. She would tell him her real name, that she was Jewish, and not French but German, and she had stolen his chocolate—everything. Taking a deep breath, she tried to start in, but couldn't. Finally she managed to say:

"Who's Nancy?" Perhaps if she began her confession with something relatively easy . . .

"What do you know about Nancy?"

"I read her letter to you." She could not look at him. "I know I shouldn't have. I'm so ashamed."

He laughed. "So you read my letter. So what."

This gave her courage to go on. "And I ate half your chocolate bar." She pulled the remaining half out of the pocket in her skirt.

As he accepted it, he laughed again.

"Want some?"

They ate the rest of the chocolate. Rachel didn't enjoy her share at all.

"Anything else?" Davey said, and waited.

"No."

"I get the impression there is."

She wanted to tell him the rest, but couldn't do it. She said: "So tell me who Nancy is."

"A girl I was going steady with."

"What does going steady mean in America?"

"I used to think about marrying her. She was so suitable."

"Suitable?"

"Our parents were friends. We had known each other off and on for years." Was that all there had been between them? That she was suitable? Davey had begun looking for truths in places he had never looked before. "She probably thinks I'm dead," he said. "Anyway, that was before I met you." And he pulled her close to start kissing her again.

But she stopped him. "Why should it make any difference that you've met me?"

"I never felt nearly as close to her as I do to you." This was still another new truth he was trying to come to terms with. "I don't want to marry her anymore, I'm sure of that."

"Who do you want to marry then?" She tried to keep her voice light, making a joke of it.

"Well"—he took a deep breath—"you, maybe."

"Me?"

"What would you say if I said I wanted to marry, well, you?"

It was a wondrous thing to hear, wondrous to think about. It sent a glow all through her. But she was a level-headed girl, who quickly saw the idea as impractical. "How can you marry me?" she said. "I'm here, and you'll be there."

"The war isn't going to last forever. I can come back, can't I?"

She was silent.

"Do you want me to?"

"Sure."

Maybe he would come back. It seemed to her unlikely, because it was so far, but maybe he would.

"You shouldn't say such things if you don't mean it."

"I do mean it."

They looked at each other. New York to France was six days by ship, followed by two days on a train. It would cost a fortune. Where would he find the time, and the money?

She said: "I wonder when that pastor is going to get here?"

He said: "So go on with your confession."

This caused a long, profound silence.

Her confession was over. She couldn't go on with it. Tell him she had lied to him even about her name? The way she felt this minute—loved, warm—all that would go. He wouldn't want to marry her anymore, wouldn't even want to be with her.

Just then they heard the banging on the front door, and she hurried down the ladder to answer it, while Davey pulled the trap all the way up and into place.

FOR a time he listened to their voices speaking French—what else did he have to do? He could not tell what they were saying, but the preacher sounded smarmy. Could he be trusted with her? Considering this thought unworthy, Davey chased it from his head. He had never known a dishonorable churchman, or even heard of one. It was for this reason that he had earlier discounted the possibility that Pastor Pelletier could be in the employ of the Germans. In the less cynical world that existed at that time, churches had real power; the transgressions of priests, ministers, and rabbis, when they occurred, could be and were smothered at once. Parishioners never knew. Men of God were considered, therefore, in America at least, and especially in the circles in which Davey had moved, above reproach.

Pastor Pelletier, whom he had not yet met, was to him above reproach. Rachel's honor was certainly safe with such a man, who would never betray Davey either, if he knew about him.

This was part of what Davey had been taught to believe.

Rachel, of course, believed otherwise. It was for her that he would endure this purgatory up here for however long it would last.

In summer the attic was sometimes used by the children as a playroom, and the floor was finished, but he had hobbled across it earlier, and the boards creaked. Only when night came would he be able to move a bit. As soon as Rachel and the preacher had gone to bed downstairs any noise he might make would be ascribed to mice. But for now he felt glued to the mattress. He was on his back looking up. Above him were the laths, and the underside of the thick roof slates. He could hear the wind through the slates, and he could see refracted daylight.

He was alone with his thoughts, and they began to crowd him.

At first he didn't have any that were not connected to Rachel. The mattress was still cold, the blankets too. He was cold. His wounds ached, his leg, and he ached for Rachel. He wanted her in bed with him. Such thoughts warmed him, and then they warmed him too much. As she filled his consciousness, the images became increasingly erotic. He wanted to smell her hair, lick the salt off her breasts. He could feel her body still, both under his fingers and around them, and he sniffed them as he had done last night, wanting to smell that part of her, but there was nothing left now, it was gone. He reached a state of arousal so intense that it alarmed him, and he shut such thoughts down, or tried to, concentrated on flight school, on basketball. He ran down streets in his head, turning corners, only to find Rachel in the next street too.

Bit by bit he forced his mind onto subjects that were important. He was alone in a foreign country, shot down, wounded—there was so much that needed his attention. Were the Germans looking for him? They would be as soon as they found his plane. What happened next? Well, there was Rachel . . .

He thought of his parents, especially his mom. Had his parents been told yet? What had they been told? How had his mom taken it? He thought of her as old—she was forty-one—and bossy, perhaps even tough, but he had seen her weep once when his brother had been in a car crash, so he supposed she would weep for him. If only he could talk to her on the phone. That would make her smile, he guessed.

Although he had been in the squadron only a few weeks, others had been shot down, so he knew the procedure up to a point. The squadron would post him as killed in action, or missing in action—which one, he wondered?—and so notify Washington, and the telegram to his parents would go out from the War Department. At home the doorbell would ring, his mom would go to it and when she saw the Western Union boy, she would know what it was in advance. Perhaps she would faint. Perhaps she would just disbelieve it. That's what he hoped would happen. He hoped also that his father would be there to take the telegram away from her, and hold her in his arms. He was his mother's favorite, he had always thought. He was her firstborn, and much resembled her, same fair complexion, same nose and mouth.

In the barracks they would clean out his footlocker looking for condoms, love letters, dirty pictures. They wouldn't find any of that. They would box the rest and send it to his parents. The squadron commander, in his case Joe Toft, would write a letter of condolence. Toft had liked him, he believed, and so the letter would be a nice one. He was entitled now to a Purple Heart, and maybe they would award him a Distinguished Flying Cross, maybe even a Silver Star. They would send those things to his parents too. Whenever his name was mentioned people would think of him as a hero. This notion made him frown. As he saw it, all he was was a guy who had got shot down.

He remembered Toft flying on his wing after he was hit. Toft would get back to the base and be hurried off to the operations shack to be debriefed. Maybe he knew where Davey had gone down and could tell them. But had Toft stayed with him all the way? Davey didn't know, for the blow to his head when he crashed had wiped out the last hour or so of memory. If Toft had stayed with him to the end, then perhaps he knew and would report where he had gone down. That assumed Toft had made it back. It assumed also that he had made navigational markings as he flew— compass headings, indicated airspeed, elapsed time. In a strange country it was pretty difficult to know where you were from towns and rivers on the ground. If Toft knew, it might be possible for Air Corps headquarters in London to make contact with the local Resistance, find out he was alive, and tell his mom not to worry. Of course the Resistance didn't know where he was either.

He wished he could tell his mother himself. As soon as my leg heals, Mom, I'm walking out of here. Lying under blankets gazing up at the underside of slates, this idea was real to him. He would walk to Spain or Switzerland, and from there get back to England. Others had done it, he had heard; he would too.

He tried to think of Nancy, but could no longer see her clearly. His mother might notify her, or she might not. Although he had been "going steady" with her for about a year, this amounted to only eight or nine dates, most of them two summers ago at the country club her parents belonged to. Her father was a department store executive and they lived in Larchmont, which was one of New York's ritzier suburbs. After that summer she had been away at college, and he had been in flight school. He had had a week's leave at Christmas, during which he had seen her only twice. He had been shipped out from Norfolk, Virginia, and it hadn't been possible to meet even to say good-bye. Lately her letters had become more and more bland, rarer too. This had bothered him a great deal. There was nothing he could do about it except to continue to write to her, which he had done.

When she heard he had been shot down, she would forget him pretty quickly, he guessed. Maybe she already had.

But if he did get back to America in one piece, he would have to break it off. Did he have to tell her about this interlude with Rachel? In the past, he had pictured himself married to Nancy, and living with her in a house like her father's, or his father's, and going on to live a life like her father's, or his father's. Rachel was so different from all of that. Rachel was, in the final analysis, a French girl—so he thought. She was a foreigner.

He no longer saw such a clear path for himself, if he survived the war. There was so much he would have to think out.

Soon he could no longer see daylight through the gaps in the tiles. As night fell, the temperature fell with it. There was only one electric outlet in the attic. He could have light or heat, but not both. He chose heat, though the heater didn't give off much. By its glow he ate some of the dried fruit and drank some water. It was as cold up here as in the cockpit of a P-51 at thirty thousand feet, he believed. He was wearing woolen underwear, flight suit, fleece-lined jacket, and he lay under two blankets. He was all right for the moment, but had begun to hope it wouldn't get any colder. He reminded himself that there were rooms in the house as cold as this. A few feet below him the preacher was no doubt sleeping dreamlessly. Perhaps Rachel was too. He envied them both, gave in to a certain amount of self-pity, and when the erotic daydreams returned—the taste and feel of Rachel again, the wetness of her—he did nothing to chase them. He fell asleep that way, and woke up a little later with his crotch soaked, the stain probably seeping through his flight suit as well, and lay in the dark annoyed with himself. The house was soundless. The temperature in the room seemed stable. The room was simply cold. His face and ears were cold. He chewed on some more dried fruit, then fell back asleep again.

This time he did not wake up until morning. What woke him was hearing Rachel and the preacher downstairs. As soon as the preacher would go off to the church he could come down, use the bathroom, wash his face and shave, and he listened hard but did not hear this happen. What he did hear was other voices. These belonged to Madame Henriot, who had arrived with all of the nine children, three of whom were about to be left with Rachel while she took the others to church. The front door opened and closed and he did not hear the preacher's voice anymore. Then it opened and closed again and he no longer heard Madame Henriot. But there were still children in the house. It was impossible for him to figure all this out, except to know that he still could not come down.

Then he heard Rachel below the trapdoor singing in English a song of her own invention. In it she told him she was taking the kids out to play in the snow, but the morning was so cold she couldn't keep them out long. She could give him fifteen minutes, probably no more than that.

The house at last was silent.

Coming down that ladder one legged was not easy, but he made it. In the bathroom he peered out through the slats in the shutters. There was a small garden beside the house, and in it Rachel and three little girls were building a snowman. He could see their breath. The children were all laughing but Rachel's face was red from the cold.

By the time Davey hoisted himself back up into the attic he felt a little more comfortable.

And so he lay there the rest of the day looking up at the slates, waiting.

XIV

THE service, Pastor Pelletier told Rachel over lunch, had gone well. He had preached obedience to the civil authorities, and as he paraphrased some of the arguments he had made he sounded proud. The Marshal was a noble personage, all of whose decisions were in the best interests of France, he had preached. One should venerate the Marshal, embrace his ideas, and obey the men with whom he had surrounded himself, for they were the best men in France. If they sometimes made mistakes in his name, this was to be expected because they were human beings prone to error. Their errors were relatively small ones. That French Jews were being stripped of their citizenship and deported was a minor detail, for there had never been many Jews in France. The foreign Jews deported did not belong here anyway. Our own young men were being deported too, conscripted as forced labor, and there were a million or more French prisoners of war still hostage in Germany. The Marshal's concern was for all of these people, not just the Jews. Meanwhile, the occupying forces were trying to be correct, and one should not antagonize them. These were hard times, they demanded patience and submission, but they would pass.

"There," Pelletier said, "how does that sound to you?"

"Very good," said Rachel.

"It's too bad you had to miss it."

"I had to take care of the children."

"You're not Protestant, I understand."

"No."

"Catholic?"

Rachel nodded.

There was a train scheduled to leave at six P.M. The afternoon was a long one. The holy man sat in front of the fire, for the most part ostentatiously reading his Bible. Once, trying to make the hours pass more quickly, Rachel went out for a walk in the snow. It was a cold, gloomy day, and the walk did not seem to help.

Later she walked with Pelletier up the hill to the station. She wanted to make sure that the train actually left, that he was gone. The village was dark by then. As they passed the Hôtel des Voyagers she noticed several German officers standing out front, one of them Lieutenant Ziegler, who waved to her. She did not wave back. There was a wind and the snow swirled about. The cold stung her cheeks.

When they came in sight of the tracks the little train with its big smokestack was there, the stack sending up steam, but the hour came and went and it did not move. Surrounded by other passengers they stood in the badly heated station making small talk, their breath forming halos around them. Pastor Pelletier kept thanking Rachel for her hospitality. He said she needn't wait with him any longer.

Rachel stayed. Finally the passengers were told to board. Through the coach window she watched Pelletier come down the aisle and take his seat on the bench, and she stood in front of the station waving to him as the little train began to move. When it had turned the corner and passed from view it hooted several times. After that it would hoot, she knew, at every crossroads. She stood listening until the hoots got dim, and finally could no longer be heard. Then she turned and walked back to the presbytery.

· · ·

WHEN she came in the door Davey, who stood on his crutches in front of the fire, turned and looked at her.

"I'm sorry," she said, "that couldn't have been very nice for you."

He shrugged.

"That awful man. He's gone now."

Davey nodded.

"You must be famished. Would you like some soup?"

"Yes, please."

They were as ill at ease as if they had not seen each other in months.

"There's some rabbit, too."

"That would be fine."

"That young man Prudhomme brought it. He's very nice."

"Yes."

The conversation during dinner was no better.

"I've never had rabbit before."

"How do you like it?"

"It tastes a good deal like chicken."

"You don't like it."

"It's good."

"They don't eat rabbit in England. Not at my school, anyway."

"Not in my squadron either. I can assure you."

"I hope you did like it. I saved half for tomorrow."

They moved back into the living room, where Rachel lifted some new logs onto the fire.

Davey said: "I suppose we should get the mattress down from the attic."

"I'll do it," said Rachel.

Having pulled the trapdoor down, she climbed the ladder. Davey, who was standing below on crutches, could do little to help. She threw the bedding down on him. He caught the heater on the fly. She pushed the mattress through the hole and he received it.

Neither remembered the parachute, which she left on the floor where it lay.

When she had climbed down, Davey pushed the trapdoor shut, and they stood in the narrow hall pinned almost to the wall by the mattress.

"Let's pull it in front of the fire," Davey said.

"What for?"

"We could sit on it and play chess. At least we'd be warm."

"Suppose somebody should come to the door."

"I don't think anybody will come this late."

Rachel looked doubtful.

"So you tell them you were lying in front of the fire to stay warm," said Davey. "It's a cold night. They wouldn't see me, I'd be in the back room."

"Okay," Rachel said.

They dragged the mattress on its edge into the living room and made space for it in front of the fire. The front door was locked, the shutters shut, the heavy drapes pulled tight to hold in the heat. Without fully realizing it, they had created a place—or an illusion—of security and warmth.

"I'll get the chess set," said Rachel.

But Davey pulled her down until she knelt on the mattress, the flames flickering on her face.

"You don't really want to play chess, do you?" said Rachel.

"No."

"I don't either."

The preliminaries were a great pleasure to Davey, but they took a long time. He loved kissing and being kissed back. He loved her weight half on top of him, he loved his own half on top of her, one leg thrown over one of hers. More time passed before he was allowed to fondle her through the bulky clothes, much less under. There was a hunger in him that had lasted since the onset of puberty—about seven years. Perhaps in her too, he didn't know, he knew so little about girls.

He had a broken leg and could not easily stand, but he could kneel, as could she. Kneeling, he began what was almost a religious ritual, a kind of prayer. The first of her sweaters dropped to the floor beside the mattress. Again it took a long time. She shook her head, which did not mean no, at least not yet, she was only shaking out her hair. A little later the second sweater followed, same thing. Later still she knelt in her bra, which was neither padded nor pointed like American bras he had seen in ads—his sister bought padded bras by the dozens. Rachel's was thin and through it he could see her nipples, and he bit gently on the cloth. She had her head thrown back and she pressed him to her by the nape of his neck.

In time he got the bra off her and stared.

She said: "Stop staring at me."

"I can't help it. You're gorgeous."

Her embarrassment did not last, she preened, put her hands behind her head and thrust them out, for she was at that moment relatively relaxed. She and Davey seemed to have reached a plateau of sorts. Perhaps she thought herself safe enough on it. Forward movement seemed temporarily to have stopped. This would go no farther.

"They're nice, aren't they?"

Davey knew little about female breasts, but said what was expected of him.

"At school, you should have seen some of the other girls."

It took time, but he got her skirt off her next. She was giggling and squealing, catching his hands then letting them escape, and there was much kissing and nuzzling in between. Now she was dressed in panties only, but when he tried to tug them down her thighs she stopped him, her legs crossed, no longer giggling, and he saw that he still had much work to do.

"Are you cold?" he asked her.

"It's not that."

He began trying to rub the smooth flat cloth between her legs. She stopped him, but when he kept returning there, her efforts became less determined, until finally they ceased, and she began to moan and writhe. He tugged at the elastic around her thigh until there was room to slide his hand under. To this she made no resistance at all. But for Davey it too was not enough.

There was more elastic around her waist. Kneeling between her legs he rolled the panties over the elastic, rolling them down until he could pull them the rest of the way down her flat smooth abdomen, then down her legs. He pulled them from under her, and although she let him do this, she had stiffened and gone silent. Suddenly her mood had changed, as if she was shocked to realize that the ceremony had got as far as this, that her defenses were almost gone.

He looked between her legs, wanting to see what was there, but she covered herself with her hands.

There was an awkward moment while Davey got out of his own clothes, a gap in the procedure, a moment long enough perhaps for her to reconsider.

Davey was involved in a seduction that was not a sure thing, that was not accomplished even yet, and so he hurried, got the flight suit off over his cast and cast it aside. Then the long johns. It was as if he were reading down a checklist in an airplane, one requirement after another, being careful not to forget something important.

Rachel's head was in a turmoil. At moments she had been dizzy with desire, unable to process thought at all, but she could now. This had all gone too far, it was her fault and she did not know how to stop it.

If she wanted to keep the boy she had to go through with it now, it seemed to her. She was not ready for what he wanted, yet maybe she was. If she refused she might lose him. She did love him. She did want him. In every girl's life there was the first him. Was this boy to be the one? What was about to happen, once it was done, could not be undone. Was it what she wanted? He wouldn't even be here long, he'd be back in England, or arrested. What about getting pregnant? What about the pastor throwing her out? What about the notion that good girls don't? Afterward the choices for her would become more limited. Innocent boys, not knowing, might still be interested in her, but she would not be interested in them. Her eventual husband might be extremely disappointed, might hate her for it.

But there was no way the pastor could guess it had happened, was there? It would not show on her face or in her voice. Who would tell him? Not her, certainly. Davey wouldn't, would he? Why would he? The pastor couldn't possibly find out. Nor an eventual husband either.

Unless she got pregnant.

What was happening had been lived millions and millions of times with only slight variations: different articles of clothing removed, different degrees of fear by the girl, of anxiety by the boy.

"Don't get me pregnant. Please don't get me pregnant."

"I won't, I promise."

Her knees framed his face, his hairless chest. It was about to happen. The most commonplace act in the world, though not to her. She could not stop him now, and in a certain sense could not stop herself. It was not that she wanted this less than Davey, but rather that she had so much more, it seemed to her, to lose.

Davey recognized her reluctance. It made him especially tender. He came down over her and pushed gently in what he imagined was the correct place, but this was an act that neither had rehearsed, and there was no result, he did not advance. What had he expected? That one motion was all it would take? That her body would engulf him? It didn't. Why did he not slide right in?

He pushed and prodded, unable to see what he was doing, unsure of himself, astonished to find that what he was trying to effect was more complicated than he had ever imagined.

He was dealing with virginity plus fear. Her body was rigid, not that he realized this. Neither of them did.

He paused, partly to think it over, mostly because he had to or explode. In all the macho stories he had heard, no one had ever confessed to such blundering as this.

She said: "Why did you stop?"

"Just give me a moment."

Virginity was evidently no joking matter. He started again. She did not help him. He would have been astonished if she had. She did not know enough to help him, that any help might be needed.

He saw her biting down on her lip, which must mean that he was causing pain, but it would all be over in a moment if he could just—

But it wasn't over in a moment.

"You're hurting me," said Rachel.

He stopped, and lay facing her, their bodies almost on top of each other, and the kissing, the fondling, the whispered endearments began again. Lying against her, kissing, caressing her, he again made her moan. She got sopping wet so that he thought: maybe that has something to do with it, and he positioned himself to try again.

"I don't think it's going to work," she said. She truly believed this, and was grateful. She believed herself temporarily inviolable, secure for this night at least, reprieved, a tremendous relief, no bridges to cross tonight, and as a result she was neither frightened nor tense, as she had been previously.

He poked and prodded, it felt more slippery than before, and pulled back, and poked again and felt her ceding, and then he went in all the way.

She had gasped. Perhaps he did too. In his joy he cried out: "Rachel, oh Rachel, Rachel, Rachel."

What they had done seemed to him beyond belief. His head was pounding, not only with joy but with insights into life and love—he felt flooded with them. I've killed other men, he thought, he didn't even know how many; I've been wounded and survived a plane crash, but what's important in life is not that, but this. This was what they kept you alive for. He was really a man now, he told himself, and Rachel really a woman. One and one made only two, but he and Rachel together had become the equal of ten or a thousand, he believed. And as for love, a man might love a girl before this, but afterward he loved her many many times more.

Under him Rachel was silent. Now you've gone and done it, she told herself. Now you've really done it. You never intended to do it, but you did. Are you so sure it won't show? What do you do next, and what is the cost to be?

"Oh, Rachel," Davey said again, "I love you so much."

She caressed his face and felt a flood of loving him back. What's done is done, she thought. It couldn't be undone, and she wasn't sure she wanted to undo it.

Though trembling and forced to breath deeply, Davey knew the most intense happiness of his life. It seemed to him that the whole world was theirs, whatever parts they wanted. And although there might be—would be—suffering for them ahead, this moment paid for it all.

This elation, these realizations, were followed by a number of other surprises. First of all that such a moment did not last forever, that it could be so quickly and completely behind him. Already he was not content just to lie there on her and in her and savor what had happened. He wanted to move in her, was compelled to, could not keep himself from doing it. He did not last long after that. He came on the mattress between her legs, and a moment later was only lying beside her.

She looked down, and what she saw made her giggle. "Well, you certainly have made a mess of the mattress."

She went and got a towel. Kneeling, she wiped it up. "So how many girls have you made love to before me?"

"Well—"

"I'm the first, aren't I?"

He felt sheepish. "I guess so."

"Well," she said. "Well well well." She was laughing. "I've had a thousand previous lovers myself, as I'm sure you could tell."

He pulled her down and hugged her to him, her breasts squashed on his chest. He hadn't known that his life would be changed, but he saw that it had been. Say hello to the other half of the human race, he thought, and knew he would never be satisfied in an all-male society again. And that was only one of the differences. He perceived, or imagined he did, that from now on he would be lonely whenever this girl was not there. It was not just that Rachel was the only girl he wanted to make love to, she was also the only one he wanted to talk to, to be with, to make plans with about the future, and he did not know how all this was to be arranged, or where it would lead.

He kissed her eyes, her nose, he held her tight, and what he felt was not fulfillment, for that implied satisfaction, and satisfaction was always momentary. He would never be satisfied. He wanted her forever. He wanted her more and more. Already he wanted her again, and with renewed desire came the realization—it came to him with startling suddenness, startling clarity, still another surprise, a revelation—that: hey, I can fuck her again—a word he would never have spoken aloud with reference to her, or in her presence—and he rolled on top of her and did it, and this time she seemed to take a big part, which she hadn't the first time, and her face got red and her body squirmed and bucked, and when he had finished she murmured: "That was really nice."

Davey sat up: "I want to see you."

Her legs parted. She let him look to his heart's content.

She said: "Tomorrow I'm going to walk through the village and greet people, and they won't see any difference."

Tomorrow she might have another reaction entirely, might worry again about the pastor finding out, about pregnancy, about

Davey going back to England. But for now, she gave in to other emotions entirely. She belonged to this boy, they belonged to each other, and she thought she was happier than she had ever been.

A plighting of troth had taken place of which neither was aware at that moment in those terms.

"I'll be looking at people passing," she said, "and I'll be thinking: Look at me. Do you see any difference? I've done it. You wouldn't guess, would you, but I've done it."

Davey laughed. They both laughed.

They fell asleep, the fire flickering on their faces, their bodies glued together, the blankets rough on their bare skin.

XV

OBERSTURMBANNFÜHRER Gruber was having trouble with Claire Cusset, whom usually he liked to please. The problem was boredom—hers, not his—which is one of the most difficult of all problems for a man to overcome.

They were in their spacious living room overlooking the river when the problem first surfaced. The servants had retired for the night. They were alone, still fully dressed, when the former nude dancer, who had just turned twenty-five, came over and sat on his lap, and began nuzzling his neck. Her hand then moved to his fly. Gruber had been reading reports, but he dropped them to the floor almost with a thump, and immediately his fingers began manipulating the buttons of her blouse.

Also she was murmuring words in his ear, but he was intent on what she was doing not what she was saying. That is, he didn't even hear her.

Then he did.

Lyon was boring, she was saying. She was bored with their life there. Why couldn't they move to Paris?

But his work was here, he answered.

But Paris was so much more fun, she said, as she continued her attentions. He liked Paris, didn't he? He had said so often enough.

And after all, they had met and fallen in love there, had they not, and—

His work here was vital right now, he managed to say, the German war effort depended on it. But at the moment it was hard for him to concentrate on the war effort.

In Paris, she said, reaching into his fly, there were things to laugh about and to do, interesting people to be with.

He could not get transferred to Paris, Gruber told her.

He could if he wanted, she pouted.

He said he didn't think so.

Was he an important man, or not?

Yes.

How important?

Very.

Then just do it.

No.

Do it for me.

To Gruber the words sounded almost like a threat. She was no longer speaking in the low, husky voice she used for bedroom activities, and her hand had been removed.

You don't understand, he told her.

She said she understood perfectly and got up and went into the bedroom and closed the door.

He waited a seemly moment, not wanting to appear to run after her too quickly. When he entered the room in his turn she was sitting up in bed thumbing through a German magazine.

He put his pajamas on—again for appearance's sake—then got in beside her, but when he put his hand on her naked thigh she said:

"I'm reading."

Despite the aroused state he was in, he got up and put a bathrobe on, and went back into the other room and resumed work on his reports.

That was the start of it. She was like an enemy artillery piece. She kept lobbing salvos into his lines. She found Gruber's friends boring, she told him at breakfast, for they only spoke German, and if he thought it was fun sitting at a dinner party all night not understanding a word of what was said, then he had another think coming. For a girl her age with her attributes their life in Lyon was boring, boring, boring.

They continued to sleep in the same bed, but when he would get between her thighs she would just lie there staring at the ceiling until he was finished.

Would she please show a little enthusiasm, for God's sake, he cried once.

But she replied that it was hard to get enthusiastic about anything, even something that had formerly been terrific, when one was bored all the time.

He was more than familiar with that vacant, upward stare. His wife, when she wanted something from him that he did not wish to give her, had behaved exactly the same: body limp, legs extended straight out, not taking part in any way, eyes looking for cracks in the plaster.

Women were all alike, he told Claire disgustedly.

To a certain extent he was tired of Mademoiselle Cusset, and almost wished she would disappear, go to Paris, go anywhere. She was always complaining about something, never satisfied with anything he did for her. But she had a pretty face and a superb body. If she left him he would be humiliated before his colleagues. Without her it would be back to the approved brothels, women every German officer in Lyon had fucked multiple times. Or else pick up some woman on the street and risk either a dose or a knife in the back, perhaps both.

So he continued to put up with her.

Paris was the place, that was her message. Sometimes the message was more genial than others. An important, fascinating man like Gruber could arrange a transfer with ease, she told him one night. They were standing on their terrace and had been looking up at the stars. Now her hands were on his cheeks on both sides. His cheeks were cold, she said. Threaten to quit altogether, her voice suggested, and then watch them jump.

There was a war on, he told her.

Not here, there's not.

True, which was why he refused to request a transfer or make any other commotion. He'd rather lose Claire—he never thought it would come to that—than lose Lyon. Lose Lyon, and war was what he would get. Right back into combat at a time when the German armies were being plastered on all sides.

He would think about moving them to Paris, he told her, and the next day took her out and bought her a new hat—there were still milliners working in Lyon and they were good. The hat was as light as pastry, white, with a thin brim and glass cherries on top, very nice, they both agreed, and it quieted her for a while, but in a day or two she resumed.

If he wouldn't move to Paris with her, maybe she would have to consider moving there by herself.

What would you do there?

Start a new life.

How would you live?

Go back to work, maybe.

What kind of work could you do, except for what you did do?

She had never minded showing off her body, she said.

But she had hated the second part of the job, he reminded her. Having to drink with all those men afterward, earning commissions on the champagne they drank.

She shrugged.

Because they always took you to be a whore.

She shrugged again.

Which you were not. Or so you pretended to yourself.

"I never took money for sex," she responded heatedly, "so I was not a whore."

After a moment she remarked that men had liked watching her dance. They had admired her. She had felt their admiration and been pleased by it.

He said bluntly that men had liked watching the way she manipulated her cunt. They had admired her cunt, not her.

She looked at him.

"I'm sorry," he said, "I shouldn't have said that."

They were about to go out. She was seated at her dressing table putting on makeup. She wore only a slip and stockings—real silk stockings he had bought for her, which were of course unobtainable by ordinary people whether French or German.

She painted mascara over her eyelashes, and in the mirror he watched her.

She smeared bloodred lipstick onto those lips he loved to kiss, mouthing the lips afterward to smooth it out.

The life of a nude nightclub dancer was not for her, he continued in a kindly voice. She should get dressed now and they would go out and have a good time.

But still it wasn't over. A week later they were eating in a restaurant—eating well, he might have added. She really should leave Lyon, she said.

He studied the menu.

Whether he did or not, she said. Paris . . .

She would need to find a place to live, he reminded her, and in Paris these days that was not easy.

Somebody would be glad to take her in, didn't he agree?

Who? he asked.

She knew some important people, and would call on them.

Who?

General Rahn, for one.

General Rahn, he told her, preferred boys.

Really? she said. She gave a half laugh. Dancing with him she had had quite the opposite impression, she said, "If you know what I mean."

Rahn liked to be whipped, Gruber said curtly. Or else to do the whipping. He had once broken some girl's nose in a Left Bank brothel. But if Claire had a good dentist lined up in advance, then by all means she should call on General Rahn.

The restaurant was full. German uniforms at about half the tables, Gruber saw, as he glanced around. The food was as expensive and succulent as before the war. Most of the other patrons were probably black market dealers or war profiteers.

Claire was still talking about Paris. At first Gruber was not listening, but after a while her voice grated on him so much that he couldn't not listen.

"You can't go to Paris," he interrupted. "It's out of the question. So please stop talking about it."

"Why is it out of the question?"

"Because I wouldn't be able to protect you there."

"What's that supposed to mean?"

"If it became known who you'd been sleeping with, some of your compatriots might become annoyed."

"How would they know?"

"They might find out."

"I don't need your protection."

"If they did find out, they might capture you."

Neither one was eating the meal.

"What do you think they'd do to me."

"Punish you in some way. If they found out."

"What way?"

"Oh, cut off your hair, maybe. Or . . ."

"Or what?"

Gruber offered the second alternative as if it were immaterial to him which punishment was chosen.

"Or cut off your tits," he said.

She stared at him.

He said: "Cut off your hair or cut off your tits. You're not going to Paris."

Claire put down her knife and fork and got up and left the table. She marched straight out of the restaurant.

Gruber had no choice but to drop money beside his plate and go after her.

THE barracks caught fire, whether accidently or on purpose was unknown. Fanned by an icy breeze that kept changing direction, it burned from the middle toward the glassless windows at either end.

It was late afternoon. The work details had been marched in from outside the camp. Men were lined up washing at the pipe that jutted from the ground between the buildings. Though the day was cold, many had stripped to the waist. There was no soap. They were trying to rub the dirt off themselves with rags that had once been pieces of clothing.

Pastor Favert, who had been waiting his turn, happened to glance into the building just as the flames leaped up. He climbed heavily inside—the window was a meter off the ground and he was not an athletic man—and began heaving out bundles, everything he could get his hands on, especially blankets, because without them this night men would freeze to death. He must have shouted a warning, for others had climbed in after him and were doing the same. From time to time through the heat and smoke Favert glimpsed men at the far end, working as frantically as himself.

He had been first in, and was last out, having saved what he could. He wasn't in there long. When the fire got onto the sleeping platforms it ignited the straw and in an instant raced the length of the building top and bottom. The heat, perhaps the flames as well, caught Favert in the window frame climbing out, and he let go. He fell rather than jumped. It became a dive onto the hard ground, and it injured his shoulder.

The fire had brought men from all over the camp. He stood in the crowd breathing hard. His shoulder hurt. His face felt scorched. In his nostrils was the odor of singed hair, his own. He tongued his mustache, which felt half burned off. On the backs of his hands, he noted, there was no hair left.

The heat, which was terrific, kept forcing the men backward. Then flames burst from the roof. They leaped up twice as high as the building itself. Unable to stop watching, the men were herded still farther back by about thirty guards with guns.

Commandant Motier had run up and begun barking orders. A bucket brigade was formed—not to save this building but to protect the adjacent ones. Favert was in the middle of it. He kept passing buckets, his shoulder aching.

The building vanished before their eyes. The fire consumed it until there was nothing left but a rug of ash half a meter thick which, as they watched, collapsed into glowing embers. Ash and embers commenced to blow through the air, from time to time igniting tufts of dried grass.

As a punishment, the inhabitants of that particular barracks got no food that night. Although no one had ever glorified the evening soup with the word *dinner,* it was better than nothing. Darkness fell. The temperature dropped further. The men waited to be assigned to some other barracks, but this did not happen, and they passed the night on the icy ground in the open, huddling together in a vast human pile under the blankets that had been saved. For a time the smoldering embers gave off some heat, not long.

The following morning the half-frozen men were transferred to Section A and dispersed among a number of barracks. Some had blankets, some did not. In the new barracks they were treated like outcasts by the resident prisoners, and they slept thereafter like spoons, three or four men to a blanket.

On the third day, time enough for Favert's identity to become known, he was approached by a man who spoke to him in German, and who wanted to be baptized.

The man's name was Rosenberg. "I want to become Christian," he said.

The pastor had just come in from helping to deepen drainage ditches in the village, and was exhausted.

"I want to belong to Jesus," Rosenberg said.

On his feet he wore shapeless shoes, the soles stuffed with paper, and on his head a shapeless fedora. He wore a camel's hair overcoat, now shiny and stained, that had once cost real money.

Favert quizzed him about his "conversion." He seemed to know a good deal about Christianity, and he sounded sincere.

"There are a number of us who feel the same," Rosenberg said. "Ten or a dozen. But please keep this to yourself, or we'll be ostracized in here by the other Jews."

Favert met the other men two and three at a time. All were Germans. All spoke piously of Jesus, but when asked to explain their convictions few could do so.

Rosenberg wanted the baptisms done as soon as possible, and kept pressuring the pastor to perform them. "And we'd like you to give us certificates of baptism as well."

"Why would you need that?" said Favert.

"So we can feel more truly Christian," said Rosenberg piously.

"I see." The pastor was not a cynical man, but he was not entirely naïve either. "I understand that there is a Catholic priest in this camp, and one or two Protestant clergymen as well. Why come to me?"

"But you are known as a friend of Jews."

Favert frowned. He didn't see himself as a friend of Jews especially, but rather as a friend of all men who suffered injustice, who were persecuted and needed help. Such people these last few years were mostly Jews, and so he had helped them as best he could. As a Christian, he was obliged to fight injustice, persecution—lies— wherever he found them. If asked he would have said he had only behaved as Christians were supposed to behave. He would have said he deserved no special praise, and at the beginning of his self-appointed crusade to save Jews this was what he had believed. However, he was well aware that his stature had grown, and kept growing. He was considered a hero by all who knew of him, and this was not unpleasant. There were Jews in the recent past who had tried to kiss his hand, and although he had not permitted this, nonetheless the reaction had pleased him.

"Please let's get it done," said Rosenberg. "Every month the trains come, and there are fewer of us."

"A baptismal certificate won't save you," the pastor said. "As the racial laws are written—both the French laws and the German—you would remain a Jew."

"Don't talk to me about the law. I used to be a lawyer in Berlin."

Favert was silent.

In a gentler tone Rosenberg said: "A baptized Christian can perhaps get transferred into Section C."

"I'm not sure I see that happening."

"The commandant might agree to it. He seems a decent man."

"Decent?" said Favert. "He left two hundred men out all night with the temperature ten degrees below freezing."

"In C one can hope to be overlooked, at least for a time. It's a chance."

"Baptism is a holy sacrament. One becomes a Christian because one believes, not to get into Section C."

"I do believe."

Favert said nothing.

"For God's sake, man, there's a train out there in the siding even now."

"I'm not sure I can do it," said Favert.

"I said I believed."

"It would be testifying to a lie."

"It's not your job to judge my sincerity."

"No, but every man must obey his conscience, and I must obey mine."

"What right do you have to decide what a lie is? Are you God? You have to do it."

Favert was silent.

"I want to be with Jesus," Rosenberg said.

Favert nodded.

"I love Jesus."

"And the other men?"

Rosenberg peered at the ground. "Them too."

Then, when Favert said nothing: "I cannot vouch for the other men."

"I don't know," said Favert. "I must think about this."

There was a rabbi in the camp. His name was Karp, and the pastor decided to seek him out.

He found him standing at the barbed wire, gazing toward the mountains, a small man, thin to the point of emaciation. He must have been about fifty-five but looked eighty. His complexion was gray, as was his long ragged beard, and he was minus his right arm, which he had lost fighting for Germany in the trenches in World War I. Being old and weak, and having only one arm, he was excused from the work details, and so spent most of each day wandering about the camp with nothing to do.

Favert stood beside him at the barbed wire.

"I like to look outwards at what is possible," Rabbi Karp said, "rather than inwards at what is not.

The pastor said in German: "I am faced with something of a moral dilemma, Rabbi, and I wondered if you could give me counsel."

"Counsel I can perhaps give. I have nothing else."

"A number of your co-religionists have asked me to baptize them."

Rabbi Karp flew into an almost immediate rage. "Rosenberg, is he the one? I saw you talking to him. The former big lawyer from Berlin. He's a Jew, and he'll always be a Jew, and nothing you do can change that."

"I understand what you are saying."

The rabbi's voice rose. He accused the pastor of trying to aggrandize himself by making easy converts of members of the rabbi's congregation—Jews like Rosenberg who in some cases had been locked up in this camp for more than four years, and who as a result were thoroughly demoralized and willing to clutch at anything, Jews who in normal life would not have listened to him for a minute. But God would never accept such men as Christians, Karp said. God knew better, and if the pastor went forward with his baptisms, he would be guilty of a horrendous sin.

The rabbi's arguments grew more and more heated. "Their Jewishness, and the solidarity that goes with it, is the only thing that sustains them in this place. But you want to take it away from them. That's what you want to do, isn't it?"

"No, of course not."

"They are faced with the greatest concentration of evil in the history of the world. Take away their Jewishness and you leave them with nothing, nothing."

The pastor had not expected a tirade like this, and at first it struck him dumb.

"Converts," snarled Karp. "Easy converts. And you call yourself a man of God." And he walked away.

The pastor ran after him, saying: "Rabbi, please, please."

But he was talking to Karp's back. He could not get him even to turn around, much less respond.

So Favert sought counsel from Assistant Pastor Henriot.

They were outside the camp wielding pickaxes, deepening ditches to the west of Le Vernet village.

"I could take them at their word," Favert said, "ask no further questions, and baptize them."

About a hundred prisoners worked at the bottom of this particular ditch, guards with machine guns standing above them in the road.

"Yes, you could," said Henriot.

"How many Jews have passed through my presbytery?"

"I don't know. Hundreds. Maybe thousands."

"Have I ever proselytized any one of them?"

"No."

"That isn't my style, right?"

"I've always admired you for taking that particular stand."

"People asked to convert, I always told them: if you still want to convert after the war, come back and I'll baptize you."

Favert swung his pick hard. The ground at the bottom of the ditch was like rock. At each swing the steel rang out.

"But in the case of the Jews in this camp," Henriot said, "baptism would perhaps be enough to save their lives."

Favert's hands stung. He was breathing hard. "If it got them into Section C . . ."

"It's a small chance," said Henriot.

"But it's a chance."

"Perhaps."

They rested on their pickaxes. Farther down the road they could see other work gangs, other guards. Favert said: "But I would be testifying to a lie. I would have made the type of compromise God does not want us to make."

"You could decide on purely practical grounds," suggested Henriot. "Since baptism won't save these men, it's of no practical value to them. Therefore, there's no compelling reason to do it."

The pastor had stalled for days, had knelt and prayed and asked for guidance, but was as confused as ever. "No, it's a moral question. It must be decided on moral grounds." Pastor Favert swung his pick. This time its nose rang on stone and bounced off.

"I can't decide for you," Henriot said.

"To deny them baptism would be, perhaps, to condemn them to death. Do I have the right to do that?"

Favert had lost weight but felt stronger than before. He looked at his hands, now thick with calluses, that no longer bled from swinging picks. "Also, baptism is a sacrament. In and of itself it is a thing of good. It confers grace, and grace is strength."

"On people who don't believe?"

"I think so, yes."

At four o'clock they were herded together, the workday ended. "Who am I to deny them a chance at life however slim?" said the pastor, as they were marched back to the camp.

But as they neared the gate they saw that the siding was empty. The train it had contained was partway down the track, a long series of boxcars moving slowly away.

Pastor Favert felt a sudden lurch inside his chest, and as soon as the work gangs had passed inside, and the roll call was completed, he ran about asking if anyone could tell him where to find the lawyer, Rosenberg. Rabbi Karp as well. He accosted a number of men, but they wanted to talk only about the train. Earlier, about a thousand men out of Section A had been lined up on the parade ground. They had been led out through the gates and down alongside the train, rows and rows of them, and forced to clamber into boxcars. This had been visible through the barbed wire. Soon none of the prisoners could be seen anymore, though the train was still there, a few guards standing on the ballast alongside. After a time the train had started.

"Were Rosenberg and Rabbi Karp aboard?" Favert kept asking, but no one could tell him. No one knew which men had been taken. No one had wanted to get close enough to find out.

When Rosenberg was nowhere to be found, Favert believed he had his answer, and he went to his bunk and sat down heavily on the straw, and a man came in and found him. The man was carrying a folded blanket, and he handed it over. It was old, and encrusted with dirt of various kinds, and the man said: "It was the lawyer Rosenberg's. He wanted you to have it."

HE turned over in the night, pulling on his wounds, which were still not fully healed. This woke him. He lay there a moment, then reached out and touched her knee, smooth skin but hard bone underneath, proving she was real, a girl's knee in bed with him. From there he touched one of her breasts, which seemed to him more proof yet. He could not get over the joy of being able to do this.

It was enough to wake Rachel, who was not used to being touched while she slept. Her hand sought him out, and he liked what she was doing, but not as much as something else. In a moment he had got to where he most wanted to be, and he began to move, and together they explored the inexhaustible wealth of their bodies.

Before they stopped there was daylight showing through a gap in the drapes.

As a result they slept very late, to be awakened by a loud knocking on the front door.

The shocked Rachel sprang to her feet. Stupefied with sleep, she looked first at the fire, which was out, then toward the sound of the knocking, and only then ran to find a bathrobe, with Davey hobbling behind her looking for a place to hide.

They did not have time to hide anything else.

The caller was Madame Henriot who had just delivered the children to school, she said, as she came into the house. She was carrying a bundle of what looked like the children's laundry. She had stopped by to see if Rachel needed anything, and also to ask for help with the kids' dirty clothes. "With nine of them in the house, I don't have much time, as you can imagine."

Mechanically Rachel accepted the bundle. "Of course," she said, even as Madame Henriot stepped past her into the living room.

"Oh," the older woman said, observing the mattress, "you're sleeping in front of the fire now."

"It's warmer like that," said Rachel. She was glancing frantically about. What else was on view that might give Davey and her away? "Let's go in the kitchen. I'll make some tea." She wanted Madame Henriot out of this room.

"Better get your fire going again first."

"Yes," said Rachel. Kneeling in front of the fire, she pushed in brush, dropped logs on top.

In the kitchen, as she made tea, made what conversation she could, she was conscious the whole time of the wet stickiness on her leg.

Madame Henriot had not seemed to notice anything, Rachel told Davey later, and they laughed about it. The girl did not mention how aware she had been of being naked under her bathrobe, but it was one of the most vivid impressions of her life so far, and it would remain in her memory as long as she lived.

She spent most of the afternoon at the kitchen sink over the washboard, scrubbing out shirts and underwear of all sizes, the frequently mismatched socks, repeatedly having to heat more water on the stove. Davey offered to help and even tried to for a few minutes, balanced on one flight boot and his cast, but he was so inept he made her laugh. He didn't know anything about washing laundry, and she soon relieved him. "Just sit over there and watch," she told him, and went on rubbing the clothes with the block of brown soap.

The soap was harsh, the bleach caustic, and the water that poured out of the kettle was sometimes too hot. Her hands were chapped and red, and when finally she had hung the laundry up to dry, she looked at them, and shook her head sadly.

THE seat of the Reformed Church in France was Nîmes, and its head was a man name Guerin, formerly a pastor, not a friend of Madame Favert, an acquaintance for many years, and she sat in his office after another eight-hour train ride and asked him to help her get the headmaster, the assistant pastor, and her husband out of the Le Vernet camp.

Guerin was seventy years old, his hair white, his teeth gray. He wore a dark business suit with a white shirt and a black tie, and to Madame Favert looked like a funeral director. He said: "I don't understand what you are asking of me."

"Would you say you are a man of some influence in France?"

The old man shrugged modestly.

"I want you to come with me to Vichy and demand their release."

"Demand?"

"Request. However you want to do it. Request forcefully." This man too had sat at Madame Favert's table, and owed her, she believed. Not to mention what the church owed her husband.

Guerin said: "I've been trying for weeks to find out where Pastor Favert and the others were being held. As soon as I found out I was going to write the strongest possible letter of protest, directing it to the Marshal's attention personally. Now that I know, I'll write that letter."

He did not immediately say so, but a written protest seemed to him the limit of the pressure he could afford to exert.

"A letter is not enough," said Madame Favert.

More than that was asking for trouble, Guerin believed. "I can't risk bringing the government's wrath down on our church," he told Favert's wife. "We're a persecuted minority, and—"

"We're Christians obliged to stand up for what is right."

The former pastor stirred papers on the top of his desk. He said: "According to law your husband is guilty of crimes. A letter is about all I can do."

Madame Favert said: "They were arrested by the French police but were never charged, proof that they were arrested at the orders of the Gestapo."

"Even worse," said Guerin.

"On the contrary. The Gestapo chose to hide behind Frenchmen. And since the hand of the Gestapo doesn't show anywhere, it can be ignored."

"I wouldn't say that exactly. Not at all."

"Under French law prisoners cannot be held without charges."

"The government these days can do anything it wants."

"Frenchmen arrested my husband, and Frenchmen can release him."

The former pastor was again stirring papers on his desk.

"All it would take is an order from Vichy," said Madame Favert, watching him.

Guerin said nothing.

"One of the members of the Marshal's cabinet is a Protestant."

"Morville," said Guerin. "Finance minister."

"Do you know him?"

Another shrug. "I've met him."

"We go to Vichy. You're the head of his church. You ask him to get those three men out of Le Vernet. If you ask him, he'll do it."

They gazed at each other without speaking. Within the church there was some jealousy over the admiration this woman's husband was accorded, the fame. Both knew it. In an organization dedicated to God there shouldn't have been but there was, and it was a considerable force, one Guerin felt obliged to consider. There were pastors who thought Favert was only getting what was coming to him.

In addition, the old man had no desire to ride for hours in one of those trains.

He said: "I'll telephone the finance minister."

Pointing her head in the direction of Guerin's phone, Norma Favert said: "All right, do it."

The old man placed the call. "It will take a while for the call to go through," he said when he had hung up. "Half an hour, maybe more."

"I'll wait," said Norma. She didn't mean wait in the hall. She stayed where she was.

The minutes passed. Guerin was unable to do any work with her sitting there staring at him.

Finally the phone rang. Guerin spoke into it briefly, then broke the connection. "The minister's secretary," he reported. "The minister was occupied but will call back." He nodded in the direction of Madame Favert. "Maybe he'll call back today, maybe not. Where can I reach you?"

Again he looked at Madame Favert across the desk—the signal she should leave. Again she stayed where she was.

The call when it came was from the minister's chief of staff, who said that the minister was too busy to come to the phone, and wouldn't even be able to return the call for a day or two. What was it about?

As on most French telephones at that time, Guerin's came with an extra earpiece on a cord. Madame Favert had stepped around the desk and was listening on the attached earpiece, and when she heard this her forefinger pressed down on the lever.

"The minister probably knows what we want," she said. "He doesn't want to make contact with us because he doesn't want it known that he's a Protestant."

"Maybe."

"We'll go there in person," said Madame Favert decisively.

"I have things to do here," said Guerin. "Important things."

"Nothing is as important as this."

"Now wait a minute—"

"We'll camp outside his door until he agrees to see us."

The old man advanced other arguments, but Madame Favert would listen to none of them.

Finally Guerin gave a sigh.

They caught the train that afternoon but reached Vichy after the ministries had closed for the day.

The Ministry of Finance was in the Carlton Hotel. In the morning they went there but were told by a secretary that Morville was too busy to see them that day, to come back tomorrow.

Instead of leaving they took chairs in the anteroom and waited. That was Saturday. At noon the ministry closed for the weekend.

Norma Favert walked through the streets. She found Vichy to be a nineteenth-century city, precisely designed and laid out, most of its buildings similar in height and style. On a smaller scale it much resembled Paris, which, this deep into the war, it had in every way eclipsed. Famous for its thermal springs, full of handsome old hotels, Vichy had for this reason been chosen as the seat of the French government when France fell in 1940.

The next afternoon she attended a free band concert in the public gardens. She was not in the mood for music, but it helped pass the time.

When the ministry opened again on Monday morning. Norma Favert and Reverend Guerin returned to the same chairs in Morville's anteroom and there they waited until the ministry closed for the day, and Guerin never stopped grumbling. Norma Favert ignored him. There must have been a back door to the offices, for they never caught so much as a glimpse of the minister.

She came to know Vichy well over the next two days. Instead of rich tourists taking the cure it now housed ministries and politicians, together with their German overseers, plus the foreign legations of many nations, together with various dealmakers, opportunists, and sycophants, and the families of all these people. As a result the city was vibrant, frenetic, bustling. Its casino seemed to be crowded every night, its nightclubs full, its thermal baths still popular with the foreigners, for Norma looked into several and did not hear French spoken except by the attendants in the white coats. On the sidewalks she noted many uniforms, especially German ones. The gardens and parks were impeccably kept, the chairs and benches aligned just so, and in the afternoons she noted nurses who sat rocking prams at the edges of the long straight promenades under the trees, just as if there were no war on at all.

On the morning of the third day the minister finally came out into the anteroom. He was all smiles, virtually bursting with cordiality, shaking hands with Norma Favert, embracing Guerin and giving him the accolade on both cheeks.

He must have realized finally that we wouldn't go away, thought Madame Favert.

He ushered them into his office, listened attentively as Guerin spoke, and then announced that he was seeing the Marshal in an hour. "I'll bring it to his attention. If you will come back in the morning I'll have an answer for you."

That night, unable to sleep, the pastor's wife walked for hours through the streets. She came upon a number of thermal springs. One bubbled up in the center of town inside a kind of glass house, filling what was almost a swimming pool. Another was nearly invisible under steam; its water, according to a sign, burst forth at a temperature of 143 degrees centigrade. She even looked into the casino when she came to it, noting that many of the players were German officers. The girls on their arms looked like prostitutes to her, and the crystal chandelier over their heads must have weighed two hundred kilos.

The next morning, having slept hardly at all, she met Guerin in the street. Together they entered the minister's office. Immediately the secretary told them he had a message for them from the minister—the three prisoners would be released tomorrow. The following day at the latest.

Guerin and Madame Favert looked at each other. Norma was not satisfied.

"Normally," she commented, "people like to give good news in person."

"Well, we really don't know this man," answered Guerin.

Morville's door was closed, and as Norma advanced toward it the secretary tried to intercept her. She brushed him off, pushed the door open, and went in.

The minister, seated behind his desk, looked up in surprise.

Madame Favert said: "So the three prisoners are being released. That's good news. Really good news." She paused, choosing her words. "I know you did your best for us, and I was just wondering. Is it something we can count on or what?"

The minister assured her it was. "The Marshal hadn't heard about the detention. To him it smacked of religious persecution. He thanked me for bringing it to his attention, then turned to Prime Minister Laval, and told him to order their release."

"You heard this yourself?"

"The order was given in my presence."

After a moment Norma Favert said: "I sense there is something you're not telling me."

"Oh no, absolutely not." Morville turned toward some papers on his desk, picked them up, put them down again. There was indeed something else, but he did not intend to speak of it. After leaving the Marshal's office, he had become aware that the Gestapo had obtained *mandats d'amener* on the three men—warrants to move them. What this was all about he did not know. An officer named Gruber, an *Obersturmbannführer*. The name meant nothing to Morville, and would have meant nothing to Norma Favert either, though she would have remembered Gruber's face in an instant. To Morville the existence of such a warrant had suggested there was a footrace on. Who would get to Le Vernet first, men with the release order or men with the warrant? The order, he hoped, but there was nothing he himself could do about it either way.

The pastor's wife did not need to know any of this, Morville decided, and so he put a big smile on, put his arm around her shoulder, and walked her to the door. Because Guerin was waiting in the anteroom, the minister was required to make a few minutes small talk, and then to shake hands with them both, but finally he got back inside his office, swung the door shut, and the incident, for him, was closed.

In the street Norma Favert thanked Reverend Guerin, and they parted. Though not entirely convinced that her husband would be released, she had done her best for him, there was no further step she could think of to take, and her children needed her now.

PASTOR Favert and his two companions were taken under heavy guard—two men with machine guns front and back—out through the barbed wire and into the administration building, where they were made to wait, and although they asked for an explanation, the guards remained mute. The signs were ominous, could not have been more so. The Gestapo had come for them, all three believed. They were about to be deported, and they were filled with dread. Deportation had become a word with extremely ugly connotations. It meant more than ripping people away from loved ones, home, familiar surroundings, and shipping them someplace they did not want to go. The specifics had changed. Deportation meant a ride of two thousand kilometers or more, days and days in a sealed boxcar that would open, probably, inside one of the death camps to the east.

That man Gruber is behind this, Favert told himself. Why, why, why did I have to bait him? I am personally responsible for whatever happens next, not only to me but to these other two men who are far more innocent than I am.

At this stage of the war the existence of the death camps had not been documented. Nonetheless, rumors of monstrous conduct by the Germans had begun to permeate all of Europe. All three men had heard them, and from many sources, some of which were worthy of belief; and, especially because of their present circumstances, all three now accepted them as true. A people who could behave as the Germans had behaved in France, stealing everything there was to steal under the term *requisition,* ripping children from parents, wives from husbands, deporting them for the crime of being Jewish, deporting young Frenchmen to Germany as forced labor, hanging hostages from lampposts—such people were capable of anything, it seemed to the three men, who now were hostages of a kind themselves.

Finally they were led into the commandant's office, and the first thing they saw was their papers in three neat piles on his desk, identity cards on top. This surprised them. And the commandant was smiling, a second surprise. They had quickly to readjust their emotions.

"I have good news for you," said Commandant Motier. "I've been able to secure your release." He saw no reason not to take credit for this. When the war ended there were going to be trials, reprisals. His own role as commandant of this camp might not be looked at in a good way. If necessary, these men might testify in his behalf.

He came around the desk and, smiling broadly, shook hands with them. "How's that for good news?"

Of the three men, only Favert was able to speak at all.

"Yes," he said, "well—"

"The order just came down from Vichy."

His two companions, Favert saw, were grinning and socking each other in the arms.

"Here," said the commandant, "take these." He lifted each batch of papers and, after glancing at the identity card to see to whom it belonged, handed them over. "There's a truck going into Toulouse for supplies in about an hour. You fellows will be on it."

So it's over, thought Favert. God did take care of us after all. He then berated himself for ever having doubted.

"From Toulouse you can catch a train home," Motier said. He limped back behind his desk. "Just sign this," he said, "and you can go. Get your things together and be ready for the truck."

Headmaster Vernier glanced at the paper he was supposed to sign. As part of the public school system he was a civil servant, and had signed similar documents in the past. "No problem," he said, and signed it, afterward passing the pen to Assistant Pastor Henriot.

Henriot was about to sign in his turn when Favert, reading carefully, stopped him. "We can't sign this," he said in a low firm voice.

"What?" said the commandant. "What?"

"It's an oath," said the pastor. "An oath we can't sign," and he read aloud from the form, which consisted of two paragraphs, the first of which required "respect for the person of our leader, Marshal Pétain."

"We respect the person of every human being," said the pastor, "so we have no problem with that paragraph. It's the next one."

And it too he read aloud: "I shall obey without question orders given to me by government authorities for the safety of France, and for the good of the National Revolution of Marshal Pétain." He put the paper down on the desk. "We have no intention of obeying certain decrees promulgated by Marshal Pétain and the government," he said. "To sign this oath is impossible for us. It would be contrary to our consciences."

Henriot beside him had put down the pen.

"The Marshal stands for the honor of France," cried the commandant.

"The Marshal and his national revolution deliver Jews to the Germans to be deported to the death camps in central Europe."

"There are no death camps in central Europe," shouted Commandant Motier.

"We have opposed the persecution of the Jews in the past and if liberated we will continue to do so. We can't sign."

Motier screamed, he ranted. The pastor watched him unmoved. Motier calmed himself down, began to plead. "Be reasonable. You have wives and children. Sign. It's just a formality. No one will ever know whether you signed or not." He paused. "How does that sound to you?"

Favert said: "You have asked us to surrender our consciences to the Marshal, and to those who speak in his name."

"It's Vichy who asks you, not me."

"An oath is serious to us. We will not sign an oath to obey immoral orders."

"I can't see why not," said the commandant in a cajoling tone. "It's not really an oath. It's a piece of paper. You know you don't mean to obey it, and I know you don't mean to obey it."

"No," said Favert.

"It goes into my bottom drawer. It goes no farther than this room. A compromise solution."

"Another of the compromises God does not want us to make."

"I have my orders from Vichy. If you don't sign I can't release you."

The pastor shrugged.

The commandant began to scream and sputter. "This is insane. You're insane." He had in fact received two orders from Vichy, he screamed, one to release them, the other to turn them over to men from the Gestapo who would get here today or tomorrow. "The Gestapo will deport you. See how you like being in the hands of the Gestapo."

Favert said: "Be that as it may."

"For God's sake, man, I'm trying to save your life."

"No," said Favert.

All this time Henriot had said nothing.

Motier ran to the door and screamed for the guards, and when they came up he ordered them to take the two prisoners back into the camp.

"You," he snarled at the headmaster even as the guards led the other two away, "you can go. Get out of here. Fast!"

As they were led back through the barbed wire, Pastor Favert felt he had just committed suicide. Henriot beside him said nothing, but the anguished Favert turned to him saying. "You should have signed. You didn't have to follow me."

"No," said Henriot, "I'm with you to the end." He gave a mischievous grin and added: "However soon that end may come."

XVI

REPEATEDLY people came and banged on the front door which, now, Rachel always kept locked. Sometimes it was one of the Favert children come to fetch something. Often it was Madame Henriot—"just keeping an eye on you," she would say in a friendly way; or one of the neighbors—"Is there anything you need?" Sometimes it was refugees, desperate people who had no relatives or friends in the village, and who didn't speak French. Not knowing who they might be, Rachel never dared speak German to them. From the little train, the refugees had come straight to the presbytery, the only address they knew, where they spoke the name of Pastor Favert, the only name they knew. Rachel could do nothing except send them on to the pastor of the next village, which was Buzet, as Madame Favert, before leaving, had instructed her to do.

Each time the knocking came Davey had to scurry on one leg into Rachel's room. He did not like the crutches and rarely used them. He got around by hopping. In the bedroom he would turn the lock and wait silently, motionlessly, until the danger had passed, the house empty again.

One day the knocking proved to be a courier from Switzerland bringing the funds that supported the refugees in Le Lignon and the surrounding villages—there were more than a dozen private homes, pensions, and residences in Le Lignon alone, not to mention all the outlying farms, that housed nonpaying "guests." The funds came from the Quakers, the Congregationalists, the World Council of Churches, certain Catholic groups, from the Swedish and Swiss governments, and from the Cimade, which was an organization of women founded in 1939 to help displaced persons of whatever kind.

The courier was a stout-looking young Swiss not much older than Rachel who stood in front of the fire and began to undo his outer clothing. Wrapped in newspaper and strapped to his waist were packages of money and he took these off and laid them on the table, after which he was no longer stout.

"All right," said Rachel, "I'll take care of it." She would deliver the packages to Madame Henriot, as she had been instructed. "Would you like some tea?" She knew the young man had been riding trains all day, had passed through all the controls without being subjected to a body search. Now he would have to make the same trip back. A cup of tea was the least she could do for him.

When he was gone and Davey had come out of the bedroom, they stared down at the packages.

"Money," Rachel said, in response to Davey's question.

It came every month, which Rachel knew, but so many refugees had sought shelter on the plateau that it was never enough to feed all of them properly; a good many went hungry most of the time. This Rachel did not know, and of course Davey did not. To the young couple these packages constituted a fortune, especially after Rachel opened one to display sheafs of French bank notes, and they began to make jokes about stealing it all and running away. What should they spend it on, where should they go? New York should be the first place, Davey said. He would show her the Empire State Building. He would take her dancing on the Starlight Roof, him wearing a tux, her in a long dress.

"Could I go to the hairdresser and get a perm?" said Rachel. "I've never had a perm."

Davey raked his fingers through the thickness of her hair. "You don't need any perm. I like it the way it is."

"And have my nails done."

"Sure. And I'll take you to a basketball game in the Garden."

Maybe she would like that. The noise and the excitement. He hoped she would. "And afterward we'll go to an expensive restaurant and eat as much as we want."

It was fun to fantasize. It was fun to decide on the presents they would buy each other.

"I'd buy you new underwear," said Rachel. "Those long johns are not too sexy."

"And I'd buy you a new bra. The one you're wearing is getting tattered."

"From you rubbing it."

But even as she joked Rachel was becoming troubled. She still hadn't corrected all the lies she had told him about herself. With the passage of time the prospect had become no easier for her. Sooner or later she would have to do it, and perhaps she should do it now.

"Unfortunately we can't go anywhere," she said.

"I don't see why not?" he joked.

"The world is in flames," she reminded him.

"Let me think," he said, going on with the joke, "there must be someplace."

"No place we could go that would be safe for us. Wherever it was we'd be hunted down."

"I would be hunted down, maybe," Davey said, "not you."

"No, both of us. You because you're an enemy pilot and I because I . . ." She paused, and then came out with it: "Because I'm Jewish."

"What?"

She could not look at him. "I'm not what you think I am. I'm not even French. I'm from Berlin, and my name is Rachel Weiss."

She wished she could cry, feeling that tears might enlist his sympathy, if not his understanding. But the tears would not come. She was too full of dread to cry. She had lost him, she was convinced of it. He won't want me now, she told herself. He would see her for what she was, not a wife, not even a good lover, just an eighteen-year-old girl who was not only Jewish but a liar as well.

"Well," he said, "I don't know what to say." And then: "Why didn't you tell me?"

"I'm telling you now."

There was a kind of foolish grin on his face and he scratched his head. His crew cut had partially grown out and for some days he had tried to part his hair on one side and slick it down. But it wasn't long enough yet and here and there tufts stuck up.

"What about the rest of it? Boarding school in England. Your parents killed."

"No, everything was true except my name. And that I'm German and . . . and Jewish."

"Well," he said. "Well, well."

His reaction was not what she had expected, and she was beginning to experience hope. "And when I said I loved you, that was true too."

"Well, what should I call you?"

"What do you want to call me?"

He took her in his arms, kissed her, and when the kiss ended he said: "Rachel Weiss, I adore you."

"I guess you should think of me as Sylvie Bonaire until—"

"Until when?"

"Until the war ends."

"Rachel Weiss, I wish we could take this money and go somewhere where we'd be safe and could get married and have a honeymoon."

"We've had the honeymoon already, wouldn't you say?"

"Sort of," he said, holding her.

"It was a nice honeymoon. I liked it a lot."

The next day Madame Favert returned home, and the honeymoon was over.

IT was night when Norma Favert got down from the train in Le Lignon station. She had been on trains all day, another horrendous trip, and instead of going directly home she lugged her suitcase up to the Henriot house, because that was where her children would be at this hour.

She came in the door and they clustered around her, the smallest ones hugging her legs. Listening to their numerous voices, holding them, she gave in to the strain she had been under, was still under, and at last wept.

She had not eaten all day. Giselle Henriot heated up some soup. Sitting at the kitchen table with her children all around her, Norma Favert dunked bread in the soup and ate it, and drank the soup and heard all about school, and other kids, and all that had happened in their lives in her absence, and from time to time she managed to tell Giselle about their husbands, that they were supposed to be released tomorrow or the next day, maybe even today.

Giselle appeared to take this news calmly. Of course they would be released tomorrow, why not, they never should have been arrested in the first place, she said. Norma found this reaction heartening, and began to be a believer herself. Why, after all, should they not be released? She was too tired to worry about it anymore tonight anyway.

A few minutes ago she had broken away long enough to telephone Rachel to tell her she was home, and the girl seemed happy to hear from her but a little strange as well, though Norma was unable to put her finger on how or why.

As she hung up, the thought had come to her that phoning Rachel was the type of warning a husband might give who was returning from a trip earlier than expected and didn't want to risk surprising his wife with another man. Norma Favert had no idea where such an absurd thought might have come from. Rachel was just a child, barely older than her own children, and totally trustworthy besides. To entertain such a thought at all, even if only for a moment, made her laugh at herself. Her excuse was that she was giddy from fatigue, giddy from seeing her children again as well.

She left the Henriot house shortly after that, her smallest child wanting to be carried, the others scampering around her as they walked downhill to the presbytery, and to her surprise here came Rachel up the hill to meet them, running the last few steps and embracing her, cold cheek against cold cheek.

"I've missed you so much, Maman," said Rachel.

"The oldest of my children," murmured Norma Favert into her hair.

"And Papa? What about Papa?"

Norma told her. "He's supposed to be coming home tomorrow."

"Thank God, thank God."

The girl relieved her of the suitcase but not of the child who clung to her neck and wouldn't let go. The night was cold but dry, the stars like the lights of isolated houses, and as they continued down the hill Rachel suddenly blurted out: "There's a wounded American pilot in the presbytery. He was shot down. He's nearly recovered now." A little breathlessly she added: "I've been taking care of him."

"How long has he been there?"

"Since you left."

Norma accepted these facts, only noting the girl's breathlessness, which she put aside for consideration later. A pilot hidden in her house—that was the important thing. It might require certain decisions, certain steps, or might not. Having him there was dangerous. So was the harboring of refugee Jews dangerous, but she had never flinched from doing it.

Norma Favert was not mystical at all, and in fact fled from the abstract. She thought not in religious terms but in terms of people in trouble, of doors kept open rather than closed—she would keep her own open no matter how tired or distraught she might be. Helping people was, she believed, the only religion she had.

"You've been with him all this time."

"Yes."

"Alone?"

"He was wounded," said Rachel.

To Norma Favert the girl sounded a bit defensive. What did this mean? she asked herself. Perhaps nothing.

"He knows my real name."

"You told him? Why?"

"I don't know," said Rachel in a small voice.

For a moment Norma studied her. Then: "Did no one ever come looking for him? The Gestapo? The Gendarmerie?"

"No."

"Who knows he's there?"

"The young man who brought him in and the doctor."

"No one else?"

"No."

"Except Madame Henriot?"

"No. I didn't tell her."

"I would have thought you would tell her." Giselle Henriot had been left in charge of all the Favert children, and to Norma this included Rachel. "Why didn't you?"

"I thought she had enough to worry about."

They were still walking downhill through the village. The light from the sky was reflected off the snow. There was no one else abroad at this hour in this cold. As they crossed the square, which was well trampled now, the snow crunched under their shoes. "Tell me about him," Norma Favert said.

"He's really nice. You'll like him."

"I'm sure I will."

"He's from New York. His father is a banker. He's twenty years old, and he has one brother and one sister, both younger than he is, and he's completed two years at the university."

Norma Favert thought: That she knows such details in itself means nothing. If she's been cooped up with him this long, it stands to reason she would know them.

"What's his name?"

"Davey.

"Davey?" said Norma.

"Second Lieutenant David R. Gannon."

"Is he tall, short?" In her head Norma was getting ready to meet him, trying to picture him.

"He has light brown hair and nice teeth. He's not quite as tall as Papa, and much thinner, even though he eats a lot."

Norma was trying to absorb all this, while also trying to decide what, if anything, she may have sensed in Rachel's demeanor. "How badly hurt was he?"

Rachel began to describe the wounds.

"You appear to have observed them very closely."

"Well, I was there." It seemed to occur to Rachel to add: "Most of the time I didn't look, though."

"The Germans didn't send over search planes looking for where he went down?"

"Yes. The other young man told us he saw them go over."

"I see," said Norma Favert, thinking: that's something else to add to the equation.

The three older children had reached the presbytery, and run inside, leaving the door thrown open.

"Let's meet this Second Lieutenant Davey, shall we?" said Norma Favert. And they went into the house and Norma closed the door against the cold air.

Hearing the commotion made by the new arrivals Davey had not stirred. He was in Rachel's bedroom with the door closed, and the girl went in and got him, leading him out by the hand. But when she noticed that this familiarity was not lost on Norma Favert, she dropped the hand and looked guilty.

Norma watched the American boy hop along into the living room.

She shook hands with him in front of the fireplace, and introduced him to her staring curious children, who came up and shook his hand in their turn. He should not be alarmed by the children she told him; even more than the other children of the village, hers had seen hundreds of refugees come and go, and had been taught never to speak of them to anyone.

After that, because she was trying to form an impression of him, she tried for a time to make small talk. He was a nice-looking boy, she thought, and he was very shy, or else he was afraid of her, though why should he be?

Norma knew some English, though not enough to be comfortable very long, and making the boy say anything at all was hard work. He had an open, innocent face, and looked younger even than Rachel, not old enough to be trusted with a car, much less an airplane.

After a short time she broke it off and went to put the children to bed, reading them a story and then tucking them in.

When she came back into the living room Davey jumped to his feet, broken leg and all, and remained standing until she had sat down herself. To Norma, this seemed proof that he came from a good family, or at any rate one that had taught him good manners.

She was exhausted and wanted only to go to bed. "Where have you been sleeping?" she asked Davey.

"I gave him my room," said Rachel.

The two young people looked at each other. They also looked extremely ill at ease. "All right," said Norma to Davey, "stay there for tonight."

"And I've been sleeping in the girls' room," said Rachel.

"The girls are back, so that won't do. You can move in with me until my husband returns."

She looked at them, saw there was something between them, and wondered how much.

"I don't think you should stay in this house much longer," she said to Davey. "Too many children and not enough privacy for you. You need a place that's both more comfortable and safer. Don't worry, we'll find you one. And when your leg heals, we can see about getting you to Switzerland or Spain."

"That sounds like a good idea," said Davey. But again Norma intercepted a glance between them.

"It's late," she said. "Let's all go to bed."

She woke once in the night and the space beside her was not only empty but cool to the hand. She listened hard but heard nothing, and she lay in the dark and waited. Presently Rachel in her long flannel nightdress came back into the room.

"I had to go to the bathroom," she whispered, when she saw that Norma was awake.

You silly girl, Norma thought, I hope you haven't done something you'll regret for the rest of your life. She saw herself as the only mother Rachel had. Nonetheless, she respected her privacy too much to question her now.

Rachel was soon asleep again. This was clear from her breathing. But Norma, tired as she was, lay awake for hours, forced to confront all that worried her, her husband of course, but prominent among these worries was a new one: Rachel. Soon enough it would be her job to see her foster daughter married, and although the girl had England and Berlin in her background, those places were cut off from her forever because of the war, and because of the isolation and poverty of the plateau. Her husband-to-be must necessarily come from this village or a neighboring one. If she had a child out of wedlock, no one hereabouts was going to marry her. Even if there were no child, if she were known to be less than virginal—and it was difficult to keep secrets in villages—no one was going to marry her, and this would become not only Rachel's problem, but Norma's as well.

·   ·   ·

AS soon as he got down from the truck that had carried him as far as Toulouse, Headmaster Vernier found a post office where he placed a long-distance call to Le Lignon—not to his own wife, but to the pastor's. The headmaster knew he would be speaking to her on an open line, that others might listen in, one or two people surely would, perhaps the wrong ears would hear, but the news he had to impart was too important to delay.

There were other people in the post office waiting for calls to go through. Back and forth in front of the telephone cabins the headmaster paced, while other connections were made and the operator at her desk, calling out names, directed people to pick up the receiver in one or another of the cabins.

Finally, unable to wait any longer, Vernier canceled the call and boarded his train. It was not scheduled to leave for two hours, but this was the only way he could be sure of getting on it at all, even in the corridor.

The train stopped frequently en route. There were a number of police controls. Sometimes, when the train waited in a station for an hour or more, he thought of trying to find a post office in which he could re-place his call, but by then he had a seat in a compartment and did not dare move. Then it was night and the post offices were closed.

He reached Le Lignon at noon the next day and went home. Seeing him his wife became jubilant. As he cleaned up and changed his clothes, he told her what had happened, that Favert and Henriot had refused to sign the oath, and were therefore still being held, and then he hurried toward the presbytery to tell Norma Favert.

When she opened the door to him an expression of joy came over her face, as if her husband was right behind him, but it disappeared just as fast when she saw that he was not.

"Life in Le Vernet is hard," Vernier began, "but the two men are in good health." There seemed to him no easy way to say what he had to say, so the headmaster simply blurted it out. "There was a paper they had to sign. They wouldn't sign it."

Norma said: "You mean my husband refused to be released?"

"It was an oath. He refused to sign it, or let Henriot sign it."

"Oh, that man!"

Madame Favert's exasperation was plain to hear, but so were a number of other emotions: loneliness obviously, and after that the desperation that came from fear.

He watched her place phone calls to the Reverend Guerin, and to Finance Minister Morville, each of which would take, they both knew, between thirty minutes and two hours to go through.

As they waited, Norma Favert brought Davey out of the bedroom and introduced him to Headmaster Vernier. Apart from her husband, she trusted Vernier more than any man in Le Lignon, she told Davey in English. "I say that so you will know that you can trust him too."

In French she said to Vernier. "We've got to find someone who will take this young man in. He doesn't belong here."

"Your husband—"

"My husband isn't here."

"I'll see if I can place him."

"He's going to find you a place to stay until your leg heals," she told Davey in English.

The telephone rang, and the connection was made with Reverend Guerin in Nîmes. Norma kept him on the line until he had agreed to phone the finance minister, demanding that he force through the release of the two churchmen, whether they signed the oath or not.

A little after that the call to Vichy went through. Morville himself was not there, or else refused to take the call. "What's it about?" the secretary asked.

The headmaster watched Norma's fingers tighten around the telephone. After hesitating briefly, she explained what had happened at Le Vernet. She wanted the minister to intervene, she said, and she urgently asked that he call her back.

And they all waited in front of the fire, hardly speaking, but no return call came.

After a time, his heart heavy, the headmaster went home.

Late in the day Norma Favert called the finance minister a second time. The secretary could tell her only that her message had been passed along. More than that he did not know.

· · ·

AT Le Vernet, Commandant Motier had also phoned Vichy. What was he supposed to do with these two recalcitrant pastors? He wanted instructions. But his call had not been returned either.

Even as he waited, two black cars running on actual gasoline—they were without the huge gasogene drums sitting on their front and rear bumpers—pulled up in front of the administration building. Motier had been standing at the window, and he knew what the cars were the moment he saw them. He had been gazing out over the camp, at the long even rows of barracks, at the clouds of grit that the cold wind scraped off the ground and blew along the alleys, at the groups of penned up men, most of them men without hope.

There were four Gestapo officers in the cars. He watched them step out, glance self-consciously around, then enter the building, where they no doubt ordered themselves conducted to his office. He sat down behind his desk and waited for them.

They had come for certain prisoners, said their spokesman the moment they had been shown in. He spoke fair French. He did not offer to shake hands. He made no small talk. There was no mention of the weather, or the condition of the roads, or how far the four men had come or where they were going.

They wanted prisoners Favert, Henriot, and Vernier, the spokesman said. He brace-bowed and presented three perfectly valid *mandats d'amener*.

They were tall, athletic-looking men. Motier looked across the desk at them. They had flat faces, flat eyes. They wore trilby hats and long leather overcoats. To the commandant they looked like they would be good at torture.

At first he said nothing, only took the *mandats* and pretended to study them. He was trying to figure out what to do, what to say. He could tell them that Vernier, the headmaster, was already free and out of their reach. Maybe they would become furious and start smashing things up; but he had more men here than they did. He could tell them the other two had refused to sign the oath and were still being held. He could mention that they were the subject of his call to Vichy that had not been returned, and then he could hand them over.

For the moment the commandant did none of these things, but instead got to his feet and left the office. One flight up he found another window to stare out of. This one looked not over the camp but toward the Pyrenees, which today shone clear, an abrupt, rust-brown wall with the sun glinting off the snow on top, the snow becoming a number of darker blots lower down where the shadows covered them. The blots seemed to have slid halfway down the rock facade, and there they clung.

He stood in the window, trying to think. The four thugs downstairs could wait. One did not have to be polite to men like that.

Men moved in and out of the offices all around him. From time to time, seeing him there, they brought him papers to look at, but he shrugged them off.

In Germany the Gestapo was authorized to operate above and outside the law without restraints of any kind. The courts and the constitution had no power to oversee or curb anything it did. In Germany its officers were guilty of outrageous acts. Here in France too, of course. But other times they tried to operate within French law, which was what they were doing now.

The *mandats* downstairs were legal. The commandant, if he handed the prisoners over, was legally in the clear.

Further legalities, once in the Gestapo's hands, were unlikely to be observed, he believed. He too had heard about "reinforced interrogations."

The two churchmen, Favert and the other one, were preachers, not criminals.

But what about after the war? the commandant asked himself. Lately the outcome had seemed to him no longer in doubt. The American armies were advancing up Italy, the siege of Leningrad had been lifted with tremendous German losses, and American bombers now hit Berlin regularly with fifteen hundred Flying Fortresses at a time. There would be an invasion soon.

He had this information from BBC broadcasts in French out of London, and so it could be believed. French newspapers and broadcasts were censored; nothing in them could be believed. Allied victories were not mentioned. German defeats were not mentioned. It was a crime to listen to the BBC. In the big cities the

Germans managed to jam the BBC frequency more or less successfully, but isolated places like Le Vernet—Le Lignon as well—were
out of range of their equipment. One had to be careful. One strung
one's aerial indoors from one radiator to another or from one balcony to another if the balconies were on a hidden side of the house,
so that the telltale aerial could not be spotted, and between broadcasts one rolled it up and hid it. The biggest difficulty, for Motier
and others, was that their radio tubes were nearly worn out, and of
course could not be replaced. To bring the broadcasts in one had to
sit beside the set adjusting the dial ten or twenty times during the
quarter-hour broadcasts.

One was careful afterward about where and to whom one
passed on what one heard.

Commandant Motier had become convinced that Germany was
losing the war. He was further convinced that when peace came
there would be a settling of accounts in France. All those who had
collaborated during the occupation would be made to pay. Collaborators' houses and stores would be burned or bombed. There
would be beatings and murders, summary trials and summary executions. The purge would eventually die out, but not until reprisals
of one kind or another had gone on for years.

How would he himself be perceived?

That he had loaded German Jews into boxcars by the thousands
would not be counted against him, he believed. Not only had he
obeyed orders from above, but also they were aliens who were
merely being handed over to their own people to be returned to
their own country. What happened to them there was of no concern to France, or to himself. When you came right down to it, no
one cared about foreign Jews.

But these two pastors were another story. First of all, they were
French, and second, they were not only charged with no crime,
they were also apostles of nonviolence who had preached nonviolence from the pulpit Sunday after Sunday; Motier did not doubt
that in the village they came from, and within their church as a
whole, they were well thought of, perhaps loved. Third, they
would be seen as men of honor who had refused out of conscience
to sign the oath that would have set them free.

Their church, the Reformed Church of France, might have political clout. How much clout, Motier did not know. Not much, probably, but some.

The two pastors could be seen, and after the war probably would be seen, not as men but as symbols. Especially if anything happened to them. Men, as soon as they are dead, are forgotten, but symbols live a long long time. Symbols can come back and haunt you.

Whoever harmed either one of them might pay dearly.

On the other hand, those *mandats d'amener* downstairs were legal. Motier kept coming back to this fact. He had no legal right to refuse to execute them. He could be brought to trial himself if he did so. He would certainly be convicted and his career would be over, his pension lost.

He thought of his pension a lot in these troubled times. He had been severely wounded, was lame, could not do physical work anymore. But if he were disgraced and without a pension, physical work was all that would be available to him.

And he was afraid of the Gestapo; who wasn't? If he thwarted those men downstairs they could well come back with troops and drag him out of here, throw him into a cell with hostages, even hang him from their favorite lamppost if they chose. They had shown him proper legal documents. Getting those documents had taken time and effort. That they had gone to such trouble proved to Motier how much they wanted those three prisoners, for they hadn't had to bother. They could have marched in here in their usual high-handed way and demanded that the three men be thrown into the backs of their cars. But they had decided on strict legality instead. Whoever had given them their orders had wanted no hitches—no possibility of hitches.

Commandant Motier continued to stare out the window. The sun was lower now, gradually lifting its jewelry away from the tops of the mountains.

After a time he went back downstairs and reentered his office. He believed he had still not decided what to do. It would all depend on the next few minutes.

As he sat down behind his desk, the Gestapo spokesman said:

"The prisoners. *Schnell.* We're tired of waiting. You hear me? *Schnell.*"

Motier gazed at them for a moment, then made his decision. Why should he turn anyone over to these pigs? He said: "It is just as I thought, sorry to say. The men you want are no longer here. I received an order a few days ago . . ."

He fished through a folder, brought it out, and handed it across the desk. "In accordance with this order they have been released. I don't know where they might be at this time. Far from here in any case. So you've come all this way for nothing. I really am sorry."

Before reentering his office he had taken the precaution of stationing two armed officers outside his door. He got up from his desk, went to the door, and said to them: "These men are just leaving. Please escort them to their car."

They were furious, obviously. He watched from his window as the cars drove away, and was surprised at how good he felt.

He waited an hour to be sure they were gone, then ordered the two pastors brought to his office.

When they came in, dirty, unshaven, thin, standing in their exhausted suits, he told them they were being released.

"We will not sign the oath," said Pastor Favert.

"Forget the oath. I'm willing to overlook the oath."

After a moment he said: "The Gestapo was here. Not an hour ago. They had warrants for you." He nodded at the two pastors. "I sent them away. But they may still be in the area. You should know that."

"Thank you for telling us," said Favert.

"Watch out for them."

"Yes, of course."

"They'll be after you from now on, I would guess. When you get where you're going, I suggest you take proper precautions."

"All right," said Favert.

The commandant came around the desk smiling, his hand outstretched. He shook hands with both of them. "I can provide a truck to take you to Toulouse. Get your things and get out of here. Good-bye and good luck."

XVII

THE Fieseler Storch came over again.

It was another bright, sunny afternoon, perfect weather for a search plane. In most parts of France winter was over, or nearly so, though not up here on the plateau. Nonetheless, the weather had been warming for some days, the temperature above freezing except at night. The thick snow on the ground was much compacted. The wind had combed the dandruff out of the spruce trees, which were green again.

The forger Pierre Glickstein had heard the engine noise some distance off, the farmer also. They had come out of the barn. The plane was behaving as it always did, searching along a grid, going out of sight, and then coming back on an adjacent line.

It had been coming over about once a week, but each time had gone away again without ever seeming to concentrate on the edge of forest that held the wrecked American plane.

"He's going to see the thing this time," the forger said. "I myself can see it from here."

The two men stood in the yard watching. The plane kept getting closer and closer, flashing the black crosses on its wings each time it banked.

When it came over the farm it seemed to stumble, as if it had run into a wall of air. In fact, the pilot, his hand on the throttle when flying this close to the ground, had involuntarily jerked back on the power.

"He's seen it," muttered Glickstein.

The farmer grimaced. His tooth was hooked over his lower lip, his eyes tracking the Fieseler Storch.

Which banked sharply, flew directly over the wrecked P-51, then came around for another look.

It made several passes, losing altitude each time.

"He's radioing that he's found it," muttered Glickstein. "Giving the coordinates. Step back inside the barn. I don't think we want him to know we've seen him."

Finally the Fieseler Storch flew away.

"In an hour," said Glickstein, "there'll be truckloads of troops around this place. I imagine you don't want to be here. I know I don't."

He started across the barn to his room, but when he looked back the farmer hadn't moved.

"Get your things together," said Glickstein. "Get your wife, and let's go."

"Go where?"

"Anyplace is better than here."

"What about the animals?"

"Forget the animals, man, think of yourself."

"They have to be fed. The cows have to be milked twice a day. I have to stay with the animals."

"Who's going to feed them when the *Boches* arrest you?"

"Maybe they won't."

"That's some maybe."

"My wife will go with you. I'll get her ready."

"I'll take all my gear. If they tear the place apart, which they will, at least they won't find that."

When Glickstein came back with his suitcase and his gear in a sack, the horse had been hitched to a cart. The cart sometimes hauled manure, and smelled it. The forger threw his things into the cart, then waited for Madame Daudet, who seemed to take forever to appear.

He watched her come out of the house, a tall thin woman whom he knew to be in her mid-sixties, though she looked older. She wore a black shawl, a shabby black overcoat over a long black dress, and black lace-up shoes with wooden soles. He had never seen her wear anything but black. She too had few teeth. She was dragging a suitcase so heavy that the forger, who tried to help her, could not lift it into the cart. She's got the family silver in there, he guessed. It's been in the family for generations and she's not leaving it.

The horse seemed impatient. The snow in the yard was hard packed, icy in spots, and the horse was pawing it and blowing steam.

"Where are you taking her?" demanded Daudet.

"I don't think you want to know—in case they try to make you tell."

Daudet nodded.

"It's a small village. If you get out of this you'll be able to find her easily enough. If you don't . . ."

The farmer and his wife did not kiss good-bye. They had lived together forty or more years, but Glickstein had never observed any outward sign of affection between them.

"Good-bye old girl," Daudet said to her. Nodding at Glickstein, he slapped the horse on the rump. "Off you go, then." He did not watch them leave but went back into the barn.

The road was in better shape than the last time, even bare of snow in places, and Glickstein was no longer as afraid of the horse as he had been. Nonetheless, the animal was in no mood to move quickly. It dragged the cart past the other farms, and then through the stretches of forest. It half skidded down the hill to the river. As it clattered slowly across the bridge it kept looking back at them, as if surprised at the noise it was making. On the other side of the river it plodded up past the temple, and into and across the square. Snapping the reins on its back, Glickstein got it to cross the narrow-gauge railroad tracks and then to climb the steep street that led up past the small college and the pensions around it. On top of the hill was a farm, Glickstein remembered, and this was where he was headed, for he thought his passenger might feel comfortable there for a time. In addition, it was a place where he might board the horse.

As it happened, the farm couple and Madame Daudet knew each other, so he left her there and went on, for his gear still lay in the bed of the cart, and he intended to dispose of it, if possible, in a place where, if found, it would not incriminate anybody. He did not know how much time he had. He was thinking of a small lake a bit farther on—he could sling the sack as far as possible out into the water. But as he came around a turn in the road he found himself face-to-face with a truckload of German troops coming the other way.

His first thought was: *merde,* how did they get here so quickly? His second was for the sack of gear behind him.

They stopped him. Two soldiers jumped to the road and leveled guns at him. Glickstein did not have time to do anything. There was forest to either side, but to try to run for it, he judged, was to commit suicide. He glanced behind him into the cart and feared he had committed suicide already.

A third man got out of the cab and came forward. He was in civilian clothes, dark trilby, long leather overcoat. This was Ober-sturmbannführer Gruber, who did not identify himself. To Glickstein he did not need to. He was identified by the leather coat he wore, that all these Gestapo *mecs* wore that was like a badge, that was more feared than any badge.

"Papers," said Gruber.

As he handed them over, Glickstein was trying to keep from trembling.

Another officer had got down from the truck. "Open your coat," ordered Gruber. "Search him," he ordered the other man.

As the forger was patted down, something rattled in his right pants pocket.

"Stop," ordered Gruber. A thin unpleasant smile had come onto his face. He imagined he had found something, contraband certainly, cartridges in a box was what it sounded like, for the possession of which this young man could be, and would be, shot.

Gruber was carrying a swagger stick with which, now, he prodded Glickstein's pocket again and again, toying with this Frenchman, making him sweat. "Yes," he said, "isn't that interesting." He kept making the pocket rattle. "Fascinating," he said. And then: "Empty your pockets."

Glickstein brought forth some coins, a dirty handkerchief, and a small tin box.

"Open it," shouted Gruber.

The forger did so. Inside were five or six cough drops.

Gruber's stick swatted the box to the road. When Glickstein bent to pick it up, Gruber kicked it out from under his hand, and it skidded all the way to the ditch.

Gruber glanced around at the other Germans. "Turn that cart around," he snarled at Glickstein. He looked embarrassed. "Go back where you came from. Nobody leaves the village."

He threw Glickstein's papers at his feet but at least did not kick them away.

Glickstein picked them up, then got back into the cart. The turn he made was so wide he nearly got one wheel in the ditch. But finally he got pointed back toward the village. Immediately he whipped the horse, which started off at a kind of prancing surprised gallop. The Gestapo *mec* had been too embarrassed to search the cart, he conjectured, but at any moment the idea might come to him. Glickstein's hands were trembling. His knees were so weak they would barely hold him up.

Behind him he heard soldiers being dropped off the truck to close the road. The truck then sped past him, scaring the horse and nearly sending Glickstein's cart into the ditch again.

He slowed the horse, thought about pitching his sacks into the woods, then heard more cars coming, and so decided against it. The cars went by at speed. One was a vanload of gendarmes, the other a black Citroën with two men in it.

They're really serious, Glickstein told himself.

He drove past the farm where he had left Madame Daudet, turning instead into the college where he tied the horse to a tree. Carrying his sack he went inside, entered empty offices and supply closets, and dispersed his mimeograph machine, his two typewriters, his ink bottles, his compass, rulers, and pens, none of which was likely to attract attention in such a place. His false letterheads, blank identity cards, and such he tore into pieces and flushed down a toilet. He was now definitively out of the forgery business.

Only then was he able to telephone the presbytery and sound the alarm. The *Boches* were already in the village, he told Madame Favert, who took the call.

She said, sounding scared: "That's not possible."

"I saw them. They've blocked the roads in and out."

"Who are you?"

"I'm the *mec* who brought in the pilot. Is he still there?"

"No," she said, "absolutely not," and she hung up.

Glickstein stepped into a classroom and sat listening to a lecture on theology. The *Boches* had found blood in the wrecked plane, he theorized. Their immediate move was to throw a cordon around the village, and the only mystery was that they had managed to do this so quickly. So much blood meant to them that the pilot had been badly hurt. Therefore he might still be in the village. Which he was, Glickstein guessed. Probably still in the presbytery, which was where the *Boches* would go first, if they had any brains. If they were going to find him, he hoped they would find him quickly and go away. The longer it took, the more dangerous it became for everybody else.

What he himself would do next, where he would go, he did not know. If his papers survived scrutiny when the *Boches* came through this school, if he was still free when they left, he knew he would have to decide. He could join the Maquis, he supposed. There was a unit hereabouts, he believed. He had heard rumors. Thanks to regular parachute drops from England, Frenchmen were better armed every day, and were getting ready to strike back.

But Glickstein was a studious young man, not a violent one. He could not see himself firing bullets at anybody, blowing up things and people. The Maquis was an option, but not one he could see himself choosing.

MADAME Favert had responded to Glickstein's call by running to the front door and looking up the street to where the road came up from the river. Even as she watched, a truckload of German troops passed by. So the warning was true.

She ordered Davey up into the attic. With his leg still in a cast he couldn't run anyplace, even if there were somewhere to run to, and she didn't know what else to do with him. She gave him a blanket to wrap himself in and told him to roll as deeply into the eaves as he could. Perhaps the Germans would climb only halfway up the ladder, and throw their flashlight beams in along the floor. Perhaps they wouldn't see him.

She sent Rachel up to the college to mingle with students her age, for that seemed a safer place for her than in a house that also contained a downed enemy pilot.

She herself rushed to the school to gather up her children. If something terrible was about to happen, she wanted them with her. Better that the house seem completely empty, she believed, safer for the house, safer for all of them. Besides, if foreign troops were going to search through her rooms, through her things, she did not want to be there to watch.

FOR a time the road and the narrow-gauge tracks ran side by side so the two pastors, as their train approached Le Lignon, saw the truckloads of troops go by in the direction of the village.

"Those troops are here to arrest somebody," said Henriot. "Us, do you think?"

"We've just been released."

"A mistake, maybe," said Henriot. "They're coming to rectify it."

This idea had occurred to Favert too, but he pretended confidence. "They don't need that many troops to arrest two clergymen." But inside he wasn't so sure.

Nearing the village the train slowed way down, and the klaxon hooted before every crossroad, at the last of which a roadblock was being set up. In their seats the two pastors swiveled around to watch.

"No one gets out of the village," said Henriot pensively.

"At least they're letting us get in."

"Which maybe isn't such a good thing."

"It will be good to get home, though, won't it?"

The train stopped in the small station and they got down with their suitcases and stood in the cloud of steam that blew back from the engine.

There had been other passengers on the train, some of them being met by villagers. Seeing the pastors there, everyone was grinning, glad to have them back, and there was much handshaking. But these people were pensive too, asking what the Germans wanted here today.

One by one they dispersed.

Having promised to phone each other with whatever news they picked up, Favert and Henriot shook hands and parted, for Henriot's house was in the upper part of the village, the presbytery in the lower.

Pastor Favert walked home through streets that were empty and silent, apart from the Germans. Everyone else had closed themselves inside their houses.

He came to his front door, let himself in and called out, but there was no response. He stopped and listened sharply but the house was so silent it seemed to him obviously empty. This did not alarm him. Norma had probably gone to fetch the children, and there was no telling where Rachel might be. He looked into all the rooms, taking possession of each of them again, and of his house. The rooms were unchanged though empty, and he went into the kitchen. One side of the stove was hot, and he filled the kettle and moved it onto the heat. He did not know why the Germans were there in such force, and of course he was worried, as who wouldn't be. But it was too late to warn anyone, too late to do much except pray, which he silently did.

He carried the hot kettle into the bathroom.

The phone rang and it was Henriot. "Your family's here," the assistant pastor said. "Why don't you come up and we'll have some tea."

There was tension in Henriot's voice, and the pastor detected it, but he thought this tension normal under the circumstances. Finding the village full of Germans would make anybody tense.

"As soon as possible," said Henriot.

"In a few minutes," Favert said, and hung up. Whatever was to happen next, he told himself, he was not going to have his wife—or anyone else—see him like this. First he was going to wash, shave, and put on clean clothes. After that he would dress in his cassock and rabat, making himself into an authority figure, and as he walked up to Henriot's house he would try to find out what the Germans were doing, and if necessary help people if he could.

Twenty minutes later, ready to leave the house, he stood in the vestibule in coat and black fedora, his cassock showing below, and tightened his scarf, pulled on his gloves, and then opened the door.

In front of him, backed by two German soldiers, stood Obersturmbannführer Gruber, whose swagger stick was raised to knock, a detail the pastor noted and wondered about: they're knocking, not just barging in here, why?

Even as he formulated this thought, two other vehicles pulled up in front, a black Citroën and a gendarmerie van. Gendarmes got out of the van. They stood near it eyeing the two German soldiers, who immediately began to look nervous.

Out of the black car stepped Commissaire Chapotel, who advanced quickly until he was standing beside Gruber.

The pastor stepped back. "Gentlemen, come in," he said.

After removing and hanging up his outer garments, the pastor in his cassock and bib led Gruber and Chapotel into the main room in front of the fire. He was more than alarmed by now, though trying to appear calm. He said: "What can I do for you?"

All three men heard the front door open again, they turned toward it, and Norma Favert entered the room.

Husband and wife had not seen each other in weeks. Both had feared they might never see each other again. Nonetheless, this was not the time to embrace. Neither even wanted to. Affection would have to wait.

"Norma," said the pastor.

She nodded at her husband, he touched her arm. Otherwise the attention of both was on the other two men.

Who had eyes, it seemed, only for each other.

Obersturmbannführer Gruber said to the French policeman: "Seeing you here is quite a surprise."

"I was in St. Agave on another matter, and saw your convoy go through."

"You've—how should I say it?—come to a party to which you were not invited."

"I thought you might need my help."

"As a matter of fact, no."

"To make sure that whatever you do is strictly legal."

The tension between the two men was not lost on the pastor, who thought: we may have found a new ally.

After a moment Obersturmbannführer Gruber turned toward Favert. "I'm a bit surprised to see you as well, Pastor. I thought you'd gone off somewhere."

"For a while I was out of town, true," Favert said. "I decided to take a cure to lose weight."

"Yes, you look very good."

"Thank you."

Norma Favert had not yet said a word.

Favert received the impression that the Gestapo chief had not come to arrest him, that his purpose must be something else.

"An enemy plane was shot down near here," said Gruber.

"When was this?"

"The day you started your weight cure," said Chapotel.

"As long ago as that?" said the pastor.

"We have information the pilot may be hidden in the village," said Gruber.

"By all means look," said the pastor, "but I don't think you'll find him."

As they weighed their options, and tried to decide what attitude to strike, all three men were under increasing strain.

Gruber had the most guns on hand, but they were not all close by. He could win a pitched battle, but it might cost too much. There were risks to his career and his personal security both, and before he made a move he needed to decide what they were.

Chapotel, watching him, had only the few men outside, but the German would have to take them into account. There could be Maquis fighters inside some of the houses. The tide of the war was changing, or changed. For Gruber, conquered France was becoming, had become, more and more dangerous.

Calculating his own position, Favert saw that he had moral force only, symbolized by his cassock and bib, but moral force had more weight than people supposed. He had the village behind him and also, he was beginning to sense, Chapotel. For the Gestapo to drag him out of here today might cause . . . what?

Who had the most to lose, the most to gain? A show of strength might be taken for strength. Who was to say in advance what was bluff and what was real?

Norma Favert, watching all three men, listening for any stirring by Davey in the attic, was merely scared. She had come to stand by her husband once more, certain that when they took him away this time she would never see him again.

Gruber said: "My men have orders to search all the houses."

"We can't stop you. I would ask that you do it efficiently, without wrecking people's things."

"Starting with this one."

"There is no need to search this house. It is empty, as you can see."

Gruber's eyes were locked on the pastor's. He said: "I'll get my men, and we'll look."

"This house—this village—is dedicated to the principle of non-violence. We harbor only those who are persecuted—"

"Jews," Gruber snorted.

"—not those who have taken up arms."

"The pilot was badly wounded."

"I have already looked through the house. There is no one here except us in this room."

Gruber's indecision, if that's what it was, showed only in that he had not yet invited his men inside to begin the search.

"People lie," said Gruber.

"Some do. I do not."

Gruber's eyes had tightened. His accent had become more gutteral as his French, under stress, began to come apart.

"If he was here, you would lie."

"I would not lie. Under no circumstances."

The dialogue had become a battle of wills, and the pastor's was the stronger.

"If he says there's no airman in this house," said Chapotel, "you can believe him."

"My wife would prefer it if you didn't ransack her house."

"Look at his face," said Chapotel. "A jury would believe him."

Gruber said nothing.

"You have his word. What more do you want?"

All three men wore uniforms that were for them habitual: the pastor in his cassock and bib, the German in his long leather coat and trilby hat, the French policeman, hatless, in his shiny trench coat.

Norma Favert looked from one to the other.

"If you violate this house," suggested Chapotel, "and find nothing, that would be seen in the village as a loss of face, wouldn't you say. For you—and for the Fatherland."

Gruber gave his short, disagreeable laugh.

"You'd look pretty silly," said Chapotel bluntly.

"There is no airman in the house," said the pastor, and the authority he projected was absolute.

"You'd do better to search elsewhere," said Chapotel.

There was a long, long silence. Then:

"For the moment I will accept your word," said Gruber to the pastor. He brace-bowed, and turned toward the door.

When it had closed behind him, Favert reached for the first time toward his wife. But Chapotel was still standing by, so he only took her hands.

"Why don't you and I go with him?" he heard the policeman say. "It might make him supervise his men. Make them behave correctly."

"No, don't," cried Norma Favert.

"Yes," said Favert to Chapotel, "good idea." And he dropped his wife's hands and followed him out into the cold.

XVIII

As soon as they had gone out Norma glanced toward the attic above her head. In the aftermath of her immense fear—fear for her husband, for her house, for herself, even perhaps for Davey—her head had gone light. Her stomach was clenched like a washboard. She couldn't move—if she did she'd vomit or faint, perhaps both—so she stood in her house in front of the fire, and fought for control.

The nausea finally passed, but not the fear. She no longer knew for sure who the enemy was. Chapotel's conduct just now was not comprehensible. Did he know Davey was in the house? Why had he saved Davey, saved them? Had he suffered a belated crisis of conscience? Had he decided he would no longer obey these people? But she did not see him as a man opting for martyrdom.

Meanwhile, the Gestapo remained in the village and might be back, probably would be back. Something had cowed Herr Gruber a few minutes ago, she guessed, but as soon as he had his soldiers around him he would get over it.

Because of the young man above her head her household was again in crisis. What had they done to deserve still another after so many, she asked herself? How many more could she stand? She resented Davey almost to the point of hatred. Her husband was not safe yet, or herself either, this house was not safe yet, and perhaps never would be again. Having singled them out, the Gestapo would keep returning. If not today, then in the future. That was what police types did, she believed, they kept going back to the same targets. Which meant that her children were not safe either.

When she could move again she went to the kitchen where, to lift her morale, she began preparing a lamb stew for dinner. In the village earlier she had been able to obtain an entire neck, and had splurged, paying what was to her a fortune, and this had been for morale's sake also. She had wanted to believe her husband would really be released from that camp. The expensive stew meat was to celebrate his homecoming. If he came home. Buying it had made the possibility real to her.

And so she laid out the neck bones. It made the equivalent of six cutlets for eight people, for Davey would have to be fed too, and the meat on them would not make copious servings. She cut up the carrots, the potatoes, the turnips, the onions. She had water boiling on the stove, and the vegetables went into it. She minced the garlic, and threw that in, followed by bay leaves, thyme, rosemary. It would all make a rather thin stew, for she had no stock or bouillon with which to thicken it. Nonetheless, it would be a treat for them all.

As she worked she thought repeatedly of Davey, visualizing him rolled in a blanket under the eave, forbidden to make a movement or sound, no doubt suffering from cramps by now, probably cold as well, but until the Germans had left the village he couldn't come down. She felt some sympathy for him and might have called up that for a few minutes he could relax a bit, but then she remembered Rachel, what she feared might have happened between them, as well as the peril he had put her husband in, put all of them in, and found that she was in no mood to do it. He's being very still, she thought, but gave him no credit for it; his life was at stake too. Let him suffer, she thought viciously, it will do him good.

It was dark outside before the pastor returned. Norma heard him hanging up his hat and coat in the vestibule, and she went weak with relief. She was again standing in front of the fire, and that was where he found her. She hadn't even turned on any lights.

He put his hands on her shoulders, his ear against her cheek. He said: "They're gone. They didn't find him."

She turned and gazed at him, noting how thin he looked, how tired.

"They didn't even take any Jews," he said. "All those frightened people standing there, expecting to be taken."

"The rigid German mind," said Norma. "Today they were looking for the pilot, not Jews."

"They'll be back for them. They must have realized today how many there must be. We'll have to be ready, work out a plan."

He led her into the kitchen, glanced at the simmering stew, and put water on to boil for tea.

"You're sure they're gone?"

"Yes. Gruber was the first to go. Chapotel and I stuck by him, until finally he just got into a car and left. The others went on with the search. Closets, cupboards, cellars, attics. It went pretty quickly. They weren't interested in women, boys, or men over thirty. Didn't even look at them. Just the men of combat age, of which there are very few left in the village." He gave a slight chuckle. "The men of combat age have all been deported to Germany as forced labor, or else they're in the Maquis."

"And now all the Germans are gone?" she said again, needing to be sure before proceeding to what came next.

"Yes."

He had prepared the tea. They carried their cups out in front of the fire. "We should phone and get the children home," he said, sipping.

"There's something I have to tell you first," she said. "Something you don't know."

He waited.

"The reason they didn't find the pilot in the village was because he's here."

"Here?"

"Yes."

"In this house?" It was almost a cry of pain, and she knew why.

"Yes, in the attic."

Even then Norma did not call out to Davey to come down. She

had to have this out with her husband first, and she feared his wrath.

"He's here in this house?" Favert put his cup down, and his face got dark. "And you let me give my word that he was not?"

"There was nothing I could do."

"You caused me to lie."

"You spoke what you thought to be the truth."

He had begun to pace. He still wore his droopy bib, his cassock, which billowed out with each step. "You made me lie, and by keeping silent you lied."

"When a man poses questions he has no right to ask, it is not a lie to keep silent," said Norma Favert. "Nor to lie either, if you want my opinion."

She saw him glancing almost frantically around, as if he would run out, find the Gestapo chief if he could, bring him back, correct the lie by turning the young pilot over to him.

"You've made me into a liar," he said.

She saw his emotion, she just didn't believe it was reasonable. "Morally speaking, you did not lie."

"Don't talk to me about morally speaking."

He sat down on the sofa, his face in his hands. "How could you have done that to me? My word is, was, my pride, my—my gold."

She went and stood over him and put her hands on his head.

He said: "Apart from you and the children, it was the only gold I've ever had."

"You're exhausted," she said, stroking his thin graying hair. "This will look differently to you in the morning."

Later they sat at dinner together, a "family" of eight, and the stew was served, and one slice of bread per person. The children were rambunctuous as always. They didn't know who Davey was, and once they realized he could not speak French they lost interest in him. He became for them just another refugee sitting around this table, all of whom had disappeared as soon as homes were found for them.

As for the pastor, Norma noted, his entire focus was on Davey. He always did this with new people, who each time came away convinced that to him they were the most fascinating and important people in the world, that he would protect and help them at the cost of his own life, if need be. People became awed by the degree of his interest, his power of concentration, the warmth he projected. It took prodigious amounts of energy each time, and did again tonight even though, after what he had been through in recent weeks, he should have had no energy left. There sat Davey, flattered, voluble, answering her husband's questions, talking about college, about England, about New York, already under his spell, never once realizing the energy drain on her husband that this conversation represented. The beaming Rachel hung on every word the boy uttered. From time to time secret glances crossed the table between them. Norma was aware of this, even if her husband was not. Soon she would have to talk to him about Rachel, tell him what she suspected, but not tonight, let him get at least one good night's sleep first.

After supper, as she doled out bedroom assignments, she noted the way the boy and the girl told each other good night. She put Davey and her son in one room, Rachel and her oldest daughter in another. That should be enough to keep the lovers, if they were lovers, separate until morning, she told herself.

Presently the fires were banked, the lights were out throughout the house, all was quiet, and Norma was in bed with her husband, and it felt oh so good to feel his big body there beside her.

PIERRE Glickstein drove the cart out of the village and up along the high road through the small forests, past the successive small farms. He was wearing his sheepskin vest with the wool turned inside, and his fingerless gloves. He stood in the cart on wooden shoes. He was hatless. It was a bright sunny day, the warmest yet. He could feel the sun on his hair, but his ears were cold, his arms too, the vest being sleeveless. There was still too much snow for him to smell the approaching spring, but the center of the road was bare, so how far off could the warm weather be? In the fields the snow had shrunk way down, and spears of grain poked through where last year's crops had stood.

The horse was moving well, clip-clop, not quite trotting, and Glickstein was no longer afraid of it at all. His fear was for the

Boches who perhaps still hung around. He was going back to the farm. He was taking a risk and he knew it, but he had to know what he would find when he got there. If he ran into a patrol the horse was his cover—he was a farmworker driving an empty cart back home. Probably they would let him go, though you could never be sure. He would thank them as servilely as possible, give a slap with the reins and drive straight on.

That the horse might turn into the farm of its own accord, resisting any efforts by him to drive it straight ahead, had not occurred to him, though a different possibility did. A roadblock would be visible from a distance, he would be forewarned; but suppose the *Boches* had left only a guard. The *mec* would be holed up inside the farmhouse, and Glickstein wouldn't know he was there until it was too late.

But if there were no guard and no patrol either, this might mean something far worse.

When he got to the farm the horse did turn in on its own, trotting fast now. Glickstein could not have stopped him but did not try, for his eyes were fixed on what lay ahead.

The horse stopped at the front of the house. It was sniffing the air and so was Glickstein.

There was no activity he could see, but then there was no reason for any. There was no guard, because there was nothing left that needed guarding. Most of the house was gone. Its front door hung charred from its hinges.

Having got down from the cart, Glickstein watched the horse amble toward the barn.

He pushed the front door open farther, then stepped in on top of the rubble. Parts of the walls still stood but the floor was gone, and the oak wall paneling that had dated back hundreds of years, and the ceiling, and the rafters, and the roof. The heavy roof slates had come crashing down on the beds. The brass bedsteads poked up, a ton of slates lying asleep on each half-burned mattress.

He moved through what had been rooms seaching for the remains of the farmer, but did not find them.

He went out. Across the field he could see parts of the crashed plane quite clearly now.

The *Boches* had torched every building. He looked into the garage. The farmer's precious car was a skeleton.

The horse had stopped outside the barn, whose half-burned doors hung crookedly. Even the horse recognized that something terrible had been done here.

Glickstein stepped into the barn. The fire here had been fiercer than in the house or the garage—because of the hay and straw, of course. The fallen slates had made cairns over each of the cows— he toppled one cairn with his foot. It was hard to be sure, but the animals appeared to have been machine-gunned first. In any case all three carcasses were crisp.

The soot and stink made it hard to breathe. Glickstein noted no remnants of the rabbits or chickens. He assumed the *Boches* had simply stolen them. Again he stepped carefully across the rubble, searching for the farmer, for there were piles that could have concealed him. With his foot he disarranged each one. The farmer was not there. Also missing were the remains of the pig.

He went outside. The harsh light made him blink, or else it was the moisture in his eyes. Even the privy had been pushed over, he noted. Behind it, the cesspool must be shining at the sky.

He wanted to wash his hands, his face, he was dying of thirst, so he went to the well. But the bucket would not pull up, obliging him to peer over the rim. The pig, minus its bloody hams, was floating down there, nose to the bottom.

For several minutes he paced back and forth, and was filled with rage. Grabbing the reins, he jerked the horse around until it was pointed toward the road. But before jumping up into the cart something made him walk behind the fallen privy, and that was where, floating in the cesspool, he found the farmer.

AT that same hour Norma and Rachel were dressing the children for church, watched by Davey, who was leaning against the wall. The pastor had left for the church an hour earlier, and by now would be standing out in front greeting his parishioners, while the pews filled up behind him.

It fell to Rachel to dress the littlest girl, who did not want to wear the hat assigned her, and kept pulling it off and throwing it on the floor. Rachel tickled her, joked with her, got her giggling, and at last the hat stayed in place. Norma had dressed three children in the time it took.

Finally they all stood in the vestibule, where Norma Favert, looking worried, her hand on the doorknob, said to Rachel: "You're sure you don't want to come with us."

"I have to stay here for the doctor."

A few minutes ago the doctor had phoned to say he was coming to remove Davey's cast within the hour. "If I weren't here," said Rachel, "who would translate for him?"

Though neither the pastor nor Norma had ever pressured her in any way, Rachel had often gone to church, and had even asked to be baptized, for she wanted to be like the rest of the family. But the pastor had always smiled and put her off. "We'll see after the war," he had promised.

"Well, we'd love to have you," said Norma Favert now.

"I know Davey has some questions he wants to ask the doctor," the girl said. "Don't you, Davey?" she said in English.

"Don't I what?" said Davey.

"Papa would certainly be glad to see you there," said Norma.

"I don't think so, no," said Rachel. "The doctor . . ."

Norma frowned. "You're sure?"

"Next week, maybe." Rachel knelt to be kissed by the little girls, then closed the door on them all.

Standing with her back against it, she thought: she knows. She can't bear the idea of Davey and me alone here together. What am I going to do?

Balanced on one leg and his cast, Davey stood in the big room, watching her, a smirk on his face. She was so troubled that she attempted to move past him, but when his arms went around her she allowed herself to be held, to be kissed.

"It's been such a long time," said Davey in her ear.

She surrendered to the warmth of him, the strength of him. "Such a long time," she murmured, "such a long time."

But when his hands started to move over her she said, "Stop," and broke away. "The doctor's liable to be here any minute."

"He may not come for hours.

"Yes he will."

"We have time."

"We don't have time."

"The service might be over before he comes."

"Maybe."

"They'll all have come back, and we—"

"We have to wait for the doctor," she said.

He looked sulky as she left him. She went into the kitchen and began cleaning up after breakfast, but almost at once there came a knocking at the front door, and she knew it was the doctor, and she smiled and dried her hands and went out into the big room to greet him.

He came in wearing the same thin coat, the same shapeless shoes, carrying the same small bag.

It took him about ten minutes to break the cast off. Underneath, Davey's leg looked boney and white.

"You can stand?" said the doctor.

When Rachel had translated Davey stood, then limped to the fireplace and back.

"Is painful?"

"No," said Davey, "yes, but not much."

"*Gut,*" said the doctor.

Davey wanted to know what he was now allowed to do.

"If the pain you can stand, okay you can do what you want."

When this had been translated, Davey gave a whoop, removed his one boot, and attempted to stride barefoot about the room. He was trying hard not to limp, but it was clear from his face that he was in pain.

The doctor left soon after.

GLICKSTEIN had got the farmer out of the cesspool, had laid him down. He sat beside him for a long time. He kept bathing his face with snow, and crying.

The ground was too hard to dig a grave, and there was no shovel anyway, for the handles had been burned off the tools in the barn. To make the body safe from forest animals, Glickstein piled roof slates over it, covered it many slates deep.

Finally he got into the cart, snapped the reins on the horse's back and the cart started out toward the road.

Although it was out of his way, he drove the cart to the inn on the road to Rence where in the past he had delivered his forged documents.

At this hour the inn was closed, but he banged on the door until the innkeeper, whose name was Lazare, came downstairs and opened it to him.

Lazare was dressed for church, as was his wife behind him, but when he saw the state Glickstein was in, he sent his wife on alone, and invited him in, and went behind the bar where he put on his leather apron and then poured the ex-forger a glass of cognac.

Glickstein had already begun to talk, but the words were disjointed and hard to understand because he was crying again.

"Drink that," the innkeeper said, gesturing toward the cognac.

The boy took a swallow, wiped his eyes on the back of his hand, and went on talking.

As the details came out Lazare only nodded. He was a big burly man about forty years old. The death of the farmer was personal to Glickstein, not to him. These were bad times. All around one, innocent people died violent deaths. One couldn't weep for them all.

"Somebody's got to go get him," said Glickstein. "Take care of him, there has to be a funeral."

Again the innkeeper nodded. It wasn't his job, and he wasn't going to volunteer for it. "Speak to the pastor. He's good at that kind of thing."

Gradually Glickstein got himself under control. His eyes dried up, and his voice became almost normal. He hadn't come here to cry on this man's unresponsive shoulder, but for something else entirely.

He said: "I want you to put me in contact with the Maquis."

Lazare answered almost automatically: "What would I know about the Maquis?"

"Come on."

"I don't know if there are any around here."

"Of course there are," said the ex-forger impatiently. "I've made papers for hundreds of them."

As the war went more and more badly for the conquerors, more and more French youths had received conscription notices for forced labor in Germany—and more and more of them, instead of reporting, had disappeared into the Maquis, where they needed new names and new papers.

"Are you sure the Maquis is what you want?" said the innkeeper at last. He had picked up Glickstein's empty glass and was rinsing it out.

"I don't have any choice," said the ex-forger. "The farmer—before they threw him in the cesspool they beat him to death. We don't know what he may have told them."

With or without Lazare's help Glickstein intended to find the local Maquis and join them. He wanted to avenge the farmer. He was full of hatred, he wanted to kill Germans. He was tired of playing only a clandestine role, of being afraid all the time. He wanted to be out in the open. He was in the mood for violent action. He wanted to fight. He wanted to kill.

"All right," said the innkeeper. "Where will you be?"

Yesterday Glickstein had found a bed in a kind of dormitory in a pension that housed other youths his age, some of them refugees, some of them future theologians from the college.

"You'll be contacted," the innkeeper said.

Glickstein nodded, got into his cart, and continued on toward Le Lignon.

RACHEL'S body was a sheen of sweat. Her hair hung down, almost obscuring her face. Her eyes were closed. Her breasts swayed. Her mouth was open, and from it came short gutteral cries. Davey, meanwhile, caressed her hips, her back, the length of her arms. He lifted himself up so that he could hug and kiss her still again, tell her still again how much he loved her.

He wanted to marry her. They were married already. He would ask the pastor to do it formally. No, he would ask the village priest. He had always been aware in a small way of what sexual gratification must be like, but the emotions and sensations he felt at this moment were not that, at least not primarily, but were something that seemed to him completely different, they existed on a level more intense than he had ever imagined. He wanted to become one with Rachel in some absolute sense, fuse his being with hers even more than their bodies were fused already, and he pulled her down on top of him, until they were glued together by sweat, and he held her to him as tightly as he could without crushing the breath out of her. Now her breasts were squashed into his chest, which felt very nice, but they were kissing each other too, and breathing on each other, and then their faces were pressed together cheek to cheek, which felt even better. He wanted to get even more inside her than he was, become part of her, which was impossible, and with this knowledge the glorious moment became tinged with sadness. This then was the high point, the apotheosis: if they lived together for sixty years they could never get any closer than this. They were already standing on the summit, and the only direction left was down.

There was a second reason why he clasped her to him. He had been trying to slow her down. He could not go on at this pace much longer, and the climax when it came would be in a very real sense the end, at least for now—he wanted what was happening never to end—the closeness might end too, or at least be diminished. At the same time he was aware of the clock on the bedside table—he did not think she was. How long would that service last? How much time did they have?

But he could not hold her, she reared up again. "You're so handsome," she said. "And I'm so in love with you, and I'm so glad my first man was you."

He grasped both her breasts, a way of holding on to her in the most personal way he could think of, and let her do what she was doing, almost let her go on too long so that at the end he was obliged to cry out in a sudden panic:

"Get off, get off."

She did, just in time, and crouched beside him watching what happened next, the arching silver spurts that came down beside his navel. For a moment Davey was embarrassed that she should witness this most intimate male act, which he had never before performed before an audience; perhaps he thought she would be revolted.

Instead she seemed awed, fascinated, could not take her eyes off it, and when the spasms stopped she put her forefinger into the puddle that had formed and stirred it around.

"Well," she said, "well."

A moment later she too glanced at the clock. "Oh, my God," she said, and jumped to her feet. "Help me make the bed."

He did, after which she grabbed up her clothes and ran into the bathroom. Davey did likewise, running in after her. There were no secrets between them now. He watched her soaping a washcloth. She washed her face, her hands, she washed between her legs. To be alone with her while she did this seemed to him as intimate as anything yet. He watched her dry herself and dress and go out.

He soon followed.

They were sitting on opposite sides of the big room when the family came back from church.

Norma Favert gazed from one face to the other. Their pose did not seem normal to her, and neither did Rachel's cheeks, which looked a bit roughened, as if scrubbed by someone's face. Norma sniffed the air. She frowned.

There were questions she looked ready to ask that Rachel did not want asked. To forestall them, the girl said brightly: "The doctor came."

"How long was he here?"

"I don't know. A good long time, wasn't he, Davey."

"Yes he was."

"Maybe an hour," lied Rachel.

"I see."

Rachel was speaking in English, Norma Favert in French.

"He took the cast off. Show your leg, Davey."

The obedient Davey did so.

"See," said Rachel triumphantly. "He can walk now and every-thing."

Still gazing from one to the other, Norma nodded.

"He still limps a little, but the doctor said he had healed per-fectly."

The children had trooped through to their rooms or to the kitchen. The pastor had gone into his office, but now, still wearing his cassock and bib, he came out again. He too glanced from

Rachel to Davey to Rachel, back and forth. He too looked suddenly suspicious, and he swept down the hall, glanced into Rachel's room, and breathed the air there.

He was gone only a few seconds, but when he returned his face looked hard.

"Davey's leg has healed perfectly," Rachel told him, "according to the doctor."

"Well then," said the pastor to Davey, "we'll have to think about getting you out of here, won't we?"

With another sweep of his cassock, he turned and went into the kitchen, his wife following, leaving the young couple to gaze at each other in silence.

In the kitchen the pastor said: "What's going on between that boy and Rachel?"

"I'm not sure."

"Something."

"Keep your voice down."

"What's the answer?"

"I don't know."

"Didn't you ask her?"

"They'll hear you."

"I don't care if they hear me."

"The children too."

"Why didn't you ask her?"

"I don't know. I couldn't."

"Ask her now."

"It's not the right moment."

"Before it's too late."

"Please."

"Maybe it's too late already. Is that what you think?"

"I don't know."

"If you won't ask her, I'll ask her." He tore off his bib and threw it down on the table.

"Not until you calm down."

"No, right now."

But as he reentered the living room, with Norma just behind him and hurrying to keep up, there came a banging at the front door.

Not only was it the pastor's practice to keep his door unlocked at all times, but the locals had formed the habit of entering without knocking.

So this wasn't a local.

The banging was repeated.

Not a local, then. Who?

With a jerk of his chin, the pastor sent Davey into the nearest bedroom, waited until he heard the door close, then went to answer.

It was Pierre Glickstein, whom the pastor had never met, but who seemed to him in a state of great agitation, for he started talking at once, a deluge of words that did not make much sense, so that the pastor's first job became to calm him down, find out who he was, what he wanted.

Hearing the ex-forger's voice, Davey had come out of the bedroom. His appearance, to the surprise of the pastor, had an immediate calming effect, for Glickstein first fell silent, and then walked over and shook hands with him.

"You've got the cast off," he said. "How's it going?"

Davey looked to Rachel for a translation.

For a few minutes the two young men conversed via Rachel.

Glickstein turned back to the pastor. "He crashed on our farm," he explained.

"Yes, so I gathered."

"That's what I've been trying to tell you. And finally the snow melted and the *Boches* found the plane and they came and burned the farm down and murdered the farmer."

Halfway through this speech, Glickstein's eyes filled up with tears. "Beat him up and killed him and threw him in the cesspool."

The pastor went over and hugged him.

"Someone has to go out there and get him. And—" The tears were running down the ex-forger's face.

"All right," said the pastor.

"—And then tell his wife. I'm not the right person to do it," sobbed Glickstein. "I'm only nineteen years old."

"Sit down," said the pastor. "We'll all have lunch, and then I'll do what has to be done."

When lunch was over and Glickstein had been sent on his way, the pastor made some phone calls to arrange for fetching the farmer's body. He would have to negotiate with the village carpenter about a coffin, order a grave to be dug, post notices for the funeral. Facing the widow would take longest, so he would do that last.

In the vestibule his wife handed him his hat. His rage, she saw, was over. He sometimes described himself as a violent man conquered by God, but his wife feared his rages and he himself hated them. When angry enough there was almost nothing he would not do or say.

"For as long as that boy remains in this house, Rachel is not to be left alone with him," he said now.

"All right."

He had taken his glasses off and was wiping them. "One or the other of us must be here at all times."

Norma decided to say: "If anything has happened between them, she was willing, I would say."

She saw her husband grimace, and knew how much this new knowledge of Rachel had hurt him, how much talking about it was hurting him now.

"It might not be so easy to find a place for him," he said.

"More than willing," said Norma.

"An enemy pilot is a terrible risk to ask someone to accept."

"She's our daughter," said Norma.

XIX

UNTERSTURMFÜHRER Helmut Haas came up to Gruber
on the sidewalk, gave his name and rank, and saluted. Gruber was
just getting out of his staff car, in fact had barely had time to
straighten up.

This was in front of the Hôtel Terminus, headquarters for Reich
Security. Bicycles went by in the street. Beside the entrance stood
soldiers in helmets, with submachine guns hanging on straps under
their arms.

Haas added: "Reporting for duty, Obersturmbannführer."

Gruber had never seen Haas before and was not expecting him.
They stood on the sidewalk gazing at each other.

In this fifth year of the war manpower was tight. Every unit was
understaffed, every commander demanding more men, none getting them. Gruber had made no request for a new second lieutenant, but evidently this one had just been assigned to him.

Who was he? Who had sent him to Lyon and why? Haas was
working for somebody. As he nodded at him, Gruber asked himself
who? General Rahn in Paris? The Jewish Section in Berlin?

They rode up in the elevator. Young Haas was as tall as Gruber,
more athletic in build, and standing, it seemed to him, too close.

Gruber peered at the floor, or at the insignia on Haas's cap. But the smooth cheeks, the big white teeth were too close, as was the spot of stubble under one ear that Haas's razor had missed. His cologne in that small enclosed space wafted over both of them.

Gruber led the way into the corner office with the flags, sat down in the big chair behind the big desk, and reached for Haas's orders, which the younger man handed across.

Gruber scanned them, but they told him almost nothing.

Reporting to a new command was a formal occasion, though apparently not to Haas, who had wandered over to the window. In the presence of a superior officer, a word from whom might send them to the Russian front, most subordinates would have been standing at attention in front of the desk. But Haas was gazing down on the river and the city.

"Nice view," he commented.

Gruber sat back, hands behind his head as if confident of his stature and his station, which he had been, though suddenly he was less so, and he studied the young man.

"Tell me about yourself."

Haas walked casually toward him, and without being invited, sat down across the desk and crossed his legs. "Where shall I start?"

"How old are you?"

Haas was twenty-three, he said. He was from Dresden, where his father was a trucking executive.

Truck driver, more likely, thought Gruber.

"Nice city, Dresden," said Gruber, and he mentioned a restaurant there, a hotel, the names of acquaintances they did not have in common. He was trying to feel the young man out, but it wasn't working.

"You've got a fine opera company there," he added, for it was one of the places he had once auditioned.

"Fat slobs bellowing at each other," snorted Haas, "most of them Jews."

"Interesting way to put it," said Gruber.

He picked up and scanned Haas's orders still again. They did not tell him what he most wanted to know.

"Where have you served to date?"

"My training, you mean?" It wasn't what Gruber meant at all, but Haas began to describe the SS school at Bad Tölz in Bavaria.

In present company, a neutral subject.

He had loved that place, Haas said. The discipline, the athletics, the idealism. Every recruit a perfect physical specimen, and chosen for that reason. Not even a filling in their teeth. And the code of honor. You could leave money on your cot and know no one would touch it. No other branch of the service had a code of honor as strict as the SS.

Gruber waited impatiently.

Happy times, the happiest, Haas said. The day he got his cere-monial dagger was the proudest of his life. "I imagine it was for you as well, wasn't it?"

And the superb camaraderie in the mess, for they were all young officers together, and about to clean up the world.

He again smiled.

In normal times, an officers' mess was the last place to which men like Haas could have aspired, Gruber reflected.

Haas was blond and blue-eyed, the perfect specimen of Aryan youth, which the dark-complexioned Gruber was not. There was something wrong with his smile, however—perhaps only that his teeth were too big. He looked like he wanted to bite somebody.

"And the girls the uniform attracted," said Haas.

This idea dangled in the silence.

Yes, the girls, reflected Gruber. In normal times, such girls would have been out of reach as well.

He pointed toward the orders on his desk. "You've come here from Holland, it seems."

"Right."

"And before that?" General Rahn, Gruber remembered, had served in Holland before Paris.

"Hey," said Haas, "I'm just a young guy. I haven't been too many places yet."

Gruber studied him, but Haas smiled blandly back.

"What was your assignment in Holland?"

"Same as it will be here, I imagine. Filling trains with Yids." And then, after a silence: "Am I right?"

"Of course," said Gruber.

"Men, women, and children."

"Men, women, and children, as you say."

"Until there are none left."

Gruber said: "What do you suppose happens to them when they get, well, where they're going?"

"That's not our affair, is it?"

Gruber stood up. "Have you found quarters yet?"

"I came directly here."

"See Obersturmführer Muller down the hall. He's the housing officer. Take a day or two to get settled, then come back. We'll see if we can't find something to keep you busy."

Coming around the desk, he gave the young man a big smile, and a handshake, and said: "Welcome aboard."

When Haas had gone out Gruber paced. Had a spy been introduced into his entourage? If so, to whom did he report? But Gruber was perhaps being alarmist. A benign explanation was also possible. Perhaps Haas or his father, even an uncle, had enough influence to ask for cushy duty—Lyon—and get it for him. Perhaps his transfer here did not threaten Gruber at all.

Perhaps.

Gruber needed answers. But he had to try to get them at no risk to his career. There was a man in Berlin who might help. Could he trust this man or not? There was no way to be sure. But answers were imperative.

Returning behind the heavy desk he uncapped his fountain pen, wrote out his message, and that night put it in the pouch to Berlin. To enable him to make best use of his subordinates, the message read, he needed to know everything about each of them. Now there was this new man just assigned, Untersturmführer Helmut Haas. Who was he? How had he got here? A background check would be appreciated—carried out with utmost discretion of course.

A week passed before a reply came back. It was short. Haas's father, formerly a trucker, was a party official in Dresden. Haas himself had joined the Hitler youth at thirteen, the SS at eighteen. At twenty he was on Eichmann's staff in Berlin. Two years later he was transferred to the staff of Rahn, then in Amsterdam. His fitness ratings were of the highest. His reports were considered at all times reliable.

Gruber crumpled the message into his ashtray. His lighter set it afire. While it burned, then smoldered, he sat staring at the far wall, his fingers drumming softly on his desk.

THE farmer's funeral brought much of the village to the temple.

During the pastor's early years in the parish, Sunday congregations were usually small. Though the people still professed to be Protestant, they had lost the habit of attending services. The war had changed that. Attendance was up overall, and village tragedies, such as the death of the farmer, filled every pew, filled the aisles, filled much of the small square outside, and the doors had to be flung open so that people outside could hear.

After appropriate hymns had been sung, and appropriate verses read, the pastor in his cassock and bib mounted to the pulpit, where he spoke of the dead farmer in the light of the pacifism and nonviolence he himself had always preached in the past. Pacifism was not passivity, he said. The nonviolence he had always urged upon them, and urged again today, was not passive, it was an almost brutal force for awakening human beings. The farmer murdered by the Nazi oppressors had borne no arms, had done harm to no one, but had borne witness to what was true and good, had resisted evil even though it had cost him his life.

Resistance without violence was both possible and practical, the pastor preached, and it was the only way to find goodness. Resistance, in order to be valuable, had to be achieved through struggle against the forces of humiliation and death that are part of mankind. The farmer had struggled, and he had lost that struggle. The cost of goodness is sometimes death. But the cost of evil is always death. Decent people who stayed inactive out of cowardice or indifference when human beings all around them were being humiliated and destroyed were the most dangerous people in the world.

"Just as the hardest metal yields to sufficient heat," he preached, "the hardest heart must melt before the sufficiency of the heat of nonviolence."

A sermon, if it was any good, was a two-way communication. He looked down and saw people with tears in their eyes, and knew his message had seized them the way music sometimes seized its listeners, knew also that they would go on with the struggle. How could the Nazis ever get to the end of the resources of such people as these, he asked himself.

"A curse on him who wishes only to be passive and therefore safe," the pastor concluded. "He shall finish in insipidity and cowardice, and shall never set foot in the great liberating current of Christianity."

Most of the congregation followed the farmer's coffin down the hill and into the cemetery, and along the gravel path between the headstones.

As soon as the farmer had been lowered into the hole the pastor drew aside first one member of his presbyterial council, and then others, asking each one if he and his wife might be willing to give shelter to still another hunted individual. All these people had taken in refugees in the past, and some still housed entire families. He made no attempt to trick them, quickly explaining that the individual in question was not an ordinary refugee, but was an American pilot.

You mean the one the Gestapo searched the entire village for the other day? they asked him.

Yes.

One and all they refused him. Some said they simply had no room. Some said they could not take Davey because it would endanger refugees already living with them. Some were simply afraid, though they did not say so. Some asked where Davey had been hidden, and suggested that the Gestapo would not give up, would come looking for him again.

All agreed that the best thing would be to get the pilot to Switzerland or Spain immediately.

Impossible, said the pastor, the pilot still limped badly. He would be a danger to himself and to his guide, and if he were caught it would compromise the entire escape network.

Turn him over to the Maquis, was the next suggestion. Let the Maquis cope with him.

Out of the question, said the pastor, for the Maquis had begun to blow up trains and troop convoys. They were killing Germans, and he refused to be part of it.

Then the best thing, they told him, was to keep the pilot in the presbytery another week or two until he was fully healed, and then guide him to Switzerland or Spain.

All this time Rachel and Norma stood together across the graveyard, both watching him, though with different emotions. Rachel had wanted to stay in the presbytery with Davey but had been made to come to the funeral. She was certain now that her foster parents knew everything—how they knew she could not imagine—and that an attempt would be made to separate her permanently from Davey.

Norma kept glancing at the girl from the corner of her eye, trying to discern how far this romance had gone, and what was to happen next.

Having talked to five of his council members, all of them unwilling to accept Davey, the pastor had decided to stop there, lest rumors start floating through the village. The five he had talked to could be trusted to tell no one, he believed. The secret was safe with them, he was sure of it.

He came over to where Rachel and Norma were standing under the bare branches of a tree. Although he said nothing, it was understood by both women that Davey would not be moving out of the presbytery just yet—news that brought a repressed smile to Rachel's young face, and that made Norma frown. The pastor took both their arms and led them out of the graveyard.

Suddenly the sound of music was heard coming from the center of the village.

Everyone looked up sharply.

Among the German soldiers convalescing in the requisitioned hotel were a number of amateur musicians, who had formed the habit of giving Sunday afternoon concerts on the market square. These were just young men, some of them still teenagers, all of whom had been badly hurt in the war, and it was assumed that their concerts constituted an attempt to curry favor with the people of the village. Attendance at their concerts was always sparse: curious children mostly. But the music could be heard in the houses, and sometimes people left their windows open to hear better.

Not today. Since it was not a Sunday, the young soldiers must be trying to apologize for the murder of the farmer, which they had had nothing to do with. Their apology was rejected by all. The mourners dispersed. Not one went anywhere near the market square, nor did their children, whom they gathered up on the way by. Their windows and doors they shut tight. There was no one at all on the streets. It was as if the German musicians were playing in an empty town, and it was not until the music stopped, and the musicians had returned to their hotel, that the life of the village resumed.

A rap on the back door. Some whispers in the kitchen. Pierre Glickstein lay on his mattress halfway down a row of other mattresses. He was half asleep, when he heard his name—Henri Prudhomme—called in a low voice.

He got dressed in the dark. His few belongings were already tied in a sack, which he slung over his shoulder. He went down the stairs without turning on the light.

In the kitchen waited a young man his own age.

"Henri Prudhomme?" he whispered.

"Yes," said Glickstein.

"Follow me."

The forest came right up to the house. They went out the back door and the trees closed over them. The other youth had a flashlight. Its beam pulled them along. There was some snow under the trees, not much. It gave back enough light for Glickstein, trailing, not to bang into tree trunks.

The forest was about a mile across. On the other side they came out on a road, where the guide held up a hand, stopping them. Most of the roads hereabouts were dirt, but this one was paved so Glickstein guessed it was the D185, which runs north and south. The guide was listening for cars, voices.

There was no sound.

Satisfied, he ran across the road and into another forest, Glickstein at his heels.

In here it was even darker than before, the trees closer together. The forest smelled of sap and pine needles. It was on a slope, and there was no snow. The flashlight was moving fast. The slope got steeper, and the needles underfoot were like glass. A branch lashed Glickstein's face. He could see nothing. Thorns tugged at his pants leg. He bent to unhook himself, then hurried to catch up.

They came out onto a meadow which they crossed, went through a grove of trees and came out onto a narrow dirt road.

"No patrols along roads like this," the guide whispered. "But if you hear anything, get into the bushes or down in the ditch fast."

Above them the moon was thin and pale. They walked along the dirt road for about two kilometers, then went through a gate, which they closed behind them, and crossed another meadow toward a farmhouse. In front of it were some trees, and as they came close a sentry with a gun stepped out of the shadows and challenged them in an accent that Glickstein guessed was from Marseille.

The farm was owned by an old couple who lived in rooms on the ground floor, the guide said; Glickstein did not meet them that night. The Maquis unit lived on the floor above, which had been arranged as a kind of dormitory.

A ladder lay against the side of the farmhouse. It led up to a high window. He followed the guide up the ladder and in through the window.

A single large room. Lanterns for light. A number of other young men stared at him, then came forward to shake hands. Flickering faces. Two were former grade-school teachers in their mid-twenties. The rest were Glickstein's age. All were French, five, he would learn, were Jews, and two were petty thugs who had served time in jail. All of them carried false papers, and were using names that were not theirs, first names only.

Pierre Glickstein, alias Henri Prudhomme, told them he would use the name Pierre. It felt good to hear the sound of his own name again, first as spoken by himself, and then as used by the others, as in:

"Pleased to meet you, Pierre—"

"Take that mattress there, Pierre—"

He counted twelve mattresses aligned in neat rows on the floor, on each of which rested blankets neatly folded into squares, with pillows on top. On the one to which he had been directed he put down his sack. He glanced around looking for guns. There were a number of old fowling pieces neatly stacked, nothing else.

In the center of the room was a large table with benches and chairs around it. The place seemed to him scrupulously clean.

So this was a Maquis camp. It seemed to him indistinguishable from the dormitory he had come from, and he was surprised.

One of the teachers came over. "Call me Bob," he said.

To use an Anglo-Saxon name seemed pretentious to Glickstein, but he nodded.

"That staircase there goes down through the house," the school-teacher said. "We don't use it at night so as not to bother the old couple."

"Okay," said Glickstein.

"Anybody comes, you go out the window, down the ladder, and into the woods. The woods are close, so you have a chance. You come out on the other side onto the D9. After that you're on your own."

Glickstein nodded.

"I noticed you looking at our weapons."

"Well . . ."

"Those things are not good for much."

"No."

"We expect a drop with the next full moon."

"A drop?"

"Parachute drop. From England. Explosives, Sten guns grenades."

"Sten guns?"

"Submachine guns," said the schoolteacher. "The English are arming all the groups. We'll have all the weapons we want."

"What will we do with them?"

"We'll, shall we say, employ them, old man. Employ them."

To the ex-forger this sounded not menacing but pompous. He received the impression that "Bob" was not as tough as he would like others to believe.

Nonetheless, he had the feeling that in coming to this place he had stepped from innocence into darkness.

XX

THE children were doing their homework around the dining room table. In front of the fire Madame Favert sat knitting. The pastor was thumbing through his Bible, looking for verses he could use in next Sunday's sermon.

Rachel said to him: "Davey wants to go out for a walk."

Having closed the Bible, the pastor looked at her. Norma, who had stopped knitting, watched her husband.

Rachel seemed to be holding her breath as she waited for a reply.

"He hasn't been out of this house since he was brought here," Rachel said. "Weeks and weeks. He says he feels like a prisoner." Wrong choice of words. "I mean—" Rachel said.

"I know what you mean."

"So can we?"

"You feel like a prisoner too?" said the pastor coldly.

"No, of course not. But somebody should go with him."

The pastor looked at her.

"It's late," said Rachel. "There'll be no one out at this time of night."

Probably this was true. The villagers were all in bed, or about to go to bed. The hotel that housed the convalescing soldiers was in the upper part of the village. They rarely strayed far from it.

When the pastor remained silent, Rachel added: "Just down to the river and back."

The opposite direction from the hotel. Down past the empty school, the empty temple, one or two empty stores. Only a few houses to pass by. The blackout curtains would be drawn. No one would be looking out the window.

Still, they might be seen.

But if the American was to get rid of that limp and be able to travel he needed exercise. And there was no risk that the "walk" might turn into something sexual. The night was far too cold for making love under the trees.

"Go for your walk," said the pastor. "But down to the river and back only."

Davey wore wooden shoes Norma had found him, and a pair of old corduroy pants. He had the use of an old coat that still had some warmth in it, and the pastor heard him in the vestibule putting it on.

As soon as he and Rachel had gone out, the pastor went to the door where he put on his own coat, hat, and gloves.

His wife stood watching him.

"I'll just go out for a few minutes," the pastor told her.

She looked at him.

"To make sure nothing happens to them."

"What do you think might happen to them?"

Without answering he nodded to her and went out.

The night was dark. Since the arrival of Germans in the village the few streetlights were no longer lit; the blackout was now rigorously observed.

The street outside the presbytery was narrow and very dark. The night was colder than Pastor Favert had thought, and he pulled his coat collar up.

Since he knew where the young couple was supposedly heading, he moved at first downhill along a parallel street. When at last he came out onto the street that led to the bridge there was enough light from the sky to discern them some distance ahead. They walked along holding hands, the boy limping, Rachel's face turned toward him as she talked or listened, and to her foster father she looked happy.

Jumping from doorway to doorway, keeping to the shadows, he followed. At the bridge they sat down on the parapet and he could see the urgings of the river, dark and black as it passed underneath them, even hear it if he listened, though the river was not what he was interested in, he was not even interested in the boy, only in the girl. There were some kisses that lasted, and then for a time the boy still sat on the parapet while Rachel stood before him massaging his bad ankle, his weak calf. Very touching, though not to the pastor. Very soon the boy pulled Rachel toward him and there were additional kisses, and he seemed to have got his hands up under her sweaters, as well.

To the pastor, immorality could only bring unhappiness, even tragedy. It always had and always would. Marriage between these two was never going to be possible, the boy would go away and never come back, couldn't they see that?

The pastor was suffering. He had always known that Rachel must someday marry. But that day had seemed a long way off, she was only eighteen, and he had envisioned a proper suitor, a proper courtship—some fine local lad, perhaps from the theology school—and at the end a proper marriage. This American, this baby-faced seducer, was not suitable in any way. Where had he come from, and why? Rachel, his darling girl. Once again the pastor cursed the war. The war had brought immorality of all kinds. On Rachel's wedding day when he would give her away at the altar—he had imagined the scene many times—he had wanted her still to be chaste, as he himself had been on his wedding day, and as Norma had been. Judging from the ardor of those kisses down there on the bridge, this affair had long since passed from the innocent into the illicit. Was it really too late? He did not know, and he began silently to pray. Whatever had happened had already happened. It was too late to change anything, but perhaps God, knowing his prayer was coming, had answered it in advance. Philosophically, this idea was sound, prayer might still work. But as he begged the Divine Presence to intercede, his prayer sounded thin to him, and he was unable to believe in a God who, having so much else to do these days, would answer it.

From the darkness of the doorway, hidden from the young people below, he stood watching and suffering and did not know what to do. He never got close enough to hear what they were saying, and when they started back, so did he, moving up the parallel street again, and in fact he was inside the presbytery, sitting before the fire when they came in.

OUT in front of the farmhouse, only half hidden by the trees, stood a flagpole. Each dawn Pierre Glickstein and his group, having congregated around it, ran up the flag while singing the Marseillaise.

After that they spent much of each day sitting around the big table playing cards, or chess, and arguing. Their subjects were the classic ones: politics, religion, and girls. Politics was further subdivided into the relative values of democracy, fascism, and communism, especially as exemplified by the present war, and the late Spanish Civil War.

The woods were at their back, but in the event of a raid by the *Boches,* or by the new menace which was in many ways worse, namely the French *Milice,* they would need places to make for, assigned directions in which to disperse. So escape routes were worked out too. What they feared most was betrayal, so from time to time individuals were sent into the villages to nose around, and to pick up what intelligence they could. This "intelligence" amounted to little more than gossip, but they spent a great deal of time weighing it. Who in the villages was sympathetic to the Resistance, and who was not? Who could they depend upon for food? In the event of a raid, who was likely to give them shelter? In this Protestant region, most Catholics were suspect, as were those with Germanic names. Most gendarmes, they came to believe, would aid the Resistance in a pinch, or at least would look the other way. This was not true of the *Milice,* an organized force of French thugs working with and for the Gestapo. The *miliciens,* being French, were able to infiltrate Maquis groups almost at will, could even infiltrate their own.

In the absence of arms, their training consisted of studying maps, and of cross-country marches by compass in the dead of night. These marches, which were triangular in shape, were laid out by the group's leader, Jacques, who was the second of the schoolteachers. The triangles measured about three kilometers to the side, and the men marched as ordered in total silence. This was supposed to accustom them to escaping in the dark if being hunted, or to finding targets in the dark, once they had arms, and targets had been selected.

This training they took seriously at first, more casually later. Once they burst onto a road to surround a mailman on a bicycle. The group's two guns were brandished by the schoolteachers. The others carried branches cut to the approximate heft and length of submachine guns. Their sudden appearance terrified the mailman, who fell off his bike, spilling letters in all directions. They had to apologize to him, help collect the letters, and then offer him a cigarette before fading back into the trees.

Saturday afternoons, avoiding roads, keeping to the woods whenever possible, and to dirt lanes and paths when it was not, they trekked across country to Grandeville, which was the center of the Resistance for the region. The route was long and not straight. There were two single-track railroad tunnels to walk through, and the rocky footpath alongside the river came to seem endless. Each time they came to a major road they hesitated, for this was the point of greatest risk. Finally they would dash across one at a time, as if under fire. At Grandeville they would pick up orders, if any, and supplies, if there had been a drop recently, and also money with which to buy food. During the return trip the sacks on their backs got heavy.

These were twelve healthy young men who got hungry three times a day, and with so little to occupy their time, their principal preoccupation became food: how to find it, how to pay for it. Because they had prices on their heads, or imagined they did, they went out only in pairs, or very small bands, moving as stealthily as possible from farm to farm scrounging. They were under strict orders from Grandeville, who took orders from London, to pay for everything they took—lest they turn the populace against themselves and the Resistance in general. They would reach a farm and ask to buy food, and some of the farmers' wives would sit them down to dinner. Others, being fearful or perhaps only mean, gave them as little as possible—enough to get rid of them. None, as yet, had betrayed them.

Provisions were always short, cigarettes especially, and the day came when the man known as Bob ordered Glickstein and three other youths to go into Leshaies, a village about twenty kilometers away, to rob the government tobacco shop there. It was time for some serious on-the-job training, he said as he handed over the two guns, and besides, they were short of smokes.

To the ex-forger, who did not smoke himself and did not understand the craving of others for tobacco, this raid was armed robbery pure and simple, and he argued against it. They were not supposed to rob people, he said, even the collaborationist government. There might be gendarmes there. Suppose they got into a shootout with French gendarmes? At best they would alert the *Boches* to their existence for no good reason at a time when they were not even armed yet.

He saw the raid as a needless and stupid risk, and said so, but when Bob informed him that he was afraid and a coward, he shrugged and said he would go.

The twenty kilometers proved a long way to walk. They were hungry, thirsty, and footsore, and night was falling before they got there.

They had the two guns. One of them was unloaded, for they had been unable to find bullets that fit it. Glickstein gave it to a youth known as Paul who seemed to him the steadiest of his colleagues. The other, which contained two bullets, Glickstein kept for himself.

Most of the streets of the village were unpaved. All of them seemed curiously empty and they had trouble finding the tobacco shop—at first they missed the sign. It was a stone house in a row of stone houses, and not a store at all. The *buraliste* sold tobacco out of a downstairs room, and the rest was living quarters. They walked past the place twice to make sure they had it located, and to search out possible escape routes, then put bandannas over their faces, and drew their two guns, and the ex-forger banged on the door calling out:

"Maquis, open up."

As he waited, Glickstein's mouth was dry, his heart pounding. It was a superb moment, and he found to his surprise that he was as happy as he had ever been. War makes all sorts of heinous conduct legitimate, even heroic, he told himself, which must be why men love it so much.

There had been no response to his first knock. This time he banged on the door with the butt of his revolver.

But again nothing happened, except that the head of an old woman popped out of an upstairs window next door.

"No one home," she told them. "Everyone's down at the village square watching the magician."

Glickstein thanked her, and they all took their bandannas off. He didn't know what to do next. None of them did. Finally they decided to walk down to the square and watch the show.

There was a good crowd. They stood well back so as not to draw attention to themselves. The magician was a man of about sixty who had not shaved in several days. They watched him pull some feathers out of his sleeve. Then he began to juggle, first three balls, then four. Then he switched to plates. He had four plates in the air at once, but he dropped one, and it smashed. After that he had only three. He had a line of patter as he worked, and some of his jokes were funny. The four boys thought he was a pretty good magician, and when he passed the hat at the finish they dropped in coins.

As the show ended, they stepped into the shadows and waited for the crowd to disperse. When it had, they went back to the tobacco shop.

All the lights were out downstairs.

After putting their bandannas back on and drawing their guns they again banged on the door and called out:

"Maquis, open up."

They heard the *buraliste* coming downstairs. Then the door opened. He was all smiles as he invited them in, got behind the small bar, and poured them out glasses of wine.

After they had drunk to each other's health, he handed over a package of cigarettes and tobacco that he had already prepared for them. It was about the size of a bed pillow and weighed five kilos or more.

They thanked him and went out and started back the way they had come. They were tired, had a long way to go, and they took turns carrying the sack of tobacco, which got heavier and heavier as midnight came and went, and the night advanced.

WHEN the knocking came at his door, the Abbé Rousset had been about to go to bed. He put his cassock back on, the only one he had. It was shiny in some places, stained in others, and it stopped six inches short of his dusty boots, but it was the badge of his office.

He opened his door, saw the two people standing there, and was confused. The girl he recognized, though he had never been introduced to her and was not sure of her name. An extremely pretty girl. From a distance he had watched her grow up. No one had ever told him she was a Jewess, but he supposed she was.

The boy he had never seen before.

He led the young people inside, and invited them to be seated in front of his fire. Not many people knocked at his door anymore. Feeling a momentary rush of importance, he asked politely what it was they wanted.

They wanted, it seemed, to get married.

Rousset's first reaction was surprise. Marriage was a subject that did not normally come up at this time of night. But why come to him? Pastor Favert performed marriages all the time and the girl lived in his house.

It was she who did the talking, though with many hesitations. She was tense, and as she spoke she leaned forward in her chair. The boy said nothing—did not speak French, the priest soon saw—and as he realized this his confusion became consternation, and then fear, which in a moment reached the level of terror. He had watched the Germans search the village, he guessed who this boy must be, and any second he expected to hear the banging on his door that would be the Gestapo.

The Abbé Rousset was sixty-six years old. He was responsible for the spiritual well-being of the faithful of Le Lignon, which amounted to only about two hundred souls, and also for two outlying hamlets whose congregations were even smaller. He was a tall thin man, stooped, sometimes unshaven, often seen with his skirts hiked up, a beret on his head, pedaling along the roads on a bicycle that had seen better days. His church with its handsome square tower dated from the sixteenth century, but the bells were gone from the tower, the church was unheated in winter and it needed repairs he could not afford. He had written the bishop for money, but none came. Every Sunday he took up the collections person-ally—came down from the altar in his vestments—but the receipts were meager. The rectory—his house—was as old as the church, and in winter as cold. Of its many rooms only two were open, and they were furnished with now shabby pieces he had brought with him forty years ago, when he was newly ordained and burned with the true faith.

At the seminary he had hoped for assignment to a big city, or at least to a town of some importance. Instead he had been sent here, which, as far as Catholicism was concerned, might as well have been the desert. The bishop never came to the village. No one did. During those early years he had often requested reassignment. Now he no longer bothered.

There seemed less and less for him to do. With the war the birth-rate had fallen off, meaning fewer baptisms. And with the young men doing forced labor in Germany, or hiding in the Maquis, there were no more marriages. He still officiated at funerals. People still died. But whereas happy parishioners sometimes contributed gen-erously, the thoughts of the bereaved were on eternity, and never mind the temporal needs of their priest.

He was no longer sure he believed in God.

He had had a housekeeper, a stocky peasant woman some years older than himself, a widow who had lived in the rectory, who had cooked his meals, taken care of him when he was sick, and who, inevitably, had sometimes administered to his other needs—these things were understood in France. But she had died. Her replace-ment, also straight off the farm, was much younger, came in only twice a week, and he had not dared approach her.

He still said mass, not only here but also in one or the other of the hamlets in his care, two masses every Sunday, though as he got older the seat of his bicycle seemed to get narrower, the ride harder on his legs. Saying mass was part of his job, as was hearing confes-sions, though few people still confessed. He rarely prayed anymore. Less and less he was asked for counseling. There was no one to talk to, no other priest for many, many kilometers around, too far for a man his age even to ride over and back in a single day. He spent less time preparing his sermons than in the past, and from the pulpit his listeners seemed to him unmoved one way or the other. No one ever thought enough of a sermon to come forward and compliment him. In the pews they stirred, they coughed. Whereas Favert's listeners, he had heard, were spellbound. People were said to copy out his sermons as he spoke, or at least take notes, which afterward passed from hand to hand, and were sent even into distant cities like Nice and Toulouse where, supposedly, groups of people sat around discussing them.

In most of the rest of rural France the village priest was a personage of importance, honored as much for his education as for his holiness, and on the day he had taken up his assignment in Le Lignon, the Abbé Rousset had expected to be received in this way. Being considered close to God, his authority would be recognized by all, he had imagined. He would be the mediator of conflicts, the settler of all disputes both religious and secular. He would be in demand for all the ceremonies, of course, invited into all the houses.

Elsewhere, not here. Here the faithful were outnumbered ten to one by the Protestants, and their priest, namely himself, was outshone by the energetic and charismatic Protestant pastor, who filled all the roles that in another village would have been the priest's. He and Favert knew each other, nodded to each other in passing, but they had never had a theological discussion. Rousset had never been to a Protestant service, and had never been invited to the presbytery.

When the German convalescents had come into the village, the sight of them had pleased Father Rousset, for he knew most would be Catholics, and he was right. They came to mass on Sundays filling two entire pews, they put money in the basket, and from time to time he would look out at them in their Wehrmacht uniforms and feel more important than before.

At the start of the war, when the refugee Jews had first begun to descend on Le Lignon, the foreigners first, and then the French ones, Favert had asked him if he would be willing to try to find homes for them among his parishioners, sheltering certain of them in the rectory in the meantime, for he had rooms upstairs that were never used.

Sheltering Jews was the last thing he wanted to do. He had replied that he would not consider it, that he would do nothing to hurt those people but that he would not help them either, and he did not understand why Favert wanted to do it, since they were not of his faith. Furthermore, the law was plain. To help them was against the law.

"All right," Favert had said, and that was the end of it, and Rousset had breathed a sigh of relief.

Thereafter he had sometimes gone up to the station to watch the trains come in, and there stood Favert, together with other Protestant pastors from miles around, and as the refugees got down from the train, some of them with baggage, others destitute, the pastors would greet them, and distribute them among themselves and go off with them. Not only would they be placed among the farms, but forged documents would be given to them, he had heard, even money to live on. This had been dangerous enough during the early years of the war when the Germans stayed above the demarcation line. It had become many times more dangerous after they occupied the entire country. But the pastors had continued to shelter Jews.

The Abbé Rousset had been certain that the law—the Gestapo, if not the Gendarmerie—would crack down on such illegal practices, crack down hard. The pastor would be arrested, he expected, and once this happened, there would be a void which he, the Abbé Rousset, perhaps would fill, assuming at last what he had always felt to be his rightful place in the village.

But in the meantime he noted that some people pretended not to see him when they walked by him in the street, that shopkeepers no longer greeted him with smiles, or wished him a cheerful *bonjour.* The subject of the refugees no longer came up in his presence, nor were any other of the village secrets mentioned where he might overhear. Gradually the realization came to him that, despite all the years he had lived among these people, he was not trusted, had become an outcast. But he had always been an outcast in this place, had he not?

Meanwhile the law had cracked down on no one. True, there

had been a botched raid or two, but Jews were never found. They were too widely dispersed, too deft at escaping with all their belongings into the woods, and hiding until the raid was over. Always they had been warned in time—how he did not know.

But finally Favert and his assistant, Henriot, and the headmaster as well, had been sent to a concentration camp, exactly as the Abbé Rousset had been expecting for so long.

He still didn't know how they had got out of that camp. They were certainly guilty. There was no question that they had broken the law. Everyone knew it. They hadn't even made any effort to hide it. And yet they had somehow been let out.

And some Jews were living in the village quite openly and were not molested—for instance this girl across from him who wanted to get married.

All this time, as the firelight flickered back and forth across her face, she had been making what was almost a speech. Focused on Davey, whose name he did not yet know, Rousset had heard hardly a word. An escaped pilot. An escaped pilot in his house! With the Gestapo perhaps already outside the door.

At first Rousset's terror had immobilized him, rendered him speechless too. As soon as he could move again he had rushed forward to pull shut the blackout drapes—they were already shut. But some minutes had now passed. There had been no pounding on his door. He could hear no commotion outside in the streets. No Gestapo agents were quartered in Le Lignon. It was so late at night that probably they were not coming.

The girl's speech sounded rehearsed to Rousset, but not well enough. She kept forgetting her lines and having to go back and start again.

In fact Rachel too was scared. She knew this man was not trusted in the village. Suppose he went to the Germans? Or even to the pastor.

Having come to the end of her speech, she said: "So will you do it? Will you marry us?"

The priest's diminished fear gave way to rising self-importance. He was God's man in Le Lignon, and must be reckoned with. His hands smoothed his stained cassock. "One cannot get married in an hour."

ROBERT DALEY

"How long does it take?"

"There are formalities."

"How long?"

"You have not thought this out."

"Yes we have."

"I don't think so."

"But we have."

"For instance, there is a war on."

"Yes, that's why we don't want to wait."

Phrases from the seminary came back to him, and he brought them out. "Marriage is for a lifetime."

"We know you have to have papers."

"One does not marry on a whim."

"We may not be able to get them all."

"A hasty marriage would not be prudent—"

"We have been as prudent as we can."

"And it would not be legal."

She was a very pretty girl. But she had to learn to face hard truths.

"We want to get married." She looked ready to cry. "We're already married."

He stood up dismissively. "Then you do not need me."

"Please."

Some of Rousset's fear had seeped back. He wanted them out of his house. He had never had any intention of helping them. He said: "There are legal impediments to this proposed marriage, and also religious ones. You are pregnant?"

The girl did not answer.

"Do you speak English?" the boy interjected. His face had been jerking from the girl to the priest and back again.

"A leettle."

It was Davey, over Rachel's objections, who had brought them here. Getting married, to him, meant before a priest, and the pastor, he judged, would never have consented to do it anyway. To Davey, priests were men you could trust. All priests, though in the face of this scruffy old man he now had doubts.

Because of these doubts, his voice came out harder than he intended. "Then let's speak English."

"You are the *Americain* pilot?"

Davey kept silent. The priests he was used to were clean-shaven, they wore clean cassocks, their shoes gleamed.

Rousset waited for an answer, but when it did not come he explained the law. Sometimes his English faltered and he asked Rachel to translate. In France the legal marriage was the civil one. Banns had to be posted three weeks in advance. One had to present documents: birth certificate, police certificate, etc. Since foreigners needed to prove themselves free to marry according to the laws of their own country, a paper to this effect was required from the foreigner's embassy. When all was in order, one went to city hall, made the vows before the mayor, and signed the register. One was now officially married. The religious marriage came afterward, sometimes the same day, sometimes the following day, and was for religious purposes only.

He saw the young couple trying to digest this.

"You speak to the Pastor Favert, he tell you the same."

"But you could perform the marriage ceremony," said Davey. "And give us a certificate to that effect."

Rousset imagined a paper floating around with his name on it, joined to that of an escaped pilot—the idea brought on a new bout of terror. If found, and such a paper would be found eventually, he would be arrested, deported, perhaps shot.

"In a religious sense we would be married."

"It would not be legal."

"It would prove that we love each other and were trying to do the right thing. It would be legal before God, and before my parents and hers. If that's the best we can have, that's what we'll take."

"You are *Catholique*?"

"Yes."

"And the . . . lady." Lady was the wrong word, but he had not been able to think of the word *girl*. "*Catholique* also?"

"No."

"Israelite?"

"That's neither here nor there."

"The church has the laws too. Before marriage the lady must take the instructions, promise to bring up the children in the true faith."

"He's not going to help us," said Davey to Rachel.

"No."

"Let's go."

In its way, the marriage of these two was attractive to the Abbé Rousset. To spite Pastor Favert. Behind the back of Pastor Favert. To perform it would have been a delight. Favert would be furious. If it had not been for the Gestapo . . .

He showed them out. When they were gone he parted the drapes slightly, stood well back so as not to be seen, and watched them through the window.

The young couple stood in his courtyard embracing. The girl had her head on the boy's chest. There was no kissing or fondling, just the embrace. It lasted a long time, but finally, hand in hand, they left.

Coming to him was a terrific risk, which they must have known. Who was to say that he would not hand them over to the Germans? Certainly the Germans would like to have them both, the one a Jewess, the other an escaped pilot.

There were arguments for turning them in, Rousset reflected. Their arrest and imprisonment would end the state of sin, the climate of fornication, in which they currently lived, and in the sight of God this would be a very good thing. More important, it would protect the village from the inevitable reprisals when the Germans found the pilot on their own—as they surely would find him in time. How much longer would it take them, a day, a week? When they did find him they would turn on the village that had harbored him, and they would destroy it. They would not leave two stones standing. As they had done elsewhere, they would perhaps massacre every inhabitant as well, himself included.

The priest went to bed. His great fear had tired him. He was too tired to think any more about this tonight. He would think about it in the morning.

XXI

At Grandeville the next Saturday Glickstein found that a man had been parachuted in from England some nights previously with orders to take command of all of the Maquis groups in the region. He was said to be a former French naval officer, and he went by the name of Eugene.

There had been a supply drop as well.

Grandeville was the biggest of the encampments. The men lived in the woods under white tents made from English parachutes. This afternoon other parachutes lay piled about, together with boxes the size of steamer trunks, some of them open. Most of the men Glickstein saw were wearing new shoes.

The members of Glickstein's section were made to wait while Eugene drew them off to be interviewed one by one.

"They tell me you are an expert forger," Eugene said, when Glickstein's turn came.

"Who told you?"

"Someone."

The new commander was a small, tightly knit man about forty years old.

"And that you're from Le Lignon."

"I've spent some time in Le Lignon, yes."

Their backs against trees, they sat facing each other at the edge of a clearing in the woods. Over Eugene's shoulder Glickstein could see all those open boxes and he wondered what was in them.

"If we need documents, can you make them?"

Glickstein realized that his credentials were being examined. He had not seen Eugene's, and would not. He wondered if anyone had. Maybe he had been parachuted in not from London but from Berlin. At nineteen years of age the ex-forger had learned to live in a world that was suspect. You trusted no one.

"Anyone can make documents, with a little training."

Eugene waited, but when Glickstein only studied him, he nodded.

"A plane went down in your village."

"The *Boches* found it."

"They didn't find the pilot, I'm told."

"Not that I heard."

"Is he alive or dead?"

Glickstein decided to say: "Alive."

"How can you be sure."

Glickstein decided to say: "I saw him."

The man known as Eugene waited, but the ex-forger, watching him, remained silent.

"Could you get a message to the pilot?"

Each response required a decision. Glickstein said: "Who wants to get a message to him?"

"London."

"Why?"

Eugene began to show a certain exasperation. "Because he's an experienced pilot. If he can fly, they want him back."

"They must have plenty of pilots."

"Not experienced ones. There's an invasion coming. They need all they can get."

Glickstein said nothing.

"Besides, they always rescue their pilots, if they can."

Glickstein still said nothing.

"So what is he, alive or dead?"

"Tell them he's alive."

"I need to tell them more than that."

"His name's David Gannon. You want the numbers off his plane?"

"Yes."

Glickstein gave them from memory, and Eugene wrote them down.

"Tell them he was hurt," the ex-forger said, "but he's better now."

"Well enough to travel?"

"Travel where?"

"Here, for instance. If they decide to send a plane for him."

"I think so."

In the place where they sat the ground was dry, but out in the clearing the sun glittered off patches of still-white snow.

Glickstein gazed toward the open boxes, the piled parachutes. He believed he had revealed too much of himself to back off now. Either Eugene was who he pretended to be or he was not. The ex-forger said: "If you're going to command these groups you need to exert control, and you need to do it now."

Eugene looked at him.

"For one thing, security is extremely sloppy."

Eugene nodded.

"The men are playacting. They think this is all a lark. They fall asleep on watches, they wander around the villages for no good reason, and they talk too much. I've stayed alive this long by being careful. I don't want to be done in because one of these jerks gets caught and starts to blab."

Eugene said nothing.

"When is the invasion?" demanded Glickstein.

"Even if I knew I couldn't tell you."

"All right. Last week they gave us six guns. When do we get the rest?"

"Soon."

"In the meantime the men have nothing to do. They sit around plotting stupidities, and as soon as they get more arms they're going to start doing them."

When Eugene made no reply, Glickstein said: "We need someone in control here. Is that you?"

Eugene did not answer.

After a moment Glickstein said: "We need to know exactly what we're doing. There has to be an overall plan. Acts of sabotage must be committed far from any village. Attacks on armed troops the same. And we should wait until we know the invasion is coming, and then all of us attack together."

Eugene regained his feet. "I've enjoyed talking to you," he said, shaking hands. "I'll take what you've said under advisement."

Convinced that the man hadn't heard a word, Glickstein followed him out into the clearing.

"I brought some supplies in with me," Eugene said over his shoulder. "Why don't you pick out whatever you need."

The ex-forger walked over to the open trunks. The parachute drop must have been considerable, four or five chutes, maybe more.

Glickstein peered down at medical supplies in one trunk, blankets in another. In a third were stacks of shoes in many sizes in unopened boxes as if on their way from the factory to a store. A fourth contained sweaters, together with banded sheafs of French money that no one was watching very closely.

Glickstein returned to the trunk of shoes. It had been years since he had owned a pair of real shoes. The ones he was wearing had leather uppers, wooden soles. By now he had grown calluses in all the places where they had chafed his blisters raw. The boxes were stamped "Thom McAn," and he rummaged through them for his size, but when he withdrew the ones he had selected he saw that the same logo was burned into the inner soles as well.

How could they have been so stupid as to send us shoes like this, he asked himself. New shoes were like headlights in France. They attracted attention, and if a man were picked up wearing American shoes, he was not going to talk his way out of it.

He tossed the shoes back into the trunk.

"What's the matter," asked one of the teachers at his elbow, "can't find your size?"

"I prefer my sabots," said Glickstein. He wanted to add: and if you have any sense you'll do the same. However, he kept silent. He thought the idea might come to the schoolteacher by itself, but apparently it did not.

Glickstein brought his misgivings to Eugene, whose reaction was to laugh. "Let them have their new shoes, for chrissake," he said.

After lunch and a distribution of money, the group shouldered the heavy packs and started back, the many pairs of new shoes shining brilliantly in the sun. Glickstein in the lead set a fast pace, trying to open up distance between himself and the others, just in case. However, they all kept up.

The next afternoon the two schoolteachers and their shoes were arrested in Le Pin, a hamlet that happened to have a post office. They were inside mailing a letter when a German staff car pulled up for the same purpose.

It was midnight before the news reached Glickstein. Someone had come to warn the farmer, who was asleep below; the farmer came upstairs and woke Glickstein. At once the ex-forger took over leadership of the group, roused everybody, and within ten minutes they had cleared out: food, blankets, guns, new shoes—everything. Glickstein took them into the woods for the night, and the next day they established camp at an abandoned farm ten kilometers away.

When Saturday came they all trekked to Grandeville again, where the ex-forger's leadership was confirmed by Eugene. In the interim there had been a delivery by the RAF. The plane—the RAF had begun using Lockheed Hudsons for landings in France—had landed in a field halfway between the Grandeville encampment and the farm where Glickstein's group was encamped. An "adviser" and a radio operator had got off. Both were English, and the radio operator—piano players, they were called in the Maquis—was a woman in her late twenties. Glickstein was introduced to them both, and was unimpressed, for they had only serviceable French; if they got caught. He looked over the gear they had brought with them: receiver, transmitter, batteries. Big cumbersome contraptions, difficult to hide or to move. Also, the plane had carried boxes of arms and ammunition, mostly submachine guns and grenades, but also some trench mortars and bazookas, and a share of all this was distributed to Glickstein's group. He was given two more men and sent back to his new encampment to await further orders.

He began to drill his men as best he could. Firing practice was out of the question; he stopped it after less than five minutes, for they didn't have all that much ammunition, and the noise the Sten guns made was overpowering. But he made them take the guns down many times, and put them together again. They practiced ripping one magazine out, and ramming in a full one in its place. Neither the bazooka nor the mortar could be shot off for the same reasons. Nor could live grenades be tossed around; the boys had to be satisfied with finding rocks of equivalent weight, and they simulated pulling the pins, counting off the seconds, then tossing them toward targets in a field.

Most of his men, Glickstein saw, were not satisfied with this training, and a few of them after a day or two refused to take part in it. This dissatisfied group didn't see why training was necessary. They wanted live action. They wanted to attack Germans, and the sooner the better, and they began to try to stir up the others, and one of the messages that passed among them, and that Glickstein overheard, was that "Pierre," namely himself, was a Jew and a coward and not fit to lead them.

IN Lyon that morning, Obersturmbannführer Gruber had received two letters, and with them problems.

The first that he opened was from his wife. It informed him that his son was gravely ill. The doctor had diagnosed meningitis, but admitted it was perhaps polio. All Berlin hospitals were below ground now, and the boy was in one of them, safe from the bombings but in intensive care. His wife was sick with worry, and Gruber, as he read the letter, considered asking for emergency leave.

He loved his children and missed them. Their pictures were on his desk.

But the war had reached a stage of great seriousness, no leaves were being granted right now, and he was needed where he was. It seemed obvious to him, and he hoped it would seem obvious to his wife, that even if he did go to Berlin, there was nothing he could do for the boy except sit and hold his hand. And with the Americans now controlling the sky, not only bombing German cities at will but bombing everything that moved on the roads as well, it was no sure thing he could get home and back alive.

Besides which, there was too much hanging over him here. The pressure on him—from Berlin, from Paris—was enormous. To leave Lyon within the next few hours would be, he believed, to risk throwing away everything he had gained so far in this dirty war. Jeopardize it all. It was the wrong time to go.

Also, it seemed clear to him that Claire Cusset, if he went away for a week, would not be there when he returned. Someone else, in his absence, would have snagged her.

The second letter in the same mail seemed to him even more ominous. It was anonymous, and had been forwarded down from the office of General Rahn in Paris. It claimed that thirty or more Jews were living openly in Le Lignon in a building known as the House of the Rocks. In the margin General Rahn had scrawled: "Did you know about this? If not, why not? Why has nothing been done?"

Reading this, he was of course shaken. Also, he was further convinced that he could best serve his family by staying where he was. His rank and command status here gave him the power to protect his family back home. In Berlin, even from this considerable distance, people were afraid of the Gestapo, and the SS. A month ago, for instance, he had been able to move Marta and the children from downtown out into the suburbs, out from under most of the bombs, if not all. The important thing was to continue to be able to protect them. Lose his job here and who knew what might happen to them.

He put aside Rahn's not-so-veiled threat, and sat down and wrote a long emotional letter to his son. The child didn't read yet. His mother could read it to him. He felt a bit better when he had signed and sealed it. He felt that he had behaved as a caring father.

With that much out of the way he turned back to the anonymous letter, this ax that hung over his head.

There must be pressure on Rahn too. Gruber didn't care about pressure on Rahn, except as it spilled over onto himself, which of course it had just done. Berlin's Jewish Section was leaning on

Rahn, and Rahn was leaning on him. The Fatherland was perhaps losing the war, things did not look good right now, but Berlin seemed able to think only about Jews. However many trainloads of Jews were sent east, it was never enough. There had never been that many Jews in France, the French had become extremely stubborn about giving them up, and hardly any of those who were left could now be found. Yet he, and men like him, the entire SS/Gestapo in fact, were expected to work night and day to find them. Meanwhile, trains were being destroyed by American planes. The Wehrmacht needed the few trains left for moving troops and supplies, but the Jewish Section wanted them for the movement of Jews. It was a constant struggle to see who was going to get the trains, but the Jewish Section almost always won. It made no sense, but an officer who valued his career did not ask questions, he did what he was told.

Gruber kept staring at the anonymous letter. He would have to go into Le Lignon and clean out the House of the Rocks, but how, when? He knew there were many other Jews hidden in the village, but they would not be easy to find, and if he failed—another failure by him—it might become known. With Rahn's spy, Untersturmführer Helmut Haas, just down the hall it would certainly become known. Better to concentrate on this House of the Rocks, which at the moment was all Rahn was looking at.

Gruber saw how he could make use of Haas, and at the same time protect himself.

In the several weeks since Haas had been assigned to him. Gruber had sent him from unit to unit, keeping him busy, keeping him distant. "Orientation's what you need," he had told him. "When you've learned who everyone is and what we do here, that will be time enough to move you into something operational."

Now he called Haas into his office. With the young man standing across the desk, he ordered him to lead a raid on a building in Le Lignon known as the House of the Rocks, which was full of Jews. Localize the building, select his men, plan their deployment, line up transport, decide on the day and hour. "When you've done all that, come back to me for further instructions."

"Very good, Obersturmbannführer."

"Your first assignment," Gruber told him unctuously. "Do well, and there will be others."

The young man was not gazing out the window now.

"I like to groom my young officers," said Gruber.

He did not show the anonymous letter with its notations in General Rahn's hand, nor did he mention it.

"Thank you, Obersturmbannführer. You can count on me."

Haas returned two days later with a plan prepared down to the most minute detail, and a topographical map of the Le Lignon area that he unfolded on Gruber's desk. Haas's finger moved over the map. The House of the Rocks was here, he said, the access roads were here, the men would be deployed here.

"Very good," said Gruber, peering over his shoulder. "What's your time schedule?"

"We go in Sunday morning, ten A.M.," Haas said. "They'll be fewer people around. And also—"

"Also what?"

"There's less chance of mistaken identity. Anyone not in church at that hour, you know he's a Yid."

"You don't have to be a Jew to skip church on Sunday," commented Gruber.

"During a war, except for Yids, everyone goes to church," Haas said decisively. "I know I do. Don't you?"

"Of course," said Gruber. He studied the young officer for a time, then nodded, okaying the plan. "Looks good to me," he said.

Haas began folding his map and papers.

"This is your show," Gruber told him. "I want you to understand that. You're in charge. At the same time I'd like to go with you, if I may."

"Of course, Obersturmbannführer." Haas looked surprised. "I always expected you'd be there."

"In case my superior experience should be of help to you."

"Yes sir. Thank you, Obersturmbannführer." Haas snapped him a salute and went out.

Gruber went back behind his desk and sat down. Given General Rahn's personal interest in the case, he could not afford not to be there. If the raid failed and he were not there, Rahn would sack him. This way, if it failed—it should not fail, but if it did—then some of the blame had been spread onto Rahn's boy, Haas.

Gruber looked across the desk at the photo of his sick child. After a moment he picked it up, held it in his two hands. "I hope the boy will be all right," he said aloud, and brought the frame to his lips and kissed the glass.

A pub in a village sixty miles north of London. Joe Toft in uniform sat at the bar. Outside it was raining. Around him people drank, talked, smoked, getting up from time to time for refills at the bar. The publican knew all their names, but not Toft's. A corner fireplace in which burned a generous fire. A damp, chilly country, but a warm room. The essence of England. Walls slick from old smoke. Rafters that had turned black. Oak tables that were old and scarred. The plink of darts striking the board. The pub was two villages from the base, which was fine with Toft. It was too far to pedal, and the men had no cars, so his was the only uniform in the place. Toft himself had hitched a ride in a lorry—the Brits' word for truck.

The village was actually quite big. Big enough to have an inn, in which Toft had booked a room, and he nursed a warm beer and watched the dart game across the room, and waited for the woman.

"Another lager, Mate?"

It was the publican at his elbow.

"I don't much care for warm beer," said Toft.

"Blokes here prefer it that way."

"Yes, I know."

"Have something else. Have a dry martini."

"In England they're warm too."

"Put a cube of ice in it for you."

"No thanks."

"You Yanks," said the publican, and moved off.

The dart players were middle-aged. Farmers, probably. Half the farms hereabouts had been taken over and made into air bases, a few with paved runways, most of them grass.

The door opened, and the woman came into the pub. Toft went

to the door to greet her. He took her coat and umbrella and hung them on one of the pegs. She had a hat, the brim sweeping up on one side, down on the other, and he hung that too, then led her to a table.

"Did you come in a car?"

"Yes. Why do you ask?"

"If you had said no, I was wondering how I was going to get back to the base."

"I just got here, and already you're thinking of leaving."

Remembering his hotel room, Toft laughed. "Please don't misunderstand me. What can I get you?"

"I'll have a dry martini."

"A warm dry martini?"

"Yes, is that so terrible?"

"Not at all."

She seemed much less formidable here than in her office, so he was emboldened to say what at the moment he felt: "You really are a good-looking woman."

"Thank you," she said, but she had frowned first.

As he went to the bar for her drink, he worried about what to call her. He didn't want to get his head snapped off.

He came back with the martini.

"You've been promoted since I saw you last," the woman said, nodding at the insignia on his shoulders. "Congratulations."

"Thank you."

"How old are you?"

The question surprised Toft. Before answering, he wondered if she would immediately think him too young and lose interest.

"Why do you want to know?"

"I just wondered how old the Americans think lieutenant colonels ought to be these days."

The congratulations had sounded sincere, followed immediately by what sounded like sarcasm.

"I'm twenty-six," said Toft, adding a year. He had recently been decorated by General Eisenhower personally, and was beginning to be impressed with himself as a war hero.

She smiled and nodded.

He assumed she was interested in him, which was why he had

booked the room. Why else would she have come this far? "How about you?" he asked.

"How old am I? I think we'll keep that a secret a little longer." But she smiled.

"Do you want me to go on calling you Miss Tompkins?" said Toft. "I mean, this is kind of a date, isn't it?"

"I hadn't thought of it quite that way. A dinner date, perhaps. Vera. Call me Vera."

"Vera," said Toft, trying the name for size. "A name I've always liked."

"Is it indeed?"

"We can have dinner here, Vera. If you think it will be okay."

"Here will be fine."

"Cheers. Happy days!" said Toft, raising his glass to her, though to him such a toast sounded stilted. Always had and always would, but that's how the English did it.

"Anyplace would be better than the food in the mess," he said.

"I'm sure."

"Well, it really isn't that bad."

In the background was the noise of the darts striking the board.

"The reason I called you," said Vera, "is because I have news of your friend." And she paused and studied him.

"Yes, yes. Don't hold me in suspense. Go on."

"First I need you to acknowledge that nothing we do or say to each other goes any further. You repeat nothing to anyone."

Was this in any way a veiled reference to what might happen later? What Toft hoped would happen later? "Yes, of course," he said.

"I shouldn't be telling you any of this. I don't know why I am, actually."

"Please," said Toft.

"David R. Gannon, is that his name?"

"Yes."

"He's alive, and apparently well."

"That's terrific news, absolutely terrific."

"Yes, I thought it would please you."

"It's just great. Wow."

"He has managed to keep from being taken prisoner."

"Better and better."

"We know where he is and can make contact with him at any time."

"Can I inform the squadron, inform his parents?"

"What was it you just agreed to?"

"It would mean such a lot to them to know."

"I shouldn't have come here."

"Especially his parents."

"I shouldn't have told you anything."

"I gave you my word, and I'll keep my word."

"Then I suggest you let the notifications happen through channels in the normal way."

"Even apart from what you just told me, I'm glad you're here." And he put his hand over hers on the table.

She withdrew it at once.

He went to the bar to get more drinks: another warm martini for her, a stiff scotch and soda for himself. He set them down on the table, took his chair, raised his glass and again said: "Cheers."

She sipped thoughtfully at the martini.

"Can you get him out of France?" Toft asked.

"Your pilot?"

"Yes."

"There may be something."

"What does that mean?"

"Don't push me," she said sharply.

"I don't mean to push you. It's just that— If you're suggesting that a mission might be sent in there to get him, I want to be the pilot."

"Why?"

"Because Gannon's one of my men."

"It's out of the question."

"Why?"

"The planes come from the Royal Air Force, complete with pilots. Every time we ask for the loan of one of their planes it's a major battle to get them to give us one. The generals don't believe they need the French Resistance, and so they don't believe in what we do. They don't want to fly our flights at all. They're not going to let some foreigner come in and take over one of their planes."

"In this context, I'm not exactly a foreigner."

"Yes you are."

With two warm beers and a stiff scotch inside him, Toft thought of himself more in the guise of a war hero.

He said: "Do me this favor. If you bring him out, let me at least be there when he lands."

"Why?"

"Let me bring him the rest of the way home. It will be good for the morale of the squadron, the group, the wing."

"I can't promise you anything at all."

The drinks seemed to have made her edgy. They had made him amorous, so he decided to change the subject. "You don't wear a wedding ring."

"I'm not married."

"Why not?"

She said: "We'd best eat dinner, and then I must be getting back."

"I thought you were off duty."

"There's always something."

The conversation was not heading in the direction Toft wished. He said: "You mustn't be in such a hurry. We still have a long way to go together." And he gave her what he meant to be a comical leer.

"Let's eat, shall we."

She got up and he followed her to the bar where the bill of fare was written on a chalkboard. Toft was a small, tightly knit young man. Standing in front of him she was almost as tall as he was. There was a broad belt around her narrow waist, and below that a skirt that flared over smooth hips and a nicely rounded bottom.

"Roast beef with Yorkshire pudding," she said to the publican.

"Me too," said Toft.

They stood at the bar waiting for their dishes. Toft could not think what to say to take the edge off her, warm her up.

He decided on: "English roast beef is pretty good usually."

"How gracious of you to say so."

"I like it, anyway."

"There are still one or two things the English know how to do. Whatever the Americans may think."

"Yes, of course."

Over dinner he asked her about herself. She spoke French, German too, she said. Before the war she had worked as a secretary in Paris, taking dictation in three languages. The war chased her back to London where she worked for a solicitor. Shortly after it came into existence the Special Operations Executive heard about her somehow, and recruited her. This was in 1940. They were all amateurs at the start, she told him. Intelligence attracted imaginative, freewheeling, dissembling types, buccaneers of a kind. Women were good at it. Lots of the radio operators dropped into France were women. Some had been secretaries like her; she knew them well and lay awake nights worrying about them. The generals had never believed in organizing and arming the French Resistance groups, but Prime Minister Churchill did, and he had forced the generals to accept the idea. Because she knew France and spoke French, and because the agency grew in size, her responsibilities grew, until she had reached her present rank.

"Which is what?" Toft asked.

Her present rank, she said, was spending endless hours at Tempsford Airfield waiting for planes to come in from France, or take off for France; or else she was at her desk waiting for couriers to come in from the giant radio stations at Crendon, or Poundon. She lived with her mother in a London suburb; her mother hadn't a clue as to what she did.

But many nights she slept on a cot in her office.

She gave a laugh. "My mother thinks the reason I don't come home nights is because I'm sleeping with a boyfriend. She said to me the other day: 'I hope he's going to make an honest woman out of you when the war's over.' "

This seemed to move the conversation onto sex, however obliquely, and Toft was cheered.

But Vera's face hardened a bit: "We have to prove our worth every day. I don't have time for boyfriends."

"I'll be your boyfriend," said Toft lightly.

She stared at him until his smile faded.

He said: "Why did you come all this way to see me?"

"I don't know. I had a day off and wanted to get out of London. It was raining. I really don't know. Does that answer your question?"

"Not entirely, no." Maybe she had contemplated a dalliance with a war hero, himself. If so, she did not seem to be contemplating one now.

"I'd best be getting back."

"Why don't I show you the sights, first."

"The sights?"

He was unwilling to give up without one last try. "I'll show you my hotel room, if you like."

"Hotel room?"

"I took a room in the inn."

"Is that why you think I came out here?"

"No," said Toft, "of course not."

"I'll drive you back to your quarters. You can show me your airplane."

"I think I prefer to walk."

"It's raining quite hard."

"Better you go straight back to London."

"Well—"

"In fact you should start out right away."

"Suit yourself."

The result was that Toft stood under a dripping tree for an hour waiting for a vehicle to come by that would give him a lift out to the base.

XXII

A<small>FTER</small> supper two youths left the encampment for Le Lignon, where one of them formerly lived. It had been raining off and on for two days. They had had enough of the rain, and were drawn by the prospect of a dry room to sleep in, and hot porridge the next morning as prepared by the boy's mother. They did not ask Pierre Glickstein for permission to go, nor tell anyone they were going, they simply slipped out and started walking. Both boys were eighteen years old and fugitives from the forced labor drafts. They feared not the Germans but a sweep by French gendarmes or the French *Milice*, but in weather like this they believed they had nothing to worry about.

The boy who lived in Le Lignon was named François Pernand. He was the son of the village mason and had worked as an apprentice for his father. He was in awe of the other boy, Guy Ardoin, whom he considered his best friend—they had known each other under two months. Ardoin was from St. Étienne and had been apprenticed to a gun maker. He loved guns and was always fondling the Sten that had been assigned him.

Ardoin was the leader of the group that had refused to do the training, and Pernand was his chief acolyte. Both boys had talked constantly about killing Germans. With the acolyte this may have been mostly talk, but Ardoin, a big hulking individual, not too bright, had a hard, vicious streak and seemed to mean it.

Pernand's mother was glad to see her son, was cordial to the other boy, she prepared beds for them, and in the morning let them sleep late.

It was mid-afternoon before they returned to the encampment, where they sought out Pierre Glickstein.

"There's a detachment of convalescent troops in Le Lignon," said Ardoin.

"Yes, I know."

"Every morning a physical training instructor takes them down the road. He marches them a hundred meters, jogs them a hundred meters, and so forth, for three or four kilometers. He keeps them out there an hour."

Glickstein nodded.

"We noticed them this morning."

"What's your point?" But Glickstein believed he knew the point in advance.

"We can set up an ambush," Ardoin said. "We pick a spot, get set, and they jog down the road right into us."

"I have nothing against killing *Boches*," said Glickstein carefully. "In fact I want to do it. But not like that."

"We wipe them all out."

"I don't think it's a good idea."

"Give me three or four men, and it's all over."

This was not the first challenge to Glickstein's leadership, and he did not think it would be the last. He saw Ardoin as a bully and a lout who was not going to accept arguments based on logic, but he decided to try logic anyway. "Much better to wait until all the groups are fully armed, and the invasion starts," he said. "Then we all rise up together. That way we can have a real effect on the war."

"We wipe out those soldiers, that's good enough for me."

Glickstein was trying not to get angry but could not help himself. "You're talking absolute stupidity."

"Who's stupid?"

As a leader, you were supposed to at least listen to the ideas of your subordinates, Glickstein believed. But this particular idea might carry the whole camp; therefore he had to squelch it at once. "Are you some kind of moron, or what?"

Ardoin had become immediately sulky. "An ambush would be easy. Nothing to it."

"And what would be the aftermath?"

"What aftermath? They're all dead."

This statement made Glickstein testier than perhaps a wise leader ought to be. "Try thinking it through."

"I have thought it through."

"You're not very smart, are you?"

The acolyte, Pernand, looked from face to face, and said nothing.

"Kill 'em all. Take four or five minutes, if that."

"We kill twenty or thirty wounded men and the *Boches* send in a division and destroy the village."

"They see our power, they wouldn't dare."

"What power? You mean you with a Sten gun? Don't make me laugh."

"The trouble with you is you got no balls, you goddamn kike."

"They kill a thousand innocent people. Kill everyone they see."

Pernand, as he listened to his idol being put down, was nodding thoughtfully. Others had gathered around. By tonight the camp would be talking of nothing else.

"The idea is nonsensical," said Glickstein, and he walked away.

That some of his men counted themselves ready to take on the German army was plain to him. Despite having no military experience at all, Glickstein knew better, and he wondered how long he would be able to control them. When he glanced back he saw Ardoin in earnest conversation with several of the others. The guy is dangerous, he told himself, don't turn your back on him.

BECAUSE it could be reached by railroad, although narrow-gauged and two cars only, and because it was surrounded by farms, although poor ones, Le Lignon had become, this late in the war, a market town. People from St. Étienne, Valence, Lyon, even from cities as distant as Paris, came in on the trains and got down carrying empty suitcases, and went prospecting for food.

The refugees, also carrying suitcases, came in on the same trains. Their suitcases were usually different—they were battered, overused, and they contained now all that the refugees had left. It was because of the already full trains and all the suitcases that the refugees were able to blend in, more or less, to reach Le Lignon without calling too much attention to themselves, and once off the train they could hurry away, still more or less unnoticed, in the direction of the pastor's house. It was because Le Lignon had become a market town that so many refugees were able to get there, and hide there, some of them for years.

On market days during the growing season the surrounding farmers would load their produce and start for the village while it was still dark. For some it was a slow trip, for they came on carts behind plodding horses. There were usually a few rusty trucks running on charcoal as well. By first light all these vehicles were entering the village. The clatter of hoofs, the creaking of wagons, the sputtering charcoal engines, could be heard inside the houses.

The farmers did not have control over what they grew and raised, for they were obliged to meet quotas set by the government, and these were stiff. The amount of meat and produce required of them had to be transported to government centers, supposedly for distribution around the country, but it was subject to "requisition" by the occupying forces as well, and sometimes—often in fact—no distribution ever took place. All of France was hungry. It was a time when feeding one's family took on new meaning.

The farmers were allowed to keep whatever exceeded their quotas, which wouldn't have been much, except that most of them had managed to hide livestock from the inspectors, and to cultivate fields the government never learned of.

It was this surplus food that drew the empty suitcases to towns and villages like Le Lignon.

Today the farmers had set up their carts in the market square, which was elliptical in shape and framed by the walls of stone buildings two hundred or more years old. Each cart had occupied the same spot for as long as anyone could remember. This was by tradition, nothing had ever been written down. By the time the sun rose up over the rooftops, villagers were out buying whatever there was to buy. Additional rush hours would occur throughout the morning each time a train came in, but for the latecomers there would not be much left but rutabagas, which is a kind of turnip, something no one liked but that many people, especially city people, lived on.

In winter—and it was still winter up here—the situation was somewhat different. There were fewer carts in the square, and on them less to buy. The farmers, and sometimes their wives, stood bundled to the ears against the cold. They stamped their feet, and waited on the villagers and waited for the trains.

There was a third category of suitcases entering the village, heavy suitcases this time, and these were carried by the black marketeers. These men were professionals, part of the new merchant class that had grown up to fill a need, and they took over tables in the backs of the village's several cafés, their suitcases on their laps, or on the floor between their feet, and they waited to be found by buyers, which never took long.

The food searchers from the cities, many of them, hurried away from the trains as guiltily as the refugees. They accorded the farm carts only a few minutes, enough time to glance around for the law, then slinked toward the inner darkness of the bars, where it might be possible to buy at an exorbitant price some immense treasure, such as a sausage or a ham.

Since normally there was no police presence in Le Lignon, the dealers ran little risk, and this was true of the buyers too, until they started home, for the food laws were strict, it was illegal to transport food without a permit, and the controls on the trains and in the stations were frequent. Selling on the black market was of course against the law, but so was buying. Infractions were punishable by fines or imprisonment or both. Worse, the goods themselves would be confiscated. A man could spend hours making his way from his home city to Le Lignon. He could fill his suitcase at great expense, and on the train back, or in one of the stations, get stopped, be made to open his suitcase, and lose everything.

Nonetheless, it was a risk people were willing to run.

On this particular day Rachel had been sent out to buy food, especially eggs if she could find any. She had enough coupons for six eggs for four children and four adults, and if she came back with them then tonight there would be a feast, a potato and dried mushroom omelet that would be thin on eggs but delicious anyway.

She found no eggs on sale in the shops.

Rachel was carrying a string bag that by now was heavy. She had found a cabbage, a cauliflower, and some potatoes that would go into soup, and in the butcher shop a piece of lard. She had given up coupons for the lard, and also for bread and milk.

She was wearing her usual bulky sweaters and wooden shoes, and her modest skirt to below her knees, but her hair was glossy, and her cheeks were reddened by the cold. She had been crying earlier, but at her age this hardly showed now.

She had asked at several of the carts for eggs, but was refused. She knew that the pastor was militantly opposed to patronizing black market dealers. He had forbidden both his wife and Rachel ever to do so.

But she wanted to please him, especially today, please the family, which she could do if she could bring back eggs. Despite her gloomy mood, thoughts of eating an omelet caused her mouth to fill with saliva. It had been a bad day for her so far, but an omelet might make it better.

She was passing one of the village's bars at that moment. Realizing from the traffic going in and out that there must be a dealer inside, she decided to go in and ask for eggs. If she was successful, she reasoned, the pastor need never know where she had got them.

She had not been in this bar before. It was very dark. There were roughly dressed men drinking wine at the bar, and three or four better-dressed men waiting their turn to approach the dealer at his table in the rear. It was even darker back there, but she knew transactions were taking place because she could both see and hear the opening and closing of suitcases. She heard the sound of a number of voices as well, all of them pitched so low she could not understand what was being said.

Finally her turn came. She was somewhat frightened to be in this place at all, frightened also to be engaged in illicit trade. As she stepped up and asked for eggs she could not quite control her voice, and her knees were weak too.

The dealer reached into the suitcase on his lap and brought forth six eggs already wrapped in a package of old newspaper. During the instant that the suitcase was open Rachel had glimpsed bottles of olive oil, blocks of butter, bars of soap.

She wanted to see what she was buying but did not dare ask the dealer to unwrap the package of eggs.

She asked the price, and the man named it.

This was double what Rachel, who had been doing the family's marketing off and on for several years, was used to paying for eggs, and she gave a surprised gasp.

"Eggs're hard to come by these days," the dealer said.

He was a man of about forty in an unpressed suit who had not shaved in some days, and he looked up at her without expression.

Rachel knew nothing about bargaining, had never bargained before, and the dealer was no doubt an expert, but she did not have that much money with her, and what she did have was not hers. She had no choice.

With a sinking heart she said "Too much," and turned to walk away, an effective ploy, though she had no idea it was a ploy at all.

"How much you got?"

She turned back.

From the age of about fifteen she had been able to sense when she had an advantage over boys and men, and she sensed immediately that she had an advantage here too, of a different nature perhaps, but otherwise the same, though how or why she could not have said.

She named the old price.

"Not enough," the man said, but again she sensed her advantage.

"It's all I have."

In fact, these were the last eggs the man had, his suitcase was now half empty, and he was anxious to get the eggs out of there before one or more of them got broken.

Rachel only sensed him wavering.

"It's for the pastor," she said. "He has refugees to feed." This was true enough, she was not lying. She herself was a refugee, and in a sense so was Davey.

When the man still wavered, she said: "I have coupons."

The man liked looking at the girl, and wanted to see her smile.

He was not in the business of collecting coupons. Nonetheless, they could be useful.

He pushed the package of eggs across the table, and the transaction was concluded.

As she moved toward the door, package in one hand, string bag in the other, Rachel felt elation, triumph. Felt that this morning's heartache, her solitary tears, had perhaps been exaggerated. She stepped out into the street—

—And almost into the arms of Lieutenant Ziegler and two other German soldiers. They were in uniform, and Ziegler carried a baton. He said: "What's in that package?" and tapped it with the baton.

It was not the job of Ziegler or the German army to enforce the French food laws. If Rachel knew this she did not at that instant believe it. Her terror was instantaneous.

In a weak voice she said: "Eggs."

Ziegler was twenty-two years old. He had been fascinated by France from boyhood, had studied French in the gymnasium at Osnabrück, his hometown, and had been rewarded with a summer in a Boy Scout camp in the French Alps. He was not a professional soldier, and certainly not a Nazi. He had spent most of the last three years in Russia, where he had received a battlefield commission for heroic action before Stalingrad. That he had survived the slaughter and the freezing winds of Russia was probably due to an American air raid on Osnabrück while he was home on leave. A bomb blew him thirty feet in the air. When he came down he was missing a third of his right biceps and part of his skull. In the hospital nothing much could be done for his arm, but the hole in his skull was replaced with a steel plate. When he was mobile again he had been sent to Le Lignon to recuperate. By then his hair had grown back, and his arm no longer hurt very much, but he still suffered terrible headaches, grotesque dreams, and wild mood swings. "Psychological problems suspected," the doctors wrote on his medical report.

Nonetheless, the young officer had received papers that very morning ordering him to rejoin his unit, which, so far as he knew, was still on the Russian front.

Rachel too had received unwelcome news that morning. It was

equally unexpected, and it signaled for her, as for Ziegler, an abrupt change of direction. Because it had come just as she was leaving the house, she had been delayed by some thirty minutes. If she had got to the market as early as planned, there might still have been legal eggs in the shops, and she would have missed Lieutenant Ziegler.

The news that had so disturbed her was brought by Pierre Glickstein, and strictly speaking it did not even concern her. It was Davey that the ex-forger had come to see, and instead of hurrying to the market, Rachel had had to step back inside the presbytery to serve as interpreter for them, because the pastor was away, and Norma Favert's English was not strong.

London had been apprised of the downed pilot's whereabouts, Glickstein told Davey, and wanted him back. A plane would be sent for him during the next full moon.

"These clandestine landings can be attempted only on nights that are bright enough to see by," said Glickstein.

"Yes, I had heard that," said Davey.

He could picture it, as could everyone in the room. The field would be further illuminated by fires burning in the four corners. The plane would swoop down, land, turn around. Its cargo of arms and other supplies, would be pushed out the door. Without even shutting down the engines it would scoop Davey up and fly him home. Maybe other passengers would board as well, British agents perhaps, or important Resistance men, or other downed flyers. That is, the flight was not being laid on for Davey personally.

The field in which it would land had not yet been determined, Glickstein told Davey, nor had the exact date. But the full moon was about two weeks off.

The flight would be confirmed on the day itself, Glickstein said. Men would come for Davey after dark and take him to the field.

Davey's immediate reaction was unalloyed joy, and this was what had hurt Rachel so much. Not a thought for her, or what she had come to think of as their love. He was chortling and whooping, practically dancing. He wanted to be away from her, that was clear. He never even considered what her feelings might be. He could not wait to get back to England, and from the way he was behaving wouldn't even miss her once he was there.

Davey asked Glickstein a few questions, and through Rachel got his answers, and then Glickstein left. Davey was smirking and laughing as he walked him to the door. He did not even see the tears in Rachel's eyes.

Norma Favert did, a harsh reality that did not surprise her. So he's leaving her, she thought, so what did she expect? That he would stay here forever hobbling about the presbytery? She saw them as two children who did not yet see life clearly. Who never guessed that circumstances changed, not always in ways a person wished, that life itself was one change after another.

The older woman left the room so the young couple could work this out alone.

"Isn't it great?" said Davey.

Rachel wouldn't look at him.

"I've been going stir crazy here," said Davey. "You don't know what it's like day after day cooped up in this house. I'll be free again. Isn't that great?"

His words struck her like spears, and there was no way she could dodge any one of them.

Rachel walked, not ran, away from him. She walked, not ran, into her room where she buried her face in her pillow so he would not hear her sobs. It took her twenty minutes to make the sobs stop.

When she came out he was still happily pacing the living room, and he wanted again to talk of London, where he would be able to get to a phone and talk to his mom. He wanted Rachel to share his joy, but she walked past him toward the door, hating him, and when he tried to embrace her she said: "I have to do the marketing."

Once out in the cold her tears dried quickly, though her heart remained heavy, and she hated Davey still.

She was much later than she had meant to be, and there were no eggs left in the shops.

That Lieutenant Ziegler was standing outside the bar when Rachel came out with her black market eggs was no accident, for he had spotted her at the market and, accompanied by his two friends, had hurried after her. When he confronted her he was not in fact enforcing the food laws, or even pretending to, but was only seeking a pretext that would make this girl talk to him. He had looked for her every time he was out of doors in the village, and if he spied her he had usually managed to get close enough to smile and wish her *bonjour.* She had never once replied, or smiled back, or even met his eyes. During his weeks in the village nobody else had ever smiled at him either, or at any of the German troops, except sometimes the children. It was extremely hard to live with. he had failed to see, or refused to see, that this was the way it was and would be, but instead he had taken it personally.

And according to his orders he was leaving the village in two days' time. If he was ever to talk to this girl, it had to be now.

What happened next was provoked by the personalities and experiences of the two young people involved, and by the events preceding it that same morning. On another day, at another time, it would have happened differently, or perhaps not at all.

"Qu'est ce que vous avez dans ce paquet?" said Ziegler, tapping the eggs with his baton.

And the frightened Rachel had replied: *"Des oeufs."*

At that point they were still speaking French.

The Wehrmacht was not the SS. For occupation troops stationed in places like Le Lignon a strict code of conduct existed. Troops were to obey local laws, be polite, help the elderly and the children as the occasion arose. They were to pay for everything they bought. They were not to molest the girls. They were to be correct at all times.

The *Feldgendarmerie* was nearby to enforce this code.

Always up to now Lieutenant Ziegler had obeyed the code, had been at all times as correct as anyone could wish. He had been attracted to Rachel, true, and on several occasions had tried to talk to her, but it had not gone beyond that.

Villagers in Le Lignon and in most places throughout France had a code of conduct as well. Insofar as was possible, one ignored the enemy troops. Men seen talking to them were suspected of being collaborators, women of being whores.

Rachel had at all times been aware of Ziegler, had felt he was stalking her, had hated it, but there was nothing she could do. Ziegler was a nice-looking boy, but he wore the wrong uniform. She had had no intention of talking to him ever.

But she just had.

Two already distraught young people face-to-face.

"Could we go someplace and talk?" said Ziegler. "Just talk."

This question released Rachel from her terror.

"Get away from me," she said. "You hear me, just get away from me." And she attempted to walk by him.

Ziegler reach out to grasp the package. If he could take the eggs away from her, he could hold her here.

He pulled the package one way, Rachel pulled the other, and one of the precious eggs broke. They observed it leaking through the newspaper. Both saw the leaking egg as a tragedy, and both were almost stupefied by it.

"Now look what you've done," cried Rachel still speaking French.

In German the young officer said: "Why won't you talk to me? All I want to do is talk to you."

By now Rachel was enraged, and she answered in German almost without being aware of it. "Because you're a pig," she screamed, "you're all a bunch of pigs. Why don't you go back where you came from and leave us in peace."

Breathing hard, appalled at what she had said, and that she had said it in German, she stared at him.

Ziegler was not an anti-Semite in the Nazi sense, but he carried the stain of the culture in which he had grown up. This was inevitable—he had been a child. Without much question he had accepted what seemed to be the vogue of the country at the time. There was no way this could have been prevented.

Now, having recognized Rachel's Berlin accent, he recognized something else too. "Refugee bitch," he cried, "Jewish bitch." He batted the eggs from her hand and when they had landed, stomped on them.

She slapped him.

He struck her with his baton.

The other two soldiers pulled him away, leaving Rachel staring down at her precious ruined eggs.

She ran home to the presbytery where she burst in on Norma Favert, who was ironing clothes in the kitchen, and blurted out what had happened.

"You did what?" Norma responded.

Davey stood in the doorway trying, and failing, to understand what they were saying.

"You spoke German to him? Are you crazy?"

"I didn't even know I was doing it."

Rachel's face was contorted, the tears streaming down her cheeks, her words difficult to understand.

"You silly girl."

"It just came out."

Norma, who still held the hot iron, looked like she wanted to hit someone with it.

"I'll pay you back for the eggs."

"Never mind the eggs."

"I'll get the money somewhere."

"We can live without the eggs. Wipe your eyes."

"What's happened?" said Davey.

"Crying doesn't do any good."

"Will somebody please inform me what's happened?"

"Don't tell Papa."

"Don't you understand the danger you have put yourself in?"

"Please don't tell him."

"Put all of us in?"

"Why do you have to tell him?"

"The pastor must be told."

"I have a right to know," said Davey.

Finally, haltingly, Rachel told him. She had cursed out a German officer and—

"You did what?" said Davey. "In German? Oh, Jesus."

In the kitchen as they heard the front door open and close, they went silent.

The pastor had been at a meeting of his presbyterial council. This had taken place inside the otherwise empty temple, and most of the discussion had been about money, the paucity of it, the need for expensive repairs to the roof. Where was the money to come from? When the discussion ended—with no solution in sight—the pastor had started back to the presbytery.

Now they heard his heavy footsteps come down the hall, and then he stood in the doorway, at first smiling at them, the smile slowly fading as he weighed the silence into which he had walked.

With Davey obliged to advance two paces toward the stove to make room for him, the pastor stepped toward the kitchen table and pulled back a chair. He said: "Perhaps I should sit down before you tell me whatever it is you have to tell me." And, looking from one face to the other, he waited.

Whereupon much of foregoing scene was repeated, though this time with fewer tears by Rachel. Her tears were played out, and in the face of this big, forceful man, her principal emotion was fear. Some sort of decision was called for now, no one knew what, and she—they—waited for the pastor to make it.

But Favert got up from the table and after that only paced and fumed. His big feet banged on the floor. Sometimes he shouted. Sometimes he approached Rachel as if to hit her, and although he had never hit her before, each time she cringed.

Again Davey stood on the fringe. Again he kept interrupting, as he tried to understand what was being said.

"I have a right to know what you are deciding," he cried in frustration.

After a sustained heavy silence, the pastor addressed him in English. "We're trying to decide what sort of reaction, if any, is called for," he said.

"She's got to get to Switzerland," stated Davey.

"One doesn't casually walk from here to Switzerland."

"You smuggle people to Switzerland regularly, I'm told."

"Some of them don't make it."

"Mostly they do."

"Each group takes preparation."

"There may not be time for preparation."

"There has to be."

Rachel was looking from face to face, her adoptive father and her lover fighting over her.

The pastor said: "It's too early to talk of going to Switzerland."

"She isn't safe here."

"There is little safety anywhere these days."

"They'll come for her."

Perhaps, the pastor agreed. He looked confused. "There's safety if she gets to Switzerland. It's the getting there that's dangerous."

He was in the grip of emotions whose strength surprised him.

Switzerland: yes, she could probably be smuggled across the border, but it wasn't a sure thing and—he saw this clearly—the cost to him would be terrible. He would lose this child who had grown up in his house, and he did not want to lose her. He loved her as much as his own children, perhaps more, the way a father might love a sickly child more than his healthy ones. When he had daydreamed of her eventual wedding, it was in terms not only of giving her away to some worthwhile young man some day, but afterward of having them to dinner on Sundays, and of fondling the grandchildren to come. Rachel could perhaps be got across the border, but he was confronted with the emptiness she would leave behind in this house. He would not see her again for years, perhaps forever. If something happened to her en route he might never even know it.

"Anything is safer for her than staying here."

"You don't know what you're talking about."

"I know she can't stay here."

"And it's really none of your business," said the pastor with annoyance.

"It is my business," said Davey. And then after a pause. "There's something you don't know."

The pastor waited. So did Norma.

"Someone else knows she's not"—he looked at Rachel, and swallowed hard—"she's not who she's supposed to be."

Pastor Favert waited.

"Rachel and I—" He stopped. "We tried to get married. We went to the priest, and—" He stopped again.

"You went to Rousset?"

"We wanted to get married."

"Rousset? You went to Rousset?" Pastor Favert was enraged but trying to smother it.

In a halting voice, Davey described their meeting with the Abbé Rousset.

Pastor Favert let out a scream. "You went to see that priest?"

Then he began shouting at them. Without using a single oath he cursed them as fools, then stormed out of the kitchen.

The rest of that morning he remained closed in his office. Rachel and Davey waited in front of the fire for him to come out, but he did not do so. Lunchtime came. The children came home from school, and went into the office to sit on his lap or play with him, or whatever they did in there. Lunch was served, but still he did not appear, until finally Norma carried his plate in to him.

"I want to go in and talk to him," said Rachel.

"He doesn't want to see you," said Norma.

Rachel hung her head. When Norma had left the room, Davey walked over to where she was standing near the big table and embraced her. He kissed her lips and then her eyes, and tasted the salt in both places.

Later that day Norma Favert went into the office, and when she came out the pastor's decision was at last handed down. Rachel was to pack a bag and move up to the Henriots'. If men came to the presbytery to arrest her they would not find her.

"What about Davey?" said Rachel.

"That's a risk that will have to be taken," said Norma.

"I'll be all right," said Davey to Rachel. "Don't worry about me."

"If they search the house for me and find him, then what?"

"We don't have any choice as far as Davey is concerned," said Norma.

Rachel was to stay with the Henriots a week or two, the pastor had decreed, according to Norma. She was not to go out of the house. She should be safe there. A week, two weeks—time enough to see what, if anything, was going to happen.

Talk of Switzerland, at this time, the pastor had also decreed, was premature.

It was night before he at last issued from his office. Davey had been waiting all afternoon to talk to him, but now the pastor walked by him without even a nod, sat down in front of the fire, and began reading his Bible.

Rachel was gone by then. For Davey the presbytery was empty. It felt as if a hundred people had moved out.

XXIII

THE House of the Rocks stood in a rocky clearing on the extreme edge of the commune. A three-story stone building surrounded by woods on three sides, and by a dirt road on the other, served as a dormitory for thirty-three boys ranging in age from twelve to twenty, all Jews, all refugees from Germany or central Europe, all students in one or the other of the village schools, plus a cook and a monitor. The cook was a woman of fifty from Hamburg, Jewish, carrying false papers, who spoke broken French. The monitor was the pastor's cousin, Georges Favert, twenty-nine, the only one in the building whose papers were real. Georges Favert also oversaw a second house closer in toward the village, which was called The Crickets. At ten o'clock on that particular Sunday morning, because two of the boys had come down with measles, Dr. Blum—the naturalized Frenchman Jean Ligier according to his papers—was present also, his first house call of the day.

Untersturmführer Haas had done his work expertly. At that hour the churches were full, the village streets empty, or nearly so, not only in Le Lignon itself but also in every village his convoy had raced through en route, meaning that no one except for a few children noted its passage, no one telephoned ahead to signal its approach. The convoy consisted of a truckload of troops, three buses in case the haul was a large one, and a car carrying Haas, Gruber, and three other Gestapo officers.

At Le Lignon the convoy turned off the departmental onto a dirt road, which it sped along very fast, throwing up vast clouds of dust. In front of the House of the Rocks it slid to its multiple stops, and a final swirl of dust blew back over it. The troops, who wore steel helmets and carried rifles, sprang out and surrounded the house, out of which people began to run, including boys of various ages, and the doctor with his black bag. But the rifles herded everyone back inside.

One of the boys who lived in the house was named Joseph Levy. He was fourteen, and kept rabbits in a hutch he had built at the edge of the woods behind the house. He was back there feeding them when the convoy drew up.

This Sunday morning he had brought his rabbits a feast of potato peelings and carrot greens. Rabbits were easy to raise, he had found. They would eat anything and they reproduced fast. Better still, he no longer became fond of any one of them the way he had at first—when he was younger he sometimes began weeping like a girl when the cook came out with her knife to collect what she saw as dinner, but what to him was a pet. But he didn't mind the killing of them now, and he imagined the reason was that he had become mature. Although the House of the Rocks was funded by a Swiss church group, nonetheless there was often not enough money, and therefore not enough food to go around. By raising rabbits young Levy was contributing to the common good, and often he received praise for it. They were just rabbits after all, and without them there would have been no meat at all.

Levy saw the convoy pull up, and instantly, instinctively, he hid himself as best he could. There was no foliage to conceal him at this time of year, but nobody was specifically looking for him back there. The bushes were thick and once he had faded back into them he was able to watch from behind a tree.

He saw the soldiers surround the house. He saw the Gestapo men get out of their car—he recognized them from the long leather overcoats and the trilby hats. They got out casually, and strolled casually toward the front door, as if they had all the time in the world before beginning whatever inhumanity came next. They went inside, and the boy heard voices shouting.

Young as he was Joseph did not have to be told what was happening, and his only thought was that the pastor had to be informed, and he ran downhill through the woods, his body and even his face getting whipped by branches, and came out on the road lower down, and kept running, badly out of breath now, through the few village streets, across the market square, and then down the hill again to the temple.

He had never been in the temple before. The pews were full. There were people standing in the back, and along the aisles. Everyone was singing. Levy was breathing hard and did not know what to do. The song ended, the congregation sat down, and the pastor climbed the steps to the pulpit and began preaching.

Levy pushed his way down the aisle.

People were looking at him. He felt out of place. He ought not to be here, a Jewish boy in a Christian place of worship, especially during a service, but his message was urgent, he could not turn back.

He had been able to spot the pew where Madame Favert sat with her children. She sat on the aisle, her children to the inside of her, and he went there and knelt close to her ear and whispered what had happened.

Her face took on a look of alarm. She whispered something to the woman behind her, then got up and started out of the temple. In the pulpit the pastor's voice faltered momentarily to see this happen, but then he continued.

Levy followed Madame Favert up the aisle and out of the temple.

Outside in the sunlight she turned to him, directing him to the door in the side of the temple which led to the sacristy. "Go in there and wait for the pastor. When he comes down, tell him what has happened. Tell him I went directly to the House of the Rocks. After that you go to the presbytery. You'll be safe there. The door is open. You go in and you don't come out for any reason, until we return."

Most of the congregation had come to the service by bicycle. There were hordes of them stacked against the wall. Madame

Favert selected her own, mounted it, and started off, pedaling hard. She went up the hill pedaling and the road curved and she was gone. The sun was shining everywhere. Joseph Levy, age fourteen, looked off at the surrounding hills and his eyes filled with tears.

THE first job was to secure the building. Untersturmführer Helmut Haas ordered it secured room by room, for some of the inhabitants were milling around and others were no doubt trying to hide. He could see some boys and a man with a black bag who was perhaps a doctor, but did not know who else might be there. As each room was cleared, only more boys so far, he left a soldier on the door to make sure it stayed that way.

Everyone was to be herded into the common room, and while this was being done he looked in on the cook in the kitchen. She was a refugee too, he thought, but when he spoke to her in German she pretended not to understand.

One of his men had brought in a carton containing eggs, a ham, bread, and a case of wine, for the interrogations were going to take several hours, and when lunchtime came his men would be hungry. He tried to explain this to the woman, but she wasn't getting it, so he left in disgust.

Finally his men reported that all rooms were now secure, except for the one containing the two sick boys.

"Sick?" inquired Haas.

"They look pretty sick."

Trailed by soldiers carrying rifles, making sure nothing had been overlooked, Haas and Gruber went through the building themselves. They pulled blankets off beds. They strewed schoolbooks around. They were perhaps looking for contraband, but did not find any. They upended suitcases, pulled out drawers, dumping their contents on the floor. Haas's foot stirred through underwear, socks, photos, letters or packets of letters. Some were in German. He pulled letters out of envelopes, glanced at what was written, then tore them to shreds. By the third or fourth room his hands had got tired, and he stopped.

"You notice there are no crucifixes or holy pictures on the walls of any of the rooms," said Haas.

"You're right," said Gruber.

"Jew pigs."

In one drawer was a small pile of money. Haas started to put it in his pocket, but reconsidered in time and handed the few francs to Gruber.

"Whoever this belongs to won't be needing it anymore," he said.

How smoothly the money disappeared. Gruber, Haas decided, was a man with class.

He dumped the contents of another drawer. Out fell a satin pouch which he picked up and opened. Inside was a prayer shawl and set of phylacteries such as every Jewish boy received at the time of his bar mitzvah.

Haas put the shawl on his head and danced around the room as if he were a woman. He was laughing hard at himself. When Gruber only smiled, Haas blew his nose in the shawl. He got off a few honkers, and laughed again. Finally he mimed wiping his ass with it.

"We've come to the right place," he said, "in case you had any doubts. Nest of kikes."

He shoved the shawl back in the pouch and undid the phylacteries, small leather boxes on the ends of long straps. Grasping the ends of the straps, he twirled the boxes around his head like a slingshot, and if the window had been open might have slung them out into the garden.

Gruber, not watching him, was glancing around at the rest of the room. Was Haas really this rabid, or was he just trying to please a superior? Gruber himself had no use for Jews, but hunting them down was to him just a job, not a crusade, just a means of advancing his career.

Haas rammed the phylacteries back into the pouch with the shawl. "Let's see who these belong to," he said, and forced the pouch into his pocket.

In the next room in separate beds lay the two sick boys. *"Raus,"* Haas shouted at them. They understood him well enough, he saw. Yids. And since they understood him, that made them German

Yids. Both were feverish, already shaking with cold as they got up, and as the soldiers tried to push them toward the door they pulled blankets off the beds in which they tried to wrap themselves.

"No blankets."

Haas shouted these words too, for he had learned that when you shouted, men paid attention. "Rip those blankets off them," he ordered a soldier. "Good. Now take them downstairs."

The shivering boys were prodded out of the room. "Don't get too close to them," Haas called after the soldiers. "Filthy Yids."

There were steps rising to an attic. Haas climbed them, Gruber trailing. It was cold up there. Some empty suitcases, empty trunks. About twenty rickety old chairs. No one hiding.

The basement, when they came to it, was unfinished, almost a cave. Broken furniture, disused bicycles. There was a furnace still hot to the touch, and beside it a stack of logs. Haas threw in more logs, watched them blaze up, then slammed the iron door.

"We're going to be here a while," he commented, and gave an obsequious grin. "Might as well be comfortable."

Gruber nodded.

Beyond the piled furniture was a thick door from which protruded a heavy iron key. Haas turned the key with some difficulty, pulled the door back, and his flashlight probed the space inside.

"Wine cellar," the young man said.

"I think this place used to be a hotel," said Gruber beside him.

"Let's see what they've got."

There was a wooden wine case on the floor. Corkless empties, the flashlight showed. There were rows of empty racks. Otherwise nothing but spider webs.

"There might have been something," said Haas.

"Pity," said Gruber.

"Time to begin the interrogations," said Haas.

Gruber nodded. He thought the young man was doing an excellent job so far, and he followed him up the stairs.

AT the House of the Rocks, Norma counted the vehicles out front, and the troops she could see, and pedaled into the compound and around to the kitchen door. There were troops there too, and they tried to stop her from entering but she pushed past them and into the kitchen, where the cook was cutting up enough vegetables to feed thirty-three boys, a lunch that now might never take place.

The two women conversed, the cook speaking in broken French. She didn't know much. She had been told to stay in the kitchen, that none of this concerned her. She had heard voices raised, she said, and blows struck, and boys crying out in pain or fear.

Norma Favert went out into the common room. The thirty-odd boys were seated on the floor, backs to the wall. At the refectory table sat two Gestapo *mecs*, who seemed to be doing preliminary interrogations of one boy after another: name, age, and so forth. Also, they were collecting the boys' papers, those that had any. There was a stack of documents in front of them, and they were adding to it. In general the French boys had papers, Norma knew, maybe even their own, if their names were not distinctly Jewish; the refugee boys sometimes did not.

Also seated against the wall were the doctor and Georges Favert, and Norma started to go to Georges to ask what was happening, but she stopped herself in time, realizing that as director of the house, he was guilty of sheltering Jews. This the Gestapo did not need to know.

From behind the door she heard a thud, and a boy cried out, and Norma winced.

The door opened. The boy who came out was about sixteen with dark curly hair. He was very tall and skinny, no flesh on him at all yet. His face was swelling fast and he was crying.

Behind him came a Gestapo *mec* and Norma saw that it was Gruber. There was a half smile on his face, as if something had left him half amused—perhaps the sounds of a sixteen-year-old boy being beaten up. He looked at her and then at the line of frightened boys waiting to be interrogated, as if searching for his next victim. He did not remember her, she saw. There had been no glint of recognition. Whereas she remembered him clearly, starting with the day he had first come to Le Lignon when she had watched him skulking around the buses that were still empty because no Jews had been found. She had been waiting for her husband to be arrested. It was what she had expected, and the expectation had made her stiff with fear. She had seen Gruber only the one other time—the day he had come to the presbytery looking for Davey, who was hidden in the attic. Again she had expected the arrest of her husband. Again her fear had left her unable even to speak. If arrested, then deportation was the best he might have hoped for; more likely the *Boches* would have put him in front of a firing squad, while making her watch.

Gruber's face was burned into Norma's memory, and she expected it always would be.

She went forward and said: "Do you have children, Monsieur?"

Gruber looked at her.

"You are beating up children. Must you?"

Gruber began screaming at her. The words came out half in French, half in German, so she did not understand them all, though their import was clear enough: a series of threats, curses—close her mouth, go to the kitchen and stay there, or she would be next to feel the might of the Third Reich.

She went back into the kitchen and in her fear and fury, wished violence on all those men out there, and she cut off slices of precious German ham, broke precious German eggs into a skillet, and cooked an omelet which she and the cook then ate. Neither had eaten an egg in a month, and their memory of the taste of ham went back even longer, but they ate in silence.

THE interrogations continued. The boys were called in one by one. As they stepped through the door they saw Gruber and Haas sitting at a table, watching cold-eyed as they advanced. Most were so frightened they were already trembling. They were ordered to stand in front of the table while Haas perused their papers. Gruber said nothing, only fixed them with a hard stare.

Haas then spoke to them in German. Most answered in French, a pretense that made him sneer, though at that point in the interrogation he made no other reaction.

His opening questions were easy: name, age, so forth, questions that had already been asked by the men outside. Questions no one could pretend not to understand.

Then came the first of the hard ones.

"Are you or are you not a Jew?"

Most denied it, for although they had come to Le Lignon as children, and had not personally been menaced until now, they knew of the roundups, the deportations. They knew what Gestapo agents had in store for Jews. And although some insisted they were not Jews but gentiles, and not German but French, few were able to maintain such assertions very long. A little pressure and they cracked. Haas was excellent at pressure, Gruber saw. He knew how to intimidate people, how to keep them intimidated as well, though with teenage boys it was easier than with grown men. At times Gruber admired his technique. Most of the boys were soon in tears. Depending on how quickly they broke down, they stayed a greater or lesser amount of time in the room, during which they suffered a greater or lesser amount of pain.

Each intimidation began with the shouted command: "Drop your pants."

Haas would walk round and round the boy who, his pants on the floor, usually stared straight ahead, waiting in terror for what would happen next.

"What's this?" he would say. He had a baton with which he would prod the circumcized penis. Sometimes he would slap at it, doubling the boy over. "You Jews might just as well be wearing a flag," he said once, and the baton struck. "You think you can pass," he told another boy, "but you can't hide this," and the baton struck again.

Gruber was used to watching interrogations. Watching did not bother him. At times he found the reactions of the boys amusing. It was hard not to smile.

Haas knew how to apply psychological pressure too. One boy, though circumsized, kept maintaining he was not a Jew. Haas sent a guard for a kitchen knife, and when it was brought to him, after testing its sharpness on his finger, he announced that liars did not deserve to have penises at all, even circumcized ones, that he was going to cut it off, and he advanced on the kid. Gruber received the impression that Haas was not joking, that he meant to do it, and he stepped in and stopped him, saying: "After all, Haas, we're Germans, we're not savages."

Haas gave a sheepish grin and whispered that he had only been trying to scare the lying Yid.

This was the first time Gruber overruled his subordinate, and he thought it would be the last, but then came a boy who was not circumcised, and who claimed under heavy interrogation to be a Spaniard. He showed a document which seemed to prove it, and Gruber tended to believe him, though Haas obviously didn't. Since Germany was not at war with Spain, which was almost an ally, Gruber ordered him to let the boy go, explaining that certain diplomatic niceties, like the rule of law itself, had to be observed absolutely, or civilization as we knew it could not continue to exist.

When Haas had each boy thoroughly cowed he would begin the serious questioning. Who else was a Jew in the next room? Where else were Jews hiding? Who in the village was protecting Jews? To these and similar questions most of the boys had no answers, or only vague ones, for the secrets of the village were compartmentalized, and to most refugees unknown.

The two officers talked it over during intervals between boys.

"We need more specific information than we're getting," said Gruber.

"We've got nothing, so far," admitted Haas.

"I'm sure there are lots of Jews hereabouts," said Gruber, "but we can't afford to go from farm to farm trying to pick up each one."

"We could spend a week at it and not fill a single bus," conceded Haas. "It wouldn't be cost effective."

"Keep trying for specific information."

And Haas did, but without success, so that he became enraged, or pretended to become enraged. "I hate liars, especially Yid liars," he said, and lashed out with the baton, whipping it across faces and necks.

He knew what every skilled interrogator knew, Gruber observed. The baton did most of the work. One did not risk damaging one's hands. Nonetheless, provoked by Jewish lies, there were times Haas could not restrain himself, and his fist snaked out and made contact with what Gruber thought of as oversized Jewish noses, it buried itself in thin Jewish bellies. It rearranged several noses, made them handsomer, Gruber decided. One boy vomited. Haas gave him a severe beating for it, then made him clean it up as well.

Haas was sweating, his face red, his hair disarranged. Gruber was glad that he did not have to do this particular work himself.

There were other questions Haas asked each boy. The first concerned the enemy pilot who had crashed nearby; where was he, Haas wanted to know, who was sheltering him? If any boy had known, considering the pressure Haas put on them, he would have talked, Gruber believed, but none did. That Haas concentrated on this subject bothered Gruber. He himself had failed to find the pilot. If Haas did find him, Gruber would have to think of a way to turn any resulting glory away from his subordinate and onto himself.

Another question had to do with the phylacteries. Who did they belong to?

Gruber himself considered the phylactery subject unimportant, but because it seemed to mean a lot to Haas, he did not interfere.

A boy entered whose papers identified him by the good French name of Colin, and who claimed to be French. He was fourteen years old, small and skinny. He had not had a growth spurt yet, and weighed not much more than a hundred pounds.

Haas addressed him as Cohn—probably what his real name was, Gruber supposed.

The boy refused to admit to being named Cohn, despite the beating Haas administered, nor did he admit he understood German, which at times forced Gruber to translate Haas's questions. The boy stood up to punishment very well, despite his small size, and Gruber began to think he might be French after all—his French was certainly better than Gruber's, who could not discern whether he spoke with a German accent or not.

The pouch containing the phylacteries lay on the table, and the boy's eyes kept going to it even as they began to swell up and close.

Both men noted this, Haas with increasing satisfaction.

"Yours?" he said at last, tapping the pouch with his baton.

The boy denied it. By then his front teeth were loose and bleeding and he could barely be understood.

"What did you say?" said Haas, giving him sword thrusts with the baton. "I didn't hear you."

Because his pants were at his ankles, the boy fell down.

"On your feet," said Haas, and he whipped him until he got up again.

Haas went to the table, pulled out the prayer shawl, and mimed what he wanted. "Wipe your ass with it," he ordered. "Wipe good."

The boy was crying so hard and his teeth were so loose he could not speak.

Haas had returned to the pouch, from which he withdrew the phylacteries.

"And what are these?" said Haas, swinging the phylacteries round and round his head.

"No, don't," mumbled the boy, reaching out for them, "please don't."

The boy had been bar mitzvahed six months before. His parents had come down on the train from St. Étienne, where they were in hiding, bringing a rabbi with them, a voyage of great risk. The phylacteries, which had last belonged to the boy's grandfather, had been in the family for many generations. For this reason, and because to a devout Jew they were sacred, the boy treasured them.

"*Schweinejude,*" Haas screamed, and he began whipping him with them. "*Schweinejude.*"

Again and again the phylacteries descended, hard boxes on the ends of straps that caused wounds, and then the door burst back and in came Pastor Favert, cassock flapping, and he ripped them out of Haas's hand.

FROM time to time as he preached the pastor could see Joseph Levy moving back and forth in the sacristy. He knew something grave must have occurred, but Norma was taking care of it. The Levy boy was waiting to explain. If Norma had immediate need of him, she would send someone. It never occurred to him that she might be a prisoner herself, unable to get a message out of the House of the Rocks.

And so he stayed up in his pulpit and preached to the end. Because his wife's sudden departure had left him distracted, the sermon was less focused than he wanted, a little shorter than most, not one of his best, and when it ended he stepped out into the church to pass the basket down each of the rows, among the standees as well. His congregation was poor, and gave little enough at the best of times. People seemed to give a bit more when he took up the collection himself—and it was the only income he and Norma had, money they desperately needed to feed not only themselves but also the refugees who kept coming to their door. He nodded his thanks to every donor.

Having carried the basket, which was not overflowing, into the sacristy, he at last learned from young Levy that the *Boches*—Gestapo and troops both—had raided the House of the Rocks, and that Madame Favert had gone there on her bicycle to see if she could help. Behind Levy's narrative came hymns praising divine goodness, and God's power over all men and all things for the service was not yet over. The pastor heard this without hearing it, like the music that plays behind a scene of high drama in a movie.

The pastor to that moment believed in God's goodness and power. He had no notion that today he would come to the crisis of faith he had feared all his adult life, and that after today, shaken to his foundations, he would never wholly believe in anything again.

Norma! That she was being held by the Gestapo he never for a moment doubted, and this upset him so much that he had cried out her name, and rushed out the sacristy door and up the hill, his skirts flying, his bib flapping under his chin, leaving Assistant Pastor Henriot to conclude the service or not conclude it as he wished. Favert himself was consumed with the need to save the boys who lived in the House of the Rocks if he could, but most of all to save Norma.

It took him nearly a quarter hour to get there. It was a long steep climb, and when he came to the gate that led to the House of the Rocks he too counted the vehicles out front—he saw the coming disaster before it ever happened, knowing he would be powerless to stop it. Three buses meant they intended to take away everybody, and perhaps the residents of other houses as well. And as he moved along the path to the building itself he noted the soldiers with rifles across their chests who stood at the front door and who would surely bar his entrance.

As Pastor Favert approached them they stepped closer together, blocking the door.

His face covered with sweat, his heart thumping from exertion, the pastor cried out to them: "Stand back." Otherwise he ignored them, striding between them without a glance. Their orders, whatever they might have been, apparently said nothing about preventing an irate clergyman from entering the building.

Favert found himself in an entrance hall. He crossed it and entered the common room, where boys, some of them with bruised faces, sat on the floor against the wall. He did not see Norma. The pastor was glancing around wondering what to do next, when a high, keening scream came from the room beyond.

There was a guard at that door too. Again Favert simply brushed past him, threw the door open wide, and strode inside.

In the room, seated at a table, was Gruber, but the pastor gave him barely a glance, because the other, younger man—Untersturm-führer Haas, he would learn later—was beating a fourteen-year-old boy with a set of phylacteries. The boy, who stood with his pants at his ankles, was weeping and cringing, and that was what had to be stopped. The hard leather boxes on the end of three-foot-long leather straps made an excellent weapon, a kind of religious cat-o'-nine-tails. To a devout Jew, and at that age the boy was probably devout, there was a sacrilegious aspect about the use to which the phylacteries were being put, and Favert, who had studied all major religions, was aware of this.

He strode forward, tore the phylacteries out of the younger officer's hands, handed them to the boy, and told him: "Go!"

Clutching his pants in one hand, the phylacteries in the other, the boy scrambled from the room.

The pastor had not thought out what he would do next, what would happen next. A man like Favert, seeing himself obliged to perform a moral act, did not have to ask himself such questions, for by the nature of the obligation he was left with no choice but to perform it, and he had.

The astonished Haas, momentarily disarmed, lunged for the table on which lay his baton. He grabbed it up and came forward swinging, not the best emotion for accurate striking. His face contorted with rage, he missed the pastor's head, fell momentarily off-balance, and then the pastor had twisted the baton out of his hand and thrown it to the floor.

Haas's shirt was wet from previous exertions. His Luger was in its holster at his belt, and now he remembered it. Taking two steps backward, almost falling backward, he yanked it out and fired. He was not six feet from the pastor but slightly off-balance, overhasty, and so furious he could barely see.

He had aimed at the pastor's face, and he missed. The shot went through the door, slightly wounding one of the soldiers guarding the boys.

From beyond the door the guard screamed, as did Gruber beside Haas, both at the same time, even as a second shot went off. This one went into the floor because Gruber had rushed forward, and batted down Haas's arm.

"Stop! Stop!" Gruber shouted.

"I want to kill him," said Haas. "I'm going to kill him."

"No you're not," said Gruber, who had jumped between Haas and the pastor. "Give me that thing!"

There was a momentary silence, made louder because the shots seemed to echo.

"Give it to me, I said."

Haas still held the Luger, and he was staring at the pastor over Gruber's shoulder, eyes fixed with hatred.

It was the pastor who broke the silence, saying to Haas in German: "A grown man beating up a child. Have you no shame, sir?"

"Give it to me," said Gruber. "That's an order."

Haas never handed the Luger over. Gruber took it out of his hand and placed it behind him on the table.

The outer door had opened, one guard had rushed in, and the other was sitting on the floor clutching his arm. Behind Gruber were French doors that led out to the driveway and the road beyond, and through them could be seen other soldiers running up from all over. Gruber opened the doors and barked orders.

"You two, come in here. The rest of you get back to your posts."

The two soldiers had entered the room. Gruber tossed his handcuffs at one of them, and pointed to the pastor.

"Handcuff that man," he ordered. "No, not like that. Behind his back."

The pastor stood tall, retaining his dignity even though handcuffed. Haas walked behind him and squeezed the cuffs tighter, as tight as they would go, forcing them so tight that the pastor, despite himself, winced.

"You two men," Gruber said to the soldiers, "take him down to the wine cellar and lock him in. Untersturmführer Haas will show you where it is." Gruber glared at Haas. "I don't want anything to happen to him, is that understood?"

The clergyman in cassock and bib, hands cuffed behind his back, was led out the French doors, around the building, and down the outside steps and under the house.

Haas's flashlight sought the key in the wine cellar door. When he had found it he turned it gratingly, then pulled open the door. Behind him was the furnace, edges of light showing around the rim of the firewall door.

"Step back," said Haas to the two soldiers, and they did, and he walked up to the handcuffed pastor and drove his fist into his midsection as far as it would go. When the prisoner doubled over with the pain and shock, Haas kneed him hard in the nose, and he fell over backward into the wine cellar.

Haas slammed the door on him, locked it, withdrew the key, and on the way out of the cellar opened the firewall door and threw the key into the furnace.

"Have you calmed down now?" Gruber asked him when he reentered the interrogation room. "Do you know why I stopped you?"

"No, I don't," said Haas coldly.

"There are a number of reasons. Are you ready to listen?"

"Go ahead, talk."

"We have a hotel full of convalescent troops in this village, did you know that?"

"No."

"The pastor is the head man of the village. He's supposedly a beloved figure. You kill him, and the Maquis will come down out of the hills and massacre all those wounded men. Is that a good enough reason for you?"

"They do that, we'll hang a thousand of them."

"But that won't bring our men back to life, will it?"

Haas shrugged.

"All right, here's another reason. I had him in a camp, the worst camp in France in fact, and he got himself out of it. How did he do that?"

"How do I know."

"He has political clout, that's how."

"France lost the war. We won. French politics doesn't interest me."

"Let me give you a word of advice. It's not a good idea to mess with political power you can't quite figure out."

"I should have killed him."

"You're young yet. You ought to listen to advice from time to time."

"If I ever get him alone, I'll kill him."

"There's one other thing I want you to see," said Gruber, and he opened the door to the outer room. The wounded soldier was sitting in a chair, his uniform coat off, his sleeve rolled up, his shirt soaked with blood. Dr. Blum was treating him. He had been shot in the fleshy part of the arm, and Blum was stitching him up.

"That's a German soldier you shot," said Gruber.

Haas said nothing.

"Next time think before you pull the trigger."

"Who's that doctor?" said Haas. "That doctor's a Yid."

"The kid with the phylacteries," said Gruber, closing the door, "do you want him back?"

Not meeting Gruber's eyes, Haas gave a dismissive wave of his hand. "I'm finished with him."

"Let's get on with the interrogations," said Gruber, "and let's speed it up. The way you're going we'll be here all week."

XXIV

THE boys who lived in the House of the Rocks and who waited for Haas to get around to them had noted the arrival of the pastor, had heard the gunshots. Through the windows they had watched the pastor dragged out in handcuffs. Most, as they approached Haas's table, were even more scared than before. Some could not swallow. One or two could barely walk.

The interrogations continued all afternoon, the same easy questions first, and then the one that had become, on this continent at this time, because of the consequences, unanswerable:

"Are you or are you not a Jew?"

Followed by: "Drop your pants."

Followed by Haas's baton prodding and slapping whichever boy's circumsized penis was now on display.

But the interrogations had become shorter than before, and Haas seemed to conduct them with a little less verve. Also, he had begun to focus in on the doctor, whose turn with him had not yet come.

"Who else is a Jew? That Jew doctor out there, I know a Jew when I see one. Who else?"

There was time out for a copious German lunch, served in shifts in the refectory, some soldiers remaining on guard, while others ate. The two women in the kitchen then asked permission to feed the prisoners, and this was granted—they were allowed to bring in bowls of soup on trays.

The questioning then resumed. Gruber watched, seldom rising from behind the table, seldom taking part, seldom speaking. Haas had taken off his necktie. He worked in shirtsleeves, the sleeves rolled up, the back of the shirt soaked through, his blond hair flying, and the degree of his energy and application was amazing. So was his hatred for Jews, apparently. Gruber saw Haas as a boor, but there were many boors who had risen to the surface in Germany at this time. He could see how the young man might have caught the attention of previous superiors, and how he might have been sent here to spy on his present one, namely himself.

Seated behind the table, Gruber was listening to warning bells, not the screams of prisoners. Perhaps, he reflected, he had come down too hard on the young man earlier. The shooting had been only an accident, and he himself could be accused of having caused it.

Gruber resolved to be more circumspect for the rest of the day, and from then on he allowed Haas every latitude.

In late afternoon Haas's interrogation reached Georges Favert.

Young Favert, as he entered the room, seemed afraid of no one. He wore two thicknesses of sweaters, rough corduroy pants, and wooden shoes. The pastor had brought him to Le Lignon several years earlier to run two of the funded houses—to handle the staff, manage the accounts, and serve as surrogate father to the boys. He had done a good job, the pastor had told him often enough. The houses ran smoothly and the boys all liked him. Still unmarried, he had that day no family to be afraid for, nothing much to lose personally, or so it seemed to him, and for hours he had been trying to comfort children and youths, some of them severely beaten, after Haas had finished interrogating them. Boys nominally in his care. Georges Favert was furious at what had been done to them, and since he had gone to school in Germany and spoke German, he had no difficulty now in expressing this fury in a language Haas understood.

"You're so brave," he sneered, "beating up children." As a beginning this was perhaps reckless, but he was in the mood to be reckless.

Gruber interrupted him. "You have the same name as the pastor. You related to him?"

"Nephew."

Gruber turned to Haas and said sharply: "Remember what I told you."

"Where's the pastor?" said Georges Favert. "What have you done with him? If you've hurt him—"

Haas said: "You are guilty of hiding Jews, but I'm prepared to be lenient if you tell me what I want to know. An American pilot—"

"You've been asking that all day. Nobody knows anything about it, including me. You got the wrong village. Where's the pastor?"

Gruber decided to say: "He's unhurt. He's been locked up some-place where he can't interfere."

Georges Favert was dark-skinned, with dark curly hair and dark eyes, and Haas studied him speculatively. He said: "That doctor out there . . ."

"A marvelous man. The first doctor this village has ever had. Goes out in all kinds of weather. If people don't have money there is never any bill."

"He's a Jew," said Haas.

Like his cousin, Georges Favert was unwilling to lie. But this did not prevent him from saying indignantly: "Who told you that, for God's sake?"

"I can smell them."

"He's an excellent doctor. He's sewn up wounds, set broken bones all over the village. He's sat by patients' bedsides all night. The people are crazy about him."

"Why are you defending a Jew?" said Haas.

"He has treated your soldiers here without charge."

"The staff doctors treat our soldiers."

"For ailments of a venereal nature, they would lose pay or leave, so they go to him instead, no charge."

"No German soldier would allow his private parts to be seen or touched by a Jew."

"What nonsense you speak. What a moron you are."

"You're a Jew too. You think I didn't see it? I saw it the minute you walked in here. Drop your pants."

"No," said Georges Favert.

Haas began beating him about the face and neck with the baton. When Georges covered up, Haas drove his fist into his belly, and then kneed him in the face doubled over.

Stepping around Georges, who lay on the floor spitting out blood, Haas went to the door, where he called in some soldiers to whom he gave orders. Two of them grasped Georges by the arms, lifting him upright, and a third soldier undid his belt and fly. His pants dropped.

Haas gave an ugly laugh.

Georges mumbled through bleeding, fast swelling lips: "I had an infection as a kid."

Haas sent the soldiers out of the room.

"Shit-eating Jew," he said, when they were gone, and he began whipping and punching Georges Favert, who tried to cover up. Subjects who tried to cover up, as opposed to those who stood there and took whatever punishment was coming, usually fared the worst from Haas.

"I'm a member of the Reformed Church of France."

"You're a Jew and that pastor you're related to is a Jew, which I knew from the start."

When his arms tired, Haas went to the door and ordered the doctor sent in.

Dr. Blum entered and handed over his papers, which Haas studied for a moment, while Blum glanced repeatedly in the direction of Georges Favert, who sat on the floor hurt and bleeding, while at the same time trying to pull up his pants.

Haas looked up from Blum's identity card. In German he said to Blum: "Ligier, is that a Jewish name in this country?"

"I understand not," said Blum in French.

"But then Ligier is not your name, is it?" said Haas in German. "More like Goldberg, Einstein, one of those names. And you understand me very well, I can see."

Not daring to speak, Dr. Blum shrugged. He thought he saw

where this interview would end, that there was no hope of escape for him, but he was not sure yet.

The documents in Haas's hands had come to Blum after weeks of anxious waiting, for at the time he had had no others of any kind from any country, nothing, nor had his wife. The joy he had felt coming home with them at last, home being a seedy hotel whose owner did not ask questions, holding finally in his hands the life-saving documents, his own and his wife's, was one of the most joyful days he had ever known, more joyful than the day of his marriage, or the day he had graduated from medical school. He felt absolute liberation. Looking at them, it was as if he had found love, which in a sense he had, for love and security are the same, and he and his wife now had a kind of security at last in a world in which security had long ago ceased to exist. He could go out in the street again even in broad daylight, and not fear being arrested, he could ride buses and trains, his wife too, he could possibly even find a village where he could work again. For weeks he used to take his new documents out at times and look at them, feel them with his fingers, study his new identity the way a miser might study his money. He had loved them the way another man might love a child, and his wife did too, he believed.

He watched Haas rip the documents to shreds before his eyes. "Since your name is not Ligier," he said, "you have no need of them, do you?"

Blum had lunged for the documents at the moment Haas started shredding them, but too late, and then he saw abruptly that the second of his lives was over. The curtain was coming down, and there was nothing he could do. He had had five years with these documents, five years of not being hunted, good years of feeling almost like a complete human being. The village had been good to him. The pastor had been especially good to him. He had always known these years would end, and now he could see they had ended. He was a Jew. He had been found out, and now there was nothing for him to do except accept what was to happen.

As he realized this—he didn't make a decision but merely saw that one had been made for him—he realized also that he still had one job left to do, and that it was a negative kind of job: he must do or say nothing that might lead these people to his wife. If she got out of this war alive, then it would not matter much what happened to him, he would have had a triumph, one of the greatest triumphs possible under the circumstances, and he could savor it in heaven. He knew he would recognize heaven when he saw it, because it would be a place where being a Jew was not a crime.

"Admit it, Jew," said Haas in German.

"Yes," said Dr. Blum, speaking German to a stranger for the first time in years, "I'm a Jew, and you're a pig, and so is your friend over there who doesn't say anything. What else do you want to know? You and men like you have brought shame upon the German race." Blum was like an Indian warrior keening his death song, and it sounded good to him. "You are a disgrace to the memory of Beethoven and Goethe and all the other great and kind and decent Germans who have come before you."

This last speech was one that came to him word for word as he spoke it, but he did not get to make all of it, because Haas slugged him in the face, in the neck, in the side of the head, and after that in many other places. Blum did not go down. He was resolved to stand there and take it, thereby showing Haas and the other man at the table that Jews could take as much punishment as men like them could dish out, for Jews were not cowards, Jews had lived through centuries, and especially now years, that no gentile could have survived, or at least not many. The punches and lashes came down on him hard at first, and then much like spring rain, the temperature of them becoming more and more pleasant, until after a time he didn't feel them at all anymore, and then came a great ripping sensation in the center of his chest, and then he was falling through gray space, and then he struck the floor, and then he was dead.

"He's not moving," said Gruber, who had come around the table.

Georges Favert had scrambled forward.

"He may be dead," said Gruber looking down.

Georges Favert took Blum's head in his lap. "You've killed him, you *salopards*."

"His heart gave out," said Haas to Gruber. "Or some goddamn thing. I had nothing to do with it."

"Well, he's all yours now," Gruber said to him, and he nudged Blum with his foot. "What do you want to do with him?"

"Leave him where he is," said Haas. "We're about ready to wind it up here anyway."

Georges Favert was weeping. He rocked Blum in his lap and sobbed tears of pain, frustration, and grief.

"You're finished?" Gruber asked to be sure. "There's nothing else you want to do here?"

"I'm finished," said Haas.

Gruber gave instructions to the soldiers, and the prisoners were led out of the building toward one of the buses—the others would depart empty. Some of the boys, as they boarded, were limping, some were helping others, and there was dried blood on most of their faces. None of them was dressed in warm clothing, and they had not been permitted to fetch any from their rooms.

With the guards removed from the kitchen door, Norma Favert had gone running out toward the buses looking for her husband. She had heard the pastor's voice earlier, but that was hours ago, she had not heard it since, and she was frantic.

She kept calling out to the boys: "Have you seen the pastor?"

Georges Favert was the last to board. It had been necessary to send two soldiers to drag him out from under the dead doctor, and to support him as far as the buses. Through split and swollen lips he told her what he knew, that the doctor was dead, that the pastor was presumably alive but locked up someplace.

Georges was pushed on board, the convoy started up and soon it had disappeared around the trees.

Already calling her husband's name, Norma ran back into the house through the open French doors that were flapping in the wind. Immediately she came upon the doctor's body. The room was already very cold, and the doctor lay there on the floor. She got a tablecloth and covered him, then rushed from room to room calling: "Andre, Andre."

But the pastor was not anywhere.

Finally she thought of the cellar. She found the outside door, and went down into the gloom and when she called out this time, a weak answer came back.

But she was unable to find the key to the door behind which he was imprisoned. There was no key anywhere, and finally she ran back upstairs to telephone the assistant pastor, asking him to bring men with axes.

Four men came, one of them Henriot, and two axes. The door was stout, but eventually they broke a hole through it, and her husband stumbled out.

When he embraced her she realized he was weeping silently into her neck, and because she knew him so well she understood that his tears were not from relief or pain or fear, but from grief. In a single day all he had ever hoped for from his life and from his village had been crushed, and he recognized his failure, and he wept.

THE pastor's office in the presbytery was small, about two and a half meters square. It had pine floors, and walls paneled in sycamore. The one window cut through the outer wall had a sill about half a meter thick.

The office was not heated, and so the pastor when he worked in there usually wore sweaters and slippers lined with rabbit fur. He was wearing them now. It was later that same day, the door was locked, and his face was in his hands. He was trying to come to terms with himself and his God.

It was in this office where, on other days, he had worked on his accounts or his sermons. It was also where, in the early days of his ministry, he had tried to solve the dense ethical problems that had preoccupied him at the time, and had formulated the philosophy of pacifism and nonviolence, of love of neighbor, that he had both lived by and preached ever since.

From the pulpit he had spoken regularly of the love that ought to regulate the life of every Christian, but the love he had urged upon his congregation was not the adoration of an abstract God. He had never been interested in the private ecstasies which were said to have illuminated the lives of certain mystics in the past. Rather he had spoken of a personal moral purity that made one worthy of love. It was not enough merely to keep one's hands clear of evil, he would preach. What was required was an active, dangerous love of fellow human beings who were in need. This love was not sentimental, nor was it a desire to feel morally noble. One either opened or closed a door to those in need. Goodness, the basis of all ethics, was neither more nor less than the accepting of this responsibility.

Aside from the distinction between good and evil, between helping and hurting, the fundamental distinction of the ethic he had tried to transmit was between giving things and giving oneself. When you gave somebody something without giving yourself, he would preach, you degraded both parties by making the receiver only passive and by making yourself a benefactor standing there to receive thanks, or even sometimes obedience. But when you gave of yourself nobody was degraded. In fact, both parties were elevated by a shared joy. Again and again his voice had resounded through the temple: "What you give creates new, vigorous life instead of arrogance on the one hand and passivity on the other."

His energy and his ideas had been contagious, and he knew this. His sermons had reeked of an almost erotic love for other persons, erotic feelings for every human being. The men and women who heard him could not long resist his words, and they could not resist him.

How fine he had sounded at the time, both to his congregation and to himself. The power of the spirit is surprising, he had told them. It was a force no one could predict or control.

But tonight it seemed to him that none of this was true, had never been true, and he saw himself as a fraud who had brought notoriety on himself and disaster on his village. Sitting at his desk he confronted what seemed to him his uselessness and guilt, and he did not see how he could go on pretending to be a man of God. He had longed for an intimate relationship with God, and had thought he had one, presumptuous thought, for now there was nothing, no love for him, or by him, in any direction he could see, and he was close to total despair.

From the pulpit he had sold nonviolence not only as Christ-like but also as practical, for it was totally disarming. It actually blunted rage, blunted evil, he had preached. As time went on he had even bragged about its effectiveness, pointing out with pride that no one could resist nonviolence, and the proof was that, although it was widely known that Le Lignon hid Jews, nonetheless there had been no massacres in the village, they had been left alone.

And they had been until today. Today, thirty-two young men had been taken away who would never be seen again, one of them his nephew, the doctor already murdered. The massacre had happened. And where was the pastor during all this, and where was God? The pastor had been locked in a closet, and God was locked in there with him, apparently. God and Jesus had been proven as powerless as himself.

Alone in his office, hearing the children through the door, the pastor searched for peace in his heart and soul but could not find it. He had liked to say he had received peace from God as a gift, but he knew he had rarely possessed it. All the major questions had kept posing themselves anew from the beginning again and again. Yet there had always been some peace, a little at least, whereas tonight there was none. Never before had he been this overwhelmed with doubt. Where was God, why had God forsaken him?

He had been humiliated in front of the village as well. The leader of the village, the man to whom all other men looked, the man whose sermons had passed from hand to hand all over southern France, had been totally diminished. Terrible events had occurred that the village had counted on him somehow to prevent. Instead he had been reduced to such impotence that he had had to be rescued by men with axes. He could tell himself that he was without vanity, that this did not hurt, but he wasn't, and it did.

He thought of his wife, who lived for others, whereas he had lived, he now believed, only for his own aggrandizement. His wife would get over this quickly enough. She was a woman who talked swiftly with a breathless heavy voice. She had powerful arms that were frequently used to move things and push herself away from tables so she could cope with human physical needs. There would be new people to save, and she would save them. She would forget the despair and defeats of the past, but he would not.

To Norma something was evil because it hurt people. To him it was evil because it hurt people and because it violated an imperative of God that was in the Bible and in men's hearts. This was what he had preached, whereas she did not even believe in God; not really she didn't. She saw ethics as horizontal, person to person, not as awe for a superior being. Whereas belief in a superior being had been to him essential. Jesus had awed him. He had wanted to put his feet in Jesus' footprints. He had wanted to obey the commandments not like a soldier obeying orders but like a lover wanting to please his beloved.

But now it seemed to him that he no longer believed in anything. His faith lay in shards at his feet, he did not see how he was to put the pieces together again, and without his faith he would not want to go on living.

By the time he let himself out of his office the house was silent and dark. His children were asleep, and the pilot was asleep in the bed that had been Rachel's. The pastor got undressed in the bathroom, then got into bed beside his wife who was snoring softly, and he stared at the ceiling that he could not see, and that was like the future he was also unable to see, and he lay there for hours and could not sleep.

One other conclusion he had come to during his long meditation: Rachel must be smuggled into Switzerland. Getting her there was risky, but not as risky as letting her stay here. What had happened today must not happen to her. He would make the arrangements and bid her good-bye. The frightened child alone in the world who had been so desperately anxious to please, who had needed him so much, had grown into a sweet and cheerful young woman. He would get her name on the list of refugees whom Switzerland would accept, and in a few days she would be gone. Over the years he had come to love her so much. This bright, beautiful person would be gone from his life, but it had to be done, a realization that he hated.

Perhaps ten years from now she would come back with her children to say hello. And that's all it would be: hello. In sending her to Switzerland he would be losing her forever, and he could not bear the loss of it. But it was the only way he could think of to save her life.

AT midnight, sneaking out of the assistant pastor's house where she shared a bedroom with two children, Rachel made her way to the bridge over the river. She was bundled up against the cold. Because she feared meeting or being seen by Lieutenant Ziegler, she had kept to back streets, and paused often in doorways to listen for other footsteps, of which there were none. Young Ziegler, who at that moment was crossing Germany in a troop train, had never denounced her, but she didn't know this, and so her heart beat fast, her palms were wet, and she was afraid.

At the river waited Davey who, as far as the pastor knew, was sound asleep in the presbytery.

By the calendar it was now spring, but on the plateau there was still snow in places, and the nights were windy and cold. The two young people embraced through many layers of clothing, and there were kisses, icy lips against icy lips, and then Rachel said:

"He's sending me to Switzerland."

"Good," said Davey. "I wanted him to. You'll be safe there."

"We won't see each other until after the war. If then."

"The war won't last forever."

"It's already lasted forever."

"There's going to be an invasion soon."

"We won't be together for years, and you don't even care, do you?"

"I want you to be safe."

"You don't, do you?"

"I'm going with you," said Davey.

"You are?" said Rachel, momentarily elated. And then: "You don't have to go with me. I can get there without you."

"I want to know that you made it across."

"He won't let you go with me."

"He can't stop me."

"He doesn't want us to be together."

"I'll go anyway."

"Oh, Davey."

This was followed by more kisses, cold desperate kisses in the night.

THE pastor was in his office, the door closed. Davey knocked and went in.

"I don't have time to talk to you now," said the pastor. "I'm very busy."

Davey said: "You're sending Rachel to Switzerland."

"How do you know that?"

The pastor stared at him, though only for a moment. When Davey said nothing he looked away.

"I see," said the pastor.

"You don't see anything," said Davey. And then: "I want to go with her."

"You can't go with her. Your name would have to be on a certain list, and it's not on there."

"I want to go with her as far as the border. After that I'll take my chances."

"You'll compromise our escape routes, that's what you'll do."

"What's this list?"

"We send Switzerland the names of refugees for their approval. We have groups there who will fund the refugees until the end of the war. Sometimes there's a mistake. Refugees make it across and their names are not on the list and they get sent back."

It seemed to Davey that there was no force left in the pastor. He sounded evasive, and he rarely met Davey's eyes.

"Is there any chance Rachel might be sent back?"

"No. I've made especially sure. You, however, are a foreign belligerent. They would never accept you."

"Probably they'd just intern me for the duration."

"Is that what you want?"

"There are worse things."

"You'd be traveling through enemy territory without papers—"

"I do have some papers."

"Without speaking the language. There will be all sorts of controls along the way. If the Germans catch you . . ."

Davey shrugged.

"You'd have to stay well away from Rachel during the trip so if one of you gets caught it doesn't compromise the other."

"All right," said Davey.

"If you make it across you wouldn't be with her. You'd be interned and she would not be."

"I want to see her cross that border. I want to see her safe."

Still not meeting Davey's eyes, seeming to give up more or less without a fight, the pastor said: "If that's what you want . . ."

"That's what I want."

There was a long silence. Then Davey said: "You've been good to me. You've saved me from a prisoner of war camp or worse. I appreciate it, don't think I don't. And after the war I'll try to find some way to repay you. But now the time has come to move on."

Again there was a silence.

"When do we go?" asked Davey.

"Tomorrow," said the pastor, "as soon as it gets dark."

THE church was again full to overflowing, and the pastor mounted to the pulpit and looked over the congregation.

"We are gathered here today to pay tribute to, and to bury, our doctor," he began. "So this is a sad day for all of us. Our doctor died tragically, and long before his time, not because he had done something wrong, but because he happened to have been born a Jew. Some of us knew him better than others, but we all knew him, because during the last five years he has been inside nearly every one of our houses, and always in time of need. He brought with him the few medicines he was able to procure, and a vast amount of knowledge and expertise, and he cured us, or sewed us up, or set our broken bones, or delivered our babies. We saw him not as a Jew or a Christian or as anything other than a good and kind man whose presence made life in this village a little less frightening, a little more secure.

"He was from that part of Czechoslovakia that has since been overrun by one of its neighbors. He studied in Germany, and I think he considered himself German. German was his first language. He had been in a concentration camp in Germany for some years, and got out, and in another one in Poland, and got out. And then the war started and he somehow got here to France with his wife, but not with his children. He did not know what had happened to his children. He was without money, without papers of any kind, when he reached this village. And he became our doctor, and we needed him, and we loved him.

"He got some papers finally. According to these papers he was Jean Marie Ligier, a Frenchman. This was the name most of us knew him by. He didn't fool us though, did he? The things he did to the French language were enough to take your breath away."

The congregation, which had been absolutely silent until now, burst into laughter.

In the pulpit the pastor smiled, waited for the laughter to subside, and went on.

"His name was Hans Blum, but we live in a time when, to go on living at all, some men, one of them Hans Blum, are forced to disavow all that they have been and are, all that they wish to be, including even their names.

"We are here in sorrow, not in anger. Anger cannot help us, and it cannot help Dr. Blum, but the sorrow we feel for the death of this man can be looked at as the last great gift he was able to give us, because in sorrow we become stronger than we were, more resolute, and in the truest sense of the word more Christian.

"Dr. Blum was a Jew, and I'm sure he would have preferred to be buried from a synagogue, not our Protestant temple. And Dr. Blum, like any Jew, would have wanted the Kaddish to be recited over his coffin. Of course we have no synagogue here, no building that goes by that name, and no rabbi, and Jewish law is very strict over who may recite the Kaddish, and when and how. It must be recited standing, and in Hebrew. It requires a minyan, a prayer quorum, the presence of ten Jewish males, because according to Jewish law, ten men constitute a synagogue and when they pray together the Divine Presence is with them and there is no need for a synagogue building or an officiating rabbi."

The pastor paused, and took heart, and some of his despair lifted, for he was being a pastor again, and it was his job to try to provoke other men to do what they ought to do.

"If we had ten Jewish men here," he said, "that would make for a minyan, and our Protestant temple would become a synagogue, and the Kaddish could be read."

He looked out over the congregation, and said: "Are there by any chance ten Jewish men here?"

No one responded, and eyes dropped to laps. He would have expected heads to turn as people looked around at their neighbors, but this did not happen.

Pastor Favert knew all these people, their faces certainly, and in some cases their names. He knew which of them had always been parishioners, and which were new to the village—relatively new—

meaning they were refugees who had found here a place where they could hide and perhaps survive the war. He knew each of the refugees because in most cases it was he who had placed them with families, and because he visited them regularly on his rounds, asking if they had everything they needed, knowing they did not, knowing how hard to bear their lives were, offering them what encouragement he could.

Looking down from the pulpit he recognized at least a hundred refugee faces. The death of Dr. Blum had drawn them here from the farms and houses where he had hidden them, and in which they continued to hide, and as his eyes moved from face to face he thought he saw them silently pleading with him. To say Kaddish for Dr. Blum, much as they might like to do it, was to declare themselves. It was simply too dangerous, and each of the silent faces seemed to say to him, please don't make me do it.

Many of them had been in hiding for years. Most never left their rooms. They were not in concentration camps, but their fear was such that they were imprisoned anyway. In general the Jewish children went to school, circulated freely, behaved like children everywhere, but the adults, most of them, were too afraid ever to go out of their houses, ever to be seen in the village streets, and even those who lived on isolated farms ventured out of doors, out into the barnyard or the nearby forest, only at night.

It was clear to the entire congregation, Pastor Favert saw, that he thought Kaddish should be said, and when he got no response he frowned.

"Let me tell you about the Kaddish," he preached, keeping the pressure on the Jews, while at the same time giving an explanation to the Protestants. "The mourners' Kaddish has an affinity to the Lord's Prayer, in that it requires men to give praise for the evil that befalls them even as they give praise for the good. It is not really a prayer for the dead. There is not a single mention of death in it, and this may seem odd. Rather, it is what is known in other religions as a 'Gloria'—a prayer in which one does not ask for anything, but only praises God's greatness. Kaddish is said over one who has died and also over one who has just been born, because the Kaddish blesses both the good and the bad, since all come from the same source. When something terrible happens—what is happening to the Jewish people at this time, for instance—the Jews pray even harder. They react in a 'kaddish' way by being stronger. The Kaddish is also a promise. At a time when people feel weak and sad or when they feel there is a terrible evil loose upon the world, that is precisely the time when they are called upon to rise up, and instead of saying 'less' say 'more!' "

Again he scanned the congregation, his gaze lingering longest on the faces of certain of the Jewish men, the ones he thought of as the strongest, all of whom still refused to meet his eyes.

"Was Dr. Blum afraid for his life during the years he lived among us? He told me once he was afraid every minute of every day, and yet he went out every day, and visited his patients every day, and trusted the community not to betray him, and it did not betray him. I wonder how many others here believe in the community as he did, and are willing to trust the community as he did."

Again he scanned the faces in the pews, in the aisles, but this time some of the eyes were raised. He said: "And now, as we prepare to lower his body into the ground, Kaddish needs to be said. And if there were ten Jewish males here we would have a minyan and it could be said."

Below him in one of the pews there was a rustle of movement, and then a man stood, worked his way out into the aisle and came forward until he stood almost beneath the pulpit, and he put on his hat.

There was a long silence, and then a second man rose to his feet, and came forward, and stood beside the first man, and put on his hat.

All over the church other men stood, and came forward, and put on their hats. In all there were thirty of them or more, and the prayer began, the men speaking in Hebrew from memory, while the pastor in the pulpit, reading from a card, translated for the benefit of the rest of the congregation.

"Glorified and sanctified be God's great name throughout the world which He has created according to His will," the pastor read. "May He establish His kingdom in your lifetime and during your days, and within the life of the entire house of Israel, speedily and soon."

The thirty or more Jews said: "Amen!" and the entire congregation added: "Amen!"

The prayer continued in Hebrew.

"May His great name be blessed forever and to all eternity," the pastor translated. "Blessed and praised, glorified and exhalted, extolled and honored, adored and lauded be the name of the Holy One. Blessed be He beyond all the blessings and hymns, praises and consolations that are ever spoken in the world."

The entire congregation in unison said: "Amen!"

The coffin was carried out of the church and across to the graveyard where the hole had already been prepared, and as the remains of Hans Blum, doctor of medicine, were lowered into it, there came the final words of the Kaddish.

"May he come to his place in peace."

And the Jews as they left the grounds, threw grass and earth behind them in the direction of the gravesite, saying in Hebrew: "Remember, we are dust."

XXV

Though they had been told she was not going far away, nor for very long, the younger children clung to Rachel as if they knew they'd never see her again. The older two kissed her casually, and went back to their homework.

Norma Favert walked the girl out into the hall, where they fell into each other's arms, both of them weeping.

The pastor, who had been locked in his office for the past hour, had still not come out.

"Wait," said Norma Favert, brushing away tears, "I'll get him."

Rachel, waiting, also brushed away tears.

She heard footsteps, and then the pastor appeared, wearing what seemed to her a false smile.

"Ready to take off?" he said. "Well, then, good-bye and the best of luck."

She said: "Papa . . ."

He said: "Be sure to send us a postcard—"

"Papa . . ."

"Tell us how you're doing."

She looked down at the floor.

"You only have about ten minutes," said the pastor. "Better get going." Kissing her casually on both cheeks, he turned and walked away. A moment later she heard him enter his office and the door close.

He's turned his back on me already, she thought.

"He's upset because you're leaving," said Norma Favert. "Remember him—kindly—please."

Rachel embraced her foster mother once more, this time dry-eyed, and went out into the night, and began walking up toward the station. The shops were closed, the streets empty. The buildings were dark, though she could see cracks of light where the blackout curtains had not been fully drawn. She kept walking uphill, and soon could hear the train huffing in the station. She was wearing what she always wore; sweaters, skirt, and wooden shoes, and was carrying the same handbag, with nothing extra in it except a toothbrush and a bar of soap. Also some toilet paper, for there would be none in any of the stations en route. On her head she wore a knitted ski cap. The night was dark and cold, and she hugged herself against it. She was eighteen years old and about to put the world of Le Lignon behind her, as she had put other worlds behind her previously, and she was scared, but excited too. Waiting ahead was Davey. Switzerland as well, and she didn't doubt she would make it there, and she wondered what it would be like.

There were going to be four people attempting to reach the border, herself and Davey, and two other refugees who had been brought to the presbytery earlier by the guide who would lead them across.

The guide was a seventeen-year-old boy in a Boy Scout uniform. His name was Raymond Bourette, and he had drawn his group into one of the bedrooms, and begun to give them instructions about the trip ahead. The other refugees, a man and his wife, were Poles who spoke no French and very little German. Rachel had to translate the instructions into English for Davey and into German for the Poles.

"Who is this kid?" Davey asked Rachel.

"He seems to know what he's talking about."

"Ask him how many people he's led across."

The boy told Rachel he made the trip about once a week, always with three refugees, or at most four, and had been doing it since the previous September. "The Boy Scout uniform is a good cover," he said. "Nobody suspects a kid my age of being a guide."

This reply did not satisfy Davey. He worried about entrusting his safety—and especially Rachel's—to this boy. Though not much older, he had been hardened, especially recently, in many more ways.

But for the moment he listened to the rest of the translation, and kept silent.

"Once I have given you your railroad tickets," Raymond said in French, "you will separate from each other, and you will follow me from a distance from start to finish. On the trains or in the stations, if someone asks for your tickets or your identity card you hand them over without acting troubled, and without speaking. It's a long trip—"

"It's about a hundred and fifty miles," interrupted Davey.

After speaking to Raymond, Rachel turned back to Davey. "He says it's four changes of trains, a bus ride, and then on foot," she said. "It takes more than two days."

"We'll be traveling by day and by night," Raymond continued. "Some of the time you'll probably be sleeping. The rest of the time, pretend to be sleeping. On the trains, in the waiting rooms, close your eyes and pull your hats down over your faces. Avoid eye contact. Avoid anyone who might try to make conversation with you, and whatever you do, don't chat in your own language with your companion. Try to relax. If someone seems to be looking at you with persistence, pretend to be asleep. There will be stops along the way in safe houses. You can speak to each other then. Once you are in a safe house you must obey all instructions. You will be hidden in attics, and you must keep movement and noise to a minimum. You are not under any circumstances to come down or attempt to go outside until your guide comes for you."

He paused, and glanced at the Poles, who clutched each other's hands and looked scared. "Write nothing down," Raymond said next, "not the name of any person, or your own name, or the name of any town, especially this one. If you get caught, you don't know where you came from or where you are going."

Raymond stopped, glanced in the direction of the Polish couple, and made a joke to Rachel. "Superfluous warning," he said. "These two really don't know where they are or where they are going." But it wasn't a funny joke, and his grin faded. "In any case," he told Rachel, "we'll be traveling mostly by night, so they're not going to see much to orient themselves with."

He turned back to everybody and Rachel resumed translating. "If you see that your guide, myself, is not with you, don't be worried. I'll reappear as soon as I can. At each stop I have to buy your tickets, which I'll pass to you as unobtrusively as possible."

Having paused again, he shook his head sadly in the direction of the Polish couple. "You're going to have to abandon your belongings here," he told them, Rachel translating. "Your valise is small, Madame," he said to the woman, "but you can't take it, I'm afraid. The sack you're carrying, Monsieur," he said to the man, "you can't take it."

He waited, watching their faces fall as the translation got through to them. They didn't have much left, but now even that was going to have to be left behind.

"Worrying about yourself is going to require all your concentration," Raymond continued. "You can't afford to worry about baggage too. There are places where you are going to have to walk distances, you're going to have to pass under barbed wire. The barbed wire is the border—the most dangerous part. You're going to have to crawl under and run without occupying yourself with your companions, not even a wife or husband. You have been warned that the passage is risky and there's no guarantee that everybody will get through. If you are arrested pretend not to understand what is being said to you. You do not know who your guide is, or where he is from; you had no guide. Even in Switzerland don't speak about your guide." He looked up, meeting each pair of eyes in turn. "If you don't want to go, say so now. If you are agreed, good luck."

He had left them then and gone to the station to buy the tickets. The refugee couple had sat on the pastor's sofa holding hands, saying nothing, while Rachel in the kitchen prepared tea, Davey standing at her side. Later there was an early dinner, soup and bread. The children sat around the table trying to be polite to the refugees, but soon saw they did not understand French, and after that talked around them. They had talked around Davey too, at first, but he had roughhoused with the little ones, and played chess with the older two, and now, despite the language barrier, he was their friend.

The pastor had taken his soup in his office, and had not come out again.

Finally it had become time to leave for the station. The Boy Scout had gone out first, the others following at five-minute intervals: the Polish woman, then her husband, then Davey, and lastly, after the tearful good-byes, Rachel.

At the station the train was building up steam. Separately they waited on the platform for permission to board. There were many other travelers, local people who recognized refugees when they saw them, but knew better than to stare, and people from the cities, mostly men who were carrying suitcases of food for which they had no travel permit, and who, consequently, were trying to attract no attention whatever; they looked nowhere, met the eyes of no one.

Rachel stood alone at one end of the crowd, Davey at the other, when suddenly the pastor appeared. He was obliged to greet people, to shake a few hands, but he was peering about and when he spied Rachel he made his way toward her. She watched him approach and did not know what to expect, and then he took her in his big arms and apologized for his coldness in saying good-bye to her.

"I couldn't bear to see you go," he told her. "Please forgive me."

"Papa," she said. She was raked by his mustache and the edge of his glasses.

"You're my daughter, and you always will be," he said. "My oldest, and no one in the world loves you more than I do."

"*En voiture*," bawled the conductor. The passengers boarded, and a minute or so later the train started down out of the village. The last thing Rachel saw of Le Lignon was the solitary figure of the pastor standing on the platform waving to her. Then the track turned and dropped below the level of the station, the train with it, and he was gone.

The locals called the train the Twister. It started down off the plateau, moving slowly. The many turns, some of them almost switchbacks, left it swaying from side to side on its narrow tracks. It honked at every crossroads, and it stopped, it seemed, in every hamlet. There was nothing to be seen at this hour out the window, so Rachel watched Davey at the other end of the car. The pastor had given him a beret, which he wore over his face, moving so seldom she thought he might be truly asleep. The two Poles and Raymond were in the other car.

The end of the line was Dunieres, a village not much bigger than Le Lignon, where passengers going on to St. Étienne were obliged to transfer to another train, and where there was a police control. The passengers were made to form two lines. French gendarmes stood two to each line, Rachel saw, and as the passengers filed through, their papers were examined.

When she glanced around for the Poles, she saw they were behind her, and to her it looked like they were trembling. Davey in his beret was ahead, and he looked very American to Rachel. Ignoring Raymond's instructions, she pushed as close to him as she could get, in case there was some way she could help him.

He didn't need help, as it happened. He showed his papers, grinned at the gendarmes and shook their hands. This surprised them. When he had passed through their glances followed him, and they shook their heads in amusement.

Watching Davey, Rachel was equally surprised.

"Mademoiselle," a gendarme said to her.

"Oh," she said, "sorry," and she produced her papers and was passed through.

She waited some distance off watching for the Poles. She saw the husband give both sets of papers to the gendarme, which he wasn't supposed to do. He was sweating. From where she stood Rachel could see beads of sweat on his brow. But the gendarme never looked at his face, or his wife's either. After glancing briefly at the papers, he handed them back and waved the couple through.

The train to St. Étienne would not leave for two hours. Most of the passengers from Le Lignon were waiting for it, and all the benches were taken. Davey and Rachel sat on the floor, their backs against the wall. They were eight or ten feet apart, as close to each other as they dared, and when they looked at each other, they were careful not to smile. The Poles had found a bench. They sat side by side, bolt upright, with frozen expressions on their faces. Meanwhile Raymond flitted about, talking to everybody. Presently Davey pulled the beret down over his eyes, and pretended to doze. Rachel got up to look for the toilet. As she passed out of the waiting room, Raymond bumped her, and while apologizing managed to slip into her hand her ticket for the next leg of the journey.

Finally their train was announced, Raymond managing to slip the others their tickets as they boarded. For the past two hours there had been no sign of police in the station at all, and there was no police control aboard the train either. By the time they came into St. Étienne, a city of 200,000 people, it was nearly midnight.

All of them looked for a police control as they got down onto the platform, Davey imagining he could brazen it through, Rachel, since she spoke French and had papers, not afraid at all, the two Poles rigid with fear. But there was nothing, and they followed the crowd out of the station.

Raymond, the Boy Scout, was waiting at the curb, and they followed him at a distance, stragglers, the other pedestrians dropping off one by one as the distance from the station increased, until they were alone, five widely spaced individuals advancing down the same sidewalk in a city that had become dark and silent, all of them now listening for a police patrol; even Raymond felt exposed, increasingly nervous.

Finally they had reached what was almost the suburbs, and Raymond stopped in front of the house of a man named Besset.

The house was big, and in the darkness imposing. It had some land around it. It had its own stables too, meaning that in the not too distant past it had had its own animals. Besset had a small trucking business, and the stables now housed his trucks.

There were no lights burning inside the stables, nor inside the house either, but Raymond stepped up to the door and rang.

The door opened and they were invited forward into the darkness. Only when the door had closed again did lights come on, and they saw that the house was not only large but comfortably furnished. Besset was a man of about fifty with gray hair and a gray beard. He shook hands with each of them, then led them into the kitchen where a pot of soup simmered on the stove. His wife had been recently arrested, he told them. He hoped he would be able to get her out, but it would take time. In any case, he was alone in the house, and had made the soup himself, he hoped they liked it, and he sat his guests at the kitchen table and served the soup, then took a huge round loaf of rye bread and cut it into pieces. He put out glasses, and a liter of rough wine.

Everyone ate. The Poles murmured to each other from time to time. Besset, through Rachel, quizzed Davey about England. Afterward Raymond, whose presence in the house was perfectly legal, went to the room he occupied on each trip, while Besset led the others across to the garages. There was enough moonlight to find the way. In his hand he carried a flashlight, and once inside he turned it on.

Above the garages was the old hayloft, which still smelled like one, which still contained piles of straw, and which that night would serve as a dormitory for the four refugees.

The loft was unheated, and in the glow of the flashlight they could see their breath. Besset began to rake straw into the rough outlines of four beds, and as he did so he apologized for what he called the primitive conditions he was offering. But during the day he had workers moving about below, and since the arrest of his wife the premises was regularly searched by the Gestapo. They came always at quitting time and examined everybody's papers, and went through his house looking, he supposed, for evidence of people living there. They examined the stables too, so he couldn't have mattresses up here, and he couldn't afford to own, much less lay out, what might seem a surplus of sheets or pillows. He could offer them only blankets and straw, and he hoped they would understand. After asking them not to show any lights, and to make as little noise as possible, and after handing the flashlight to Davey, he went down the stairs and they heard the door close.

The Poles were pushing their two piles of straw together to form a double bed. Davey said to Rachel, whose face he could barely discern: "Should I do the same?"

She gave a low laugh. "Sure, but don't get any ideas."

The two Poles lay together under the blankets talking softly.

Davey got in beside Rachel, and kissed her. The blanket was rough and the straw crackled.

Davey began doing things to her under the blanket.

"Stop," she whispered. "There are people five feet away."

"They can't understand what we're saying."

"No, but they can guess what you're doing."

"I want to make love to you."

"I want to make love to you too, but we can't."

After a moment she again said: "Stop."

"They can't see us kissing."

"You'll get yourself all hot and bothered."

He managed to get her skirt hiked up.

"I hate to think of the wrinkles in the morning," she murmured in his ear.

He got her underpants down her legs without making the blanket move too much. She unbuttoned his fly. They were face-to-face, breathing on each other, and she threw her leg over him, and then they were joined. For five minutes, perhaps longer, neither moved, though the kisses, the murmured endearments never stopped. The Poles had stopped talking and were either asleep or listening, but Davey and Rachel never noticed. In time Davey could hold off no longer. He pulled away from her and caught himself on his handkerchief. They rearranged themselves under the blanket, Davey buttoning himself up, Rachel trying to pull her skirt down to where it belonged, smoothing it as best she could. She dragged her underpants up one leg under the skirt so they would not be visible— would not give her away to the Poles when she got up in the morning.

For both of them it had been the strangest sexual experience of their lives. Of course they had not had many, but this one they would always remember.

For Davey it was one thing more, and he lay awake troubled. Rachel was asleep in the crook of his arm, and he looked at what he could see of her face and was filled with love for her. They would wake up with the daylight still in each other's arms. But he could not get rid of the feeling that he had made love to her tonight for the last time.

. . .

THE train from St. Étienne reached Lyon-Perrache just before six
P.M. They filed off the quai and into the waiting room with its monstrous crowd of travelers. It was hard to find a place to stand,
much less sit down. This was the most dangerous part of the trip,
Raymond had told them, apart from the actual crossing of the border, for every time he had been there previously the hall had
swarmed with men in leather coats and trilby hats slowly, methodically, checking papers. There could be *flics* from other police agencies too, including the Milice, who were the worst, for they were
French. Unfortunately they were going to have to sit it out there a
good long time, for their train to Annecy, the next leg, did not leave
until midnight. They would have six hours of pretending to be
asleep.

He had warned them to be wary of everybody.

Now as they reached the waiting room, they had to wade
through a crush of people even to get into it. It was not going to be
possible to pretend to doze, at least not at first. The benches were
all taken, there was no wall space to lounge against, nor did they
even have luggage to sit on.

Raymond went to buy tickets to Annecy, and came back, and
when he had passed them out he warned them again to have their
papers ready to be controlled by the Gestapo, and he ordered them
to separate from one another. The Poles moved some distance off,
but did not separate, and they did not appear able to take their eyes
off the nearest Gestapo agents, who were approaching, though
slowly.

Just before separating from Rachel, Davey said to her out of the
side of his mouth: "Stay away from those Poles." He had tried to
speak without moving his lips. "They're not going to make it."

Davey too watched the Gestapo agents approach, from time to
time turning to grin at Rachel, who was about ten feet away, but
with so many people between them that at times he could barely
see her. Over by the archway which delimited the waiting room
there was a cluster of *Feldgendarmerie,* he noted, and now, signaled by one of the Gestapo officers, they came forward and there
was a commotion, and they dragged someone out.

Trains came and went, the crowd in the waiting room thinned out, and it became possible to sit on the floor against the wall. Davey pulled the beret down over his eyes and pretended to doze. Perhaps he did doze. A tap on the shoulder brought him to his feet, and he showed the papers Pierre Glickstein had made him. He was neither nervous nor afraid. The papers had passed inspection once, and would again. Davey didn't speak French, but this Gestapo guy probably didn't either.

The man nodded at him, handed the papers back, and moved on.

Davey pulled the beret down over his eyes again and, except for quick glances to make sure Rachel was still okay, he stayed that way until the waiting room clock showed him that it was time to stand up and begin looking for the train. Raymond had told them that if they wanted a seat they should board at least forty-five minutes early. Davey waited on the platform until Rachel came by him and boarded. To his surprise the Poles boarded too. Either the Gestapo had not read their fear, or they had not been controlled at all.

Rachel went into one compartment, Davey into the adjacent one. At length the train started, and it was possible to doze for real. There was only one more control, this one by the *Feldgendarmerie*. At about three A.M. men came through the train demanding papers which they pretended to examine in the weak blue light.

The ride lasted all night and at six-forty in the morning, the dawn just breaking, the train came into Annecy, slowing down and crossing empty streets. They got off. The station was nearly empty, the streets too. Across from the station was the Protestant temple, and Raymond led them into the presbytery, which was adjacent, and the pastor there put out bread, honey, and hot café au lait.

After finishing his breakfast, Raymond went out, and walked around to the Catholic church to see the Abbé Pollet, who told him that the driver of the nine o'clock bus to Collonges-sous-Saleve was expecting them, and that the trip should go smoothly. Raymond went over to the bus station and bought the tickets, then went back to the presbytery and gave them out.

A little later he led his group to the station. Other passengers were waiting, and when the bus pulled up, all boarded. Raymond's group spread out all over the bus, none within five rows of any of the others. They were feeling confident now, for they were within thirty kilometers of the Swiss border. If they had got this far safely, what could go wrong now? They watched the pretty countryside passing by the windows.

According to the bus schedule, the ride was to be nonstop, but at the entrance to Collonges the driver pulled up at the street that led to the Catholic church and rectory. Raymond got off without looking behind him, so all the others did too. The rectory was less than a hundred meters down the street. Raymond knocked on the door, and the priest let them in, and led them immediately up into his attic. In the attic were some chairs, a bench, a mattress on the floor. The priest shook hands with all of them. His name was Grolier. It was then about eleven A.M.

From the dormer window, Raymond pointed toward Switzerland. There were a few fields, and then the barbed wire that indicated the border. Then came a row of poplars, and behind them widely spaced could be seen Swiss soldiers on guard. The Poles, looking out, seemed to have stopped breathing. Freedom was that close. To Davey, freedom had never seemed very distant, and he was well aware that the last part of any journey was the hardest.

"When do we go?" he wanted to know. He said it in credible French. *"On va quand?"*

The answer was nine P.M.

"Another long day," commented Davey.

The priest and Raymond sat together on the bench and talked about frequency of patrols, and other technical details. But then the tone turned ominous, which Davey sensed.

"What are they saying?" he demanded of Rachel.

The conversation between her and the priest was a long one. When it ended she explained to Davey that in the last few days the Italian guards who used to patrol the border had been replaced by Germans. This probably made the crossing more dangerous than it had been. Perhaps much more dangerous.

"Why?"

In the past, Rachel told him, if the Italians caught refugees trying to cross, they sometimes handed them over to local gendarmes, who were sometimes sympathetic. A number of those caught had lived to make a second try. That would not be the case if one were caught by Germans.

"Should I tell the Poles?" asked Rachel.

"I don't think so," said Davey. "They're spooked enough already."

"Spooked?" said Rachel.

"Scared."

"You Americans," said Rachel. "The way you talk."

Davey glanced at her sharply, realizing she was scared herself.

Raymond in his Boy Scout uniform went out and walked along the Collonges-Annemasse road to reconnoiter by daylight the point halfway between two guard posts where tonight he would send his Jews—he assumed all four were Jews—under the barbed wire. The wire, as nearly as he could tell from this distance, had not been reinforced. There was a villa off to the left that had been emptied out at the start of the war. It too looked the same as always. Presently a patrol passed him: six soldiers in coal-scuttle helmets armed with rifles. They looked him over suspiciously. Even for a seventeen-year-old Boy Scout it was risky to be on this road at all, so he turned and walked back toward the village. He was halfway up the street leading to the rectory when the patrol passed again out on the road. He had timed it. The gap between patrols was about twenty minutes, same as during his last trip. He went into the rectory and up to the attic, and the long day began to pass.

The Polish couple spent much of it at the window gazing out toward Switzerland. Davey and Rachel sat on the bench and in the manner of young people everywhere talked of the future, of where they would live and how many children they would have. But Davey became increasingly tense, less and less forthcoming. Rachel ascribed this to concern over the crossing, and chided him for it.

He gave her a thin smile and said: "No, it's not that." And then fell silent again.

There were certain decisions he had made. The need to reconsider them was what preoccupied him. He kept turning them over and over in his head. What had seemed clear to him earlier in the week, or even two hours ago, no longer seemed clear at all. He owed it to everyone to describe what these decisions might be, but could not make himself say anything at all. He kept gazing at Rachel, and could not bear the notion that after today he might never see her again.

Darkness fell. Zero hour was three hours away, then only two. The Poles were now visibly nervous. So was Rachel, whose conversation mostly dried up, as did her saliva apparently, for she licked her lips more and more often.

Davey was merely silent.

The Abbé Grolier brought up dinner: soup and bread. The Poles hardly touched it, nor did Rachel; Davey ate his own portion and most of hers as well.

Raymond came up into the attic, where he brought them all together. "Translate this," he said to Rachel, and she did, first in English, then in German.

You are going to crawl under the barbed wire, Raymond told them, and once on the other side you are going to run toward Switzerland, toward the lights you see over there, toward the first Swiss guards you see, and once in their custody you will be safe. Whatever happens, don't wait for anyone else, don't come back to help anyone else, don't even look back.

"Is that understood?" he asked, and everyone nodded. He looked at his watch. "About ten more minutes," he said.

He led them down the stairs to the front hall. Father Grolier went out to the road to watch for the passage of the patrol. Just inside the door the others waited.

"The weather's clear tonight," Raymond commented.

"Is that bad?" asked Rachel.

"A heavy storm would be better."

Davey drew Rachel aside. "I want you to promise me something."

She looked at him. The lights were out in the hall and they could not see each other clearly.

"If I ask you to do something, I want you to do it immediately, and without question."

Rachel was immediately frightened. "I can't promise something like that."

"If you love me, I want you to promise."

"I do love you. If anything happened to you I wouldn't want to live."

"Nothing's going to happen to me," said Davey.

The priest came running back to the house. Raymond, who had been watching for him through a crack in the door, threw it open and the priest swept in, cassock whipping the jamb.

"Patrol just passed," he said.

"Promise me," said Davey.

"I love you," said Rachel. "I promise you my whole life."

"Let's go," said Raymond.

Davey kissed her. Now comes the hard part, he thought, for he did not intend to cross with her.

The Polish couple embraced as well, the woman lifting her veil to kiss her husband. They looked very scared.

All the lights in the rectory were out. They stepped from darkness into darkness, and ran down the street toward the road following Raymond.

At the road he stopped them, and they all listened hard, but heard nothing. They ran along the road for about two hundred meters. Now they could see the lights of Switzerland across the way, not far off. There was a ditch quite far below the road.

"Everybody down in the ditch," said Raymond.

They lay in the ditch in total darkness listening for the return of the patrol. Presently they heard it on the road above, the drumming of hobnailed boots.

When the night was silent again, Raymond jumped up and ran across the field toward a copse of trees, the others following. The lights of Switzerland, a beacon in a blacked-out continent, were much closer now.

In the copse they stopped to catch their breath, and to wait for the patrol to pass on its way back. Raymond pointed at the barbed wire, at the place where they were to slither under.

"Now!" he said to Davey and Rachel. "Go now. Go."

"I can't go with you," said Davey to Rachel, taking her in his arms. "There's a plane coming for me. I have to go back to the war. I don't have any choice, don't you see?"

"I won't leave you," said Rachel.

"Hurry!" said Raymond.

"All I want is to see you safe, and know that we'll be together again after the war."

"No," said Rachel, "I won't go."

"You promised. Do this one thing for me. That's all I ask."

Rachel was crying. "You ask too much."

The Polish couple was looking from Rachel to Davey, not understanding. Raymond didn't understand either, but he knew there was a hang-up of some kind, and the minutes were passing. He pushed the Polish couple toward the wire. "Go," he told them. "Run."

They ran.

Rachel was clinging to Davey and would not let go.

Fifty meters from the copse the Polish woman lost her hat, and stopped to pick it up. The two of them raced for the wire but ran out of breath when still meters away, and slowed to a walk. From the copse they saw the woman on her hands and knees, the man lifting the bottom strand of wire, and then the woman stood up on the other side, but instead of running toward safety, she waited for the man, who was still flat on his stomach and whose clothes seemed to be snagged on the wire.

The woman waited and waited, but the man seemed unable to free himself, until in exasperation and frustration Raymond screamed from the copse: "Run, run."

The woman started to run then, but the man still did not follow, and she ran back toward the wire again, and then a searchlight came on, and she was surrounded by blinding light coming from the formerly empty villa off to the left. Also from the villa came commands in German, one of them: *"Halt!"* which everyone in the copse understood.

The woman stood there rigid, and then the man got to his feet beside her and held her, a frieze, the searchlight blinding them both, at the same time binding them together forever, while leaving them with no doubt as to how short forever might be.

"Let's get out of here," cried Raymond. And he got to his feet and ran for the road, tumbling into the ditch when he got there, Davey and Rachel landing almost on top of him.

"Is there no way we can help them?" said Davey in an anguished voice.

"*Aucun,*" said Raymond, which means "none," and Davey saw that he was weeping. "They're finished," Raymond blubbered, and for the first time Davey saw him for what he was, a seventeen-year-old boy becoming old before his time. "We're going to be lucky to save ourselves," Raymond said, which Davey understood without understanding the words.

They heard the patrol cutting across the field to make the arrests, and when it passed behind the copse and was hidden from them, they got up and ran down the road into the village and banged on the door of the rectory. The Abbé Grolier sat them down and interrogated them. This was followed by a long somber silence while they contemplated what had happened. It was as if they were attending a wake. "Those poor people," the priest muttered, "those poor poor people."

There was nothing more anyone could say.

The silence ended with the priest saying: "Let's get practical." He thought the Germans might now institute a house-to-house search, he said, especially if the Polish couple talked, which, in their despair, they perhaps would. He thought Raymond and his two remaining refugees should get out of Collonges at once, get to Annecy and get on the train back to where they had come from. This was important for their own safety, and it was important also that they stop any other refugees from coming this way for a while. The priest had a car, he said, and would drive them to Annecy himself. He knew there was a train from there to Lyon just before midnight. With luck he could get them there in time to be on it.

The priest's car was a 1936 Citroën that had been altered to run on charcoal. It was in the garage beside the rectory.

It had a boiler in back, and a gas collection chamber in front, both mounted above the bumpers. Sacks of charcoal were strapped to the running board. Davey had never seen a car like this before.

It took twenty minutes to get the fire going hot enough to produce the gas that ran the engine which, once started, ran with a putt-putt noise that Davey at any other time might have found amusing.

After leaving the village, the priest kept to back roads, and he ran without lights. Top speed seemed to be about thirty kilometers an hour, and on the hills considerably less. There were many hills. Under any stress at all the engine missed badly. Once it stopped altogether, and they had to get out and throw in more charcoal, then wait for it to catch fire.

They reached Lyon-Perrache at a quarter to midnight. The priest gave Raymond money, and he ran in and bought the tickets. "The train is still in the station," he said when he came back. He distributed the tickets, and they all thanked the priest, and Rachel embraced him.

"I sometimes think this dirty war will never end," he said, and got back into his car and left.

On the return trip Rachel went into one compartment, Davey into the next one. But after a moment Rachel came in and sat beside him, and held his hand. She hardly let go of his hand all night. There were controls along the way, but they showed their papers and were not molested. At length Rachel fell asleep, her head on Davey's shoulder.

The young man did not sleep, but stared out the window as the countryside passed, the dark fields, the even darker villages and towns. The problem was not himself but Rachel. What did he do now? By first light, as the train pulled into Lyon-Perrache, he thought he had decided.

Even at this hour the station was crowded, but he noted no *Feldgendarmerie*, no Gestapo agents circulating. He was hungry. They were all hungry. The station canteen was just opening, but only Raymond had coupons. He bought what he could and they shared it, and over this meager breakfast Davey asked if knew how to make contact with the Maquis group near Le Lignon. The boy said he did.

"Will you take us there?" said Davey.

"Her too?"

"Both of us."

XXVI

I n Lyon, Obersturmbannführer Gruber had received another order from Berlin. Jews again. Another trainload. Shipment to be ready in ten days' time.

Gruber put the order down and began to pace his office. Where was he to get so many? The internment camps, once full of foreign Jews, were now depleted. French Jews who had survived this far into the war were well underground. Gruber looked out the window at the city below. In the past it had been possible to depend on informants. Plenty of Frenchmen had been willing to denounce Jews. But informants were scarce now. The Resistance, as it grew stronger, had murdered a lot of them, and for the most part that particular source had dried up.

A thousand Jews.

I've already found all I could, he thought petulantly, and once again he began to worry about losing his post: losing Lyon, his big apartment, and the busty Claire. In exchange they would put him in combat in front of Russian tanks. Or American ones. The previous train had gone out about two hundred Jews short, his fault, according to Berlin. Another failure, and . . .

Needing an ally, he thought of Helmut Haas, and asked for him to be sent in.

A few minutes later the blond, blue-eyed young man entered the office.

"You sent for me, sir?"

In looks the perfect example of German youth, Gruber thought, studying him.

Behind Gruber's shoulder was the big red flag with the swastika on it, furled of course, and Haas, it seemed to him, had come very close to throwing it a salute.

Gruber was under no illusions about this former member of the Hitler youth, this son of a party official, this protégé, according to all the signs Gruber could read, of Rahn in Paris, and probably others in Berlin.

Gruber showed him the order, waiting while Haas read it.

"Where are we supposed to find a thousand Jews?"

"Probably that many in Le Lignon alone," answered Haas.

Gruber shook his head. "You worked all day there and found thirty."

"Thirty-two, Obersturmbannführer."

"All right, thirty-two. At that rate, to find a thousand would take you a month. The train would have come and gone."

"All we'd need is enough men to seal the place off. We'd find them."

"I'm not so sure."

"Perhaps you're right, sir."

The sudden obsequiousness caused Gruber to glance up sharply. After a moment he said: "What other ideas do you have?"

"If we want to keep Berlin's goodwill we must find Jews, and find radios. It's what the war effort demands as well."

Lately Berlin had begun sending out directives about the clandestine radios whose coded transmissions to London were intercepted every night.

Haas said: "Jews running them, you can bet on it. Find radios and you find Jews."

Gruber said: "Those transmitters are hard to find. There aren't many of them and they keep moving."

"I'd have trucks out looking for the signals night and day."

"Finding the signals is not what's hard. It's finding the transmitters."

"I'd have the trucks out."

"Be somewhat wasteful in terms of man-hours, wouldn't you say?"

"It would impress Berlin, which is important."

"Yes, of course."

"I'd subordinate everything else to finding Jews and finding transmitters."

The young man obviously knew nothing about running an office as big as this one. "What about our other jobs?" said Gruber.

"What's more important than Jews?"

Gruber said: "You're right."

There followed a rather long silence.

"How do you think the war is going for us?" asked Gruber.

"A few strategic withdrawals here and there," answered Haas. "Otherwise, fine."

"Do you think there'll be an invasion?"

"I'd like to see them try it. Our west wall is impregnable. We'd throw them right back into the sea."

"Yes," said Gruber, "of course."

When Haas had gone out, Gruber picked up the order again. As he saw it, he had two choices. He could promise to provide a thousand Jews, and give excuses later when he fell short. Or he could send a message to the effect that there were not that many Jews left in all of France, and that meeting such a quota was virtually impossible.

He decided on this latter message, and wrote it out, but did not immediately send it. He needed time to think first. Was such a response wise or not?

The next morning when he came to work he ordered the message sent.

As it happened, it went into the dispatch bag with a report prepared secretly by Untersturmführer Helmut Haas which was twelve pages in length, but whose import could have been contained in two sentences: (1) Obersturmbannführer Gruber knew of a village where thousands of Jews were hidden, but refused to move against it, and (2) Obersturmbannführer Gruber was a defeatist who believed Germany was losing the war.

Three days later Gruber was relieved of his command and ordered to return to Berlin for reassignment. And Haas was promoted to Obersturmführer, made acting commander of the Lyon *Kommando der Sipo und SD*, and given orders to proceed as soon as practicable against the Jewish village mentioned in his report.

Haas had a plan for this that was already prepared. Gruber had never mobilized enough men, he believed. Haas would not make this mistake, but would block every road, path, and lane around Le Lignon, and then move in house by house toward the village center. Not a single Jew would escape him.

But to implement his plan he needed more men than he had, meaning he would have to get them from the Wehrmacht.

Though Haas's rank only the equivalent of a captain, he telephoned Colonel General Kleindienst, who commanded Army Group G—the southern half of France.

He was put through directly. The Wehrmacht general congratulated him on his new promotion. "What can I do for you?" he said. "How can I help?"

Haas said he needed a reinforced battalion, including half-tracks and machine guns, and he ordered Kleindienst to provide it at once.

A battalion was about eight hundred men, a number that seemed unreasonable to the general, who protested he was understrength. The equipment also would have to be gathered, and—

"At once," said Haas curtly.

The general's tone changed, and he begged for a week's delay.

"First priority," said Haas.

The general went on begging.

His new authority allowed Haas to be magnanimous to generals, if he chose, so he cut him off, saying: "You have five days," and he hung up on him.

According to a report Haas had seen there was a clandestine radio operating very near Le Lignon. While waiting for his battalion, he decided to go out and capture it.

THE group commanded by Pierre Glickstein had grown to twenty boys and men, all now heavily armed. They lived in the woods on the slope of an extinct volcano known as Le Lizieux south of Le

Lignon. They slept on the ground under English parachutes held up by sticks and tree branches. They bathed as best they could in a nearby stream that was icy cold. There was no latrine. The latrine was the woods behind them, which bothered Rachel greatly. The kitchen was an open fire that could be lit only at night lest its smoke give away their position. They sat on logs grouped around it and had conversations they considered profound and intense, of which Davey understood nothing. They now had Sten guns all around. They had trench mortars and bazookas that had come with directions in English that none of them could read, with which they were expected, when the time came, to blow up bridges and locomotives, thus bringing German troop movements to a dead stop.

However, most of them wanted to use their new weapons as soon as possible. All were fretting from inactivity. All were anxious to test themselves and become heroes.

Davey fretted too. There were three tents in all. He and Rachel shared theirs with six other young males who tried to afford Rachel some privacy when they thought of it, which was not often. Because he had much to think about, Davey would have liked some privacy from time to time too, but Rachel would not let him out of her sight, and if he started out of the encampment she would come with him, holding his hand. She had asked nothing about his plans, as if fearing what the answer would be, and he had volunteered nothing, but he was plainly as troubled as she.

The moon was getting bigger every night, and they watched it.

Every three days Pierre Glickstein moved the encampment. It was activity, a way of keeping the men from boiling over, for certain of them regularly proposed schemes—an ambush, a raid on an isolated German outpost—that to Glickstein sounded impractical or harebrained or both, and that guaranteed reprisals against the civilian population. Also he was paranoid about informers. They still had to go out for food twice a week, and almost anyone with whom they came in contact could tip off the *Boches* to where they were.

For all these reasons, he kept moving.

The weather was exceptionally good. The snow was gone and the ground was thawing fast. It had been sunny every day, and warm enough at midday for some of the men to go shirtless. At night, if one lay out on the ground, one could look up at billions of stars, most of which, as soon as the moon came up, would disappear.

According to Eugene in Grandeville, the flight from London was still scheduled for one of the three days around the full moon, assuming the weather held. More munitions, and another radio and the team to run it were coming in, and the American pilot would be going out. To Eugene, Davey constituted an encumbrance, and he was anxious to get rid of him. The invasion could not be far off now, and as soon as it started, every Maquis group in France would rise up against the *Boches*. When that happened, he didn't want Davey on his hands.

The impending flight from London would touch down in Pierre's territory, Eugene decided, for his own had been used too much lately. The ex-forger was ordered to find a pasture long enough and smooth enough to take a two-engined bomber. The specifications were given him as to what was needed: length, width. There must be no ditches or hidden boulders, nor trees too high to come in over, nor telephone wires that might snag the wheels. As soon as the noise of engines was heard overhead, Pierre's team would light the bonfires delimiting the landing area.

The whole thing sounded routine, almost simple.

Davey took Rachel aside and explained all this to her. It was then about ten o'clock in the morning of another bright sunny day. He took her to where a number of great rocks protruded from the hillside. A sentry was sitting against one of them, his shirt off, his eyes closed, the sun baking his face and chest. They stood nearby and looked out over the countryside: pockets of forest, tiny farm buildings clustered together, and rolling fields that had begun to show a tinge of green.

The full moon was forty-eight hours off.

Tomorrow night or the next night—the night after at the latest— a bomber was coming in loaded, Davey told Rachel. When it turned around to go back it would be empty. There would be room aboard for them both. He was not leaving her behind. He was not leaving France without her.

"We just climb on board," she said.

"Exactly."

She did not seem much cheered. "I'd be surprised if it was that easy."

"It will be that easy."

"They won't take me."

"Why shouldn't they take you?"

"I'm nobody to them."

There being no answer to this comment, Davey took refuge in specifics. "It'll be a Lockheed Hudson. At the start of the war that was the frontline bomber. It will hold at least eight people."

Rejection was familiar to Rachel. She had had many in her young life. She said: "You'll go, and I'll never see you again."

"No, absolutely not."

"I think you're deluding yourself." To Rachel rejection was normal and only what one could expect. "When the plane comes in it will be good-bye."

Davey had been worried enough before telling her. He worried more now, for she had seen the situation almost as clearly as he did. The plane would land and he would not be dealing with Americans, who enjoyed breaking rules. There would be a crew on board—English plane, English crew. The pilot would be obeying orders, none of which covered taking Rachel. If he refused to take her, that was that. Davey would not be able to force him to change his mind—to force her onto the plane.

The next day at dawn Pierre Glickstein went out on a bicycle, and when he came back much later he had found his field. He was enthusiastic. It was perfect, he said.

That same night, running on carefully hoarded gasoline, the truck that would take away the plane's cargo came into the encampment. In it was Eugene's radio operator, an Englishwoman named Lily, together with her gear. As the woman set up her radio in one of the tents, Davey talked to her. She told him that all arrangements had been made, that he'd be back in London in a jiffy. He watched her transmit the landing field's map coordinates to London in Morse code. Her messages had to be short and cryptic, she explained conversationally. The Germans had tricks for trying to find radios. When they picked up a transmission they would turn off the electricity in one village after another, or one part of a city after another. If the transmission cut out, they knew they had the right spot, and they would swoop down on it. They wouldn't get her that way, though, for her radio ran off these big car batteries, and she pointed to them.

The enemy also had detection devices circulating in trucks, she noted. These were more dangerous, since one never knew if a truck might be close.

She sounded fearless, and her fingers worked the telegraph key. Then she looked up at him and smiled—the transmission was over, and she shut down the radio.

Other young men had also stood watching, and she turned to them: "Show's over, mates," she said in English. And then in French: "C'est fini, les gars."

In their tent in the night, wrapped in separate blankets, only their heads close together, Davey said to Rachel:

"It will be easy. You'll see."

"Maybe."

"In about twenty-four hours we'll be in England."

Lily shared the same tent, as did a boy with a sinus problem who, in his sleep, snored loudly.

But in the morning it was raining, and it rained all day, the tents becoming soggy, and then beginning to drip. The sentries came in grumbling. There was no point standing guard, they said. It was cold and wet out there and they couldn't see much anyway. The whole valley lay under fog.

Pierre Glickstein ordered them back, but they refused. If somebody had to go, let somebody else go, they said. They were freezing and needed to warm up.

Discipline in Maquis units was never strong, and often non-existent.

Davey said: "I'll go."

"I'll go with you," said Rachel.

If he had hoped to shame the French boys into doing what they were supposed to do, the tactic failed. For hours he and Rachel huddled in a groundsheet under a leafless tree, unable to see even halfway down the valley, and the rain never let up. With darkness a ground fog settled in, and when at last they were relieved and got back to the encampment they learned that Lily had sent a message to London canceling the flight for that night.

AT Le Lignon four French Jews, a couple and their two children, had come in on the evening train. At the station they waited a while, but the storm did not let up. Finally, they lifted their suitcases and set off for the presbytery through the driving rain.

They were soaked when they got there.

Having invited them in, Norma Favert hung their outer clothes to dry in front of the fireplace, set four extra places at the table, and sat them down to dinner with the family, which, in Rachel's absence, had been reduced by one. Pastor Favert had got on the phone immediately, and from his place at the head of the table he told them the results of his calls. Of course they could all stay here tonight, and for as long as the rain lasted, he said. Tomorrow the children could move into one of the funded houses in the village. They'd be with other children their age, and from there they would be able to go to school every day.

Having said this much he paused, for he had been unable to place the parents anywhere in the village. For the first time people who had room, and who had received refugees in the past, had refused him.

"At the moment," he told them, "not a bed in Le Lignon seems to be available. But the pastor in Buzet, one of the neighboring villages, does have a place for you."

He saw their faces fall.

"It's not Le Lignon," he said quickly, "but it's not all that far. Arrangements can be made for you to see your children regularly."

There came a knock on the door.

Since the locals, after calling out, walked right in, this knock, any knock, was ominous.

Having hustled the refugees into the nearest bedroom, Norma rushed about removing their dishes and silverware from the table, while the pastor, making his footsteps ring out, but walking deliberately slowly to give her time, went to the door and opened it.

The caller was Commissaire Chapotel, who said at once: "Please don't be alarmed, Pastor, I've come on a personal matter."

The pastor looked at the wet suitcases stacked in the hallway. So did Chapotel.

"Is there a place where we can talk?"

As he led the policeman into his study, Favert was still alarmed but, because of Chapotel's manner, less so. He closed the door.

"Take off that wet raincoat," he said. "Please sit down."

He hung the policeman's hat and coat on a peg. "Would you like something hot to drink?"

"No, thank you."

"We don't have anything alcoholic, I'm afraid. Some soup, some tea."

"No, thank you."

For a moment they looked at each other in silence.

"I've been suspended from duty," said Chapotel.

The pastor did not know what reply to make.

"I have no gun, no badge, no police card."

"When did this happen?"

"Yesterday. I'll probably be arrested."

"Oh I hope not."

"It's really strange to be unarmed after so many years of carrying a gun at all times."

Favert could not imagine being armed, much less being unarmed.

"I tell you this so you will believe the information I am about to give you. And take steps accordingly."

The pastor waited.

"The German commander, Gruber, has been removed. No replacement has yet been named. The new man, Lieutenant Haas, the one who was here, has been promoted to Captain and is temporarily in charge."

"All right," said Favert, and he waited with dread for what was coming next. He expected to hear that another raid was planned on the children.

But Chapotel's message was different.

"Haas doesn't like you."

Favert shrugged.

"He's conceived the notion that the way to get rid of you is not to arrest you but to have you assassinated."

"Assassinated?"

"By Frenchmen. No one is to know it's a German plot. He's hired two French gangsters to do it. Former clients of ours. We know them well."

Favert could not think what to say.

"They're members of the *Milice,* both of them, but they're gangsters. Haas thinks if Frenchmen kill you, there'll be no outcry from the populace."

Favert stroked his mustache.

"How much do you know about the workings of the police?"

"Very little."

"We have this information from informants, members of the underworld themselves. We know the prospective assassins' names. We know how much Haas is paying them. The only thing we don't know is when and how they plan to kill you."

Favert managed to say: "It's hard to think that anyone would want to kill me."

"I arrested them, was suspended from duty for it, and they were released."

"Well," said Favert.

"I think Haas is wrong. Kill you and the Maquis will come down out of the hills and do real mischief."

"You think so?"

"Most of them are kids dodging the forced labor draft. You know that as well as I do. They didn't want to go to Germany as slaves, so they go into the bush instead. Lot of them around here. Think they're soldiers. Want to kill Germans. They want to shoot them in the back is what they want to do. Their officers, if you can call them officers, can barely control them now."

Favert nodded.

"These assassins gun you down, they'll take it as the excuse they're looking for to go berserk."

The pastor was sitting in front of his desk, his chair turned to face the policeman. He said: "Surely you're exaggerating."

Chapotel leaned toward him, his manner urgent. "You don't believe me."

"I don't know," said the pastor.

"So what are you going to do?"

"What am I supposed to do?"

"You can't stay here, man!"

"My place is here though."

"Not anymore it's not."

"This is where my work is, where I belong."

"How can you be so naïve?"

"If I run away now, all that we have done here so far in this war will come apart. Without my leadership—"

"No man is indispensable."

"In Le Lignon, I'm afraid I am indispensable."

"Come to your senses, for God's sake. I'm trying to save your life. And the lives of all those kids who will get killed trying to assassinate German soldiers to avenge you, and all the hostages who will be hung or shot if they succeed."

Favert started nodding, and found he could not stop.

"How can I convince you that you can trust me?" Chapotel stood up, and though the room was tiny, began pacing. He pointed to his raincoat on the peg. "You see how wet my coat is? That's because I not only don't have a badge or a gun anymore, I don't have a Sûreté car anymore either. I came on the train and walked down from the station."

"Yes," said Favert.

"Does that convince you I'm on your side? No? How about this? There were four refugees on the train with me. Jews, I suppose. They were carrying suitcases—the ones now stacked in your hall. I don't care about any of that. I'm suspended from duty and about to be arrested. And you're about to be murdered."

Chapotel had run out of breath and was almost panting. "If you don't care about yourself, think of your family. They come in here and spray bullets around, maybe they kill your wife or one of your kids as well."

Favert rose to his feet. "It's too late for you to get back to Lyon tonight. Where will you stay?"

ROBERT DALEY

"I took a room in a hotel near the station. I thought I'd stay here
a few days, keep phoning my wife, see if they've come for me." He
gave a brief laugh. "It seems that I too have become a refugee in Le
Lignon."

"Have you had dinner?"

"No."

"Come and have dinner with us. We don't have much, but
you're welcome to it."

They went out into the big room. "I think our friends can safely
come out now," said the pastor to his wife. He was trying to make
his voice sound jovial. "And we'll set an extra place for Monsieur
Chapotel."

THE pastor went out and down through the night and the driving
rain to the temple, which to him was the house of God, and let
himself in, and shook rain off his umbrella. He put on only one
light, then knelt in front of the altar with his arms outstretched and
prayed for guidance. Men who would murder him were on their
way. Should he run away from his post, from his duty, and from
people who needed him, and thereby go on living? Or stay where
he was and accept for better or worse whatever God had in store
for him?

Often in the past he had come to this temple, or a previous one,
seeking guidance, and each time the answers he had prayed for had
been forthcoming, and the major decisions of his adult life had almost always been made in such places when on his knees. And so
tonight he knelt in the semidark, with the rain pelting the roof,
alone in God's presence in God's house, and again he prayed.

He was in the habit at such times of speaking to God aloud, and
he did so now, his voice barely audible, a murmur, for God was not
deaf: "Lord, I'm just an ordinary man but I want to do the right
thing, I'm trying to do the right thing, if only I can see what the
right thing is. Help me, Lord. Lord, what shall I do?"

Always in the past God had answered him, he believed—not
aloud, of course, but as a muted voice deep in his being, almost in
his ear. Through prayer it had become possible for him to see the

problem, whatever it was, clearly. Always he had come away from such prayers refreshed, heartened, and decisive.

But now, though he listened, no voice came back. Apart from the pounding of the rain there was no sound anywhere, nothing. He could not even decide whether to tell Norma what the situation was, although obviously whatever decision he might make concerned her most of all.

He remembered when the first of the refugees had come to Le Lignon. How he had prayed at that time. It was easy enough to save the first three or four, but he knew there would be more, that all of Europe was turning, had turned, against these poor people, that there was nowhere else they could go, and that soon, unless he closed them off at once, there would be thousands on his doorstep.

So he had prayed. "Lord," he had prayed then, "if it be Thy wish, lift this burden from me. I am not man enough to care for so many, and my village is not rich enough, nor even big enough. Lord, Lord, please."

He had known well enough what was the right thing to do, but without being able to see how it could be done, nor why he should be the one who had to do it. It would be not a burden but a cross, the heaviest cross imaginable, and so, refusing it, he had gone on praying. "I am a poor man with a wife and children to feed," he had prayed. "This village is poor, the soil poor all around it. The people I would have to ask to help can barely make ends meet as it is. They are not educated. They are not even very religious. Your temple is half-empty every Sunday."

Not yet accepting the burden, the heavy cross, he had gone on praying: "And what about the danger of it? Do I have the right to ask my village to take such risks? I don't think so." But then, as he continued to pray, it had seemed to him that he did have the right, the duty as well, and then he realized that God was asking him, no, telling him, that he would have to do it, to take in thousands of desperate, homeless people, most of whom were not French, did not speak French, and could do nothing to help themselves, so that finally he had bowed his head, and conceded, and his prayer turned into questions that were merely practical. "But how am I to do it, Lord? What steps am to I take, and in what order?"

And this too, through prayer, had become clear to him. There were organizations from whom he might get funds, and other pastors of the region whom he could ask to help. They would all climb up into their pulpits and tell the faithful what the situation was. They would describe the injustice and terror being perpetrated on a whole race of human beings for no reason at all. They would warn their parishioners that these hunted individuals were coming here to the plateau for help, and that they would come in great numbers. God and the Bible, the sermons would conclude, demand that we help. Will we be found wanting?

And as he had prayed that day, he had realized that the people themselves would do the rest, that God would see to it.

And so it had come to pass. Already during four and a half years of war, many thousands of refugees had come into Le Lignon, mostly on the little train, and they had been distributed over the entire region, and not one had ever been turned away.

Tonight on his knees with arms outstretched he was looking for a response from God that was similarly strong and clear. Did he run, or did he stay. "Help me, Lord," he prayed. "Lord, if I am your son . . ."

If he ran he feared that this edifice of his, the simple goodness represented by his village and the neighboring ones, this refuge of the innocent and the oppressed that he and they had constructed, would fall to pieces. Its spirit would crack. Without him it might turn suicidal. For four and a half years refugees from the *Boches,* most of them Jews, had just kept coming. And they were still coming—witness the four new ones tonight. His parishioners had already taken such risks, had already done so much, that it was almost not fair to ask them to do any more. But he could ask them, and they would do it for him. Without him, their pastor, to stiffen their resolve, their Christian backbone, many of them, perhaps most of them, would choose now to take no further risks, would close their doors for good on those in need. And it seemed to him that if the village and the plateau did not carry on its work to the end of the war, then all that had gone before would be lost, would come to seem a failure, an effort that had not been sustained. It would stand for the glory of no one, not an edifice at all, just an attempted rescue that had succeeded only for a time.

His knees began to ache, his arms as well, but still his prayer was not being heard.

To make sure that the work, his work, went on, he would have to stay. Tonight, in its way had been proof. Finding a home for the Jewish couple to go to tomorrow had been difficult. "They won't take up much room," he had said on the phone. But the people had made excuses. This had never happened in the beginning, but his parishioners now were tired of living under such stress. Only if he stayed would his work continue, and if he stayed and was killed he believed the impetus provided by his killing would keep the work going just as if he were still there.

The temple floor was hard, and the altar in this light as dim and distant as God himself.

But perhaps, as Chapotel said, he was not indispensable, though in all humility he had always believed that he was. Humility, to Favert, was the noblest of the cardinal virtues. It was what he had always tried for in his dealings with other men. He counted himself humble, tried to be humble. But now, in the absence of any response to his prayers, it occurred to him that possibly Chapotel was right, that he was not indispensable at all. Perhaps his pride, unknown to him, was so immense that it had drowned out God's voice trying to reach him. Perhaps any other man, Assistant Pastor Henriot for instance, could do his work as well as he could. Or even better. At what point did egotism overwhelm humility and blind a man, make him stupid?

Through such convoluted reasoning his mind moved in circles, and nothing resembling an answer to his prayers came back to him. He was not warmly dressed, the temple was unheated, but he had knelt so long, held his arms outstretched so long, that he was sweating heavily. His shirt was stuck to his back. There were drops of sweat on his brow.

No answer from God must mean stay, he decided. He saw no way out, he must stay. It would mean meeting the murderers on some village street, or on the doorstep to his house, alone and defenseless. He could do it, and if that was what God wanted, would.

And afterward?

Henriot would take over. The people liked and trusted Henriot. The course he should follow was already charted.

And Norma and the children?

Was he more indispensable to them than to his parishioners? The church would take care of them. Norma might even marry again. He hoped she would.

But suppose he fled.

He saw it as quitting a task only half done. He could also see it, he supposed, as the only choice he had. How could he, a pacifist, a prophet of nonviolence, deliberately make himself a focus of violence and bloodshed, provoke in fact what could so easily be avoided? How could he permit the commission of a crime that would weigh on the consciences of the two young murderers all their lives? How could he be responsible for all the other deaths that would most probably be exacted in reprisal?

How could he live with the notion that the murder might well take place before the eyes of his innocent wife, his young and innocent children? He could visualize without much difficulty the murderers bursting into the presbytery as the whole family sat at dinner, and if that were to happen, how could he imagine that the bullets would reach only himself and not Norma and one or more of the children as well? They could be hit, and perhaps not even killed. Perhaps his smallest daughter's hand or arm shot off, his son perhaps crippled for life.

By now his outstretched arms weighed a hundred kilos each. The pain in his knees was shooting up into his pelvis.

He thought in despair: God doesn't listen to me anymore. Why won't God make the choice for me? But this thought smacked of blasphemy, he recoiled from it, and finally, in the absence of answers, he ceased praying, and got to his feet. He put the light out, locked up the temple, and as he plodded home through the rain it seemed to him that God had failed him, and the reason must be that his faith was gone, he no longer believed strongly enough, no longer deserved God's help.

If God wouldn't decide for him, then Norma must, and as soon as he had come in the door of the presbytery, the children having been put to bed long ago, and the refugee family quiet in one of the bedrooms, he took his wife into the kitchen and told her everything and asked her what he should do.

Her response was to put her arms around him, her face in his neck. And then he realized she was weeping, and this surprised him. She was a strong woman, in some respects a hard woman, a woman with the strength always to do what had to be done. He had known her to weep only two or three times during their married life. Always before it had been from rage or frustration, whereas there was a different quality to it tonight. Now it was from heartache.

"Why do we live in such times?" she blubbered into his neck.

But in a moment she had finished her weeping and she stepped away from him and said: "You must go. We can't have the children seeing men come in and murder their father."

He saw that this was the only argument that meant anything to her, that she had cut through directly to it, and that it overwhelmed all others.

"All right," he said. "I'll go now."

"Go where?"

"To Jean-Paul's hotel for tonight."

"That's the same one Chapotel is at."

"Jean-Paul has always been a friend. Maybe he won't charge me."

She gave a wry smile. "He'll think we've had a terrific fight and I've thrown you out."

"I'll tell him what's happened. He can spread the word."

"And tomorrow?" she asked him.

"And tomorrow to some other town. Probably many other towns. I'll get word to you where I am. From now on lock the front door."

"I never wanted to lock it."

"Well . . ."

"Yes, of course."

He went out again into the rain.

XXVII

It rained the next day too. The men built fires under the parachutes. The smoke went out the center hole in the canopy. Later another message was sent by Lily—too many from the same spot, she said in a worried voice—canceling the flight for that night too, and there was much speculation among the men. The landing depended on the light of a full moon, and now, when and if it reappeared, the moon would be past full.

Almost certainly then, tomorrow was the last possible day this month.

Davey was worried about one thing more: the ground around the encampment felt spongy to his foot, and airplanes, landing, were heavy.

After supper the same two boys, Ardoin, the apprentice gunmaker from St. Étienne, and Pernand, his acolyte, left the encampment and made for Le Lignon where Pernand's mother would feed them and give them a warm, dry bed. Once again they had had enough of the rain. Once again they did not ask Pierre Glickstein for permission to go, or tell anyone they were going, they simply slipped out and started walking.

Pernand's mother was as glad to see her son as the last time, she prepared beds for them, and in the morning again let them sleep late. By the time they came downstairs the mason had already left the house. Outside, they could see through the windows, it was still raining. Madame Pernand prepared them breakfasts of porridge with hot milk and honey, and as they ate it she regaled them with the latest gossip.

That the *Boches* planned to assassinate the pastor, who was therefore on the run. That he had left the village early this morning in a gasogene truck—she named the farmer who drove it.

That a *flic,* the same one who arrested the pastor the last time, had moved into Jean-Paul's hotel.

"Who's Jean-Paul?" said Ardoin.

"The Hôtel du Midi," said Pernand.

"Is he with us or against us?"

"Don't know."

Madame Pernand was looking from one face to the other, so Ardoin's mouth clamped shut and he stared into his porridge.

But when the woman was in the kitchen refilling their bowls, Ardoin whispered to Pernand: "We should take him down."

"Take down who?"

"The *flic.*"

Pernand choked on the bread he was chewing, and had to cough repeatedly. "He's French," he said, when he could talk.

"He's a collaborationist."

The blood had left Pernand's face.

"The collabos are worse than the *Boches.*"

Pernand managed to say: "Sounds good to me."

"If he's in a hotel, how would we find him?"

"It's not a big hotel," said Pernand. "It's a small hotel. How many rooms in Jean-Paul's hotel?" he called out to his mother, a rather long speech during which his voice cracked only once.

Madame Pernand arrived with more porridge. "Seven or eight," she said.

"How would one recognize the *mec*?" said Ardoin.

"I know what he looks like," said Pernand.

Madame Pernand was again looking from one boy to the other.

"I saw him the day he arrested the pastor," said Pernand. "We were all standing out in the snow watching."

Ardoin nodded sagely, and said no more.

But when breakfast was concluded he asked if Pernand could get him a bicycle.

"What for?"

"Go back and get our guns."

Pernand's own bike was in the cellar. He got it out. This in no way seemed a grave or important act to him. It could not be seen as having consequences. They pumped up the tires.

The hulking Ardoin pedaled back to the encampment through the rain. This morning there were sentries out, so he was challenged, and Pierre Glickstein was waiting for him as he wheeled his bike in under the trees.

"Who gave you permission to leave the camp?"

"*Va te faire foutre,*" said Ardoin. The English equivalent might have been "Fuck off."

"What are you doing?" said Pierre. He had followed Ardoin into one of the tents. The boy had pulled out a knapsack into which he stuffed two Sten guns.

"The *flic* who arrested the pastor is in a hotel in the village."

"What's he doing there?"

"Pernand and me, we're going to take him down."

"There'll be other *flics* with him."

"You think I didn't check that out? He's alone."

"If he's a flic, he's armed."

"He won't have time to do anything."

"He'll shoot back."

"He'll never know what hit him."

When Ardoin, ignoring him, started to move toward the bicycle, Glickstein said: "We'll have a council."

"I'm going off and do it," said Ardoin.

"You'll wait," said Glickstein, as forcefully as he could.

He called a council of what he believed to be the five most responsible young men in the camp. Ardoin was left fuming outside the tent.

The oldest member of the council, who was twenty-two, and who went by the name of Louis, said: "Anybody doubt the flic's a collabo?"

"He was just doing what he was told," said Glickstein.

"Definitely a collabo," said a youth who went by the name of Pascal.

Taking themselves seriously, they spoke almost in whispers so that neither Ardoin nor anyone else could hear.

"I say we take him down," said Louis.

"Let's talk this out first," said Glickstein.

"If he arrested the pastor, then he's a collabo," said a third youth, Marcel.

They sat under the soggy parachute on blankets folded into squares. Outside the rain continued to fall.

"*Flics* don't have much choice."

Louis said: "The trouble with you is you're . . ." He hesitated, then said: "squeamish," a milder word than Glickstein was expecting.

"Take him down," said Marcel. Already voices were beginning to be raised.

"You're talking about a man's life," said Glickstein. "Let's be sure of what we're doing."

"Talk," said Louis. "That's all you ever want to do. We've got guns, let's use them, for Chrissake."

"How long are we supposed to sit here doing nothing?" said Marcel.

"All right," said Glickstein, "we've agreed he's a collabo." The ex-forger was trying to regain control of the meeting, and of the band. "The next question is what, if anything, do we do about it?"

"We take him down," said Louis.

"If we do," Glickstein said, "the *Boches* will take and execute hostages."

"They won't," said Louis.

"When Frenchmen kill Frenchmen, they love it," said Pascal.

Louis, who was from Lyon, said: "In Lyon there were cases. The collabo went down and the *Boches* did nothing."

"They laughed," said Marcel.

Glickstein turned on Marcel. "You don't know anything about it, you weren't there."

"They laughed," repeated Louis. "That's exactly what they did."

"We take him down," said Pascal.

"We just walk up and shoot him?"

"Sure," said Marcel.

"You don't want to do it, move over," said Louis.

"He deserves to be executed," said Pascal.

"What this group needs is a leader with balls," said Louis.

"We execute him," said Glickstein, looking around at the others. "Is that the verdict?" He glanced at the fourth boy, Leon, who said nothing, and who would not meet his eyes.

"All right," said the ex-forger, "then I'll do it myself." If the evil that controlled Europe was ever to be extinguished, he told himself, a certain amount of killing was essential. The council was almost the equivalent of a trial. It had passed judgment. Verdict and sentence had been handed down and were almost legal. The collabo was going to be executed by someone, and it seemed to Glickstein that if he left the job to one of the hotheads, he would lose control altogether. Without him, the group would rampage through the region. Innocent hostages would pay the price.

The others wanted to come with him to exult in the murder, but Glickstein shouted them down. Too many of them would attract witnesses, and the *flic* might get away, he said. He needed Pernand and Ardoin only, the one to identify the *flic*, the other as backup. The rest of them were to stay in the camp. Sticking a handgun into his waistband, he got behind the wheel of Lily's truck, Ardoin beside him, the lout's heavily loaded knapsack on the floor of the cab. Lily came running up and stood staring as they drove out.

By the time they reached Le Lignon Glickstein had convinced Ardoin, or thought he had convinced him, that the Stens would throw out too many bullets, and would be dangerous to bystanders, that the job should be done with handguns only.

They picked up Pernand in front of his parents' house.

They parked the truck a short distance up the road from the Hôtel du Midi.

By then it was lunchtime.

Pernand led them up alongside the hotel until they could peer through the window into the dining room.

Chapotel, the only diner, sat at a table eating lunch.

"That him?" said Pierre Glickstein.

Pernand nodded. He looked sick.

"Since you're known in the village, you go back and wait in the truck," Pierre Glickstein told him. "Sit with your hat pulled down over your face. When we go into the hotel, start the engine."

Pernand did not have to be told twice. He looked grateful, and then he was gone.

"You," Pierre said to Ardoin, "you back me up. You don't do anything until I do, is that understood?"

Their eyes locked. The lout neither agreed nor disagreed. This seemed the best Pierre Glickstein could hope for, so he nodded, and started back along the building toward the front door.

They went into the hotel. There was no one behind the front desk. In a hotel this small most times there wouldn't be. The owner was probably the chef, and also the waiter.

"Wait here," said Pierre.

He went down the narrow corridor and into the dining room.

There was no one there.

Chapotel's table was empty. What now? It was some time before the ex-forger could make himself turn around, take steps to leave the dining room.

CHAPOTEL was in the hall telephone cabin talking to his wife in Lyon. He had been waiting all morning for the call to go through. A moment ago the phone had rung. He had heard it from his table and had rushed to the cabin. The outside operator told him to hold on, the connection was about to be made. While waiting he had seen Pierre Glickstein go past the cabin, had even noted the tension the boy was evidently under, for he seemed to be almost stumbling along, looking neither right nor left, passing close by and not noticing him. A career cop did not miss signs of such tension as that, though in this case Chapotel thought it had nothing to do with him, and he forgot the ex-forger at once when the operator came on again and said:

"*Parlez.*" Speak.

His wife. Was she all right? Had anything happened?

The Gestapo had come for him that morning very early, she said.

She had been still in her nightdress. No, she said to him, calm down, they had not molested her. They had ransacked the apartment looking for him, and when he was not to be found they had deliberately smashed some things, the antique vases his mother had left him, the radio, the glass breakfront. They would keep coming back, they promised. But she was fine, she really was, she said. But how are you? What will you do?

Chapotel didn't have enough money to stay on at the hotel very long. He said he would have to go into the bush, make contact with the Maquis, and from there perhaps he could contribute to the defeat of the *Boches*. It was something, he confessed, that he should have been doing all along.

He hung up on his well-loved wife because phone calls were expensive, he had seen her only yesterday, and there wasn't much more to say.

Leaving the cabin he almost bumped into the same tense kid he had noted earlier. Jewish, from the look of him. But again he thought the tension had nothing to do with him. He said:

"*Pardon.*"

And Pierre Glickstein said:

"*Pardon.*"

And Chapotel continued the rest of the way down the corridor, the kid following, and walked past the still unmanned front desk and outside onto the stoop to stand under the marquise and look out at the rain and smoke a cigarette.

The kid stood almost beside him, not smoking, not speaking, two meters away, still tense. A second kid, who to Chapotel had the face of a real oaf, came up the driveway carrying an old knapsack, which, from the way he carried it, contained something heavy.

The kid beside him cleared his throat, then said: "You're the *commissaire* that arrested the pastor."

Chapotel looked at him and said: "Who are you?"

"Answer the question."

The voice had become firmer, arrogant. Chapotel did not like the tone at all. He was old enough to be the father of these kids, this one on the stoop and his pal, the one with the knapsack, who was now closer—they were obviously together. Also Chapotel was a career policeman. His role was to ask the questions, not answer them. He was not in the habit of submitting to an interrogation by children, and had no intention of doing so now.

He was watching the kid with the knapsack. When he turned back to the one beside him he was looking down the barrel of a drawn revolver. His first thought was that he himself was unarmed. It caused a sinking feeling in the gut. His second was that these two were teenagers, that their intelligence and restraint, if any, could not be relied on. Teenagers tended to be violent and irrational, or perhaps merely stupid. He had best be very very careful what he did next.

"You're a collabo."

"Who says?"

"You arrested the pastor."

"You'd do well not to make accusations you can't back up."

Given the situation—a crazed-sounding boy holding a gun on him—of course Chapotel was frightened, who wouldn't be? But they didn't know how frightened he was, nor did they know he was unarmed.

"You and your kind are responsible for the reign of terror the *Boches* have perpetrated on all of us."

"You're nuts, kid." He still thought he could brazen it out. People were afraid of cops. Look at them hard and they caved in. During his twenty-year career he had faced down more hoodlums than he could count, many of them, like this kid, holding guns on him they were afraid to use.

The only difference was that those in his past had been felons, whereas these two counted themselves patriots. An important difference. Patriotism rendered any crime not only possible but beautiful and good.

"Kill him," said the kid with the knapsack, who stood now about three meters away.

"You're one of the ones who have poisoned the blood of France," said Pierre Glickstein. But the gun in his hand was no longer so steady.

"What poetry," said Chapotel. "What idiotic shit."

"Take him down," said the kid with the knapsack. "What are you waiting for?"

"I suggest you put that thing away," said Chapotel to Glickstein, "before you hurt yourself."

"Pull the *sacre* trigger," screamed the one with the knapsack.

Chapotel reached over and took the gun out of Pierre Glickstein's hand.

And quickly turned toward the other kid, who from the very beginning had seemed by far the more dangerous of the two. But he wasn't fast enough. Already the knapsack lay limp on the ground and he was facing a Sten gun already sending out bullets, which were breaking up the door behind him, because the boy had never before fired such a gun and could not at first control it. The noise of the gun, together with that of the disintegrating door, was stupendous.

That was the first burst. The boy yanked the gun down and around and fired again. Chapotel did not have time to do anything before the second burst cut him almost in two.

Instantly he was dead. Although thoughts are sometimes quicker than the speed of light he had had no time for any, not one.

"He would have killed you," said Ardoin to Glickstein. "I saved your life. You owe me." And he began to giggle.

Pierre Glickstein leaned over the railing and vomited into the bushes below.

Still giggling, Ardoin walked up the stoop and sent a third burst into Chapotel's skull. The bullets went through to the stone and bounced up. One of the ricochets struck Ardoin in the arm, causing him to let out a squeal and drop the gun.

The ricochet had torn through his coat, which he removed, the better to examine himself. His arm was bleeding, but not badly. He had stopped giggling. The sight of his own blood made him proud. He felt he had been wounded in action.

He put his coat back on and bent to pick up the gun, which he grasped by the barrel. The pain was instantaneous and excruciating, and when he tried to shake the gun loose from his hand, much of the skin of his palm and fingers went with it. He whimpered and whined all the way back to the camp, and Pierre Glickstein, as he tried to come to terms with the murder in which he had just taken part, knew he would have no further trouble from him for a while.

THE rain stopped in the night. By nine A.M. the clouds were gone, and a bright sun appeared. The air warmed fast, which worried Davey. Speaking through Rachel, he said to Glickstein, whom he now knew as "Pierre": "You better show me that field you found."

"It's two kilometers away," said Pierre.

"Nonetheless—"

They went out on three bicycles, two young men with no language in common, and their interpreter, who was Rachel. Pierre was glad enough to have her, he said. If they happened to be stopped by a patrol, having a girl along would seem less suspicious than two young men alone, especially since one of them wouldn't be able to understand even the most innocent questions.

As they rode along, as translated by Rachel, Pierre said: "If you hear anything coming, a car, a truck, a tractor, *tout de suite* into the forest."

It was a dirt road, and on this part of the plateau, unfortunately, there was not much forest to either side.

They stopped often to listen for oncoming cars.

"This is crazy," said Davey. "We're three young people pedaling along a country road, not one of us is old enough to vote, the sun is shining, we're not doing anything, and we're scared to death of being arrested, and after that killed."

But they reached the field the ex-forger had found, and while the others stood on the road with the three bikes and watched, Davey paced it off. Something green was just beginning to push its way out of the earth. He was a city boy, and had no idea what the crop might be, nor did he care. Instead he walked along counting his steps and calculating. He had never flown a Lockheed Hudson, nor indeed any multiengine plane, but he knew the bomber's approximate wing spread, approximate landing speed, and what its approximate weight would be when it struck the ground. The field was long enough, wide enough, but the ground was spongy. He got a stick and rammed it into the earth. It went in about six inches with ease. The bomber's wheels would dig in farther than that, and then it would probably go up onto its nose. Even if it landed successfully, it would never be able to get up enough speed to take off again.

If he himself was worried about a soggy field, certainly London would be too. Two nights in a row they had received adverse weather reports from Lily. They were people who could count. Forty-eight hours of rain on top of a spring thaw. Unless they received a detailed, reassuring transmission, they would probably cancel the flight. No reassurance, no landing.

The flight could be put off until the next full moon, sure, but by then wouldn't most of these fields be freshly plowed?

Davey came back, took his bicycle from Pierre, and straddled it. "You've found a perfect field," he told him through Rachel, "but it's become too soft to take a multiengine plane."

Every field in the area would be as soft, he judged. "We've got to find a road," he told the other two. And when Pierre waved toward the road they were on, he shook his head. It was too narrow, there were telephone wires along one side, and it was bumpy, having heaved from the winter frost.

Davey knew what was needed—a flat road with no wires or trees, paved if possible—but didn't know where to look, nor did the others, for none were natives of the area.

But Pierre had his military map with the squares marked off, which at least showed which roads were straight and which led where, though none of the other important details, and they spent the rest of the day pedaling about, examining every promising lane, ducking into the forest each time they heard a vehicle approaching, provided a forest was close. If it wasn't they waved innocently as the vehicle passed, none of them German as yet, hardly breathing until it had gone by.

They went east, then north, then east again, searching the dirt roads first, because the paved ones would almost certainly have a row of poles along one side, and on them there would be more danger of running into a patrol as well. Lunchtime came and went. They had no food with them. Their thighs were on fire, but in addition Davey's bad leg began to ache and then to burn, hot pains shooting from his ankle up his shin into his knee.

Their search kept widening. Before long they were three miles from the camp, then six, then another three, and the pain of the pedaling reached a level where Davey thought: I've got to stop, or I'll never make it back to the camp.

Keep going, he told himself. You can't stop.

They came to a place that was wide open, the road high, the fields dropping off to either side, the horizon marked by the high swollen hills that were the extinct volcanos, and they got off their bikes and Davey looked the road over while Pierre Glickstein glanced hurriedly in all directions, nervous about how exposed they were to any passing patrol.

"Hurry up," he kept saying.

On each side were farmhouses surrounded by outbuildings, but they were well back from the road. There were no wires or poles. The surface seemed solid to Davey, fairly smooth as well, and it looked long enough. He thought he could land a P-51 on it, no trouble, or any of the other planes he had flown. There were ditches to both sides, but if the pilot could hold the plane in the center of the road that would not matter.

He laid his bike down on its side and began to pace off the road, his leg aching. He figured he needed three thousand feet minimum, a thousand paces, and he strode them, counting, while the others waited for him.

It took another thousand paces to get back to the bike. He was limping badly, so that Rachel said to him: "Are you all right?"

"Sure," he said, and forced a smile.

"Mark it on your map," he told Pierre. "There are one or two potholes. We'll have to get here early with some shovels."

BACK at the encampment he found Lily, gave her the coordinates, and helped her write the message to send to London. It admitted the rain and the softness of the fields, but then described the road's length, its solidity, and the current weather: wind direction and force, high sky, bright sun. The message contained no true weather forecast, for they had no access to one.

Davey thought the message, when it was ready, sounded confident, as reassuring as needed.

But Lily looked at it askance, for it was almost a hundred words long. "This will take me ten to fifteen minutes to transmit," she said. "If there's one of those detection trucks in the neighborhood, watch out!"

Davey nodded, and they began to whittle at it, but there was too much information to convey to get it much shorter.

After shaking her head in annoyance, Lily put it into code and began to tap it out.

Soon the sun dropped behind the volcano to the southwest, and in a little while it was dark, and they waited for a reply from London, but the hours passed, and it did not come.

A convoy consisting of two trucks and a van, all built by Mercedes, all three still running on gasoline, not charcoal, was about fifteen kilometers away, parked beside the road in the dark, waiting. The convoy was headed by Obersturmführer Helmut Haas. On wooden benches inside the trucks sat a total of thirty SS troops, their weapons between their knees, most of them smoking. There was no conversation, not a murmur, for Haas had ordered total silence. From time to time their unextinguished butts arched out the back of the truck into the night.

One of the trucks was fitted with a machine gun on the roof. This was the command vehicle. It had an open cab in which Haas could stand and look out over the windshield while directing the battle, if there was to be a battle.

Haas thought he had more than enough firepower for the rabble he expected to meet.

Sandwiched between the two trucks was the van, from whose roof sprouted a number of direction-finding antennas. Inside sat two men in earphones working dials. It was the van that had brought the group this far, and they were waiting for the clandestine radio's next transmission to move in still closer.

XXVIII

Having landed at Tempsford Airfield, Joe Toft was led into a Quonset hut. The usual big room heated by woodstoves at either end. There were rows of empty chairs facing a stage and a curtain that concealed no doubt a map. To Toft it was an operations shack much like the one at his own base. Some men sat on the edge of the stage looking disconsolate, and others sat in the first row of seats, including Vera Tompkins who, hearing him come in, stood up and came toward him.

They shook hands.

"First of all," Vera said, "I want to apologize for the way I behaved the last time we met."

"You don't have to apologize."

"I wasn't very nice to you."

"Well, I enjoyed our dinner together."

Realizing that he was still holding her hand, he dropped it hastily.

"If we brought your friend back from France, you wanted to be here," said Vera. "That's why I called you. I felt I owed you that much."

"You don't owe me anything."

"As it happens, I'm afraid I brought you here on a wild-goose chase."

"I'm sorry, I don't understand."

"The flight's off. There's not going to be one."

The room smelled of woodsmoke, and also of whatever perfume she had on. That a woman like this had perfumed herself surprised him. He had met her only twice, but had been unaware of perfume either time. Why tonight?

They sat down in a row of chairs and she showed him the three messages from Lily, the two previous ones canceling each night's flight because of heavy rain, and the one today, much longer, that described the new landing area.

"The pilot refuses to go," said Vera. "He doesn't believe the message. He says he's not going to risk his plane."

It had been raining here for two days too, but was not raining now.

Toft looked up from the message. "Who signed this? Who is Lily?"

"A girl who used to work for me. She's very good, very reliable."

Toft looked across the backs of chairs at the people in the front of the room—no doubt the people who were supposed to go out on the flight that would now not take place.

He said: "Order the pilot to go."

"I don't have the authority to do that. Besides, he's a wing commander."

"Isn't that a lot of rank for a job like this?"

"A flight lieutenant would be more usual."

"Let me talk to him."

"It won't do much good, I'm afraid."

"Where is he? What's his name?"

The wing commander was named Brown. Toft found him on the flight line walking around an oil-spattered Lockheed Hudson. He was watching the plane's control surfaces as a co-pilot in the cockpit moved them up and down.

Toft introduced himself.

Brown was about thirty-five, a tall man in a rumpled RAF uniform. He said: "So you're the famous Joe Toft," which was not a good beginning, though for a time after that they spoke to each other cordially enough.

Then Toft said:

"That's one of my men you were going to bring back."

"Is it, now," said Brown, already reacting with a certain stiffness.

"Yes."

"Get him next month, or the month after."

"He may be in a prison camp by then, or worse."

"It's been raining for two days there. On top of ground that's been thawing for a month."

"I was with him when he went down."

"I can understand why it's important to you, but the answer is no."

"I'm sure you could make it in and out."

"Did you see the message?" scoffed Brown. "Suggests we land on a dirt road. The roads will be mud. The wheels would go in up to the hubs. Probably full of potholes, as well. Go off the road into the ditch."

There was some merit in what Brown said.

"These people here, if they were going to parachute in, I'd take them."

"But they haven't had parachute training," guessed Toft.

"Right. I suggest they get some. Do you know how narrow those dirt roads are? If we did land, there wouldn't be room to turn the plane around to take off again."

There was merit in this too.

"Some woman named Lily," said Brown.

"She didn't write this message," Toft said. "This message is my pilot's work, and if he says you can land on that road, then you can."

"Your pilot wants out. What do you expect him to say?"

Toft paused, searching for the correct argument.

"I'm not going to risk pilot, co-pilot, crew chief, and an aeroplane, not to mention the prospective passengers, under such conditions. I don't see where these flights are important to the war effort anyway. Let the French stew in their own juices, I say."

Toft was silent.

"I'd best be getting off," Brown said. "Good to have met you."

Toft gestured toward Brown's plane. "Lend me the plane and I'll fly it."

"My aeroplane? Not bloodly likely."

Toft wanted to hit him. Instead he said: "You leave me no choice. I'll go in my own plane."

"That one over there?"

It was the T-6 two-passenger training plane he had come in. Numbers of them had been loaned to the British at the start of the war. Every air base now had several. When not involved in training exercises, the generals used them as taxis.

The two men peered across the hardstand at it.

"You're putting me on," Brown said.

"No."

"You don't have the range, old man. When you land, if you get there at all, you'll have empty tanks."

"Carry the fuel with me, refuel on the ground." The plan was taking shape in Toft's head. The rear cockpit could be stuffed with how many jerricans of fuel? There was a small luggage compartment as well.

"Narrow undercarriage on those things," said Brown. "Tend to ground loop a lot. Roll into a pothole, and she'll be standing on one wheel, a wingtip, and a broken propellor."

"You know something, I've never ground looped an airplane."

"Call up the Jerries."

"In my life."

"Have the Jerries bring over a new prop."

"You don't have the nerve to go in there. I do."

"You're one of these blokes with a desire to commit suicide, I see. That's fine with me," said Brown, and he turned and strode toward his bomber.

Toft walked slowly back toward Vera, who had stood in the doorway watching. He believed he knew the corridors into France that were undefended, or little defended. He knew how to avoid being intercepted by night fighters along the way. He told himself that even in a slow, unarmed plane he could get through. He would need a hundred gallons of fuel to get back, maybe more. Could he

THE INNOCENTS WITHIN

strap that many jerricans into the backseat? It would make the plane loggy, but he thought it would fly.

He said to Vera: "I have a favor to ask you."

"It depends what," she said cautiously.

"I need some fuel."

"That's not much of a favor."

"Here's another one, then."

Vera waited while he decided how to phrase his request.

"Your people in France are expecting a flight, right?"

"Yes."

"All I ask is that you don't cancel it."

"Don't tell me," said Vera.

"I'll need maps, the recognition code, weather."

"You're going yourself."

"I thought I might, yes."

"In that?" She gestured toward the training plane.

"Yes."

Her reaction was much the same as Brown's. "You trying to commit suicide, or what?"

"Not at all."

He had shot down twenty German planes, and now would fly more than six hundred miles behind enemy lines to rescue one of his pilots. The idea appealed to him.

He was thinking not of suicide but of exploit.

AT nine-fifteen each night, using one of its most powerful transmitters, the BBC broadcast the war news in French. Across the channel—indeed, all over occupied France—people sat glued to their illegal radios, trying to hear through the gaps and static caused by the jamming, repeatedly jiggling the dial to bring the voice in.

The war news each night was followed by a long series of personal messages.

The "personals" meant nothing to most people, though everyone tried to figure them out, and some of them were so cryptic they sounded amusing, or even silly.

The cows are blue in Belgium.

Three trees are ready.

Thirteen horses to the left.

Some messages were dummies. Others were codes understood by those for whom they were intended. They signified the time and place of parachute drops or landings, or gave instructions, or warned of agents or situations that had been compromised. By this method London carried on much of its communication with agents in the field. It was simple, direct, did not require complicated encryption, and the only equipment needed by the agents was an ordinary radio.

In Pierre Glickstein's encampment the message they were waiting for was one of the last. Everyone clustered around the set. The static was bad and the words were in French, but when the message came even Davey, who had been told what to listen for, heard it.

"The river runs backward."

Their truck had high wooden sides, and they loaded it: the radio, ammunition, a box of grenades, two shovels, a crosscut saw and some axes, and all their Sten guns of course. Also some of the other new toys they had never used, and probably didn't know how to use, including the mortars and bazookas. Lily drove, with Davey and Rachel in the cab beside her, twelve men in the back and four others clinging to the running boards.

The presumed airstrip came out of one forest and after a long straight run entered another. It was altogether about a kilometer and a half long, and needed to be defended at both ends. Pierre distributed the crosscut saw and the axes, and placed men as far as possible into each of the forests with orders to fell trees over the road as roadblocks, and then settle down with guns to prevent any vehicle from advancing until the flight from London had landed and then taken off again. In the event of an attack they were to defend the roadblock, delay the *Boches* as long as possible, and then melt backward into the trees.

It sounded both heroic and antiseptic. Delay, not kill or blow up. Or get killed or blown up.

The forward group was the smaller, five boys, two axes, Sten guns all around, grenades in all their pockets.

It was dark under the trees and dark out on the presumed landing strip too, for the moon was not yet up, and after dropping off the forward group, alone now in the truck, Davey drove along looking for potholes, jumping out with a shovel each time he came to one, filling it, pounding the dirt flat with the shovel, and then moving on. But before he had finished this work the moon rose, and from one minute to the next, it seemed to him, the night disappeared, to be replaced by a kind of day that was so bright, the air so crisp and clear, that he felt himself visible for miles across the meadows, an easy target. The same would be true of the plane when it came in.

Already the lights had gone out in the farmhouses set back from the road on both sides. All were dark. The farmers and their wives, having noted all this activity, wanted nothing to do with it, whatever it was.

At the edge of the forest, concealed by it, Davey and Rachel, Glickstein and Lily settled down to wait, and they waited a considerable time. Behind them they could hear the crosscut saw cutting down a tree or trees.

The minutes crawled like hours, the hours like days. Despite his sore leg, Davey paced and calculated, and Rachel watched him. As spring approached the days had become longer, the nights shorter; tonight it had been dark by seven. A bomber taking off from the south of England might reach here as early as ten. Probably not so early, but it was possible.

Lily, meanwhile, sat crouched over her radio, listening for any further message that might come, and from ten o'clock on she sent out a regular signal that the arriving bomber could pick up and ride in on, fifteen minutes of signal, fifteen of silence, lest the enemy pick up the same signal and ride in on it too.

But ten o'clock passed, and eleven, and then midnight, and there was still no indication of any incoming plane.

TOFT flew south over a country that was entirely blacked out, not a light anywhere. Because of the moon he could see the water courses and at times the reflections of the rooftops. Otherwise, it seemed to him, he might as well have been flying over a desert or the ocean.

He was flying low, not the most economical way to do it, using up fuel too fast, but it made him harder to spot by anyone below, too quickly visible and then not. He had avoided every big city, every known concentration of flak. He had not been intercepted so far, had drawn no fire nor even any interest as far as he could tell. He had the foldout map on his knee, but navigation was mostly by dead reckoning—he held the correct compass heading, factored in airspeed and elapsed time, and tried to guess at the winds. He had managed as well to perceive certain landmarks below. He knew approximately where he was.

He hated that this plane was so slow, but on the horizon under the moon there now appeared the high humps of the volcanos he remembered from the last time, meaning that he was nearly there now, and he kept fiddling with his dials trying to bring in the radio beam he needed in order to find the road he was to land on. If he couldn't bring it in, couldn't find the road, he hated to think what happened next. He would have to find just any road, and if the plane survived the landing he would have to pour fuel into the wing tanks by himself, the heavy jerricans hoisted one by one out of the back cockpit and poured, which would take a while, and then try to take off again, provided no one came upon him first.

But there it was, the radio beam: dah-dit to one side, dit-dah to the other, a steady hum in the middle. Though the beam cut off too soon it made Toft smile, and he began to fly square patterns, about five miles to the side, looking below for the flares that would delimit the landing strip.

"THERE he is," cried Davey. With a flashlight he gave the code letter in Morse. At his end of the strip there were three piles of twigs spaced a hundred yards apart. They had been doused with kerosene, and he limped forward and lit them one by one. At the far end of the road, seeing the flames leap up, the youth known as Pascal lit the fourth pile, which would indicate the touchdown point.

Davey brought Rachel over to Pierre Glickstein to say thank you and good-bye, for he imagined there was not going to be time once the plane landed. He expected it would be on the ground no more than a minute or two, the time it took for its passengers to clamber down with their gear, and for him and Rachel to jump up inside—if the pilot could be made to take Rachel.

"Please tell him how much I appreciate what he has done for me."

Rachel spoke to Pierre, who smiled and nodded.

"He carried me into the pastor's house on his back," said Davey. "Tell him I'm aware of that, and if this war ever ends I'd like to come back here and see him again, and—"

But Davey was distracted. The oncoming plane didn't sound right, and then it came close and passed under the moon, and he saw with consternation what it was, recognized its type instantly, not a capacious bomber at all but a two-seat training plane, one of the first planes he had ever soloed, a T-6. His mouth closed, and the rest of his speech to Pierre Glickstein remained unsaid.

TOFT came down low, and made one pass over the strip, noting from the flames and smoke the direction of the almost nonexistent wind. The strip looked all right to him, so the next time around he put the plane down, flicking on landing lights only at the last moment, and dousing them soon after, braking as quickly as possible in case there was a hole ahead, then taxiing forward to where men were dousing the fires. The lights of a truck suddenly appeared instead.

Toft stopped, shut down the engine, and climbed clumsily out, parachute pack sagging behind him, and an individual in wooden shoes and a beret came up and stood wringing his hand, and it was Davey. American men never embraced at that time; a handshake was the limit.

Nor did Davey ever use words then considered coarse or vile. "You old sonuva gun," he said. "You old sonuva gun."

Momentarily he had forgotten his consternation about the plane—its size, speed, and everything else about it. The two young men were grinning and socking each other in the arms, and Rachel, who had come forward, turned and walked back toward the trees.

Then: "I expected a bomber," said Davey soberly. He glanced behind him at Rachel's back.

"Well, the Brits chickened out. You'll have to be satisfied with this."

"Any trouble on the flight down?"

"Piece of cake, as the Brits say."

Lily came over and shook hands. "I'm Lily. I'm the radio operator. You were supposed to bring in some people and some radios."

"They're not coming, I'm afraid."

Lily looked at him.

In his Mae West and harness Toft looked heavy-assed, unbalanced. "Maybe next month," he said.

From deep in the distant forest came the sudden crackle of small-arms fire.

"What's that?" said Toft. The moon was very bright and he peered in the direction of the shots.

"You'd best hurry if you want to get off again," said Lily.

"We put a roadblock in those woods down there," said Davey. "They must have seen something."

"The Jerries are here, you mean."

With the first sound of gunfire, the men had run for the woods behind them. Only Lily, Rachel, and Pierre Glickstein had remained close.

"Hey, you men," Toft called into the woods. "Help us turn this thing around. Hurry up. Quick."

"I'd best get the truck out of the way," said Lily.

"All of you," Rachel shouted into the woods in French, "get out here. Help turn around the plane."

She and Glickstein grasped the edge of the wing, joined a moment later by most of the others.

"Who's the girl?" said Toft.

"The radio operator?"

"No, the girl pushing."

"Just a girl."

"I can see that."

The wingtips of the T-6 were chest high. With Toft and Davey lifting the tail, and the others pushing the wings, they turned the plane in its own length until it was facing back the way it had come.

[4 2 0]

"You're going to have to take off downwind," said Davey, staring toward the distant forest, where heavy firing continued.

"Help me refuel," said Toft, "or I won't be taking off at all."

Using the stirrups, he jumped up onto the left wing. The back cockpit was stuffed with jerricans. They were big and they were heavy. Hugging the top one, he hoisted it out. On the opposite wing, Davey did the same. The two men knelt to either side of the cockpit, inserted spouts into place, tilted the cans and began pouring fuel into the wings.

"Stand back everybody. This is high-octane fuel. There's a certain danger of fire."

The two men kept hoisting jerricans out of the cockpit. It was slow work. "Fast but carefully," Toft called.

"No spillage, right."

"We're going to need every drop to get back."

They heard repeated occasional shots, the sounds of a battle either not entirely joined or almost over.

Hugging cans, kneeling, they poured as fast as they could.

The gunshots had stopped. For some minutes there was no sound but the slurping of the fuel.

The big cans were tossed empty to the road where they bounced and rolled toward the ditch. As he hoisted still another over the lip of the cockpit, Davey saw that Rachel was standing about ten yards away.

He began giving himself orders.

Tell him about Rachel. Get it over with.

From the other side of the plane, he heard Toft say: "Nice-looking doll. Think I could make it with her?" Davey heard another empty jerrican bang on the road. "Is she the moll in this outfit? Does she service everybody, or what? Pity I can't stay."

This was perhaps the best moment Davey would have to say what had to be said.

"I was shot up and had a broken leg. She took care of me."

"Oh," said Toft. "I see."

They poured in silence.

"And a romance developed," said Toft.

"Sort of, yes."

"She let you bang her?"

Toft's head rose and he grinned across the cowling.

"She's going with us," Davey said firmly.

Toft heard a certain steel in Davey's voice that in the past had not been there, and it made him pause. He said: "You're kidding."

"No, I'm not."

Standing at full height on the wing, Toft looked down at Davey kneeling. "You're crazy."

"Not crazy either."

"Davey, it's a two-passenger plane."

"There's room. She can sit on my lap."

"It's out of the question."

"She goes, or I don't go."

Toft tried a joke. "I come all this way to get you, and you send me back empty."

"Empty, yes."

"It's a military airplane. It's out of the question."

"She's going."

"We can't afford the weight."

"You used up seven hundred pounds of fuel getting down here. She weighs about a hundred and ten. She's got no baggage, and neither do I."

"Davey, they'd court-martial me."

"Me too, maybe, but she's going."

Davey heard the bang of the final jerrican as Toft threw it into the ditch. His head appeared above the cockpit. "You about finished there?"

"Yes," said Davey, "finished." He tossed his own can down, screwed in the gas cap.

"All right, get in the cockpit. That's an order."

"I can't go without her."

"Get in the cockpit."

"Not without her."

"That's an order, I said."

"No."

"Davey—"

"She's pregnant."

"Jesus Christ, Davey."

From the distant forest came renewed gunfire.

"Rachel," Davey called, "come over here. Hurry."

"Sitting on your lap her head would be sticking up into the slip-stream," said Toft. "You wouldn't even be able to close the canopy."

"There's a way to make room for her." In the rear cockpit was the extra parachute Toft had brought with him for Davey. It was about six inches thick and would form the cushion on which he sat. Davey lifted it out of the cockpit, and slung it into the ditch.

"There," he said, "now there's room."

"You care about her that much?" said Toft.

"Yes."

Rachel, the moonlight on her upturned face, had approached the plane. Davey had never seen her look so beautiful.

For just a moment the two men stared at each other. Then Toft said: "Climb up onto the wing there, Miss. Get into the cockpit, Davey. Now you, Miss." And then to Davey: "You're going to have cramps in your thighs before this is over."

Toft settled himself in the front seat, strapped himself in and pushed the starter button. The small, two-blade prop stuttered, hesitated, stuttered again, then caught and turned into a blur. At once Toft released the brakes and the plane started forward. Toft in the front chair and Davey in the rear waved to Pierre Glickstein, Lily, and the others they could see. After that they watched the air-speed indicators. The plane became light, and then Toft lifted it up and it was airborne. Flying over the woods at the end of the strip it came briefly under fire. The muzzle flashes could be seen not very far below. Then it was past. Slowly it gained altitude. At a thousand feet Toft leveled off, and they started home.

XXIX

Pierre Glickstein's eyes followed the plane's bright orange exhaust flames up toward the moon, until it turned away and he lost it. At about the same moment he saw a vehicle come out of the far woods.

"The *Boches* are here," he said, but when he glanced around he saw he was already alone.

Clearly the enemy had got through the roadblock. What might have happened to the five men manning it he did not know. All of that was some two kilometers away, and there was nothing he could do about any of it. His job was to protect the radio, protect Lily, and protect his remaining men. It would be nice to kill some *Boches,* but this particular spot seemed to him difficult or impossible to defend.

The oncoming vehicle was big enough to have men in it. How many he could not say. Then he noted troops with rifles. They appeared from behind the distant farm buildings and fanned out in the fields to either side of the road. At this distance they did not seem dangerous, but he knew they were. There was a machine gun mounted on the roof of the truck, and a man standing up in the truck's cab, but Pierre did not perceive either one until the gun opened up. The muzzle blasts threw a halo around the standing man, and the bullets dug up pieces of road in front of Pierre. He heard them strike, and a clod of earth slapped at him. It surprised him to realize that he was not scared, at least not yet.

He turned and ran for the woods. About a hundred meters into the trees he came upon the truck. Lily at the wheel was nursing it backward, but the road was so narrow and the darkness in there so intense that she was having a bad time. There were ditches to both sides, and she couldn't see what she was doing. The truck was their way out of here, and if it slid into the ditch they were finished.

None of the Maquis men were in sight. Pierre Glickstein had a flashlight, and he walked behind the truck lighting the edge of the road for Lily, until she had reached an indentation in the trees that she could back into. Finally she had the truck pointed in the right direction. Pierre jumped onto the running board and Lily drove as fast as she dared as far as the roadblock at the edge of the woods, where she was forced to stop.

The roadblock was a spruce tree whose trunk, where it lay across the road, was a foot in diameter. When Pierre saw its size his heart fell. The roadblock had been built at his orders, but he hadn't expected them to cut down a forest giant.

His men were standing behind the plumpness of the tree, and he began shouting for them to drag it aside so the truck could get by. A number of them grabbed branches and tugged, but the tree was too big, and wouldn't budge. The crosscut saw lay on the bed of the truck, which was how the men had felled the tree in the first place. Jumping up onto the truck, Pierre threw it toward his men and it fell twanging. There was an ax—he heaved that as well.

With the ax one of the men cleared an area in the center of the trunk, and two others began sawing.

"Hurry," cried Pierre, "hurry."

He saw that this was going to take time, more time probably than they had.

TOFT in the front seat was making his calculations. Not only compass course, airspeed, and altitude, but what the enemy might do.

England was about six hundred miles due north. There was a fire-fight in that woods back there, German troops against Maquis, what else could it be, and the Germans would have a radio. They had seen him take off. For all they knew he was carrying a general or government minister, perhaps even De Gaulle himself. They would alert the nearest Luftwaffe squadron—there was one at the airfield north of Lyon, he believed. The squadron would scramble—how many planes? Three, probably. Knowing he was in the air, and could fly in one direction only, they would wait for him where? And in response he would do—what?

Davey in the backseat, with Rachel on his lap, watched the dials, watched the sky, and made the same calculations. What evasive action could be planned? But the choices were painfully narrow. England was at the extreme limit of the plane's range. They would have to fly a straight line to get there at all. At maximum speed, which was about 210 miles an hour, the engine would guzzle gas, and any plane they met in the air would be half again faster anyway, perhaps more. Cruising speed was about 170 miles an hour, but Toft would have to cruise slower than that to stretch the fuel. They not only could not outrun anyone, they couldn't outclimb anyone either. The plane's ceiling was about 24,000 feet, at which altitude they might escape detection. But it took too much fuel to get up there, they had no oxygen, the cockpit heater was inadequate, and at that height Rachel, who was not dressed very warmly, would freeze to death. So would he, probably.

There was not a cloud in the sky to hide in.

PIERRE Glickstein grabbed the bazooka out of the truck, plus two projectiles, one in each pocket, and as he ran back to the edge of the woods he was trying to remember how to use it—the directions as translated by Lily. The bazooka, he remembered her translating, was a one-man antitank weapon, and this seemed right to him, for it was not heavy. It could be aimed like a rifle, and if it hit that truck, would destroy it. Yes, that's what the directions had said. Since the ex-forger had never fired a bazooka, and no one he knew had ever fired one, he did not expect to hit anything at all, but it should make a terrific noise. If it could pierce the wall of a tank of course it would, and that would, at the very least, make the *Boches* come on slower. He would have to delay them at least ten minutes. Ten minutes might be enough.

When he came to the edge of the woods he saw that the truck was much closer and the troops, fanned out to either side, were much closer, and he could plainly see the man standing up in the cab—this was Helmut Haas, though he did not know it, had anyway never heard of him, Haas, who in three days' time would be encircling Le Lignon with eight hundred men. The moon was still exceedingly bright.

Though careful to stay several meters back in the trees, Pierre Glickstein could see the machine gunner on the roof as well. He presumed they could not see him. The truck was in the lead, about fifty meters in front of the troops, and the man in the cab, Haas, was shouting orders to them, making them move forward, shouting first to one side, then to the other, in what Pierre thought of as that ugly, ugly language of theirs.

No one had ever said Haas, who was more exposed than anyone, was not physically brave.

The ex-forger loaded the bazooka, then got himself set up, the tube on his shoulder, aimed straight down the road. He was resolved to wait until they were all much closer than this, perhaps so close that he couldn't miss, would actually hit the truck. But in a matter of seconds he lost his nerve. To wait any longer seemed to him insane, they were too close already, not only the truck but the men in the fields as well, he would pull the trigger and run, and he would pull it now.

And he did, but forgot the second part of his promise to himself. Instead of running he stood there with his mouth gaping open.

The rocket fell short. He believed he saw it strike the road and go skidding forward, and then it skidded or bounced into the truck, which in an instant stopped dead in its tracks and then exploded. There were pieces of steel flying about, a wheel went bounding off, the truck seemed to collapse, and then it was burning fiercely. There was no more man standing up in the cab, no more machine gunner on top, and even some of the troops closest to it had gone down, whether hit by shrapnel or just seeking cover he could not tell.

The destruction he had caused seemed to Pierre so wanton, so out of proportion to the weight of the tube that had lain on his shoulder and now hung from his hand, so unconnected to the simple unimportant, irresponsible act of pulling on a bit of metal which was the trigger, that he did not run, was too stunned to run. At the same time he felt an emotion even stronger than astonishment, and it was glee. He was delighted with himself, they did not have to worry about that truck anymore, he had done what he had to do, had faced combat, become a hero in his own eyes at least, but as a result of all these confused emotions he not only did not run but actually took a step or two forward, as if to see his handiwork more clearly, to bask in its flames, admire it without any reserve at all.

Whether he was visible to the troops in the fields would never be known. Only a few seconds had gone by, the troops had recovered from their own stupefaction, and they did what they had been trained to do, they went to ground and from there sent forth a wealth of bullets that flayed the trees and bushes all around Pierre Glickstein, a steel rain coming at him sideways, and before he could move again a bullet caught him in the throat, and he fell down.

Still facing the woods which contained for all they knew a regiment of sharpshooters, and with no one left alive to order them forward, the troops ran for cover behind farm buildings, firing all the while, and there started to regroup. The truck still burned on the road, the dead or wounded lying nearby.

It was Lily who raced up and found Pierre Glickstein. The boy was choking on his own blood. She screamed for help. Two other boys carried him to the truck and laid him down in it, but he died almost at once. He had tried to speak. Lily, who had bent down close to his lips, thought it was something about the plane reaching London okay. But she could not be sure.

Previously the ex-forger had saved Jews individually. This time, without knowing it, he had saved the entire village.

"We don't even know his name," Lily said. "It isn't Pierre, you can be sure of that." She was crying. As the truck rolled along she searched his pockets until she found his identity card. "Henri Prud-homme," she said.

TOFT figured his only option was to stay down close to the trees, so this was what he did. He made one other decision as well. Because logically the enemy would guard the straight line north, he first flew east, dropping down off the plateau and crossing the Rhône, a ribbon of white marble under the wings, and only then, just inside the moonstruck wall of the Alps, having added thirty or more minutes to the flight, he turned north.

Davey held Rachel in his arms and looked over the side of the cockpit at the blacked-out towns and villages passing below, the long empty stretches of farmland in between, the river running dead straight off to their left, the plane's noise waking people in bedrooms. Davey knew about radar, if Rachel did not, and wondered if the Germans had any this far south. If the plane was making blips on a radar screen the operator would notice them any moment, and would reach for a phone, and a few minutes after that their flight would end, their lives too, probably.

Their only chance, it seemed to Davey, was if the Germans had no radar in this region. Low and slow, the T-6 flew on, and even Rachel, sensing perhaps the tension in Davey, waited to be discovered and then shot down, but an hour passed and then another, and they were still aloft, still unmolested, still presumably unseen.

But a little after that Toft in front pointed off to the northwest, making Davey quarter the sky over there until he saw what Toft had seen; a flight of three planes outlined against the moon, insects buzzing around under a lamppost.

Rachel, having seen them too, did not have to be told what they were.

"Can they see us?" she shouted in Davey's ear.

"If they look over here, maybe."

"But they haven't seen us yet?"

"I don't think so."

"Will they?"

"I don't know."

"If they come after us, what then?"

"They shoot us down."

Rachel in his arms gave a shrug. "They won't see us," she shouted.

Davey, watching the distant insects, said: "I never should have brought you."

"I came of my own free will."

"Please forgive me."

"There's nothing to forgive."

Since she shouted this in his ear the words sounded less romantic than they might have on the ground. But if he got out of this alive, Davey thought he would remember them all his life.

As they continued north, the enemy squadron hung there under the moon, and another thought came to Davey. Not only were the Germans not expecting a plane this far to the east, but they would not expect one this slow. If they had scrambled too early, their fighters were not going to be able to stay up there much longer.

The enemy fighters were even farther away now, harmless as the bugs they so much resembled, and even as he watched, they spiraled down one by one, and were gone.

"They never saw us," shouted Rachel. She bit his ear, and when he jerked it away she began to giggle.

And an hour after that heavy clouds appeared above them. The plane's nose rose, and they climbed. The clouds, it turned out, were at twelve thousand feet, and wispy at first, as Toft snuggled the T-6 into them. It was cold at that altitude, but they knew that for as long at the clouds lasted they were safe.

If the fuel held out. Davey studied the needles and though he said nothing, did not like what he saw.

Obviously Toft was watching the fuel gauge too, for he had throttled way back. The plane's most economical cruising altitude being five thousand feet, he had dropped down to the bottom of the cloud cover, so low that at times they poked out of it and could see the ground.

The cover was solid all the way to Holland. It broke when they were over the North Sea, at which time the fuel needle was on empty. Toft radioed the base to get his exact position, and landing instructions. He lined up the runway from ten miles away—it too shone in the moonlight—and flew straight in. As they taxied toward the operations shack the engine sputtered and stopped, it had been that close. They still had half a mile to taxi, and when the wheels refused to roll that far they got out of the plane, and stood on the grass.

"England," said Rachel, and she started to cry.

The flight had lasted over four hours. Davey was so cramped that if he hadn't been so young he would have fallen down. As they walked the rest of the way in, Toft and Davey were laughing and slapping each other on the back. Rachel's tears had dried, and she was cold sober. At eighteen she was contemplating facts of life she hadn't known existed.

Toft signed in. At this hour there was only one operations officer on duty. He came out and shook hands with Davey, and welcomed him back. He didn't know what to make of the girl, and no one told him anything. He gave Toft the keys to a jeep.

The night was absolutely silent. Most of the day the countryside hereabouts boomed with airplane engines, but now it was still, not a sound anywhere. Sniffing the air, Davey got whiffs of burnt aviation fuel, and of cut grass, familiar odors that brought a smile to his face. The dawn would come soon, and it seemed to him he could smell that too. He was home, and Rachel was beside him— he took her arm and hugged it to his chest.

At the wheel of the operations jeep Toft drove them to the village where he had once met Vera Tompkins, and they woke up the woman who ran the inn. She looked down at them out of an upstairs window, and greeted them with ill grace.

"This girl needs a room," Toft called up.

She came down and opened the door, a woman of about fifty with her hair in curlers.

"Just the girl?" she said.

"Just the girl."

"I run a respectable place," she said.

"I know that," said Toft.

"She can have a room, but you boys can't come in."

"We're getting married," said Davey.

"Come back when you do it."

Davey drew Rachel aside. "In the morning I'll probably have to have a physical. I'll come as soon as I can. They owe me three months' back pay," he said. "We have plenty of money."

"What will we do tomorrow?"

"If I can I'll get a jeep, we'll go sightseeing."

"Where will we go? Can we go see my school?"

He and Toft waited till the light came on upstairs. The window opened and Rachel leaned out. She blew him a kiss, and he blew one back.

Toft was waiting in the jeep.

"What's the procedure for getting married?" Davey asked him.

"You apply to your commanding officer. He has to approve it and send it forward."

"Who's my commanding officer now?"

"Me," said Toft. "Send me the request. Maybe I'll approve it." He started up the jeep.

Davey did not know how to say what he wanted Toft to understand. Finally he just came out with it. "Thanks for coming to get us, Joe."

"Nothing to it," said Toft. "Piece of cake."

XXX

PASTOR Favert's first stop was Buzet, the village nearest his own. He knocked on the door of the presbytery and asked for shelter. Pastor Perrin and his wife installed the refugee in their attic, and began to bring him his meals there.

The news of the murder of Commissaire Chapotel reached him. Alone in the attic he began to weep. They were tears of rage and frustration. They were tears of grief, both for the policeman and for himself. His life had been saved by this man, a debt that now could not be repaid.

To Perrin, his host, he made a kind of confession such as Catholics practiced. He was responsible for this new death too, he said. All his past choices seemed to him to have been wrong ones. He had lived a life of arrogance and pride, not love of fellow man at all, and others now were suffering in his place.

The confession did not soothe him. Pastor Perrin was not competent to absolve him, and the only counsel the other man seemed able to give was on a practical level. Chapotel's death would bring the Gestapo to Le Lignon still again, and they ought to be worrying about how long Favert could stay in Buzet, and where he might go next.

Perrin sent his wife on her bike into Le Lignon for news.

First of all, she reported when she returned, Norma was fine, his children were fine, but the Gestapo had searched the presbytery, and had found an American parachute in the attic. At present the village was swarming with Gestapo and French Milice. The Sûreté had not been allowed to come into the case. The parachute proved, the Gestapo claimed, that Pastor Favert was in league with the terrorists who had assassinated Commissaire Chapotel, and he had been charged with murder.

None of his parishioners believed this, Madame Perrin assured him. Nonetheless, posters had gone up announcing a reward for information leading to his arrest: anyone found harboring him would be shot.

He tried to convince himself that this was no more than another test sent by God. With God's help he would get through it, but the faith that had sustained him in the past was no longer there.

Having decided that his presence in Buzet was too dangerous to the Perrins and their children, Favert shaved off his mustache and put his glasses in his pocket, though without them he could not see much, and that night, as soon as the houses were dark, he left the presbytery and the village and began walking. He had his Bible, and candles to read it by, and a little money. He was now forty-three years old. He had his health and his strength.

From then on he moved from village to village, mostly on foot and at night, keeping to the back roads, diving into the forest or a ditch when he heard something coming. Once an SS convoy, running with tape over the headlights, surprised him and he stood beside the road ready to acquiesce in his own arrest. But the convoy took no notice of him, did not stop.

At first there were occasions when he spent the night in an isolated presbytery and could wash out his underwear and socks, have a hot meal and perhaps a bath. If there were children, he might read to them, or tell them the story of some saint or martyr before they were put to bed. Afterward he would talk to the other pastor and his wife about the war, the church, the future. They would encourage him: the invasion was not far off, they believed, the war would end soon after. But Favert believed only that his presence endangered his hosts, and in the morning, before the village realized he was there, he would be off again, walking fast until the village was behind him, and then looking for a place to hole up for the day.

For as long as his money lasted and his clothes remained presentable he was able to buy food. He would go to the back door of a farmhouse and knock. People were often cordial and some, without knowing who he was, offered shelter.

When the money was gone, and his clothes had become disreputable, he would scrounge in fields for a cabbage or potato that might have been overlooked, that had lain under snow all winter. He would eat it raw, whatever it was. Other times he went hungry.

He wrote letters addressed to intermediaries which he hoped would reach his wife. He was fine, he told her, though increasingly he wasn't.

He slept in attics or barns, never the same attic or barn for more than a day or two. His hair reached his collar. A ragged beard grew. His toes had long since poked holes in his socks. His once white shirt had gone gray. His shoes wore through, his necktie lengthened.

In each of the villages he came to he looked for the poster with his name on it. He was getting farther and farther from Le Lignon, hoping to get outside the orbit of the posters. He even crossed into the Ardèche, the neighboring department, but the posters followed him, and seeing them, he kept moving.

Once he happened upon an abandoned farmhouse. He was too tired to go any farther, and considered giving himself up so he wouldn't have to run anymore. But there was a well with fresh good water, and in the kitchen he found a sack of chestnuts. A bit dried out, somewhat mildewed, but edible. He built a fire, not caring who might see it, roasted the chestnuts and ate his fill. The next day, hungry again, he went on.

His candles were all gone now, but he still had his Bible. When the dawn came up, or at night for as long at the light lasted, he would read in it, usually in the Old Testament, and usually the Prophets. He was looking for courage and strength but found mostly guilt, his own and Europe's, until it seemed to him that he alone was carrying on his back the guilt of the entire continent.

He had saved three to four thousand refugees, no one knew how many, but this did not help him. There seemed to him no place he could stop, be shriven and be safe. He would walk forever.

He had become himself a wandering Jew.

AUTHOR'S NOTE

FICTION is not fact, and in the truest sense of the word, history and biography are not fact either. A man lives sixty or seventy years, perhaps more, but his biography, which purports to be his life, takes a few hours to read. A crime, together with its solution, trial, and punishment, lasts months, a war may last even longer, but both in book form are reduced to a few hundred pages.

This novel is based on events, and on some of the people who took part in them, in and around a village called Le Chambon sur Lignon on the high plateau of France's Massif Central between 1939 and 1944. But although there may be more truth in it than in the one or two "nonfiction" accounts so far written, and I hope there is, it is a work of fiction, not history, and should be read as such. The geography of the story does not always match the real geography. I have sometimes telescoped, sometimes expanded the real-life time frame. To fill the needs of the story certain characters and the roles they played have been invented wholly. All of the names of real people and also of real villages have been changed.

Nonetheless, *The Innocents Within* is as accurate to that time and place as I could make it, and many of the important scenes herein, especially as they relate to the pastor, actually happened. The work of the forger, the escape route to Switzerland, and life in the Maquis were as described. The House of the Rocks was raided by the Gestapo, and the pastor's cousin was taken, together with Jewish children, and they did not return.

When the occupation ended the pastor, whose name was André Trocmé, returned to Le Chambon. He died in 1971 and is buried in the cemetery behind the church in which he preached. His wife, Magda, who survived him by many years, living on into her nineties, lies beside him.

After the war both Trocmé and his assistant pastor, Edouard Theis, were awarded Israel's Medal of the Righteous of the Nations, which bears the inscription: HE WHO SAVES ONE LIFE IS CONSIDERED AS HAVING SAVED THE WHOLE UNIVERSE. In addition, trees were planted in their names along the Alley of the Just on Har ha-Zikkaron, the memorial hill in Jerusalem.

At about the same time a bronze plaque was raised opposite Le Chambon's Protestant temple, which can be seen there today. It reads:

HOMMAGE

TO THE PROTESTANT COMMUNITY OF THIS CEVENOLE REGION, AND TO ALL THOSE WHO FOLLOWED ITS EXAMPLE, BELIEVERS OF ALL FAITHS AND NONBELIEVERS WHO, DURING THE 1939–1945 WAR, UNDER THE OCCUPATION, STOOD UP AGAINST THE NAZI CRIMES AND AT THE RISK OF THEIR LIVES HID, PROTECTED, SAVED BY THE THOUSANDS THOSE WHO WERE PERSECUTED.

The plaque is signed: The Jewish refugees of Le Chambon, and the neighboring communes.

ABOUT THE AUTHOR

New York Times bestselling author ROBERT DALEY has written more than twenty books, including such highly acclaimed works as *Prince of the City, Year of the Dragon, Portraits of France,* and, most recently, *Nowhere to Run.* He served in the Air Force after college and knew firsthand certain of the planes that figure in this story. Later he worked six years as a *New York Times* correspondent based in France before resigning from the paper to concentrate on writing novels. He and his French-born wife keep homes in Connecticut and Nice.